DEAD AIR: First Flight

DEAD AIR:
First Flight

A Zombie Novel

by Samuel C. Garcia

SILVER DAGGER PRESS
LOS ANGELES

ISBN-13: 978-0615611990

ISBN-10: 0615611990

Contact: Silverdaggerpress@yahoo.com

DEAD AIR: First Flight

Prologue

I arrived in Thailand December 20th ten years ago when I was nearing thirty-one. I was taking my mid-tour leave and chose to go to Bangkok. For years, the War on Terror had sent us around the world to kill bad guys and protect freedom, the typical BS. I had toured the Middle East as a CW3 UH-60 Blackhawk pilot, had seen the jungles of South America as a young Marine sergeant in the infantry prior to that, and of course went all over southern California when based out of Fort Irwin as a LUH-72 Lakota pilot. Those were the good old times, times when I went where I pleased with nothing to hold me down; it was a time when I always looked forward to tomorrow. That's not so much the case anymore.

A single soldier at the time and an orphan as far as I could remember, I thought I'd pay Bangkok a visit – since I had no one in the States that looked forward to my arrival from the war. I heard many crazy stories of the Far East from many old Huey pilots back at flight school, saw many Vietnam movies in the 80s as a kid, and read my fill of Chuck Norris jokes in the Port-o-Potties when out in the field on training exercises. So naturally I was a little curious to see what the whole commotion was all about. If it was anything like the movies, I guessed I was game for it. I've always thought of myself as an explorer type and that is probably the main reason I went there, probably why I joined the military to begin with. If it wasn't for my curiosity back then, my need for adventure, I'd be one of them right now wandering the streets of some ruined desert city looking for my next meal, rotting under the desert sun, baked so hard I would probably resemble a mummy – if I was lucky enough not to get my fucking head blown off.

****

Passing through the customs of the well-lit baggage claims, I left Suvarnbhumi Airport, which was quite new at the time. It was around 0100 hours, or one a.m. when I was away from the flagpole, whatever, it was two hours more than I had liked to take at the airport since the clock was already ticking for my return to duty in that sun-baked land. The streets were clear of traffic as the taxi drove down the highway around a hundred mph. The orange glow of the streetlights soothed my mind as images of the king of Thailand flashed before me along the side of the road. The mural of colors and vibrations from the taxi lulled me into a state of peace. As my mind and body calmed down, I could not sleep for the cabbie played his Northeastern Thai music full blast as we raced down the road as fast as he could because he was trying to earn a bigger tip from me. Loud as it was in the party cab, and after he tried to get me to visit the nearest brothel, I began to doze off as the lights blurred in front of me while we flew down the highway at ludicrous speed.

I felt good watching the lights blur before me, calmness fell on me as I leaned my head on the cool cab's window. Calmness was something I had rarely felt over the last few months. There were no SAMs, no guns, no IEDs or kabooms, and I didn't have to wonder if this would be my last trip flying through the desert mountains, where the dreaded Golden BB waited patiently with my name engraved on it.

I had flown every night, it seemed; and, as the time went by in the cab, I realized that I was not wearing any NVGs, I did not see green tracer fire on the green phosphorous screen, I wasn't blinded by white-hot explosions that toasted the rods in my eyes and instead of seeing the world in a green forty-degree field of vision. I saw orange, red, purple, blue all types of neon colors and much more for the skyline of Bangkok resembled a collage of fireworks woven together in an awesome spectacle just for me. I saw all colors except green – green the color of hell, the color some might say of rot.

****

After several toll booths and a few dark streets under the Bangkok Sky Train which is just a monorail with a cool name, we turned right onto a road with a giant mall to our left. It was one of the biggest malls I'd ever seen but an average one for Thai people, who called the mall Central World. The Christmas lights were still on and a robotic Santa Claus climbed up and down a rope attached to the top of the building by a large metal pole. Next to it was a beer garden. Chang, Leo, Singha, all types of Thai beer, were present, and the customers drank the night away as the bands around the garden played on. I thought about checking it out, but never did happened.

In choppy English, the taxi driver asked. "You stay Bangkok City Inn, mister, yes?"

Trying out my choppy Thai, I replied, "Chai Khrap, Chid Quaw Kang Na Sappan Loi leo Quaw."

The man smiled. I guess my Thai was as funny as his English.

I hoped I'd said, "Yes, keep right. At the Bridge ahead turn right."

Google Earth was amazing.

After checking in, I went up to the third floor threw my stuff on the floor and fell asleep. It was the last night I would ever sleep with both eyes closed. It was the last night of civilization, as we knew it.

****

December 21

I woke up around six in the morning, took a shower, ate breakfast downstairs in a restaurant connected to the lobby and then off for some sightseeing. I visited the Grand Palace, which reminded me of the San Antonio missions but much more extravagant. After that, I took the Sky Train to a mall called MBK and then back to Central World, where I found a gym on the ninth floor.

I bought a two-week pass — since I felt a little sluggish from the long trip — and that is where I met Payoong. She was an actress, apparently, but I had no clue at the time. I was American and knew nothing of Thai movies. I first saw her on the elliptical machine while I ran on the treadmill, a few machines down from her, to close out my workout. It was a good view of the Sky Train, which ran below us outside with hundreds of passengers standing around dazed like characters in the bus from *Shaun of the Dead*.

Now, however, my attention was on Payoong. She was the most beautiful women I had ever seen. I remember that I watched her from the corner of my eye; beautiful as she was, it was something beyond her beauty that enticed me — as corny as it may sound — but it felt like it was meant to be. It was then, as I closed out my workout, that I decided it was now or never and went over to talk to her.

A smile came from her as she saw me get off my machine, a clue that she had been checking me out too.

I avoided using the Thai my friends had picked up in Pattaya years back as sailors and Marines on shore leave, and quickly made an impression on her. Before long, I had a date that night to look forward to. That was the night many years ago that the world I knew ended.

Chapter 1: *Flight from Khao San Road*

Sai, the nickname he went by from when he was at the orphanage, was a short man compared to most U.S. Army soldiers of the time. Short due to a Native American/Hispanic ancestry – but he'd never let his size stop him. His ancestors were born fighters; they'd fought for years against several invading armies and now here he was in the U.S. Army fighting again against those who'd threatened his people, the American people as a whole this time.

He was roughly 5'6", sometimes 5'7" on a good day. Marine DIs always laughed he was trying to squeeze an inch on them back when he was at the recruit depot as an eighteen-year-old. He had a stocky built from years of weightlifting as a teenager. He'd hit the gym like all good football players and did his best to keep up with the giant players on his high school team, the Rams.

Sai had just dressed up and had gone downstairs to the lobby of Bangkok City Inn, where a man with spiky dark hair wearing a red bellboy coat opened the door smiling. He walked out the door perfectly synchronizing his timing with Payoong's arrival. She was driving up in the back of a green and yellow taxi.

Stepping into the taxi, they made their way to Khao San Road as they left the Chit Lom District where his hotel was located. Khao San Road was the club scene for the farang (foreigners) in Bangkok and had a nightlife that rivaled the infamous Bourbon Street in New Orleans anytime, any day.

After arriving and walking the strip of neon lights of Khao San Road at dusk, the night rolled in. That is when they began to have a few drinks at one of the local clubs. There were dozens of people sitting outside in the patio area chatting in many tongues. German, Swedish, Japanese, Spanish, English, and so forth were represented in the bar. On the second floor of the bar it was no different, for people from all over the world inhabited every corner of the club having a good old time that fateful Bangkok night.

The couple went to the second floor where a famous Filipino band was playing every genre of music they could think of; many of the songs had been famous American hits at one time or another. Like all clubs, the music was almost deafening, but here they had a tendency to do that only on every other song.

"P'Sai, call me Yoon." Payoong smiled as she held her arms around Sai's neck, the band easing down to play a slow dance in Thai.

It did not take a brain surgeon to understand what the lyrics of the Thai song meant, for it was played for all the lovebirds who danced their final song in that room.

"Yoon." Sai smiled, raising his right eyebrow just a little to catch her attention.

Staring at her, he searched her eyes for the cue to move in for the kiss he desperately wanted to give her.

Smiling at Sai with a twinkle in her eye, she stayed traditional, doing her best not to give in to the inevitable.

For an actress, who was considered liberal minded in the States, Yoon was the direct opposite due to her traditional Thai upbringing by her grandparents.

****

Unknown to Sai and Payoong, some of the workers who had managed the club from behind the scenes had already departed after the Thai Emergency Broadcast System had interrupted a soccer game on television. Commotion had begun to rise without the bar patrons noticing. Gossip spread from employee to employee and some began to leave through the front door without catching any of the customers' attention.

With the band continually playing, the lights dim, and romance heavy in the air, the staff and customers on the dance floor were unaware of what was going on. Below in the kitchen and dining area, waiters and waitresses began to trickle out, leaving the foreigners clueless as to what was coming. These employees felt they needed to get ahead of the panic that would arrive shortly.

The farang drank, talked, joked, and ate — failing to realize the diminishing staff in the area. Many of the younger farang were just too distracted by the Thai bar girls out to earn a buck. These women were the sirens of the bar scene who lured men in to buy and buy more drinks on the promise of a happy ending.

Up above, Sai began to notice the lack of people. A waitress began to pull on the bartender's shirt only seconds before the first shots were fired.

He scanned the room as he danced with Yoon, wary of the lack of employees and the dwindling number of people on the dance floor. He began to feel the hairs on the back of his neck rise as a crescendo of fear began to electrify within him. Jolts of adrenaline started racing through his body.

Something was in the air, a kind of electricity, a sixth sense of something to come that he could sense from all his years under fire.

The band continued to play as Sai returned a smile to Yoon; and, just like that, the pounding of a fifty-cal in the street went off.

Bam! Bam! Bam! Bam! Bam!

Bam! Bam! Bam! Bam! Bam!

The blasting went off in a rhythm of five, as someone fired away from outside the building. The vibrations could be felt trembling through the air as each round left the barrel of the gun, causing every atom to vibrate within the vicinity of the sound waves.

Bam! Bam! Bam! Bam! Bam!

Instinctively and without hesitation, Sai hit the deck and pulled Yoon to the floor. Yoon's hair flew up in an almost zero-g *John Woo* effect as she freefell straight down. It was slow motion for Yoon, the sudden pounding outside, the actions Sai had taken as she was yanked to the ground, her mind not even registering what had just occurred outside of the bar. Confused, she let out a yelp of surprise before she hit the floor hard beside Sai. In awe, she looked up at the crowd still computing what was going on in her mind.

A few individuals had dropped to the floor around them while others remained frozen like deer caught in the headlights of a truck. The sound and flashes of light had blown their senses and stunned their brain as the danger pounded away from outside in a continued rhythm.

The drummer of the band moved to the window as many people slowly began to seek cover. Curious about the sounds outside, he began to open the window, but his face disappeared sending his body back headless as the fifty-cal operator opened fire on the second floor of the club.

Tracer rounds tore through the bar patrons that were nearby as the female lead of the band broke into hysterics beside her headless boyfriend who had spilled the contents of his head all over the floor.

As quickly as the firing had begun, it ended with the sound of another .50 cal discharging along with many rifles opening up farther down the road.

Satisfied a second later that the firing threat was over for now, Sai stood up from his prone position, crouching into a low profile. He pulled Yoon, who had just brushed the hair from her face, to do the same. She moved behind him looking at his back when she turned her head towards the screams of hundreds of tourist and Thai people running through the streets of Khao San Road just outside the club on the street level.

Their screams having been drowned out earlier as her focus had previously zeroed her in on the gunfire. Her tunnel vision was now lifted and she became aware of the world around her once more. Her senses became in tune with everything – from the blood sprayed on Sai's back to pleas for help around the bar – as people called out in all languages.

She looked back to Sai who was pulling her towards the stairwell as others began to move in a flurry of activity, mostly panicking. Yet some continued to stand staring out the shattered windows in a state of shock. Women were screaming and men were yelling all around as she continued to move.

Yoon felt nothing, except she knew she needed to follow Sai. She felt her legs moving as an explosion outside sent an orange light into the dance floor too briefly to show the dead and wounded who were now on the floor.

With each burst of light, the heat from the blast flowed through the shattered windows as the light lit up the room like an oven after hours on bake until a second later the temperature turned back into the ninety-five-degree weather with high humidity.

Upon arriving at the stairs, the couple ran down from the second floor to the bar/dining area, leaving the people upstairs to their fates as chaos continued just outside the club.

Why not stay upstairs in the safety of the bar, Yoon thought. The answer was that Sai's training had kicked in and all bets were off as he began evading the gunfire. It was always best not to get caught by your enemy, no matter who it was.

As most of the bar stayed inactive, hiding, cowering in fear, Sai took advantage of the moment as he pulled Yoon to safety. It was like the water had receded from the beach prior to the killer tsunami of 2004. Those who reacted survived, those who took no action died. Now another tsunami was on the way that would prove much more deadly than any that had come before to the human race.

Moving through the bar area, the unmistakable sound of the .50 cal firing went off again and again as Sai finally recognized the weapon in the back of his mind along with several sharp reports of M-16A2 service rifles firing on the street level.

The glasses and liquor bottles rattled as the gunfire intensity increased in volume outside, while Sai and Yoon ran behind the white marbled bar taking cover.

A sinking feeling bellowed in Sai's gut as he made it past one of the female employees who was crouching behind the bar. Her eyes closed, her hands over her ears with tears rolling down her cheeks, she looked at the couple as she continued to cry her eyes almost begging them for help as the gunfire continued.

Sai gestured for her to follow and moved on. The girl just sat behind the counter in a state of shock her eyes full of fear. There was no time to waste and, as the firing continued, the employee watched as the couple moved on leaving her behind with glass bottles rattling above her.

Upon reaching the end of the first part of the bar, Sai immediately saw several people cowering underneath tables to his left. He looked up above them through the window and hesitated to see bodies being blown to pieces. Some kind of fucked-up war was raging in the streets and Sai did not feel safe in a bar with a window so large displaying the contents as a showcase.

The patio had been obliterated – chairs, tables, and bodies thrown around as if a Texas twister had passed through with guns blazing. Soldiers could be seen firing in the streets on farang and Thai alike not more than thirty feet outside of the bar. Torsos, arms, and heads turned into puffs of red smoke as a mob charged a Thai military vehicle and surrounded the soldiers just outside the bar entrance.

It was some kind of riot, close to a hundred drunken enraged fools charging blindly towards the armed vehicles – completely stupid in Sai's perspective. As he watched the charge, a flash of bodies caught his eye running towards the bar room window. A small group made up of foreigners was running toward the bar. They ran straight toward the long rectangular windows near the entrance that displayed the club inside like a grocery store. They ran as if their asses were on fire, with a speed a track team coach would be proud of.

This track team, however, proved to be more like a football team when the members broke through the team banner before the big game. The rabid crowd exploded through the window with shrieking screams at a high velocity. The farang were European, from what Sai could tell, as they smashed their way inside the club with glass and wood raining down on their backs as they fell over a booth and destroyed a table that broke their fall. They rolled onto the ground as the debris settled on top of them. The shrieking had stopped, the gunfire seemed to have died off for that split second, and it was a moment of extreme horror when the figures began to move once more covered in blood.

All eyes of the bar patrons were upon the intruders as they began to scramble to their feet, the debris falling off their bloodied bodies.

Yoon watched, still holding Sai's hand as the European party crashers found their footing and rose from the floor. Their bodies moved slowly as they stumbled up, pieces of debris and blood falling from their backs as they zeroed in on their targets. That's when the sound of the area rushed back into the bar.

Perhaps being still for that second, that moment in time, had saved Sai and Yoon's lives or maybe God was on their side. Who knew? What felt like an eternity was only a split second when a woman caught in her lover's embrace screamed and broke the silence. The European party crashers' eyes focused on the couple hiding below a table a few feet from them when the closest party crasher charged the couple. It was a woman in her late twenties with lips pulled back and blood continuing to roll down her face mixing with the snot and drool coming from her eyes, mouth and nose. An inhuman scream came forth from her mouth as she signaled the attack causing the other European Party crashers to instantly smash through the table as the boyfriend tried to fend off the attack to no avail.

The man was pulled towards the shattered rectangular window as he attempted to fight his attackers off kicking and yelling; his girlfriend was grabbed by the hair as she tried to scramble to her feet. That is when Sai began to pull Yoon once more, not waiting around to see if the European party crashers had buddies.

The girlfriend was violently pulled back to the floor by her hair and like a pack of rabid dogs the party crashers began to maul her as she tried to fend them off with her hands and legs. Her eyes caught a glimpse of her lover disappearing behind a few more individuals who entered the club from the rectangular shattered window.

Around the bar, a man rushed in to help the couple as others stood and watched in awe, not wanting to get involved or just not knowing what to do. The hero kicked a woman off the girlfriend who was now holding her throat, blood gushing out onto the floor with every beat of her heart. Her eyes in a state of panic as tears blurred her vision, and with what was left of her energy she gargled out her screams as the party crashers continued to bite her legs, arms, and torso – moving their heads like sharks tearing the flesh off a whale while engaged in a feeding frenzy.

The hero tried to grab another European party crasher, this time a tall German-looking man who had a sharp piece of glass still stuck in his neck. The German man turned his attention to the hero from the dying girlfriend and with the same viciousness and ferocity; he attacked the hero and sent him to the ground biting into the hero's face repeatedly, tearing at his nose and cheeks.

The operator of the .50 Cal turned his attention from the bodies in the street to the shattered windows of the club. There were silhouettes of screaming bodies moving from within the club as the party crashers attacked more of the rubberneckers. The operator began to spray fire into the club, sending tracer rounds flying down range wildly through the room hoping to kill all that resided within its club's confines.

The room fell apart as debris shot in all directions from the impact of the rounds, the bottles exploded into liquor fountains, spraying the walls while bodies fell apart all around like children's building blocks. Round upon round blasted its way through the bar indiscriminately hitting tables, concrete, skulls, plates, bodies and arms.

****

Pulling Yoon, and running to the back of the restaurant dodging tables, chairs, and people, the bullets tore through the air past Sai as the European party crashers continued to wrestle with the couple. It was then that the operator zeroed in on the party crashers and out of the corner of Yoon's eyes she saw the party crashers and the couple burst into a red mist moments later. Their limbs and gore splattered around the room as more people rose to their feet to seek cover, showing the gunner that more people had been hiding in the bar than he was led to believe.

Sai turned right at the counter of the bar slamming his body on a cabinet full of glasses and then pulled Yoon through the swinging door into the kitchen as an explosion from a building on the other side of the road sent a killer wave of flames over the .50 Cal operator and into the club Sai and Yoon were in.

The building shook as the flames poured into it like waves of water. Survivors of the initial blast were covered in flames screaming, skins boiling from their bodies as they cried out in agony.

The .50 Cal operator was frozen as if caught in the act red-handed; his charred body did not move as he continued to burn, his eyes forever staring into the flames of the bar to see a dozen or more people rolling around in the crimson fires.

As the flames poured forward, the door swung open as Sai and Yoon were thrown off their feet into the kitchen – sliding across the tile floor and into a stove. The air was immediately sucked out of the bar room causing the door to swing shut once more and all went dark.

****

Crying in the darkness of the smoke-filled kitchen, Yoon pushed up off the tiled floor, debris falling off her shoulders and pain shooting through her body. She brushed her face, now covered in silt, and looked to Sai.

She saw Sai moving next to her; he was recovering from the blast as well. Before she knew it, she felt his arm around her she felt him pull her up from the floor.

The smoke was heavy now; her eyes burned as Sai led her again out of the path of the plume of smoke.

"Yoon, you okay?" Sai asked from in front of her.

She could tell he was shouting, but her ears were still ringing and his voice was muffled.

"You okay?" And the noise of the world was back again, the crackling fire in the bar raging, the screaming from next door as people burned to death, the gunfire in the street still continuing even after the explosion, and Sai shaking her nervously trying to get her back to reality.

"I'm okay," Yoon said as she hugged Sai, hugged him hard – relieved to be alive.

She had no idea what had happened but was glad Sai had been there when it had. She buried her face in Sai's chest and let loose with tears. Never before had she seen such horror in the span of no more than forty seconds.

Panic was creeping into Sai's mind but he quickly flushed that from his thoughts as he tried to remain calm, which was hard due to a man screaming in the fire through burning lungs next door.

If it wasn't for Sai being blessed under fire years earlier he'd probably be crying as well, he thought. His hands were shaking, his adrenaline was up, and he was scared; but being scared led to death, and only with a clear mind could you have any chance of surviving.

The smoke was pouring into the kitchen, forcing Sai to take control of the two shell-shocked bodies, Yoon and his. He brushed the silt from his cheek as Yoon cuddled with him next to a polished stove that began to reflect the light coming through the smoke from the flames next door.

The smoke told Sai what to do next; it was time to move, time to get the hell out of here as the gunfire continued to pound its way through the streets all around Khao San Road.

"Yoon, you okay, we need to get moving," Sai said, as he looked around the kitchen as more light was now entering the room.

"Thirty to forty-five minutes." It was useless information. Sai mumbled to himself, the time it took your eyes to fully adapt to the darkness.

There was an eerie light pouring through; something did not feel right to Sai due to the way people blindly charged the Thai military vehicle. He had heard of that kind of psychotic behavior during the Korean War but never thought he'd see it. And what was up with those European party crashers? Was it drugs? A gunshot sent his mind back into the game.

"Yoon we need to get out of here now!"

Another explosion from another building erupted followed by the distinct sound of a UH-1 Iroquois/Huey that could be heard coming from the distance somewhere above. The pounding of the blades sent echoes through their chest as Sai looked up at the ceiling and back at Yoon as it grew closer to them.

The blades chopped through the air with their distinctive trademark sound and another few explosions erupted seconds later, causing dust to fall on Sai and Yoon from the ceiling. The pans and plates came tumbling down as another explosion erupted nearby causing some of the kitchen cabinets to shift, forcing the cabinets' doors to fly open vomiting their contents onto the ground.

"Yoon, we need to go now. Do you know where we can go?"

"No, but I have an aunt who lives in Sukhumvit," she replied, as she wiped tears from her eyes.

The screams began to grow again on the main street of Khao San Road. They were not like screams that Sai had been used to in the war zones where he'd been. What troubled him was the high pitch screech they made, something truly unnatural. Something was wrong with the way the screams were, and Sai could feel something evil lurking out in the shadows waiting for them.

"Farang! Pye! Pye!" a cook shouted from deep within the kitchen, while holding a butcher's knife not more than five feet from the couple.

In the darkness, the cook, who was wearing a now-dirty apron, ran across from Sai and opened a door into what looked like an alley. The blue moonlight entered the kitchen giving Sai and Yoon a clear picture of the exit. The cook stood there for a second looking towards Sai and Yoon and shouting "Pye!" before pounding his feet out the door and running away from the burning club.

"Yoon, it's time to go now."

Getting to his feet, Sai pulled Yoon to hers and began to lead her to the door while crouching to avoid the smoke that was continuing to pour into the kitchen.

As they moved to the exit, the door where they had previously entered the kitchen began to shake violently as someone screamed from behind, pounding on the door from the opposite side. The door shook on the now-welded hinges as the individual pounded senselessly on it.

Sai instinctively turned to help, but then gunshots from the other side changed his mind. Something pounded hard against the door, threatening to take it off its hinges; a struggle was going on just beyond the door as if several individuals were tearing to shreds whoever had started beating the door.

"Let's go!"

Sai led the way again and ran out into the nighttime sky of the alley. The power had gone out all around the Khao San district and the blue moon lit the way. Above the buildings, flashes of orange light coming from the flames of Khao San Road lit the skyline surrounding the alley. The buildings glowed orange, a raging fire burning out of control in the street.

The fire must be huge, Sai thought, pausing to take in the scene before continuing to follow the cook.

The couple began to follow the cook deep into the bowels of the alley. Screams and gunfire continued to rage on and grow in a crescendo of death as they moved down the empty alleyway.

Running through the darkness, Sai slowly regained his night vision as Yoon wiped the tears from her eyes once more when a voice on a loud speaker began to talk in Thai.

Sai knew some Thai, but was not an expert. He heard the word Tahan, which meant soldier; but, other than that, nothing came to mind. That is when Yoon stopped running and pulled on Sai's left arm. Sai stopped and looked at her waiting for the translation he knew was not good.

"Sai, the soldiers are going to shoot anyone who is out in the streets," Yoon said in disbelief.

"Fuck," Sai grimaced lowly as he bit his lip, his eyes scanning the area as he quietly tried to figure out what to do next.

He looked at Yoon, but did not want to push her over her breaking point by showing the stress was now getting to him.

The choices were clear to him, risk dying in an explosion by the army while hiding in a building or be blown to pieces by a .50 Cal in the streets – or, worse, being torn to pieces by a rioting crowd of nut jobs.

Sai's training said evade, if this was a coup, which he thought it was, then all law and order was gone and rapes and murders were soon to follow just like Mogadishu and Sierra Leone.

"We keep going," he replied, thinking if only they could reach another block from Khao San they could outrun this mess.

As Sai finished those words, the Thai cook, who was just a little farther up the alley, was grabbed by a feral pack of screaming rioters.

"SHIT!!" Sai shouted to himself, as from the shadows of the darkness more rioters came running to the cook.

The rioters tackled the man to the asphalt and began to pull and tear on him, when another group of rioters began running down the alley towards Sai and Yoon's position. It was obvious there would be no surrender or arguing with these psychos, and taking flight was the best option.

Looking around, Sai knew he was fucked as he saw going back to the club as his only option until a fire escape ladder caught his eye from the building a few feet away.

"Grab the ladder," Sai ordered Yoon, as he pulled her over and picked her up in one smooth motion.

The fire code in Thailand was definitely lacking, for the ladder did not come down as advertised. Rusted shut from years of neglect and moisture, it did not budge an inch.

"CLIMB UP!" Sai said, as he turned his head towards the mob that was almost on top of him.

Yoon, being an actress and a regular at the gym where she met Sai, pulled herself up with little help from Sai – which pleased him most definitely, as the rioters grew closer. Their feet, mostly without shoes since many were Thai and their sandals had long fallen off, slapped their naked flesh against the cold concrete. It was a strange noise, one he was not used to. As the flesh continued to slap the concrete, the mob raced towards them with mouths open, lips pulled back and rage pouring from their eyes.

Sai looked back, then up, and then jumped up, hitting his head on Yoon's shoe while Yoon was in the process gaining her footing.

Losing momentum from hitting her, he paused before doing a pull-up and dropping his elbows when he felt a hand touch his boot briefly, the fingers of someone below sliding across the sole – failing to grab onto something useful. Sai looked down at the mob that howled at him below trying desperately to jump up and grab hold of the fire ladder. Their eyes were blank, and they had a crazed, rabid look about them that spelled out doom for Sai if they were to be captured by these men and women.

Below Sai, the rioters watched as Yoon found her footing above them and began to go up the stairwell. Sai watched as one of the people below began to reach the rungs of the ladder. The others tried their best to follow suit.

The first to reach the ladder was a Thai man covered in blood, which appeared as black slime to Sai in the dark. Enraged, with his teeth showing and his face twisted by the light, he began to pull himself up the ladder using a comrade who had tripped as a stepping stool. As he negotiated the first two rungs, his head popped up in the hole of the steel standing where his eyes locked onto Sai's boot that raced towards his face.

The man's head hit the back of the iron standing which Sai was sitting on and a sick, wet, crunching sound could be heard upon impact, which then resulted in his body falling onto the crowd. The body rocked on the wave of hands like a 1980s concert before disappearing below the ocean of hands to the ground. The others just used him as a step like any other who had fallen below the crowd that was increasing in number below Sai and Yoon. Each of them showed no signs of emotion, other than the need to kill the couple.

The mob was not discouraged in the slightest as the Thai man's body fell on them. Another man, a foreign man, started up the ladder, as a Thai woman held onto his trousers – trying to use him as a human rope. The foreign man's head popped up into the opening and he too received Sai's boot to his face, not once but twice until the same crunching sound could be heard and the combined weight of the woman sent them falling into their comrades below. Unlike before, the two bodies smashed through the crowd sending several people down to the ground causing a mound of bodies to form below the fire escape giving the other pursuers a better chance of following Sai and Yoon.

Yoon, already on her feet, pulled Sai up from his butt with her arms under his armpits, his back against her chest, pleading with him in Thai to follow her up the iron stairway.

Sai made it to his feet and followed Yoon up two flights of stairs as another person, gender and race unidentifiable to Sai in the dark, made its way up the ladder followed by another then another.

Yoon continued to sprint up the ladder unknowingly passing a room with an old Australian couple glued to their battery-operated radio in their hotel room listening to the BBC.

****

On the radio, a British man reported live in Hong Kong.

"That is right, Cassandra," he said with a very heavy accent. "What we are seeing here is a crackdown by the Chinese government. The rioting which began early this morning in Peking near the historical national monument of the Forbidden Palace has escalated along the coast south towards Hong Kong, Shanghai and several smaller cities where countless numbers of people have taken to the streets." He paused as gunshots were fired. "The military has been flying aircraft for the last few hours here, bombing parts of the city." The thunderous roar of something in the distance could be heard. "Rebels and many other factions have taken to the streets and are out here killing each other in what may very well be the start of a civil war."

A woman's voiced interrupted. "Well, Harry, the rioting looks more like a civil war with each passing hour as Communist troops clash with one another. Once again, for all of you just joining us around the world this may very well be the birth of a free China..."

The elderly couple continued to listen as the woman's voice continued to put a spin on the news.

As the woman's voice continued talking of the politics of China, the first person chasing Sai and Yoon made its way past the window but a second figure took noticed of the elderly couple. It stopped and stared at the couple in the dark room as the radio gave away their position. Without warning, it smashed its way into the hotel room setting the trail for the rest of the mob just like an ant finding a meal for the rest of her sisters.

****

The old couple's screams were drowned out as a helicopter flew over, this time giving Sai the familiar view of a strafing run about to take place. The gunship was a thousand feet up in the sky and was diving down towards Khao San Road, first firing guns followed by rockets.

"Guns! Guns! Guns! Rockets! Rockets! Rockets!" Sai thought to himself.

The tracer rounds were only markers for the pilot and were followed up by the more expensive payloads of rockets.

The gunship fired its rockets and tracers into Khao San Road as Sai raced up the side of the building. While climbing, Sai could see tanks rolling down the street from the direction of the Grand Palace. The tanks were firing their main cannons at a crowd that was charging at them.

The tracers and flames from the rockets continued to rain down over Sai as he looked up to see another gunship diving down behind the first as the prior one turned in a sixty-degree turn to the right and within thirty seconds would be making another pass down below.

Sai looked sharply at the battle scene but was quickly reminded of the mob he had just escaped when he heard footsteps closing in once more coming from below.

Sai backhanded the Thai woman who was chasing him, and she fell back down the stairs. Tumbling as she fell down the stairs, she managed to break both her legs before coming to a rest on the rail, her right arm was bent in a wrong angle, the bone protruding from the flesh.

Her belly had been shredded with bite marks, but that was hidden to Sai in the darkness. She hissed as she looked up at Sai, who was now running once more up the fire escape. Her milky eyes cried for blood as she grinned her broken teeth that had pieces of flesh hanging between them, displayed like a wild beast. With her one good arm she began to pull herself up the stairs but was quickly trampled by her peers who did not even think twice about using her as an extra step in the staircase.

Yoon, now reaching the roof looked back as Sai ran up behind her. Sweat rolled down her cheeks as the cool night air blew through her hair. All around her in the background plumes of smoke with giant fireballs erupted into the sky from the opposite side of the building facing Khao San Road.

"They broke through that window," she said to herself, before Sai grabbed her arm and headed toward a door on the roof.

She had been referring to the elderly couple that had been ransacked in their hotel room. In the darkness of their room, nearly twenty people were tearing the couple apart and devouring the flesh as their comrades pursued Yoon and Sai up the staircase.

Unfortunately, the door that Sai and Yoon had run to on the roof was locked. Sai turned his head back toward the stairwell and saw a figure reaching the top.

He was reminded of the news on CNN, where a soldier was dragged down the streets of Baghdad and hung from a bridge. That was not going to happen to them, and with a new jolt of adrenaline racing through his body he knew what was next.

Sai turned to the door once again and slammed it with his body repeatedly. With the speed and weight of his body, the door came crashing down with a loud bang after several hits. Now with the door down and the screams coming up the fire escape behind them, Sai and Yoon quickly entered the dark doorway as the shadowy figure charged forth at full speed.

The couple immediately turned left at the doorway where they found an open stairwell leading down into a dark abyss. Moving in the dark they began to feel their way down the stairs with their hands and sprinkles of light from the fires raging outside to guide the way. They negotiated the first few steps down the stairwell before the figure following the two blasted its way through the entrance of the stairwell. The figure crashed into a railing and flipped over and down the stairs. The man's body slammed against every rail on the way down breaking bones and leaving pieces of its flesh behind before finally slamming into the concrete floor with a wet bounce.

An eerie orange flickering glow filled the stairwell as the duo continued their descent. They moved closer to the street level with each step as screams began to echo in the hollow stairwell from each level where the rooms were located.

****

The rioters had infiltrated the hotel lobby and were now going room to room on each floor attacking the hotel guests as the battle raged in the street. People ran through the halls of the hotel in a scene of pure madness. Naked hookers were taken down by the hotel staff; old perverted foreigners slaughtered by the maids. Women and children pleaded for their lives as the rioters cornered them in their rooms while some of the men tried to team together to withstand the onslaught.

Through the chaos, the two made their way down the stairs when a little girl around the age of five appeared from the shadows of a dark corner of the stairwell. Dressed in a blue skirt and hair down to her shoulders, she held a stuffed elephant and had fear written on her face. She'd been a guest and was somehow separated from her family during the madness that resided inside the hotel of death.

Crying and speaking in Thai to Yoon, Sai had no idea what she was saying. But whatever it was, it did not matter for from two floors above a man came yelling into the stairwell screaming in Thai terrified beyond reason.

Looking up, Sai saw arms and legs dangling from that floor as the man tried to jump to the ground floor when a bunch of hands grabbed him and pulled him back into the hall. The terrified man screamed as he was dragged kicking and punching back into the hallway with people biting and tearing at him the whole way.

Screaming at the top of her lungs, the little girl gave away Sai and Yoon's position. Almost immediately, a man came falling between the stairs hitting every railing down to the first floor. Then several people started descending the stairs as a woman fell from the same floor hitting every rail on the way down as well, followed by another, then another – each one leaping towards the group below.

Yoon grabbed the girl and started down the stairs as Sai smashed his elbow into a red firebox that contained a fire extinguisher and a small fire ax. Grabbing the ax, Sai followed behind them as bodies rained down from above, and as they came to the ground floor exit they could see the emergency exit door was already open.

Carefully, the trio stepped over the bodies of their would-be attackers, who had jumped over the rail. A few bodies still twitched with life as they avoided them, moving towards the exit with a crowd running down the stairs in hot pursuit.

The three exited the building to the intense heat and smoke-filled air from burning cars and bodies on the road. There, a tank pulled up and with a bright searchlight trained on them, the turret began to move in their direction.

The little girl cried in Yoon's arms as Sai pushed them forward, shielding his eyes from the light with his hand just in time. The cannon fired into the stairwell behind them, where the mob was exiting the building in pursuit. The round slammed into and out of the first person and rammed into the wall near the exit.

The blast disintegrated the mob by the exit and sent the three sliding across the road.

****

With his ears ringing and in a state of shell shock, Sai looked down the road from the opposite side of the tank, which appeared to be an old Patton tank from the Vietnam era. Hundreds of people were now charging the tank, but something was wrong with them. Bullets ripped through their bodies, limbs went flying, and the piercing screech of their battle roar could be felt in his chest.

While dazed, several figures appeared behind Sai and grabbed him. Sai panicked, still in shock – fearing the mob was on top of him when his hearing rushed back in.

"PYE! PYE!" a soldier around eighteen years of age shouted as he pulled Sai towards a two-ton truck behind the tank.

Panic stricken, the soldier spat out in Thai, and as he looked around the charging crowd began to move closer while he struggled with Sai. His fellow soldiers and the tank fired their barrage into the mob as he and several others dragged Sai to safety.

Snapping out of his daze, Sai saw the stuffed elephant lying on the ground next to Yoon, who was not moving.

"Yoon!" Sai shouted trying to get to her.

Struggling to help her amongst the soldiers, the back of the M-16 rifle butt stock came crashing down on his head as one soldier decided to calm Sai down.

Now slumped in the soldiers' arms, they dragged Sai behind the tank towards a two-ton truck, where a soldier was giving the little girl to another soldier on the back of the truck. On the back of the truck standing by the tailgate, another soldier pulled on Sai's clothes and pulled him up. He slid Sai to the center of the truck as the little girl moved out of the soldier's way.

The little girl cried in the arms of an old lady who was now taking care of her and watched as another truck pulled up behind the tank with soldiers jumping out to support the tanks. Behind the tanks, a crowd of refugees waiting for their evacuation began to load up on the trucks.

The truck pulled away as the tank fired round after round at the crowd. The mob swarmed the tank, as the crew valiantly tried to fend them off. Closing the hatch of the tank, the gunner abandoned his post on top of the tank, but not before leaving a grenade above for the psychotic mob.

The people pulled and pulled on the hatch, when a loud bang sent metal shrapnel and body parts flying off it only for more members of the mob below to mount on top of it again and continue their rampaging assault.

The remaining soldiers formed a skirmish line protecting the evacuees to the very last second.

****

Num sat in the back of a two-ton as Sai's truck drove by in the opposite direction. The young eighteen-year-old had heard the rumors of what was going on, but like the other young soldiers had no idea what really awaited them at the quarantined checkpoint.

He watched as truck after truck of civilians passed him going the opposite way. Some people had been mauled and were in the process of being bandaged, but most were just frighten and in a state of shock. The deuce and a half came to a stop in front of several wooden road barricades with orange blinking lights covered in barbed wire and signs in

Thai the military had hastily put up. Two tanks and a few police officers were there to greet the soldiers as they dropped the tailgate and jumped to the black pavement.

The streetlights fluttered, and as Num's boots hit the ground they went black. Only the fire of Khao San Road lit the horizon in that area. The echoes of the crowd panicking in the distances and the sounds of gunfire sent shivers down Num's spine as he looked in that direction.

Num took his station behind the roadblock and waited for orders as the tanks switched on their searchlights. Their beams lit the road to find only emptiness ahead of them. Several other tanks had gone through to reinforce a road block half a mile closer to Khao San Road moments before Num's arrival and were now keeping the infected busy. The odds of seeing any more survivors was quickly diminishing with each second that passed.

Another truck arrived and an Officer began to speak in Thai to the soldiers and the police officers from the bed of the vehicle.

"This is the second roadblock, gents, Charlie 2. Down the road is Charlie 1, and our orders are to kill anyone who tries to leave the quarantine zone, and I do mean anyone who is not driving a vehicle. I want a skirmish line set up here." He pointed to the ground with his rifle and drew an imaginary line behind the barricade. "I want the SAWs there and there." He pointed to the top of two trucks that were parked on opposite sides of the road flanking the two tanks.

The soldiers took up their positions and minutes later the sound of a vehicle came into earshot.

"Sir, it's Sergeant Wan!" shouted a private with a handheld radio. "Charlie 1 has been overrun, they are falling back!" Fear rang in his voice.

Num heard the commotion and knew they were next. He bit his lip when he saw a deuce coming up the road with men firing from the back of the truck in the opposite direction.

Num could not see what they were shooting at but soon the shrieks rose above the gunfire.

His eyes grew big and as the two-ton veered off the road and through an opening in the roadblock fear began to build. The two-ton came to a stop in the center of the road behind the barricade and the soldiers disembarked to join Charlie 2's men.

An NCO ran past Num and ordered his men to fall in behind the barricade as the tanks opened fire.

"Sergeant Wan! What the hell happened?" the officer shouted from behind the roadblock.

"Thousands of those fuckers! Sir!"

With that reply, Wan opened fire as he aimed over the shoulder of the officer with his rifle.

A wall of screaming people charged into the gunfire. Their bodies were pulverized by the cannon fire of the tanks and shredded by the SAWs. Yet the wall of bodies continued forth as they charged over their fallen brethren.

"RETREAT!" the officer shouted as the enemy closed to within fifty yards, charging like Olympic athletes.

Gunfire was not going to stop these things; it did not even slow them down, as what could be thousands charging their positions moved forward.

Wan grabbed Num who was about to run on foot like a dumbass and pulled him into the cab of the deuce.

"Drive," Wan ordered, as other soldiers began to jump up onto the bed.

The soldiers scrambled up top; but before most could get up, the rioters took them down. Only a handful made it up before Num was forced to press the gas and drive off.

Like before, the tanks were to slow to retreat and their drivers could not see where to go as the mass of bodies that now covered the tanks swarmed into a frenzy of motion.

Panicking, the tank drivers smashed into buildings, causing large portions of the buildings to come tumbling down, trapping the tanks. The last thing the crews heard hours later was the sound of bloody fists continuing to bang on the steel hull.

Chapter 2: *Fall of FOB Victory Monument*

Minutes had gone by since the two-ton had left Khao San Road, and in front of the Grand Palace, which was still lit in a golden light under emergency generators, Sai slowly regained consciousness. His blurry vision began to sharpen from a golden blur to distinct shapes that rushed past the vehicle.

Clearing his eyes, he awakened to see the little girl who was sitting on the old lady's lap staring down at him. The little girl was covered in dirt and dried-up tears and had a thumb in her mouth, a sign that she had been severely traumatized.

The back of Sai's head hurt like hell; he touched his head to find blood that had dried up into flakes.

Damn it hurts like hell, he thought to himself, *what the hell happened?*

The little girl's eyes locked onto Sai as she watched him touch his head again. Sniffling, she looked on as the stranger rubbed his head, causing her somehow to think of her father, which only caused her to tear up again.

Sai's senses finally rushed back to him like a tidal wave.

"Yoon!"

He snapped out of his daze and looked in all directions at once.

Looking around in a frantic motion, he found that Yoon was not in the truck with him, causing him to sit straight up; he saw two-ton after two-ton heading the opposite direction towards Khao San Road with their complements of soldiers in full battle gear. They were of all ages, mostly young, though, probably from the countless rice paddies of Thailand when they got drafted. No college meant your ass was in the army in that kingdom.

"Yoon!" Sai shouted as he tried to get up to his feet, only to have the soldier behind him put a hand on his shoulder forcing him back down.

The soldier was a man in his early twenties who looked as if the stress was about to break him. Standing next him was another soldier in his teens, probably just another one of Thailand's draftees.

Sai sat still in the center of the truck with the others sitting on benches around him. He quickly scanned around before turning his attention again towards the soldiers who were now looking at him.

"I need to find Yoon," Sai said in a low voice as he tried to stand up, resulting in the older soldier holding him down firmly with a hand on his shoulder. "Look you don't understand, I know where she is," he said, attempting to reason with the man as his pissed-off meter began to fill with every word he said.

There was not a chance in hell the two soldiers in the back nor the ones in the cabin were going to turn the deuce around to look for a single girl, and Sai knew it but still he pleaded his case.

"What the fuck is happening?" Sai asked the soldier, as the truck moved to a lit part of the city that was still on the power grid, growing more agitated with every passing second.

"I need to find Yoon!" He raised his voice with the soldier but only received a dumb look from him for he did not speak a bit of English.

"Listen, you dumb fuck, I'm going to beat the living shit out of you if you don't turn this buggy around!" Sai threatened, knowing the soldier did not understand a word he was saying, only the expression on his face showed his anger.

Sai grew furious as he stood up to their level, the two soldiers still trying to hold him down. But with Sai's muscle mass, he easily lifted the two soldiers and prepared to give them an ass whooping.

A loud voice came from behind Sai as he was getting ready to strangle the two men.

"The news said this has been going on since this morning, old chap," a British man interrupted, as he looked smiling at the three trying to break the tension that would lead to trouble.

Sai turned his head and leaned over to the old man. "What?" he asked, still pissed.

The British man was an older man, a little on the jolly side, thin glasses and a thin blonde mustache, dressed in a white Hawaiian t-shirt. A tourist or a pervert, it did not matter, what did matter was that the man was talking and he might have some information on what the hell was going on around here, even though Sai was preoccupied with the whereabouts of Yoon.

"I take it you're an American young man?" the man said with a heavy accent as Sai turned his head to look back towards Khao San Road, towards Yoon.

"Still in a little shock are you now?" the British man continued, almost as if he were talking to himself. The people in the back began looking at him as if he had something important to say, probably since he was the only one talking as they continued to move deeper into Bangkok.

Sai raised an eyebrow and turned his head, as a little sweat rolled down his cheek, and answered.

"I guess."

"You are a soldier, correct?"

"Yes, a pilot in the army. Listen, there is this girl, I need to find her." Sai replied, agitated that the two soldiers were now holding him firmly helping him sit back down once more. He could only hope that Yoon was on another truck because he feared that his failure to protect her had cost her life. "Can you tell these assholes to let me off this truck?"

"They may not be U.S. Marines, but these Thai chaps just saved your life and that girl you keep talking about is probably on one of the trucks down the road. Several trucks were loading people from where we picked you up."

Sai gained an ounce of hope as he looked at the truck half a block away. All he could see were silhouettes and headlights from the two-ton as it passed a group of soldiers on foot heading the opposite way.

The truck continued on as the man gave the news to Sai about what had been going on in Asia all day. Sai remained distracted however, thinking of Yoon whom he had left on the floor of a battleground. As information flowed from the British man's mouth, the truck's occupants of all nationalities took it in as Sai scanned the trucks behind him.

It did not take long until the two-ton came to a stop near Victory Monument. Victory Monument was a large circular drive. On one side of the road a half circle track from when the Sky Train was built; around fifty feet off the ground and in the center of the circular road was a large monument to the military for their victory in the Franco-Thai war in 1941. Statues of Thai soldiers lined the centerpiece, which resembled the Washington Monument in D.C., except smaller in scale.

The circular road had always been a busy center for Bangkok any time of day, and now the traffic had been backed up and the cars were bumper to bumper with the drivers blowing their horns nonstop. Many families were now in refugee mode, pulling carts, traveling on bicycles and motorcycles between the cars, turning the traffic into a full gridlock of bodies and vehicles.

Police and soldiers patrolled the surging crowd along with German Shepherds, even though they did not truly understand what they were patrolling for. Yet even without such knowledge, they did their best to control the chaos that was before them, all the time wondering why the gun ships circled above like carrion birds waiting for their next meal.

The pilots were in a holding pattern above rotating counter clockwise over the monument, waiting for ground units to direct their fire, to fire at something that was little more than an eight-digit MGRS grid on the ground to them.

From their circling perch, they saw first-hand the flood of people below. A living tide growing by the second as many civilians left the safety and comfort of the surrounding buildings to become part of the river of refugees that flowed through the streets in waves.

****

It was close to midnight now, and from the direction of the Grand Palace Sai could see the anti-collision lights of several F-16s tear through the sky. Their thunderous roar vibrated the ground as they flew across the Bangkok skyline.

Crossing the Grand Palace, the jets pulled up and a few moments later 500-pound bombs ripped up the area of Khao San Road and the Grand Palace. What some would say was the heart of Thailand was now gone, and all who witnessed the blast prayed the King and Queen made it out alive.

The jets had dived down from the sky screaming excitedly for the hell they would bring to their targets below as they released several pairs of bombs. The bombs pierced the nighttime sky whistling to the ground towards a surging mob that was overrunning the Grand Palace guards. The shockwaves of the bombs echoed throughout Bangkok in tremendous echoes.

From miles around and even on the outskirts of Bangkok along the rice fields, heads turned in the direction of the bombs going off. The sky would light up like lighting as each bomb hit and a thunderous boom was shortly followed. The light from the blast reflected off overcast cloud layer, which gave the onlookers an ominous look that produced dread.

Something was surely coming to life in Bangkok and the bombing was the birthing pains. Those who were not aware of what was going on were now aware that something was happening as they woke from their beds and quickly turned on their television sets and radios.

"The insurgents must have taken the palace," Sai said to himself, still not knowing what was really happening, his head turned away from the direction of the bombing, which continued for more than a minute.

"Insurgents? Were you not listening? This is not a civil war, this is something new and definitely something no one has ever seen before," the British man quickly explained. "You Americans and your insurgents, how absurd."

The British man continued to talk until Sai's attention caught something disturbing.

A minute had gone by as a new wave of bombing began and Sai began to see an increasing amount of people running from the direction of the Grand Palace/Khao San Road and past the two-ton several cars away.

Sai looked sharply but could not see Yoon in the back of any trucks behind him as he continued to scan. The people running only meant one thing, hell was quickly approaching, and if she was alive he needed to find her.

"I need a gun."

Sai stood up to the soldier who was watching the people running, almost shitting in his drawers. Sai felt naked without a weapon and knew the time to get one would be sooner rather than later.

There was a commotion in the cab of the truck as the radio came to life in Thai. The passengers who were Thai turned their heads in quick response listening to the vital information that the foreigners could not understand.

"Khun Tahan mai?" The soldier looked like he was about to have a heart attack as he asked Sai. By no means was it the high and tight that gave him away.

The British man then spoke up in Thai.

"Tahan Nackbin American..." the British man continued.

Sai knew those words but not the rest. He heard American Military pilot.

The soldier looked at Sai and then looked at the crowd coming from that direction.

"Solda?" he asked Sai.

"Chai" Sai replied.

Sai knew he was talking to the Thai equivalent of a private, when the soldier knocked on the cabin of the two-ton as the radio continued to issue instructions.

He spoke in Thai and Sai heard Puun, which meant gun.

He must be asking the sergeant Sai thought to himself as the soldier continued to talk to the man in the truck. This might be his lucky day.

An M-16 was now hanging outside the right window as the man inside gave it to the private. The man inside quickly rolled up his window as he readied his 9-mm berretta.

The Private grabbed the rifle and looked at Sai.

"Shoot in head, make dead."

"What the fuck?" Sai mumbled, as an eyebrow rose up.

Sai grabbed the rifle in disbelief. These guys just gave him a rifle, something that would have never happened in the U.S. military but the situation was far worse than Sai knew. Not far away, the army was already handing out weapons to Thai men and farang who were or looked like they could be soldiers from other countries in order to slow the contagion that was now on the move across Bangkok.

The radio was actually blasting to all units within the vicinity of Victory Monument to give out weapons in accordance with the general who was in charge of the Bangkok Theater.

"All units within a 3-k radius of Nest 12 must immediately recruit local and foreign nationals to aid in the defense of Nest 12. Break. You have been authorized to issue out arms. Break. All Thai males between the ages of 17 to 29 will be drafted and sent to Nest 12. Break. Further orders are on the way; keep the net clear."

In Thailand it was customary for high school males to attend a military summer camp that was neither basic training nor a hike in the woods with Kumbaya shit.

So the generals had ordered the arming of the civilian population and mobilization of all able bodied males within earshot of Nest 12 which was one of many FOBs, or Forward Operating Bases, around Bangkok that were being used as satellites for the HQ which existed somewhere outside of the city.

Sai stood up and looked out the back of the two-ton when the Private handed him two magazines. Several more men were given weapons and told to protect the truck in Thai.

"That's why I retired to Thailand, friendly chaps." The British man smiled as he took out a handkerchief to wipe the sweat from his forehead, interrupted by the young Private who handed him a combat knife. "Well better than nothing I suppose."

More and more people began to run by when Sai noticed two individuals tackle down a woman several cars away just like the European Party Crashers at the bar in Khao San Road had done.

The Private opened fire, hitting several rounds in their backs but the people still clawed and bit the woman.

Sai pulled the bolt back and chambered a round and smoothly took aim and fired, and he too hit the back of one of the rioters with a single shot.

They were not falling in his disbelief as he fired another shot that hit the shoulder as the rioter violently bit the woman repeatedly. *Is this fucker wearing body armor?* Hell no, the guy looked skinnier than a twelve year old girl.

He fired again when a lucky shot from the Private finally hit one of them in the side of the head sending brains, blood and gore onto the white car next to them. *Shoot in head make dead, no shit!* Sai thought.

This shit was not happening Sai thought to himself as he took aim and sent another round down range and missed luckily his second round struck into the back of the other attacker's head.

"This is not going to be easy." He was a pilot, not a ground pounder anymore for god's sake.

Sai along with all other Soldiers, Marines, Airmen and Sailors around the world had been trained to hit center mass, a head smaller than a basketball running at you could only be brought down at point blank range or with really good aim. These people moved too fast for headshots and Sai took a gulp at the thought of what was happening all around him. It was slowly sinking in, very slowly, that's probably why he was in the Army and not in the Air Force; these attacking people were already dead.

Sai looked to the Private who was dripping in sweat while the other soldier grabbed more weapons that the sergeant handed him from the cabin. Just screwdrivers, wrenches, box cutters anything that could be wielded as a weapon from a medium size toolbox.

As the soldier handed out the tools, gunfire erupted from a two-ton several cars away. The distinct reports of the M-16s pierced the air almost as the fourth of July had begun. The soldiers of the two-ton were fending off a group of aggressors who were attacking those in the back of the truck. Bloody limbs swung violently as fingers and hands were blown off by the defenders. Like Sai's truck everything was being used as a weapon as they tried desperately to keep their attackers from climbing into the bed of the truck.

****

The milky eyes of the dead did not blink; they did not flinch as they reached out for their prey while all manner of weapons came crashing down upon them. Their eyes were like sharks, dead and soulless, it wasn't until their lips retracted exposing their jaws that one could see something beyond human was driving them. Only a hollow shell filled with evil was all that remained.

The passengers under attack on that truck screamed in all languages as the first of the dead ones climbed over the railing, a boy no more than the age of ten with a huge gouges on his cheeks and neck grabbed a gray haired elderly woman from France and with his bloody hand pulled her skull to his mouth. His teeth shattered as he tried to bite through bone and even as they shattered with her skull in his mouth he managed to break through into the brains. Blood sprayed out onto the woman's gray hair as if she had dropped a drink on herself. Screaming in terror and pain the old lady felt her skull give way as the boy sank his teeth deeper into her. Shattered bone broke through the bloodied scalp as her head slowly caved in.

A man next to the panicking elderly woman grabbed the child by the hair and pulled him back causing him to take some of the brain matter out of the dying woman's head. The man then picked the boy up; the boy quickly opened his mouth, the brain matter falling out onto his shirt and started snapping at the man. Quickly the man launched the boy into the crowd below. The boy slammed into the people at the base of the truck who quickly tossed him aside sending him smashing through the windshield of a taxi parked behind the truck. He wiggled for a second then stopped, killed by his own brethren.

Sai and the others in the back of his truck opened fire on the attackers of the other truck in an attempt to help them. Their rounds slammed into the bodies only to produce little results as small red explosions continued to pepper the crowd.

****

Sai was aiming for the head of one of the dead near the cabin of the truck when he noticed Yoon jumping from the top of the cabin of the truck and onto the hood. From his gun sights he took aim and fired at a man who tried to reach out for her. She looked frantic as she slid down the windshield and onto the hood as Sai released another round this time hitting the man in the temple.

Sitting on the bumper, Yoon looked around to see the dead were focused on the occupants on the bed of the truck, with the coast clear she jumped off the bumper and onto the road ahead of the truck. A hand immediately reached out for her ankle from below the two-ton but failed to grab her as she began to take flight through the maze of cars. She did not look back once as she escaped the slaughter that was now taking place on the bed of the truck as the dead continuously poured over the railing to the living.

****

Yoon had been lucky at Khao San Road, just in a matter of seconds after being knocked unconscious by the explosion. The mob turned their attention onto the tank that had fired at those who had left the hotel exit.

While Sai was being thrown into the truck, a soldier had recognized the movie star as one of the living and seeing her unconscious body gasping for air under the dust and smoke he ran for her. The soldier quickly dragged her towards safety while firing his M-16 at the incoming crowd and with the last seconds of his life he dropped his weapon and tossed Yoon onto his back and ran for the truck while the dead swarmed the tank.

Just feet away from the truck with Yoon in the fireman carry a hand grabbed the soldier's boot and he felt teeth sink into his calf. With the last ounce of energy he military pressed Yoon over his head and with all his might tossed her to a soldier near the truck. His comrade caught Yoon and carried her into the truck as the unlucky soldier was tackled to the asphalt by the undead tide.

At Victory Monument seconds prior to the dead swarming her two-ton, she had seen Sai shooting along with another soldier at the men who were attacking a woman near her position. She had been sitting on the two-ton when she had seen him, emotionally alone since she had awakened on the truck, which felt like ages ago. She rose to her feet and started moving towards the front of the truck. That is when the mob attacked the two-ton, while fighting against other panicking people who were trying to pass her by pulling her back she was forced to punch a young man who grabbed her hair trying to use her as a ladder to move towards the cabin in order to save his own life. His nose caved in under her fist and he let loose his death grip allowing her to continue to push forward.

Now here she was running through the surviving crowd as people fled in all directions jumping over cars and using them as a kind of sidewalk.

"Yoon!" Sai shouted at the top of his lungs putting a hand over the rail of the truck while simultaneously leaping down to the pavement.

Immediately after hitting the road Sai was pushed aside onto a stalled Toyota by a man who was trying to save his family. He regained his bearings as he saw a bloodied hand reach out from below the Toyota towards his foot.

"Shit!" He kicked the hand and began to run through the crowd as the shrieking war cries of the dead came from all directions he raised his rifle at everyone who came close not sure who was friend or who was foe for the confusion was maddening.

Through the mayhem just inches from Sai people were being taken down to the ground, people were killing each other, punching everything that came to close for all around him killing had become the norm as humanity dissolved.

The little girl watched as Sai shot a man at point blank range in the face as the people in the back of her truck began to fend off several attackers who were now jumping up from the side of the truck.

Up above the UH-1s were now beginning to open fire in the direction of the Grand Palace, first the crew chiefs fired from the sides of the Hueys, tracer rounds disappearing into the carnage below not slowing the tsunami one bit as it continued to pour its way through the streets towards Victory Monument.

Where Sai was running was just a few splashes of the undead wave, just the spray of the wave for over a mile away where the helicopters fired, nothing with a pulse was moving towards Victory Monument only the dead walked as they pursued their prey.

Sai glided through the cars that still had people inside cowering from the madness outside. The cowering were in a state of shock just like at the bar earlier. They were confused and frighten and did not react until it was too late.

Sai pushed through several panicking civilians and punched another who tried to grab his rifle all the while trying desperately to keep Yoon in his sights as men and women bumped into her causing her to veer out of his vision every other second.

Making his way killing another person Sai heard the siren wailing from the center of Victory Monument. He felt as if he was in London during the blitz as aircraft continued to rain down hell only a mile away. The ground shook and he lost his footing on more than one occasion as the bombs exploded. He felt the pressure waves push him aside as if he was a reed in the wind. His vision blurred, his body shook as concussion after concussion sent vibrations into his body yet after each blast he pushed on towards Yoon determined to reach her.

A man jumped up on a yellow car's hood besides Yoon just after another bomb had hit, Sai hastily sent three rounds down that direction and one hit his eye socket causing the back of his skull to explode with gray matter onto a window of the yellow car as a kid watched from within. The body slammed into the window and to the road and disappeared underneath the surging crowd around Yoon.

Lucky shot Sai thought, very lucky the man stopped on the hood before leaping onto Yoon. Dead or not Sai did not know but the man looked like he was going to be a threat to her and with no time to think he had fired three rounds.

Yoon ran to Sai screaming his name at the top of her lungs. In a short time, they seemed to have grown quite close due to the pending situation. Instead of hugging and kissing like some romance movie, Sai grabbed her arm and made a 180-degree turn in the opposite direction.

She ran behind Sai holding onto the back of his shirt after Sai let go of her arm to aim at another crazed woman foaming at the mouth covered in cuts. He fired hitting her in the chest sending her to the ground to be trampled by running civilians, not sticking around to see the outcome they continued towards the direction of his two-ton that was leading away from the undead tsunami.

"Forgive me, Yoon!" Sai shouted back not knowing if Yoon heard while in commotion the Private from the truck put the selector lever his rifle into full auto and began to spray down one side of the truck. It was clear that the boy had lost his cool as he burned through his 30-round magazines.

Sai turned to watch as the two soldiers in the cabin jumped out firing at the mob only to be thrown to the ground as the rioters surrounded three sides of the truck but not the front due to the lack of live meat.

Sai fired as well trying to help the two-ton that had saved him, but the crowd was on top of them and not much could be done, the mass of bodies swarmed and his shots went wide hitting the creatures in the back and arms with two direct hits putting two down for good.

Like Yoon, the little girl had some how had managed to crawl onto the top of the cabin and slid down the windshield escaping certain death again as the two soldiers and few civilians in the truck bed fired down at the mob that continued to swarm and grow larger with every second that passed. She slid down the windshield and her butt hit the top of the hood of the truck.

The infected scaled the sides of the truck and found their way into the juicy flesh within while up above a Huey launched rockets over their heads towards Khao San Road. Screeching at the top of their lungs the infecteds' hands were being shredded by the frantic passengers, and as their flesh being torn off their hands they still managed to pull themselves over the rail and into the bed.

The British man screamed as his throat was torn out yet still he tried to fend off the attack with his combat knife, the blade finding the ribs of the young girl who had pinned the man down. A few passengers down the old Thai woman stopped an elderly man from following the little girl over the top of the cabin, holding his ankle with all her might she struggled with her grip. The pain of two men biting through her arms was too much to bear. Screaming, she held onto the elderly man, who was covered in blood; shreds of flesh missing, she held strong – giving Sai enough time to put a round into the man's head. The old lady let go of the man's ankle when he flew back into the bed of the truck as the infected continued to attack her. Through a crowd of hands she saw the little girl's butt as she slid down the windshield and beyond sight and through the frenzy of hands across her face she saw the street lights explode into sparks bathing the area in darkness, her vision faded into oblivion.

Sai ran towards the hood of the car where the child now sat crying, her mouth wide open, tears rolling down her cheeks that were now flushed red with fear, her head swiveled back and forth as she screamed in

Thai probably calling out for her mother not realizing she was already dead; that is when another man slid down the windshield behind her with jagged fingers reaching for her. Seeing the man reaching for the child Sai immediately butt stroked the man across the face with the stock of his rifle. The impact sent his teeth flying through his cheeks and onto the windshield. With one hit his jaw had been shattered and with another his head caved in causing the windshield to give way. The man had been alive but Sai would never know of the murder he had just committed.

Yoon, almost as if she was on the same wavelength with Sai grabbed the child and started running as Sai covered their escape leaving the infected to cut down the people to pieces in the back of the truck. The attack continued until every last one of the people in the truck was turned into disfigured human train wreck.

The two-ton was dead now, and the three were fleeing as the mob began to smash their way through car windows desperately reaching for the tasty morsels inside like they were sardine cans just lying around the street.

****

No one was spared from the onslaught, kids were ripped from their mothers' arms kicking and screaming while fathers fought to the death against an enemy who would not die. The savagery of the attacks was far beyond the level of any animal attack. At least with lions, tigers and bears you always had the chance of scaring them off, this was not the case as people tried everything on them to no avail. Tanks, bombs, and cursing at them had no effect; some even tried to reason with their attackers, it was a kill or be killed world now and only the strong and smart would survive.

The dead feasted on the flesh of their victims, breaking teeth on the bones of their meals not minding it one bit as they continued to devour the flesh. In the chaos of the massacre that was taking place all around, people sought shelter wherever they could. Some under trucks watching people run by, watching people fall and butchered by their peers and when the infected caught notice they would surround the cars and all try to crawl underneath at the same time tearing these would be survivors to shreds.

Almost a quarter of a mile of running through the maze of cars, Sai, Yoon and the little girl had outrun the mob again. People who stayed in their cars helped slow down the mob which gave the trio the precious time necessary needed to push on past the initial contact with the dead.

The gunships above opened fire behind the trio as they reached the center of Victory Monument this time a lot closer as a few more fighter aircraft soared high above waiting for their battle orders. Tracers flew through the air down at the rampaging crowd followed routinely by rockets. Cars and men were shredded alike, the twisted metal entangled in a mosaic of burnt flesh. The trio could feel the heat coming off the blast of the rockets as cars exploded sending heat waves in all directions.

The back of Sai's neck stung as each blast toasted the hairs on his neck while the concussions continued to send pressure waves through his chest but not as bad as the bombs that were now waiting for orders to be dropped.

If people were panicked before now they had gone into overdrive as they left their vehicles. Gunshots opened up all around and Sai knew deep down inside that if he turned and fight like a good soldier would, he would only end up dead if not from the infected but from the Thai Army for sure who was on the verge of killing everything in sight.

Rushing past the built up defenses at the center of Victory Monument that surrounded the statues, the word zombie finally entered the back of his mind, if that is what they were; then the quarantine had failed at Khao San Road which meant the end of Bangkok as the people knew it. That word had eluded him since his first head shot, too busy surviving to even give a shit of what they were, but here he was, and here they were and they surely must have eaten their way past the tanks and were now heading towards downtown Bangkok which would packed full of new recruits for this forming undead army. Perfect place for recruiting for unofficially the city had over 14 million people living in it.

The crowd surged in the streets as bodies were crammed together to create a sea of people with waves upon waves pushing smashing crashing against parked cars and buildings. The screams and explosions sent the little girl into shock. Her eyes were wide open with fear, never blinking, never crying for she was now beyond the point of crying and at the brink of madness. Sai reached over to Yoon who was beginning to struggle being shoved around like a rag doll by the crazed mob as she held the little girl trying desperately not to lose Sai in the living sea of people. Sai picked the little girl up with one arm while he held the rifle with the other as Yoon secured her grip on Sai's shirt, losing him would mean certain death in this frenzy of moving bodies.

The river of bodies continued to flow through Victory Monument with infected sprinkled throughout the sea. The mass crushed cars as hundreds ran on roofs of vehicles trying desperately to jump from one car to another to keep out of the living sea that flowed between the vehicles. Below Yoon's feet, the ground was soft with trampled bodies of hundreds and she was unaware that as she followed Sai she had already walked over several of the infected who were permanently crushed under the weight of the living sea of refugees pinned to the ground unable to bite.

Not a tall man by any means Sai was having trouble looking over the shoulders of the mob and with his rifle now facing down there was no way he could lift it if one of the infected was just inches away, all he could do was pray it would be fast. If they continued down this path, they would be seriously fucked; there was no telling how many in the traffic were already infected and were turning this instant. Nor could they tell how far the infection was down the road as the Tsunami of the living sea poured in one direction down the road being forever pushed from the rear by the oncoming slaughter.

Thousands upon thousands rushed as gunfire continued to erupt everywhere, from the roofs of buildings soldiers fired into the fray, not even aiming, panicking, all hell had fallen and all orders were evaporating as their leadership was taken out.

Zipping by Yoon's head, a bullet hit the side of a man's face sending him flying to the left; several more puffs of red spray flew into the air as others in the crowd were hit, their bodies slowly falling to the carpet below.

On top of a car, not far from Yoon a soldier had been pinned to the ground by several people and as they brutally bit into him his hand never left the trigger of his weapon and every shot hit someone below in the crowd near Yoon until the magazine was spent.

The tide pushed Sai, Yoon and the little girl towards an abandon bus. It was an old fashion bus painted green with no air-conditioning, the kind you'd expect in a third world nation but comfort did not matter and Sai immediately led the group into it escaping the living sea.

Sai smashed the doorway of the bus in, to find a trail of blood leading down the steps to his feet. He ran up the steps followed by Yoon and the little girl who had found her way back into Yoon's arms again. Sai quickly cleared the bus finding only body parts on several of the seats but nothing else and relaxed a bit. They caught a breath when Sai closed the rear door of the bus and began to make his way to the front of the bus past the body parts again. At the front of the bus he looked out the windshield and from his vantage point he could see stairs leading over to a Sky Walk that connected to the Sky Train not to far from the bus. The crowd was flowing around the stairs, very few finding their way up.

"We need to get up there Yoon!" Sai turned from the driver's seat back to Yoon and the little girl, pointing with his right hand over his shoulder to the stairs. He still was barely catching his breath and sweat still dripping from his head.

Yoon nodded in response and held the little girl's head tight with her hand.

"We'll hop from car to car!" he continued as he continued to sweat profusely, "Can't fall or we're done!" He gulped as he wiped the sweat from his eyes. The bus rocked for no reason and then he turned his head back towards the stairs as the screaming outside continued to sound more and more like white noise on a television set. "We got to go now!"

Sai kicked out the windshield of bus and moved to the hood denting it in the process and there he was again back into the night air of hell. Hell as it was, he realized that the nighttime air was much better than the sweatbox of the bus. He had to see the bright side of things.

Yoon handed Sai the little girl and made her way beside Sai being careful not to cut her hands on the broken glass. As Sai readied himself to move Yoon saw several infected people to the right of the bus. Stuck in the living sea all they could do was bite the shoulders of those around them. The people screamed in anguish and horror, knowing that there was nothing they could do to stop the simplest of attacks. So tightly packed the infected were multiplying faster than ever through nothing fancier than to bite the person next to you.

"I see it too. Stay to the cars!" Sai shouted as he slung his rifle behind his back and grabbed the little girl with both hands. Holding her he jumped to the car in front of him over infected and living alike. The crowd just watched as Sai's boots made it to the island followed shortly after by Yoon.

Sai readied himself for the next jump and noticed a woman that had been moving with the tide of the living when he was in it. She was now biting into someone's neck and Sai counted his blessing for being on top of the car now. Thankfully the bus gave the trio the option of island hopping or that lady would be sinking her teeth into him.

Sai jumped again and again along with Yoon and found they were nearing the staircase next to a Boat Noodle shop that was in the process of being ransacked by people trying to hide.

The area was packed but not nearly as the street that was funneling people over a bridge towards safety. Sai put the little girl down on the truck bed that they were now standing on and unslung his rifle preparing for a fight as Yoon took the girl into her arms and looked around making sure nothing was sneaking up on them.

Quickly Sai jumped down from the truck sending someone or something to the floor and began to bulldoze his way through the crowd as Yoon followed behind. He was like an icebreaker ship as he moved making a pathway for Yoon and the little girl to follow.

A few quick seconds later he was making his way up the stair case and he butt stroked and infected woman who had turned her attention from feeding on a child to Sai. Her face caved in under the plastic butt stock and she fell backwards slamming the back of her head into the cement staircase resulting in a nice new indention that crushed her brain.

"RUN!" He grabbed Yoon and helped her up the staircase, ever vigilante of what was to come.

Skipping every other step and dodging those who were fighting it out with the infected they made it up as the thunderous blast began to rip the area near the center of the monument.

Claymores were going off every few seconds as the soldiers in the center of the round monument began to fall back to the behind the barb wire perimeter they had built up earlier.

Scrambling over the wire in their retreat, many soldiers were getting entangle, becoming easy prey for the dead that pursued them now.

The trio ran to the top of the stairwell and headed towards the train station, while below the battle had become lop-sided. The soldiers who fought bravely to the end were now dead and with the street packed with cars the rest of the army was having a hard time getting to the scene of the battle being miles away to be of any use to those who were left. The FOB was in the process of being over run as the Trio continued to run towards safety.

A Huey hovered out of the corner of Sai's eye as they continued to run; soldiers fast roped their way into the carnage below setting up a last stand at the monument's FOB with a last ditch effort to hold the revered monument.

Upon reaching the ground the soldiers opened fire as civilians and soldiers worked together to build a makeshift circular barricade out of debris, cars, and bodies inside the barbwire perimeter. Standing in the center a Thai Colonel pulled out his 9 mm Beretta as he continued to issue orders from the base of the monument as his battalion dwindled in front of his eyes. His boys were being taken out all around him so the Colonel joined the fray picking up a rifle that had been dropped just seconds before.

The trio was now passing person after person, along with the two man sniper teams that lined the catwalk of the Victory Monument. The trio made their way to the Sky Train which was now shutdown abandoned by the employees and security guards due to it being out of power as blackouts began to spread across the grid of Bangkok.

Behind the trio snipers continued to fire every other second, trying to decipher who was infected and who was not, but in a crowded ocean of bodies determining who was one and who was not one was an impossible task and soon after the trio passed them continuing their evasion the radio blared out from the Colonel in the center of the monument with new orders. Fire on everyone, friend or foe, the monument was falling.

They fired at everything, women, children, men, infected or not they launched round after round down range as the Colonel fought on below with now less than fifty men still alive in a swarm of thousands.

In the FOB the last stand was falling and the snipers could see that from their perch that the battle was nearly over. The ocean of people below was the living dead, who were jumping over the overturned cars, breaching the barricades and wall of bodies to get to the soldiers at the monument's center.

The soldier's fixed bayonets and formed a circle, shoulder to shoulder as the first of the dead penetrated the barricade charging to be greeted by three bayonets that held him in place. The infected man was quickly followed by two, then five, and an avalanche of the undead began to break through the barricade.

The Colonel looked up at the Hueys as they circled above, and with sweat rolling down his cheeks he ordered them to send rockets into his position. The battle for Victory Monument was over and all he could offer his men was a quick death, a release from the pain they would endure from the hands of the dead.

As the first of the dead tackled the Colonel, rockets came crashing down pulverizing all that remained at the monument's base and the structure came tumbling down landing on hundreds of people as the trio made their way to the Sky Train platform. The explosions lit up the trios' backs.

Sai had no plans to wait around for the power to come back on to the train station and with the help of landing lights from the helicopters circling above he jumped down onto the tracks and helped Yoon and the child down as onlookers watched not knowing what to do as panic began to make its way up the Sky Walk towards the Sky Train station.

The trio started to run towards Sai's hotel, Chit Lom, several miles away and in the direction of Yoon's aunt's house.

The snipers on the Sky Walk over the monument found themselves being preyed upon by the living dead as the creatures made their way up the staircase and towards the platform devouring those in their path.

People began to jump to the tracks as the trio had to escape the hell at Victory Monument while the snipers and few police still alive on the Sky Walk battled it out, doing their duty to the end to the defend the fleeing civilians.

Running across the Sky Train's tracks Sai could see over the edge, there he watched as tanks crushed cars below to get to the lost battle at Victory Monument while jets continued to scream by from above with afterburners breaking the sound barrier and chattering windows of buildings surrounding the Sky Train's tracks. Next the thunderous explosions went off, the air sucked from the area temporarily as they dropped their payloads into the streets where the FOB had been

The blast sent pieces of cars, pavement, people shooting through the sky in all directions, hundreds of feet into the night time air causing giant plumes of black smoke to rise that reflected the light from the raging fires below.

Where the Colonel had made his stand a second bomb fell, flesh was ripped from bone in a blinding hot white light, disintegrating like ash as the pressure wave shattered the Sky Walk that the trio had ran just minutes ago to get to the Sky Train.

Minutes had gone by and now young people and fleeing soldiers began to pass Sai and his group. Running for their lives had given everyone an endless supply of energy, but Sai was carrying a child and even with Yoon's help he felt fatigue pulling the blanket of tiredness in, yet even with his lungs now burning and muscle failure in his arms he continued on for he had been in a race of survival ever since leaving Khao San Road and he was not going to come in second.

Below and close to Victory Monument, NCOs and Officers began to fire on the soldiers who were abandoning their post. The military was in the process of mass desertions after hearing what was going on at Nest 12. Even with bullets in their backs, it was better to be killed quickly than to be devoured alive and so they ran.

For almost thirty minutes the people on the Sky Train tracks ran and soon MBK was coming into sight when a searchlight from a Huey spotted them fleeing. The blinding light pierced their eyes as the people tried to shield themselves from the white light with their hands.

The light flashed over Sai several times as if they were looking for the dead within the mob, and it was not long until the Huey launched several rockets into the Sky Train tracks behind the survivors. The Sky Train tracks had been severed and the dead ran off like a stampeding herd to their permanent deaths below. Charging forth they did not care if the tracks were still there, they were going all the way at one hundred and ten percent.

The dead had almost been on top of them and if it were not for the Huey they would have over taken the living in a matter of minutes.

"Thanks guys!" Sai shouted at the top of his lungs thankful for a guardian angel watching over his shoulder.

The Huey pilot smiled as he turned his attention down the road to launch some more hell from above.

Below the Sky Train, where the tracks had been blown in half, the army fired up at the tracks tearing the dead to pieces and sending body parts raining down. Some survived the fall only to be met with a barrage of bullets.

The pilot in the Huey had bought Sai, Yoon and the little girl time and at the MBK station the trio climbed off the tracks and ran down the escalator to the Sky Walk before they continued to push towards Central World and Chit Lom.

****

The army was now everywhere below them and as they continued on Sai thought it best to now to seek the Army's help, especially since the area looked dead free. Maybe they could get them on a transport out of there, but Yoon protested even as she saw civilians loading the two-tons like the ones that had brought her to Victory Monument below.

She needed to get to her aunt and the feeling in her stomach told her that time was running out for them. The dead may soon be knocking on their door soon.

Stopping and looking at Yoon, Sai thought about ditching the kid with one of the Army trucks below, especially since carrying her across Bangkok did not seem to appealing.

Sai looked at the little girl who was now sucking on her thumb and realized the girl was too old to be doing that but with the shit she had been through that night he could understand. The little voice in his head kept telling him: *If you leave that girl she will die, she'd be torn to pieces, and it would be your fault.* With that thought in mind, the grouped moved on towards Yoon's aunts home.

The distance they still had to go seemed so unrealistic. His insides screamed *what the fuck, what it fuck are you doing dumbass,* that was the selfish part of him, the scared part of him was telling him to run, *fuck Yoon, fuck the little girl and save yourself.*

Sai continued to run with that mental battle going on in his mind, but the honor he still had left, that piece of chivalry told him to do the illogical thing, find Yoon's family, save Yoon and save the little girl, even if it will cost you your life. Stupid decision or not Sai was not going to run out on these two and so he pressed on.

Their legs burned as they continued towards Chit Lom, each step a scream from their muscles to stop, just walk, and just give up. Each breath was a stabbing wound to the lungs, just walk, go to sleep, don't worry just rest a bit and before you know it you'll be one of them.

****

Near the Bangkok Train station Hua Lomphong, the traffic had become dense as the two-ton came to a stop. Wan checked the rounds in his magazine and decided against putting in a fresh magazine in.

Scared as Wan was, he still remained true to the NCO creed of Thailand and remained professional, a shiny example to Num and the other soldiers who found themselves under him. The men had been terrified, some in a rocking stupor, some letting their bowels loose and so forth. The only comfort they had known was leaving Khao San Road and heading towards semi safety.

Num had already driven through Charlie 3 and 4. Three was in the process of abandoning the post and four had already been abandoned only a few warning signs, a yellow strip of tape telling people to keep out and a few wrecked cars that had been shot up were all that remained.

The train station had been converted into a rescue station for those caught in the chaos on the east side of the river. The World War II era train station on a normal day looked like the scene for a romance movie where a soldier boarded the train and the girl ran after him only to cry and blow kisses. The scene was kind of the same except that as the trains departed with overwhelming numbers of passengers, others ran after them trying desperately to board them, some even becoming victims to the sharp wheels of the trains themselves.

Under the large pavilion like center of Hua Lomphong, sand bags had been place around the entrances, with gun emplacement facing the doors from within and others outside facing the surging crowds. Men and women in white biochemical suits examined those that were entering the station thoroughly before letting them through under the watchful eyes of the military.

The station was packed beyond anything Wan had ever seen before in his many times riding the trains. Suitcases, animals, plastic bags of food, children all being rushed along by the soldiers, it looked like a rodeo of sorts, or a slaughterhouse to be more exact. The cattle being rushed through the wooden fences and through a maze to end up getting their head's pulverized if they were infected.

The scene outside was like all others, the traffic in a gridlock, thousands of civilians rushing between the cars like a stream of water. As crazy as it was, the dead had not entered the vicinity; there was an order to the chaos that the dead brought. For when they arrived, panic would fill the rear of the mob from where they came and slowly that panic would push forward like a wave of water, that was their order to the chaos which was spreading throughout Bangkok. The tsunami of death was expanding.

Wan and what was left of Charlie 1 and 2 were now a combined squad of men. Wan was the ranking man sine the officer disappeared, being the NCO of the group he led them pass the sandbag security wall that had formed a perimeter around the train station that was made up of hastily built fences, overturned vehicles and plenty of barb wire. They moved passed the howitzer emplacements that pointed down the road where the trouble had all began and then went into the building as medical teams continued to search each and every individual before entering the station.

He found an officer sitting at a table who was surrounded by many sergeants all awaiting orders. The man was flustered and drenched in sweat as he tried to manage all the requests that were pouring in when Wan arrived.

Wan tried to get his attention but with the constant demands being poured in he was quickly passed over until he fired his sidearm into the air. The civilians erupted in screams for a brief few seconds and when all looked clear they continued to move like cattle into the trains again.

The gunshot caught the officer's attention and he looked up at Wan with opened eyes. The surrounding NCOs grew quiet as they all turned to Wan.

"I was at Charlie 1, we were overrun, Charlie 2 was over run, Charlie 3 was abandoning the post as we drove through and no one is at fucking Charlie 4 the enemy is fucking coming sir they've got a clear shot to here!"

The officer swallowed his saliva not knowing what to do. His mind was blank; as a junior grade officer he never truly had any experience to rely on. He was lost, breaking down inside, the pressure had been tremendous and now Charlie 4, the last point between those things and the makeshift rescue station was gone. They were wide open for an attack, which was the last thing he needed on his plate.

"Victory Monument is gone, Grand Palace is gone. The battle line is now reported to be MBK, Watergate Amari Hotel and the river. We, We, We, need to evacuate. We need to run! We need to get the fuck out of here!"

The officer began to grow hysterical and panic swiftly went through the ranks as a few NCOs immediately made a run to the remaining train. The officer had broken down, the pressure was too strong, stronger than anyone could have realized; he was only in charge because the other officers could not be found; he was a logistics supply officer for god's sake, not a goddamned infantryman!

Wan looked at the remaining NCOs who still held their bearings and back to his men behind him as the officer ran to the train.

"What I say?" Wan chuckled as he looked around causing the others to laugh as well. It was a dumb joke but enough to make the men at ease once more. "Men, I'm taking over this cluster fuck and we need to defend these civvies. We defend them and then we leave. I want to know how many tanks we have and I want your men to flip the cars on their sides to form a second perimeter around the entrance to this complex. Get all your men out on the wire, and I want a 360-degree line of fire around this building. Get your sharpshooters to the top and in the next twenty mikes we need to seal off the building from the outside. Only soldiers will be allowed in and out from then on."

"What about the civvies outside the barricade?"

"I estimate the way those fuckers run they will here in twenty five mikes. Means that the majority will already be dead and those closest to us will be under heavy attack, we can't save them all and if we let several infected in without passing through a wall of lead all hell will break lose. I know its FUBAR, and I know many of you want to board the next train out of here, but we are soldiers, we are the Royal Thai Army men, we will defend these civvies and when our job is done we will pull out. Make no mistake about this men, we are here to by time for these poor bastards and we have no choice, this train station will fall, its just a matter of time, tell your men we are leaving in forty minutes. By then most of the civvies here will be evacuated, my goal is to save as many as we can and save our men."

Chapter 3: *The Meltdown*

From the National Stadium train station next to the shopping mall MBK, Sai, Yoon and the little girl ran down from the Sky Train tracks to the Sky Walk. Not far from their location the Army was already in a world of hurt. The defense of the Victory Monument and Nest 12 had fallen to an ever-increasing number of the dead, and the dead now poured through the streets like poison. Over the smoking craters and moving beyond Victory Monument they flowed in a never-ending river of bodies towards the Chit Lom district. The shrieking screams filled the streets and were used by the dead to alert one another that prey was within their field of vision.

From high above the fallen Nest 12, the pilots circled like carrion birds as the undead parade moved on. Nothing below had a pulse anymore but still they moved.

The cameras of the news helicopter zoomed in on the crater where the monument once stood. There the dead bumped each other into moving in one direction having been drawn to the gunfire a mile or so away.

The cameras turned towards the direction the undead horde had been continuously moving towards. Little more than two miles down the road the sound of a battle drew them like flies to shit. The dead were not heavy thinkers but they knew that if they just kept walking in that direction they too would join in on the buffet of blood.

In the chaos, panicked men and women ran for their lives through the labyrinth of cars. Every few seconds, one would be plucked from the living river by the undead occupants stuck within the cars. Those who acted like crocodiles were those who had died from their wounds after bleeding out in what they thought would be sanctuary in a vehicle. From there, they had reanimated and began the cycle anew as they snagged people through the windows almost like plucking gazelle by a river in Africa.

Pulled by the hair, clothes and flesh, the human gazelle screamed as their flesh was violated by human teeth. Their throats drowned in blood as their jugulars were ripped apart exposing the bloody white tissue within.

On top of another two-ton surrounded by traffic not far from where the last victim was pulled into the car Thai soldiers fired at the crowd scared out of their minds. Their rounds shredded the living and the dead alike as their weapons became red hot to the touch.

The smoke of gunpowder added to the low visibility in the area causing the soldiers to fire flares every minute as the darkness grew. From above, the helicopters watched as a fog made of gunpowder flowed through the streets. The shadows of thousands twisted in a Gothic ballet as the flares slowly landed into the tsunami of bodies sending rays of light into unholy figures.

In the crazed gunfire those unfortunate civilians to be hit by the soldier's bullets that still had a heartbeat became easy prey for the growing number of dead.

A Tall Man shot in the legs was hopping through the traffic when a five year old boy sank his teeth into the man's butt, immediately the boys parents pounced on the Tall Man going for the vital spots simultaneously. The family feverishly bit into the Tall Man causing his lungs to fill with blood. His eyes watered up when he tried to take in a breath, his throat was now crushed and his body cried for a breath of air. His body struggled against the family trying to survive when his vision began to fade and the pain subsided. It had felt like an eternity but now the Tall Man was dead lying in a pool of blood as the family fed.

From the first bite a plagued swam throughout the body just moments before the blood pressure dropped to zero. Reaching the brain the plague attacked everything in sight, a battle rage in a millisecond as white blood cells rushed to defend the vital organ. There once all the defenses were destroyed and the life force faded, it waited in the darkness of the abyss until it began to spark up as an electrical force surged through the brain. It was as if it was jumpstarting a dead car battery. Sparks lit up the brain and a surge of power traveled throughout the body flowing with dark energy.

Lying in a pool of his own blood, surrounded by the family who continued to feast on him, the Tall Man's eyes opened with an eerie milky texture that was crawling all over his brains. It was almost the look of eggs with veins protruding from within. His iris was completely gray where it had once been blue for reasons unknown and only two dark spots remained where the Rods and Cones were located within the eyes. His mouths opened and a horrible screech came roaring out to signal his undead birth. The family immediately stopped feeding and looked towards where the soldiers that were still firing on the back of the truck. They charged forth out of the Tall Man's sight leaving him to his awakening.

Forcing his broken body to sit upright the Tall Man oriented himself to the direction of the livings screams and gunfire. He began to push himself up forcing his bloody legs underneath him so he could stand up. Wobbling for a moment, a woman pushed him aside as she ran off towards the soldiers; a fat man in a Hawaiian T-shirt followed her.

That moment he saw what he wanted, what he needed as the leading pack of the dead fell under a rain of bullets.

Brains exploded from the leaders of the pack's heads, sending pink and gray flesh onto those behind them as if it were Songkran Water Festival of Thailand.

The Tall Man charged forth behind the Hawaiian man with the growing number of attackers charging all around him for one objective. The Tall Man saw a flare pop up into the sky from within the truck and he grew excited, his hunger would be quenched if he could just reach the truck.

The fat Hawaiian T-Shirt man was pumped full of holes some escaping from his back to pepper the Tall Man with blood yet both still pushed on towards their targets.

First one of the undead creatures reached the truck only to be shot in the head, then two, who took rounds into the shoulders and arms followed by five one being the Hawaiian shirt man who was full of bullet holes in his torso after running the gauntlet and finally came Tall Man. In less than thirty seconds the soldiers on the truck were in hand-to-hand and a few seconds later they were covered by the dead, pain is what they felt first followed the warm flow of blood and urine spilling down their legs into their boots. Pain in the legs, pain in the arms, pain in the chest, the face, then the pain slowly subsided and the gurgling screams of blood silenced and moments later they too were screeching for living flesh as the undead circle of life continued. The soldiers too began to follow the man in the Hawaiian T-Shirt and the tall man as they charged once more to their next victim

At Khao San Road, the only living presence was those in the Patton tanks. The drivers drove blindly as hundreds of the dead covered the tanks not giving them an inch of remorse as the heat in the tanks became unbearable.

Cannon fire was shot blindly into the crowds as projectiles went in one side of the mob and out the other side before exploding on a harden surface. The main gun was now supper hot and those that hung on left their flesh on it as they slipped off the cannon.

The tanks had become submarines under the sea of dead, and blind there was no hope for survival, even as their treads crushed countless number of dead. For when the fuel was gone all life was gone.

Above the city another wave of F-16s and old A-37 fighter/bombers began their bombardment. Napalm sprouted up over the living and the dead when the bombs exploded. The wave of jelly filled flaming gasoline stuck to everything. The living that had not been blasted from the fires squirmed as they rolled under and around the burning cars trying desperately to douse the flames. The dead who were not disabled pressed the attack on the helpless victims of the Napalm attack, they continued to feast until their bodies broke down or their brains boiled.

The helicopter pilots in the area could smell the flesh of those cooking in the city as an inferno began to spread, many beginning to think of finding their families and getting the hell out of here.

****

The bridge near the Grand Palace exploded as two missiles slammed into it. The cables snapped along one side almost immediately. A few cables at a time at first, followed by the other side's cables as the bridge rocked more than thirty degrees from side to side until the pressures caused all the cables to break. The bridge began to shatter and sections of it began falling into the river along with the cars and frightened passengers. The large tower that held the bridge together began to tumble over sending large concrete chunks crashing on people who were floating in the river killing many instantly.

Not far away from the still collapsing bridge, near the base of an old fortress that was built Europeans a century earlier. People threw themselves into the river trying to swim to the other side. They leaped like penguins into the water in a nature show. In the hundreds they jumped into the river as the remaining cops and soldiers battled it out with the undead attackers from the rear.

Some individuals floated on suitcases, kicking with their legs trying desperately not to drown for the river was extremely wide. Many of those people had never swam a day before in their life but it still was better than the alternative. Some had backpacks and children as they tried to take them across the river only to find out they could not hold on to both.

Not far from where they entered the water these people ditched their backpacks as they swam with their children only for muscle failure to take them. Sinking underneath the water they tried desperately to keep their kids heads above the water and as they sank they pushed on the butts and backs of their children, hoping someone would have enough mercy to take them away. Nobody came and a layer of bodies was forming just below the waters as the riverbed began to fill.

Under the water, the carpet of the dead twitched as undead life came into those who had been bitten and who had fallen pray to the murky waters. The drowned infected opened their mouths bubbles escaping from their lungs as they tried to scream out which caused their lungs to fill with water. These water borne creatures looked up through the murky water to see silhouettes of the living swimming above. The swimmers outlines were highlighted as bombs continued to drop in the distance that lit up the nighttime sky. Every blast of light was like a dinner bell and the dead responded. Water drenched hands rose to the silhouettes from the dark depths, hundreds of pairs reaching out above all out once.

On the surface of the water, the human penguins continued to cross the river in a large mass of bodies that never stop entering the water. They used the freestyle, breaststroke, dogpaddle, and any style they knew to get across the river. The penguins swam and that is when the hands of the dead reached up for them like predators in the dark arctic oceans. First to go was a teenage girl with hair down to her shoulders, a Hello Kitty necklace floating behind her neck and still in the clothes she had been sleeping in. She'd been following her father in the river when a hand grabbed her ankle. Before she could scream she was pulled below, only a yelp followed by a gulp of water alerted her father that something had happened.

Her dad, a man in his late forties turned to her and began to scream her name as the human penguins continued to swim past him.

There he was treading waters as a blast from a bomb outlined his body to a fat woman reaching for him below. He felt a sharp pain in his thigh as the Fat Woman bit into him. Several hands, one with his daughter's necklace wrapped around its fingers reached up and began to pull him down. He screamed as he fought the hands that embraced him as the other human penguins watched.

Alerted from what had happened, the penguins began to scatter in all directions; but one by one they were being pulled down below. Many now could feel hands, the fingers of those below rubbing against their feet just inches away from certain death.

Along the river, patrol boats from the Thai Royal Navy and Bangkok Police Department scanned the surface with searchlights. It was not long until they realized what was lurking below the depths as people disappeared from the surface before their eyes. They relayed what was occurring to one of the FOBs on the bank opposite of the infection. Moments later they received orders as some of the sailors and officers tried to pluck people out of the water.

The ranking officer of one of the boats began to open fire on the swimmers; he could not order his men to do something he could not. He ordered the crews to open fire on the swimmers and kill all that had been plucked out of the water in a desperate attempt to stop the infection from crossing the river. The plucked survivors cowered in fear as the sailors and police executed them on the spot.

It was the fall of Dunkirk all over again taking place even farther down the river away from the Navy and Police boats, civilian boats were in the process of shuttling people across the river. The symphony of boats moving in both directions could have been easily mistaken for people just having a good time at a small theme park playing bumper boats.

The battered refugees tired, exhausted and bitten traveled across the river unknowingly transporting the deadly virus as they took passage on the boats.

Boats and canoes traveled back and forth as the brave captains came to shore to pick up refuges armed with pistols and baseball bats. People would swarm out to the boats before they would even dock. Several of the piers that were still standing had hundreds waiting to board the larger civilian vessels.

When the vessels came within feet of the pier the refugees would attempt to jump onto the vessels, many who could not clear the jump fell into the water and were crushed between the vessels and the pier.

Swamped with passengers that rushed onto the vessels, the deckhands pushed off the piers with the ships being extremely overloaded. Some so grossly over loaded that they began tipping to one side or the other while some of the smaller boats just capsized right off the bat.

As the vessels left the bank towards the other side of the river the Captains had no choice but to plow over hundreds of people that were swimming to the other side. The propellers of many of the smaller ships stalled out from the flesh, hair and clothes that wrapped around the driveshaft and blades. Stalled they became nothing more than useless islands of people waiting for death.

Some boats were even worse off as they made their journey across the river. People could be seen jumping from them as blood splattered onto the lamps lighting up the deck in a pinkish red light. Someone had died, took a bite out of their neighbors resulting in mass chaos on some of the larger ships that resulted in floating dead ships.

It was not long until a lone patrol boat found the Dunkirk scene taking place and called it in, the radio operator on the other end of the radio ordered in two Hueys that had been circling nearby waiting for orders to turn their attention to the civilian vessels.

Their landing and searchlights lit up the river as they raced towards the scene. The civilians unaware of what the Hueys intentions were, waved at their heroes and called out for their rescue until the water around the boats began to explode like hundreds of fountains erupting at once as tracer's bullets followed by rockets were thrown down into the river by the pilots and crew chiefs.

The civilians scream, some jumped from their boats into the water, some hid behind the rails of the vessels as the rounds came down splintering wood and bone alike. Some of the refugees were Thai soldiers who had escaped Khao San Road, and other battles that had been taking place. They raised their weapons aiming for the Hueys and opened fire.

Their tracers flew into the dark sky as the helicopters dodged every round easily.

The muzzle flashes and tracers were easy to see from the air and the crews quickly zeroed in on the hostile fire and took them out with a spray of led.

Bullets ripped through the soldiers as the crew chief opened fire with his M-60s. The soldiers roared as the bullets impacted their bodies continuing to fire back until their heart stop beating.

****

Close to Victory Monument deep within enemy held territory, the battle of the Alamo was taking place in several high-rise buildings. People had flooded into the lobbies seeking refugee from the mayhem in the streets as the dead pounded their bloody fist into bloody stumps on the side of the building. Police and soldiers held the doors shut in a last ditch effort to barricade the dead from entering the buildings.

Men and women threw desks, tables, vending machines and computers against the shattered windows on the ground level in an effort to keep the dead out. Hands were reaching into the buildings through every nook and cranny of the barricade desperately trying to snag some prey. On the numerous roofs of the quarantined buildings hundreds of people tried desperately to signal the helicopters as many MEDIVAC, Army Helicopters and other forms of Utilities helicopters that had been brought in for the evacuation landed on the roofs.

Some of the police still wearing their motorcycle helmets fired every round they had from their revolvers. Chunks of flesh blasted off from the attackers' backs, as the dead charged forth like cheetahs; headshots had become nearly impossible when a mob charged in the swarm. The soldiers fixed bayonets near the stairwell of one building as the last of the cops fell along with the civilian Rambos in the lobby who thought they could make a difference.

Screaming at the top of their lungs the soldiers charged into the dead crowd in a tight Riot Control formation only to add to their number to the dead Army. Even their valiant efforts became undermined as the swarm of dead engulfed all who opposed them. They were covered by the mob, as tightly packed as the soldiers formations were the dead did no penetrate the phalanx formation instead the dead crawled all over there brethren like ants creating a bridge over the soldiers.

The lobby was packed with bodies, wiggling dead bodies, five people high in some places and not an inch of open space anywhere as the dead army continued their assault into what could be only described as the Alamo.

The last to go in the Alamo were those civilians that had been fortunate enough to receive a firearm from the police or soldiers. The stairwells had became a mosaic of bodies as the dead charged up the stairs over the desk, vending machines, and computers that the civilians threw into the stairwell that only slowed the inevitable. A vicious battle was taking place for the dead had to earn every step on the way up to the meat. For every step they took their bodies were shredded by bullets, pounded from falling office debris from higher up on the stairwell, stabbed, shot at by water hose and punched in a blood and tooth scrap.

As vicious as the defense of the Alamo was in the stairwell, even with ten dead creatures dying every second thousands more were crawling through the lobby towards the stair well. The inside of the building became a living anthill, as bodies turned into tunnels in the stairwell as the dead moved towards the battle. They had fought up ten stories already; thousands of dead corpses formed the undead ladder now in the open stairwell.

Bleeding from bites, broken bones, exhausted beyond normal means, and fighting on pure adrenaline the civilians battled on as their number continued to dwindle by the second.

Old ladies, in their late sixties were now all that remained of the combatants, most of the men were gone now, only women and children remained on the upper floors and as the dead reached the thirtieth floor, the result was as predicted, a massacre.

The dead sank their teeth, gouged the eyes of their victims as panic spread through the upper levels of the impending doom. People hid under desk in offices, the stalls of the restrooms, the air condition vents only to be found by bloody hands later on.

Rushing up the stairwell and pushing everyone up top towards the helipad that had been evacuating people all night, the landing zone became over crowded for any more helicopters to land.

Hovering above, a blue civilian MEDIVAC helicopter watched as the civilians that were pushing up the stairwell to escape the dead were causing waves of movement on top. The people on top on the helipad under the pressure from those of the stairwell that still pushed to the roof began to fall off the sides of the buildings a few at first and then by the hundreds as the dead made their way to the roof.

There was nothing that could be done and as the MEDIVAC helicopter yawed to the right the pilot relayed the story of what had happened to his LZ back to HQ. He nosed over the helicopter and flew away.

People cried out as the MEDIVAC aircraft flew off into the night sky, still being slowly pushed to the edge of the building.

In less than a minute only dead hands waved to the helicopters as they continued to evacuate the surrounding buildings who were slowly falling victim to the dead as well.

****

Outside the city in provinces like Khorat, the people were glued to their television sets while others were evacuating into the countryside fearing the worst as news reports showed the carnage from the news helicopters over Bangkok. The city was burning in many areas and panic people swamped the streets in an uncontrolled manor

The Thai Royal Air Force was now falling apart in Nakhon Ratchasima, which was over a hundred miles away. Those who were not flying were not reporting for duty in the numbers they should have. Ground Crews, Pilots, Security Forces were all abandoning their post creating huge logistical problems.

F-16s, which had just dropped their ordinances returned to land for fuel and rearm, found no one left to help; the fuel teams and weapon loaders had long abandoned their post. Even their commanding officers had deserted them to an empty airfield with only fragments of work force still in the area. With no support, the pilots quickly fled the airfield and as their jet engines burned out they ran to the parking lot, jumped into their cars and peeled out of the base towards their families.

Many of the deserters had family in Bangkok, Nakhon Ratchasima, Chiang Mai and so forth. The system had broken down and slowly the airfields stopped launching aircraft as fear drove many to the military to their homes. They saw it had been a hopeless cause, for the initial barricade had fallen and now Bangkok a city numbering in the millions was now on its way to become an army of the dead.

Some bases were still in full operation however, having most of the personnel living on base made it easier to control the amount of desertions as the gates were sealed. Those bases that had many service members' families living with them gave the military personnel the reason to stand strong in the installation. Commanders began to issue their own orders instead of following the commanding Generals. The defense of their base was becoming priority, especially since many of the civilians on board the helicopters were now landing in the make shift refugee camps that were now popping up on the airfields.

****

In London, the people lost their BBC Hong Kong correspondents on their televisions when a bright light engulfed the city and cut the signal.

Several nuclear blasts went off on the coast of China as the military attempted to sterilize the area when their armies was devoured.

The Korean Peninsula was now in a full-blown war; hours before the North had attacked Seoul in a barrage of shells from North Korean cannons. The US military had already hastily retreated to the ports in an attempt to abandon Asia as orders came through to head back to the states when reports of infection began in the city of Inchon.

Japan's airspace was in the process of being severely violated as Chinese aircraft carrying refugees demanded to land. Some crashed into the islands of Japan as fighter jets shot down the 747s seeking refuge. Even South Korean, Chinese bombers and fighters were trying to escape the jaws of death trying desperately to reach Japan only to end up in dogfights over the sea as the Japanese Defense Forces engaged them.

Everything that could carry family and civilians was now heading towards Japan as people fought fiercely at the airports of the infected areas for a ride. They fought for planes that never had a crew, charged into the cabins of planes and waited, waited for a pilot who would never come.

As parachutes fell from the sky from the military aircraft that had been shot down by the Japanese Defense Force, AAA, and small arms greeted them on their decent. Most of those who had ejected landed with body parts missing or much worse after going though the gauntlet of flying led.

Taiwan had been overrun during that afternoon by the Chinese Navy and their cities now burned as Chinese Marines entrenched themselves in not knowing the reason for the attack. The government kept them in the dark; they had no clue the dead were on the move. The Chinese Mainland was shortly abandoned by the government and moved to Taipei. The Chinese Navy destroyed any ship or aircraft that came close, including one American frigate.

****

Governments around the world began to prepare for the worse as the crisis continued in Asia. The Americas, led by the United States shut down all air and sea traffic and their Navy began to retreat from all four corners of the Earth to set up blockades along with their Mexican, Canadian and South American counterparts, including the Venezuelans and Cubans.

The coast of England saw movement all day as the soldiers and Royal Marines entrenched themselves to fight off the wave of civilians that would be trying to cross the channel when the infection hit Europe.

****

Sai, Yoon and the little girl were nearing Chit Lom when the cries of the dead slowly began to die down, drowned out by the endless buildings and skyscrapers that blocked the sound several miles away. Still they were reminded of what they were outrunning as jets, helicopters, tanks, and APCs made their way towards the direction of the dead.

Sweating in the morning heat at two a.m., their speed had decreased drastically. The three had been going full speed for what seemed like hours and even Sai with his training was now on fumes. Slowly they came to a walking pace as soldiers ran past them on the Sky Walk towards the battle many with fear written on their faces.

Looking around Sai knew it was a matter of time before the dead would pass those soldiers who ran to stop them. Hopefully their sacrifices would not be in vain.

****

The dead had first come in a few scattered attacks along the perimeter but the intensity was quickly growing.

Wan stood at the roof of the building with a pair of binoculars looking down the street where the dead were coming from as another train prepared to leave. The building had become less crowded since two trains had already left and the choppers were now inbound to extract him and his team. The doors had been sealed off, leaving the defenseless civilians to fend for themselves in the streets. It had been heart breaking to do this evil deed, but Wan had to defend what he could, and with only one train left, no more could be saved.

The sharpshooters fired down below and like Victory Monument they began to put down everything, dead or alive whoever was outside of the train station was on the hit list. Their bullets exploded heads left and right at first, then their strategy switched so they could just slow down the dead for the sheer volume was not going to be stopped by plugging one or two in the head anymore. They fired at the leaders as they approached the fence, trying desperately to slow down the attackers as the howitzers began to fire down into the mob.

Below the tanks had nudged themselves on four corners of the train station and kept up a constant fire as the soldiers near by defended the barricade outside of the building as if they were on ramparts of a medieval castle.

Just beyond perimeter the sea of bodies smashed against buildings and vehicles alike, there was not enough ammunition for what the soldiers were facing.

Wan fired a green flare into the air to signal the retreat into Hua Lamphong. The men abandoned their post first followed by the tank crews that were in turn followed by the dead. The fence was crushed as the dead plowed through it, the over turn cars were almost useless as the dead knocked them over as if they were dominoes.

Rushing to the entrance that had the sandbag emplacements with .50-cals the dead were being lit up as they rushed through the first two perimeters. Their bodies danced as the rounds pulverized them — breaking, twisting and distorting them into unrecognizable mush.

The blast from the machine guns sent their targets back into the Dead Sea; it was like a hammer and nail being beaten against a rocketing freight train of bodies.

Before the dead could get to the main door and the .50 Cals, a tank parked itself in front of the entrances, trying to seal off the building. The .50 Cals ceased fire as their operators climbed over the tank and into the small opening of the door followed by the tank crew that had escaped from a hatch on the bottom of the vehicle.

Inside the building, Num fired his rifle through the cracks of the entrance into the mass of hundreds of arms and faces trying to come through at the same time.

The tank crew ran to the train and the train was ordered to leave along with what military personnel it could carry.

Train engine 459 began to creak forward foot by foot as many of the soldiers grabbed on to any part they could holding on for their lives. That is when one of the entrances to the station flew open.

Out of the corner of Num's eye, he saw several soldiers tackled to the floor and his feet took flight up the stairs of the building followed by what was left of the soldiers on the train platform, over two hundred dead people flooded the platform instantly followed by thousands more.

The soldiers on the train opened fire as the dead began to chase the train, which had not yet picked up speed. The broken bodies pushed forth as the train continued to move and the dead eventually gained on her.

The first few were put down but it was not long until they began to climb all over the sides of the train as it left the station.

Wan could see the gunfire from within the cabins as civilians threw themselves off the train trying to escape certain death only to be tackled by those who still charged them.

The thumps of the rotor blades of Hueys inbound brought hope to the soldiers who made it above as they sealed off the door to the stairs and boarded the birds. They saw the true carnage that they escaped as the pilots pulled up on the collective causing the bird to lift off. To their shock an endless supply of dead roamed the streets all trying to get into the train station.

Fires had broken out everywhere, the night sky was strong with burnt flesh and every street North of Hua Lamphong had become a battleground. Soldiers and police officers fought side by side as the strobe lights of the cars continued on long after their deaths.

The pilot passed a message back to Wan from a notepad sheet on his kneeboard.

"Headed towards Rescue Station Minburi, actually a few miles north of Minburi, all military survivors are linking up there to be reformed for another quarantine surrounding Bangkok called the Cage."

Wan crumpled up the paper and tossed it out of the Huey. He sat back, closed his eyes and leaned his head against the hull of the aircraft. It felt good to be alive; it felt good to be airborne. The sweat was finally disappearing and he opened his eyes to see his city burn.

Chapter 4: *Extended Family*

Looking at the Central World Mall, which still had power, the three needed to make a detour. They needed a motorcycle or something to drive to the Sukhumvit district. The Sky Walk would end four hundred yards past Central World Mall, and they would be taking their chances once again in the never-ending traffic below. There was no telling how many people had been bitten only to escape Victory Monument and succumbed in a dark alley or vehicle around the mall. The clock was ticking for the dead were coming.

Central World Mall was the Goliath of malls, something most Americans had never seen before, and walking through the fifteen-story mall could easily take a day.

Along with several hundred people who were moving from the Sky Walk to the mall's second story entrance, the three ran between the crowd and through the glass doors into a white glossy center. The scene was not like Victory Monument; the only ones running were the trio. It was apparent to Sai that the dead had not yet reached the area; compared to Victory Monument it was an extremely calm and orderly place.

Order had remained in place due to the cops and mall security directing traffic within and beyond the malls walls under the watchful eyes of a few soldiers and their attack dogs. A tank with its searchlight on was parked at the Beer Gardens, which Sai had seen the night before – only now it was in a state of ruins. Its searchlight scanned the crowd for any signs of disturbance, as the turret rotated right and left looking for something to shoot.

Upon entering Central World they immediately saw nurse's stations, hundreds of tables with emergency provisions set up along the walls and people sitting inside all the stores gossiping within. Each conversation was about what they had seen or heard on the radio or television. The mall was some kind of rescue station from what the three could tell. It was hastily set up sometime after the infection had broken through Khao San Road's defenses. Rescue Station or whatever it was the three were not going to wait to see if it could withstand an undead attack so they immediately turned right from the glass doors and down a long white hallway with people lining the sides waiting to use the restrooms that were in the process of being backed up.

"This way." Yoon turned, pulling on Sai's hand as he held the little girl who held onto him as if she were a Koala Bear. They ran past everyone in the hall as the lights began to flicker causing the crowd to crescendo with panic, then die off as soon as the flickering stopped.

"Thank God women love to shop," Sai muttered to himself, referring to Yoon who was now leading Sai out of the hall, turning to the right towards the entrance of a large department store. She surely knew her way around this mall.

Pushing people aside the three moved into the department store called Zen, it was kind of like the Japanese version of Sears except over 9 stories tall and each level being roughly the size of two football fields lined up next to each other.

Passing through the merchandise, she headed towards the escalators, which were swamped with people going up, trying to get off the deadly streets.

Sai recognized the place from his workout earlier that morning, with the gym being on one of the top floors. He continued to follow Yoon as he saw people who had cuts and scratches walking deeper into the mall walking the opposite direction from the escalators.

The crowds pushed up the stalled escalators, making them impossible to use properly; the loading limits had been exceeded hours ago. Slowly the passengers had to walk up the steps as their legs became entangled with one another. Yoon figured the best option would be to slide down the handrails as best they could for walking down was no longer an option.

"Follow me." She said as she negotiated the glass railing that connected with the escalator. She put her butt on the rail and began to slide down when someone bumped her back causing her to slide over the edge of the black rail, but like a cat she quickly turned and grabbed on with both hands; then, using a hand-over-hand maneuver, she made it down to the first floor as people looked at her from below wondering what the hell she was doing.

Sai and the little girl were next. Sai being bigger than Yoon knew he would not get very far with his butt on the rail.

Looking down at the little girl he forced her to release her death grip koala bear hold and put her on his back. She sandwich the M-16 with her body which was already slung on his back with muzzle facing down and with her arms she wrapped them around his neck. Sai pressed his chin down almost to the point of crushing her little hands so she could not slip loose easily if she were to loosen her grip.

Sai pushed the crowd out of his way and threw his body over the escalator railing. He began to go hand over hand down to Yoon when on the second floor the crowd erupted with screaming as the first of the Victory Monument victims succumbed to his wounds.

The man had just reanimated seconds after leaving the escalator where Sai was now going down. His body must have been carried by the refugees up the stairs kept upright due to the lack of space between people only to be released to the floor when they arrived on the second floor. His body had fallen face first onto the marble floor, the people around him just walked around not thinking it was of their concern. That is when he bit an elderly man on the leg unleashing the outbreak into the mall.

Sai was nearly halfway down now as people jumped from the escalator only to break their legs on the looted jewelry glass counters below. Those on the escalators fought to go down as the rampaging dead man attacked one after another, ripping throats out at his leisure. The crowd from below continued to push up the escalator while on top they tried desperately to move against the tide.

Two of the undead bastards were moving around already, one occupied with escalator people, the other running after victims deeper into the bowels of the mall.

The panic had brought out the police to the area within Zen but they arrived too late due to surging crowd that ran away from the dead.

Sai made it down when one of the undead near the escalator fell to the ground floor behind him. Lifting his chin the girl fell to the ground and Sai unslung the rifle, turned around and took aim; he fired once and the dead man fell back into the already broken counters, where several wounded people cried out in pain from their broken legs.

Central World was about to become a battlefield as soldiers and cops on the second floor continued to battle with the decreasing number of dead at Zen. Preoccupied by the dead in the department store they did not see the growing number of dead coming out of Forever XXI in the center of the mall where another outbreak had begun. An elderly woman had died in one of the dressing rooms from her bites and when she had awoken in death she went on a shopping spree for flesh.

Soon machinegun fire could be heard throughout the mall as Sai threw a mannequin at one of the windows of Zen to escape to the outside since the doors were packed with bodies still coming in unaware that the dead were growing in number from within.

Back in the humidity of the Bangkok night, the trio headed southeast towards the Sky Train as they made a right from the broken window and across the street of stalled cars. They passed another expensive mall called Gaysorn Plaza after they crossed the street and stuck underneath the Sky Train tracks as the road continued in the direction of Sukhumvit.

Moving east down the street and passing their fellow freaked out pedestrians, Yoon's eye found an abandoned Tuk Tuk near a shack on the side of a bank that stood beside the Sky Train tracks.

The Tuk Tuk, a motorcycle/taxi/dune buggy was hidden halfway in the shadows next to the building behind several bushes. They had already moved about three hundred yards from the mall when she had found it. She turned to look at Sai who was oblivious to what she had seen still looking over his shoulder in the direction of Central World as gunshots continued to go off.

Yoon changed direction instantly causing Sai who was holding the little girl with one arm and the rifle to change course, he had no clue what she was up to as he followed her lead.

"Yoon!" Sai shouted wondering why she was taking a detour as more sporadic fire erupted in front of Central World. Some of the dead left the ground floor chasing the people through the streets catching the eyes of the traffic cops who responded in kind by opening fire with their revolvers.

Yoon stood beside the blue Tuk Tuk with the gold stripe looking around as if she was searching for its' owner. It was like the hundreds Sai had seen all day but for some reason abandoned, hopefully it worked.

"You know how to drive, Sai Mai?" she asked him as he looked at it.

"Umm, I don't even know how to start it," he said with a puzzled look on his face. It was a motorcycle basically with a small bed/seat attached to the rear with a Fiberglas cover decorated in Thai writing and Buddhist markings and that was the familiar part.

"I better drive then," she said with a serious look as her hair blew gently in the night wind, a change for the good for once tonight.

"Sure, I've got shotgun!" Sai put the little girl into the back of Tuk Tuk then followed her in managing to hit his head twice before sitting down in the back of this small three wheeled motorcycle taxi. His legs felt great as they thanked him for the sudden shift of weight off his legs to his butt as he sat comfortably in the Tuk Tuk. Oh he savored that moment in that brief period of time.

Yoon was fidgeting with something up front that Sai could not see, causing the engine to roar to life as vibrations ran through the third-world Harley Davidson.

Hold on!" she shouted with excitement and then pressed the gas.

Sai and the little girl jerked back as the Tuk Tuk jerked forward and onto a sidewalk where people hastily got out of the way as Yoon blew the horn. She shouted in Thai and gestured with her hands for people to get the hell out of her way. She then swerved to the right to jump a curve and now the Tuk Tuk was weaving in and out of traffic. Yoon hit a few cars, scratching their worn-out paint jobs on the sides and sending sparks wildly into the air. Behind Yoon, Sai held his rifle with large wide eyes as he sat quietly watching Yoon while the little girl put her head into his lap closing her eyes.

****

Central World was quickly becoming a blood bath as bloody hand-to-hand combat was taking place on all levels of the giant structure. Thousands who had hid in the mall were now fighting for survival, as the dead seemed to come from every direction. There was no order to the chaos like the dead tsunamis in the streets. Instead people ran in random directions trying to find anywhere to escape.

On the top floor where the atrium was and a large Christmas tree stood down below on the bottom floor, people threw themselves over the ledge as they tried to escape the creatures that were coming out of the movie theater. The jumpers' bodies slammed into the marbled floor beside the Christmas tree resulting in a sickening thump as bodies and marble collided in a sick twisted percussion.

Hiding in a dressing woman, a government worker dressed in a white uniformed cried as the lights continued to flicker off and on. Outside the department store, clothes and blood flew into the air as people were tackled and trampled. The screams had become an orchestra of death, like a never-ending song and as the mall's power went out the woman cried and cried letting the darkness engulfed her.

****

Minutes had gone by since Yoon began driving and now they had gone four city blocks weaving in and out of traffic. It was not long until they arrived underneath another Sky Train station. An inferno lay out before them as a Fire Truck burned consuming the vehicles around it. The wall of flames created waves of heat that rolled underneath the tracks of the Sky Train. Yoon slowed down to a stop as Sai looked into the fire to see a fireman dead in the back of the burning truck, his helmet had the number 39 and would be the only thing that anyone would be able to use to identify him.

"Fi Kang Na," Yoon whispered to herself, her eyes fixed on the flames dancing ahead of her. Without warning, a large wild-haired man, a living man, grabbed her arm hard, almost to the point where he could have shattered her bone.

Without hesitation Sai thrust his rifle to the man's face, the barrel creating a huge gash under his eye that caused blood to gush from the wound. The man grabbed his face and stumbled backwards onto the hood of a blue car behind him. He began screaming in Thai as he continued to stumble around the car and out of sight.

The trio watched the man disappear then looked back to the inferno that was spreading from car to car ahead of them. It was now obvious that they would not be able to proceed by Tuk Tuk past the raging inferno. They would need to set out on foot once again. The trio needed to move fast for the background noise was becoming louder with gunshots racing from Central World to them.

Sai was first to step out of the vehicle as Yoon struggled to leave the Tuk Tuk for she was almost at her breaking point now. It would have been over if she could just drive pass the fire truck, they would be safe; they could get to her aunt's house that much faster. The pain would have been over and now the pain of running, the stabbing knife in her lungs would be just seconds away again.

"Time to go Yoon," Sai tried to say with a soothing voice, realizing the pain Yoon was in. He reached a hand for Yoon as the little girl stood by his side holding on to his leg. "You got us far enough, you did well."

Yoon dismounted the Tuk Tuk, disheartened that they were on foot once again. She looked to Sai, who was still holding her hand. Sai turned to lead her on a detour down one of the side streets, when a gunshot hit the Tuk Tuk next to her head.

The crazy-haired man who tried to grab Yoon a minute earlier was firing at them from a few cars over, pissed off and holding his wound with his free hand he shouted at the three in Thai. His hair was ragged, he foamed at his mouth looking as if he had overdosed on some drug, his eyes were bloodshot and he shouted in gibberish as he fired randomly towards the trio's direction.

Not sure where the gunshot were coming from, the three began to weave between cars again as the man continued to fire from several cars over managing to hit a lady to the side of Sai in the shoulder and as quickly as the gunfire had begun it was over. The crazed, man for whatever reason, had stopped firing; perhaps the fool was just out of bullets or maybe the drugs had just got the better of him.

Yoon was now turning left on a street that looked like all others. Away from the fire truck's inferno onto the dark barely lit street it was a temperature change of nearly thirty degrees, and welcome relief to their skin that had become extremely dry underneath Sky Train tracks that doubled as a large oven.

"We'll take the river!" Yoon began to lead them again when several 500 lb bombs went off near MBK close to two miles behind them now.

The MBK mall erupted in bright orange explosion, lighting up the area where the trio was, the sound wave echoing off the surrounding buildings for miles around causing windows to shatter throughout the city.

The mall, now on fire exploded again as two more bombs fell from the sky, totally destroying the structure. It had been overrun moments earlier as thousands of infected creatures attacked it. The last survivors of the military knowing that death was something they could not elude anymore while hold up in MBK called in the air strike. The dead creatures had charged up the ninth floor where the arcade and comic book shops along with many fast food restaurants were, but before the dead reached the soldiers the explosions had leveled the building.

MBKs' fiery plumes reach heights of over five hundred feet with jets racing by as the structure cremated the bodies of those within. The plume of fire could be seen over the buildings from Sai's left shoulder as if a volcano had erupted nearby as he ran north towards the river.

"We've got to move faster!" Sai shouted towards Yoon not wanting to lose precious minutes to out run the dead of Central World Mall for the bombs would surely be landing there as well in a matter of minutes, especially now that it was in the process of being overrun.

****

Not far ahead there was another tank and a military blockade. Running past the crowds, Sai noticed rows of dead bodies – with rounds in the head – lying on the sides of the street. Continuing on he saw two soldiers carrying a body to put it with its buddies in the row of corpses. The bodies were not like those of the dead he had seen, they looked almost normal if it wasn't for the bullet hole in their forehead. The soldiers had been killing all those who showed any signs of infection as people tried to pass the checkpoint. The crowd was being funneled like cattle towards several gates.

A soldier with a white mask covering his nostrils and mouth stopped Sai, Yoon and the little girl at one of these gates after they fought their way to the front of the line. Another soldier flashed a flashlight and gun at them as he ordered them to stay still. With a flashlight the masked soldiers' free hand searched their bodies hastily for bites and did not even look twice at the M-16 Sai was carrying which made Sai feel kind of awkward. The masked soldier performed his inspection fast, perhaps knowing that there was a series of checkpoints that the people would have to go through if they wanted to leave the city.

"Okay, good, go now!" he said.

The trio quickly responded, continuing to run relieved that the hold up was not to long. It had been a line of soldiers with hastily erected fences on the street that held the mob behind the trio. People sprinkled through the line after being cleared to reach a relatively calm street if it were not for all the stalled empty cars. The trio passed the tank with the crew sitting on top with weapons, waiting for something other than cleared people to break through.

The soldier that had stopped the trio stopped another family and his nine-mm berretta went off just fifteen yards behind the trio as they continued to run.

A lady fell dead as her child cried beside her dead body screaming for her mom to wake up. Sai cringed as he ran with his dependents knowing full well what had happen behind him. He bit his lip realizing nothing could be done as another shot from the gated checkpoint went off. The girl was now lying still beside her mom with no more tears.

****

It was not much farther ahead when Yoon took a turn to the right and down an alleyway. Sai briefly thought about those he had outrun in the alley at Khao San Road when he entered the dark alley and hoped he would not repeat that scene once more.

The alley had been empty; there were no vehicles to negotiate for the first time that night, just slums of homes, a few crates, and puddles. Cigarette smoke was heavy in this area as the occupants of the slums huffed and puffed away. Eyes watched the trio quietly from the darkness of the slum as the trio made their way deeper into darkness away from the crazed street they had come from.

Not knowing where he was going Yoon had been taking Sai parallel to the river, which was hidden behind several shacks along the alleyway to their left side just north of their position.

An orange flash of fur moved by the trio's legs, making each of them jump as cat ran by and more figures began to appear in the shadows as the residents began to step out of the darkness to watch the intruders.

Why were they not fleeing, the trio wondered, maybe it's because they lacked TV, but that could not be right for somewhere in the shadows someone was listening to a radio. Even in Thai, the voice was obviously that of a reporter.

In the shadows they continued to move past figures and Sai's pucker factor was elevated as he felt a large number of eyes staring at them now. That moment he felt a state of panic fall on him as he imagined them to be undead eyes staring at them.

The hairs on the back of Sai's neck shot straight up as his imagination began to run away. Everywhere were blank eyes staring right at him, he could feel it, the panic was setting in until the warm red glow of their cigarettes brought him back to reality. The soft glow told him that they were not dead but just the residents of the slums watching the strangers in their neighborhood and nothing more. He was in shantytown now, and people were not used to seeing outsiders running through their town; thankfully Yoon had managed to find the edge of the river.

The trio had came to a stop in front of a shack and now Yoon was talking to an elderly woman who had no teeth and was hunched over leaning heavily on a wooden cane. Yoon gave her a bracelet and the woman smiled gesturing to an old canoe she had used many years ago when she traveled back and forth to the floating market as a teenager. It looked like it was a cross between a plastic kayak and a Native American long boat, just perfect for the trio to use with extra space for Yoon's family as well.

Sai put the child down, and along with an elderly man the two men carried the boat to the river and lowered it into the water. It wasn't exactly a river but a canal or khlong in Thai.

The man smiled at Sai and told him something in Thai and deep down inside Sai felt sick. *Did these people know they were going to die? Did they know they would need this boat?* He felt his insides drop as he put the canoe into the water, in the back of his mind he hoped he was not screwing these people over

Yoon was first into the boat and Sai lowered the child but before he could get in the old man stopped him.

Sai turned to the man who held a paddle in his hand in which he gave to Sai.

"Take, live," the elderly man said, as he smiled, then began to mumble to himself as he chewed on his gums.

"Khap khun khrap," Sai replied, as he received the paddle and climbed down into the boat.

The elderly man and woman were aware of what was about to happen to them but perhaps it was due to their age they chose to stay behind and live the last few moments comfortably with their neighbors, smoking and drinking the night away. It was not logical, not at the least, how could they just wait to die instead of trying to run. That is when it hit Sai. Everyone in shantytown was elderly; there were no children or anyone under the age of sixty. Perhaps the young had already taken flight to the streets, the elderly had probably forced their love ones to leave knowing full well they could not make the journey on foot and their company would only hinder their loved ones escape from Bangkok.

The trio left shantytown feeling guilty for the elderly but nothing could be helped for they needed to survive.

Sai paddled and paddled as the streets above the canal turned into a war zone. In the darkness of the river splashes could be heard but no movement was seen above the water surface when the trio turned their heads to see the commotion.

Unknowingly to Sai several of the dead looked up at him from the watery depths. They watched as Sai and his boat rowed by with small wake waves trailing behind distorting their view. The moon outlined their canoe and with each paddle by Sai the dead grew hungrier and hungrier. Their dead hands reached up towards the boat but they could not reach for their lungs were filled with water and they had become anchored to the canal's bottom. All they could do was wave at their prey as they made the trio made their escape.

****

Time had gone by and Sai's legs were resting once again as Yoon pointed to the shore to the right of Sai. "Pull up to the khlong's wall, my aunt's house is not to far away."

Sai paddled towards the direction of the bank and came up to a cement wall that lined the canal that was about three feet above the boat.

There was no gunfire in this area yet, that was a good omen for the three as they docked with the wall. The traffic and thousands of refugees were making their presence known on the main street above, which was normal for the chaos that resided within the city. Sirens were wailing as cops and fire trucks directed the traffic above. The lights of the emergency vehicles flooded the dark canal with red and blue flashes as the strobes rotated.

Upon reaching the wall, Sai stowed the paddle and helped Yoon climbed up and into the alley.

Minutes earlier, Yoon and Sai had discussed the original plan, which was just to find shelter within her aunt's house but the last few hours had changed all that. If they stayed there it would only be a matter of time until the dead found them and then what? Even if the dead could not get in, they'd be doomed, starved or die of dehydration in a few days; the only option was to escape from Bangkok with her family.

"Sai, stay with the boat. I'm promise it will be alright." Yoon turned to face Sai, immediately holding her left hand up in a gesture to stay put.

"Yoon I should come with you," he answered grabbing his rifle getting ready to disembark from the boat.

"No, if you come someone else will get the boat Sai." She had a point, but going out into the street alone would also be dangerous for her. "Please Sai, I'll be alright, you need to stay here." To further her point, people in the shadows of the bank a shadow stood watching, watching and waiting to see if he'd be dumb enough to leave the boat unattended.

Sai looked at the boat and knew she was right. The canoe was probably their best bet in escaping Bangkok. He could not go in her place for he did not know the way to her aunt's house and he could not leave the little girl to defend the boat which unless she was related to *Hit Girl* from the movie *Kick-Ass* she did not stand a chance.

"Yoon, take this," Sai said as he gave her the rifle.

"I can't, I don't know how?" she replied.

"Yoon the safety is off now. All you have to do is point and shoot." He told her as he gave her the rifle forcing her to take it. "If you point it at something you better shoot it."

Yoon took the rifle and looked at Sai saying everything she had to say with one look and quickly did a 180 and sprinted off into the darkness towards her aunt's house Moments later she disappeared into a dark alley out of view from Sai's view.

"Be careful Yoon."

****

Wan and the survivors of Hua Lamphong had arrived at the Minburi Rescue station only to be quickly reassigned to a company who were to patrol the jungles north of Bangkok. They would serve as a second line of defense forming a second ring farther from the city just in case the infected had broken through the Cage which was on the outskirts of the city in the suburbs if you could actually call the clusters of homes and buildings surrounding the Bangkok that.

Num was relieved to be in the back of a two-ton racing out of the city away from the dead. The battle weary soldiers had lucked out once again and were given a break from the death that thrived in the streets of Bangkok. Under the cover of darkness in the early morning their convoy moved out of the Rescue Station as they passed wave upon wave of civilians who held up their hands trying to get a ride in the convoy's direction away from Bangkok.

****

Wanchai, Lek and Klauy who had been hiding at Chandrakasem Rajabaht University were now once again on the move. That evening the three students along with a few others from their class were working on a project when the attack had happened. They had watched everyone they knew die before their eyes and the three had hid in the ladies restroom as the violence continued around their university.

Now they were on their way again making it Northeast towards the Minburi Rescue Station. Moving in the allies they tried to stay undetected to those that roamed the streets. It wasn't until after they had eluded a few dead creatures that had come out of a Dunkin Donuts that they found a young woman hiding in a dumpster. Her crying had given her away; when they found her, she was in a stupor, surrounded in filth, rocking and whispering to herself.

As the night rolled on, they move towards sanctuary, stopping only when the battle cries of the dead grew close then pressed on once more as they died down.

An hour after an army convoy left the Rescue Station, the four found what the Rescue Station would soon be facing. An army of the dead was marching the same direction following other survivors towards the station.

It was then that they decided to cross the river they had been paralleling. They would bypass the Minburi Rescue Station, which would be doomed in a few hours to a horrible death.

****

Forty minutes had passed since Yoon had disappeared into the darkness. The little girl slept on Sai's lap as the crowd and traffic continued. In the distance Sai's ears zeroed in on the low pops of gunfire. How far, he could not tell, the sheer volume of buildings in the area had a way of muffling the shots. A few more shots went off, some sounding close by.

I should have gone. Sai thought to himself as he looked nervously around at the shadows that kept changing under the emergency vehicles strobes up above.

How long should I wait? What the fuck was I doing?

Sai knew he needed to get to the embassy and report to duty like a good soldier, but in doing so he would surely be killed along with Yoon and the girl. There was no telling how far the infected had got already. *Was it just Bangkok?*

They needed to escape; find somewhere outside the city until help came, *but what if this reached America already? What if the world was already dying? Of course our military could stop it for we are the best and no one comes close. But what if I had a family would I actually report for duty?*

Scenarios began to play through his mind; he was planning for the long haul: food, water, weapons, shelter, people. He needed all this to survive this mess.

As he thought and kept vigilance on the riverbank above a hand reached out of the water and before it could grab Sai's shirt the little girl screamed.

Alerted and almost pissing his pants at the same time Sai dodged the hand as a dead teenager's face came out of the water. Water poured out of its mouth and cheeks from where he had been bitten. Before it could scream out, Sai dropped his paddle on the boy's face. The force of the swing crushed the boy's forehead in one blow, almost splitting the skull in two.

"Shit, thanks!" he said, as his heart pounded in his chest.

"HEY!" Yoon shouted, causing Sai's heart to skip a beat once more.

"Jesus!" Sai readied the paddle looking up, as the little girl assumed the koala bear position once more.

Two kids stood next to Yoon, a boy around the age of sixteen or seventeen and his sister near fourteen or fifteen. The kids looked as if they had been crying.

"Where's your aunt?" Sai asked Yoon.

"She never came home from work this evening. They've been alone the whole time," she said as her voice broke up.

Sai could see Yoon was struggling; he knew what must have happened to her, but she could still be on the road trying to get home even at this moment.

It was a judgment call, but Sai had to make the best decision for all of them and decided they were safer coming with him on the jungle boat ride from hell then waiting on the river to see if their mom would come.

"Okay. Yoon, we need to go now, bad company is coming," he said, as he glanced back at the black water.

They handed Sai three backpacks, each full with canned food, water and some clothes for the children that they had hastily gathered from the house.

****

While Sai was waiting in the boat forty minutes earlier, Yoon ran up the main street one block and turned left into a neighborhood that hardly had people moving about. The power had already gone out and the only light was from the moon and the occasional scooter that drove by.

Inside the homes, families huddled in the darkness, relying on their steel fences that resembled cages to foreigners to keep the dead and other would-be intruders out.

Calming down as she passed an elementary school on her right, she was looking to see if the road leading to her left was clear, when she heard weeping from one of the homes.

A woman was weeping as her husband died in the cage fortress of their home.

Quickly, Yoon made haste and passed the house as she ran towards her aunt's. A motorcycle narrowly missed her as it zoomed by in the dark.

Upon approaching the gate of her aunt's house, Yoon yelled inside to alert her family of her presence.

Movement appeared inside and her male cousin appeared holding a flashlight in one hand and keys in the other.

"Ta, Mae unai?" Yoon asked as she hugged her cousin and looked for her aunt.

"Mai, pye ngyuan…she left this morning and we've been calling her all day." He answered in Thai as he stared at the weapon Yoon had slung on her shoulder.

"Ta, where is Wien?" She continued in Thai when she saw a flicker of candlelight coming from within the dark house.

"Wien! Come here!" Yoon said as she walked toward the house within the safety of the fence. Ta following close behind after he locked the gate once more.

Inside the house, Yoon hugged her cousin who had been crying since it all started scared out of her mind.

****

The day before, during the afternoon as Sai and Yoon prepared for their date, the news had reported riots along the coast of Thailand out of Pattaya and Bang Saen. That is when the phone lines and cell phones went dead at Yoon's aunt's house.

Ta, waiting for his younger sister at the bridge where the bus dropped her off daily listened to the rumors that were beginning to spread as people walked about talking.

Nervously he waited as a large greyhound bus with cartoon characters of *Dragon Ball Z* pulled up to the sidewalk. Schoolgirls exited the bus in their blue shirts and black skirt uniforms.

Wien came off the bus to see Ta waiting for her as always. Upon exiting the bus, the waling of a fire truck screamed by with the sirens heading south before turning right onto the road under the Sky Train in the direction of Mo Chit. Engine 39 pushed by as one of the fireman sitting in the back of the truck with his helmet on smiled and waved at the kids.

As night fell from the sky, the two waited for their mother to return. She was now running a few hours late as the sirens continued on at the main road. Sitting the darkness of their home for hours since the power went out; Ta held a butchers knife and flashlight as his sister cried in her bed surrounded by stuff animals. He watched as his neighbors packed their car and burnt rubber from their house to the main road only causing him to cringe in fear.

From their home the siblings heard the commotion on the main road as people yelled and fought in the traffic, the horns blew and the sirens continued when what sounded like fireworks coming from the road could be heard for over an hour before dying off.

Deep down, Ta knew they were not fireworks but he comforted his sister and told them it was just a celebration and nothing more, trying to hide the truth from her.

Hours had passed and midnight came and went, Wien fell asleep on the couch as her brother stood guard, listening to the dogs bark in the neighborhood and as he began to bobble his head with sleepiness he heard Yoon's voice coming from the gate.

****

"Ta, get your backpack and your sister's bag, and run into the kitchen and grab all the can food and water you can," Yoon ordered when she thought she heard a screeching howl a few houses down.

Wien grabbed a sweater and stood by the door, while Yoon found a bag and packed her cousins clothes.

In the narrow streets of her neighborhood, Wien saw a man running by deeper into the neighborhood, followed by a boy roughly her age that did not see her watching in the dark.

Minutes went by and Yoon was now prepared to exit the caged house and get back into the dangers of the small roadway.

With their backpacks on securely and Wien holding her cousins shirt with one hand, Ta at the ready with a his butcher knife they left the safety of their home and moved at a slow jog down the street. They jogged quietly towards the main street, which Yoon had come from only minutes earlier.

Nearing the four-story elementary school, two figures jumped out of their house towards the three. Screeching for their flesh they were stopped by the iron gates of their home keeping them in as they fired their arms up and down wildly through the slits like rabid animals.

It was the husband and wife, the wife being the first victim of the husband who reanimated to spend eternity within her in their caged home.

Yoon raised her rifle, but soon realized the two were trapped. Quickly she picked up the pace knowing that the infection was already in the area.

"Remember Ta, aim for the head," she said as she huffed and puffed her way past 4 a.m. on her watch.

The cars were on, the engines and fumes of the main road caused an almost suffocating feeling as the three entered the river of bodies running between cars.

Along the way they passed several bodies, mostly old people who had been trampled to death and in several cars the reanimated tried to grab those running by but with their seat belts still on, the attempt was almost impossible. Of course those dead people did manage to bite a few people passing by, doing their part to help spread the plague. Once escaping the bitten person continued to run in the river of bodies only to die hours later and bite another.

Several undead were in the river of bodies flowing between cars, but the three managed to navigate their way into the dark alley that led to Sai and the little girl without attracting their attention.

Unlike the first time Yoon went through the alley, no one was present. It became eerily clear something was wrong as she and the kids made their way to the boat.

As the turmoil in the streets continued an old man charged the three catching Yoon off guard. Waving a bat at her and the children, he struck the shacks made of tin and debris that been thrown together that some called a home.

His mouth foamed as he charged them like a demon, his eyes bulged when he managed to corner Yoon and Wien.

Raising his arm as Yoon raised the rifle to try and shoot, his eyes turned crossed eye and a blade popped out of his chest.

Standing behind him, Ta tried to pull the knife out when the old crazed man backhanded him, sending Ta into the shack just as one of the undead took the old man as his target.

Simultaneously Yoon fired the weapon, two rounds hitting the old man's chest and to her shock a third round hit a teenage boy in the throat who appeared out of no where attacking the crazed man.

Unscathed by the shot, the teenager growled and mauled the old man as Yoon fired a round, which missed and struck the ground beside him.

Unaware that he was being shot at, the boy violently shook his head as he took the life of the old man when the muzzle of the rifle hit the boy's temple and the warm led went in and pulverized the brain.

Quickly Yoon turned her attention to the old man and fired a round just as his face twitched to life.

Wien followed quietly behind Yoon as Yoon stepped over the two dead bodies and began to run towards the boat hoping the dead hadn't reached Sai and the little girl.

Wien quickly grabbed a pipe to use as a weapon, still not sure of what had just happened. Ta, pulled the knife out of the old man's back and wiped the blood on the teenager's shirt, ready to stab him if he moved.

The two siblings had become pale but had survived their first undead encounter.

Rounding the corner they heard a splash and saw an "Indian Dang" or Red Indian looking foreigner with a little Thai girl holding a paddle sitting in a large canoe.

Chapter 5: *The Dead Lands*

After introductions were made Sai, found himself responsible for four people other than himself. He paddled down the dark canal as hell continued to reign above. Buildings exploded as gas mains ignited, machine gun fire came from every direction and the Royal Thai Air Force continued to bombard parts of Bangkok in an effort to slow the infection.

As he paddled on through the dying city he was reminded of a sick twisted version of the *Jungle Boat* ride from Disneyland. He saw a man on a telephone pole next to the river that he had climbed. Below him were thirty "savages," all dead men and women howling at him trying to claw their way up. He kept sliding down a few inches but quickly climbed back up as the dead hands reached for him.

At one of the countless bridges he passed he saw a fuel truck that was dangling from the bridge with fuel erupting from its bowels. The fuel fell off one portion of the bridge creating small a waterfall. Passing it the phrase *"It's the backside of a Water"* came to his mind. A smirk crossed his face and he paddled on.

The river was full of dead creatures that resembled the piranha. In one part of the city where the power was on as they continued on the river, Sai could see a woman in a blue sweater looking up at him from below the dark water. He squinted as he looked down to see other flashes of color as red sweaters, yellow jackets and white dressed shirts with people staring straight up at him.

When they came to a dock near a large Wat (Thai Temple), people had gathered to pray for their safety, which had turned out to be a bad idea. The dead had overwhelmed it like they had all other buildings. Now they gorged themselves feasting on what remained of the pilgrims. They ripped and shredded the flesh off the limbs that had been torn off their victims as the torsos wiggled in undead life watching their attackers feed on their appendages.

The travelers on the canoe did not go unnoticed, for halfway through the bloody slaughterhouse of the Wat one of the creatures noticed them. It immediately dropped the piece of meat that could not be identified.

The flesh fell out of its mouth and onto the concrete before it let out it's screeching signaling to the others that fresh meat had arrived.

A stampede of the dead burst forth from the bowels of the Wat towards the canal. Sai responded by hastily paddling for his life as the first of the dead leaped towards them. The creatures landed three feet from the canoe soaking the passengers. Sai moved the boat to the far side of the canal opposite of the Wat's bank and pushed down the river as nearly fifty creatures entered the water.

Below the canoe, like a brigade of army ants they began to form an undead bridge as they used each other to get to the canoe.

Yoon took the rifle as hands began to appear from out of the water. She flipped the safety off just like Sai had shown her and with a round in the chamber she aimed and fired. One shot one kill, 49 more to go.

"Sai hurry!" she yelled as her cousins began to panic in the boat.

"Ta sit down!" Sai grabbed the boy with one hand and pulled him back to his seat. Ta had grown excited or may have just been panicking when he stood straight up almost causing the canoe to capsize.

Wien held the little girl as if she was a teddy bear and began to sink into her seat as the world closed in around her, she did not hear herself screaming for she had zoned out everyone in the boat. Her world had no noise.

Sai paddled harder than ever as a flurry of white water rose around the canoe. With each stroke of the paddle he hit a person under the water. It slammed into faces, arms and hands, beginning to splinter under the force of the impacts. He could feel the bottom of the canoe being slammed by the hands that tried to flip them over.

As quickly as it had begun it was over as the dead disappeared into the depths of the canal. The bridge of the living dead gave way to their weight as they tried to keep up with the canoe. The last of the hands tumbled into the darkness still trying to reach for the food that was getting away.

It may have been a tense moment for the crew of the canoe but it was nothing compared to trying to escape on the streets. To Sai's surprise the canal had very little living traffic. The occasional motorboat passed by as they pushed on but that was rare. He felt guilty and sick to his gut as people continued to scream out in terror up above, his little get away could have probably saved more lives but if the living occupants of the canal would have advertised their get away it would have been no different from the chaos in the streets above.

A heartbreaking moment came around 5 a.m. upon passing one of the countless neighborhoods; a boy around the age of twelve broke out of his hiding spot and made a bee line to the canoe as it moved by. He screamed in Thai calling out for help as his little legs pounded the asphalt.

His yells alerted the dead within earshot of him and the creatures began to run out from the surrounding homes with their battle cries. He had begun his sprint almost four hundred yards away as he exited an abandoned ice cream cart that he had managed to squeeze himself in.

Yoon took aim and fired at the closest threat to the boy who had somehow managed to dodge several tackles and was now within striking distance of the canal's bank. That is when several of the waterborne dead made it to shore cutting him off. They splashed out of the water catching the boy by surprise; his bloodied feet came to a screeching halt as his butt landed on the street.

All the occupants of the canoe watched as the boy's screams turned into gargled cries followed by silence. It had been just one of many incidents that would occur over the next hour as people tried to reach the canoe.

****

Six a.m. had come and past and the crew of the canoe had arrived in the area of the Minburi district. The skyscrapers were beginning to fade away and so were the dead, but the intensity of speed boats surfing by the canoe was beginning to bother Sai who knew that any one of them could send their boat to the bottom of the river and into the hands of the dead.

The sky was now gray with a little light blue shining between the clouds, the sun slowly rising on the horizon sending shades of red into the sky. The frequency of speed boats going by had continued to increase in the last thirty-minutes, the secret of the canal must have gotten out, perhaps the living in the city streets had no choice left but to try the canals as a last resort.

Not far behind where the group was traveling on the canal, a woman had succumbed to bites that covered her body. She had awoken on the speedboat she'd been fleeing on in the canal and was not alone.

Immediately she turned her attention to the driver of the boat, a man she had met while trying to escape. Rising from her slumber she slowly turned to the man and then like a snake she struck him. She dug her teeth into his shoulder causing him to fight back feverishly.

The three other passengers began to panic as the driver let go of the wheel. The boat began to veer to one side of the canal and bounced back off the bank. It immediately traveled to the other side of the river and hit the opposite side as the man fought for his life.

The three passengers jumped from the back of the boat as the driver's ears was ripped off, now hanging from the woman's mouth like a dog with a bone.

****

Ta was first to point out the trouble, pointing his finger towards the incoming boat and shouting in Thai.

Looking over his shoulder, Sai saw the boat less than one hundred yards away coming full speed at them. Immediately he tried to paddle out of the way but it was too late.

Smashing the side of the speedboat against the canoe, the force managed to send the canoe's occupants flying into the water as the speedboat fished tailed. The propeller narrowly missing the little girl's face with just inches to spare as the speed boat fish tailed over them before heading towards the opposite bank once more.

The world went brown and black in the silky water as the bubbles passed above the little girl's head when the speedboat went by. Disoriented from the impact she could no longer tell which way was up, or which was down, for she had begun to panic in the murky depths.

Tumbling out of control amongst the bubbles she felt her hair being pulled. The roots stung as the force of the pull threatened to scalp her. She felt her body moving in the opposite direction of where she was trying to swim and in the darkness she prepared for death until she surfaced above the water.

"GET TO LAND!" Sai shouted pulling the girl to safety by one of her arms now.

The water splashed around him as he pulled the little girl along the surface, looking around he saw smoke rising from the burnt remains of the speedboat that was now going under the water after colliding with a log on the opposite bank. A roar of screaming coming from all directions as he saw people running on the banks of the canal and the helicopters still flying above in the direction of Bangkok.

Sai turned the other direction, away from the boat to see Ta and Wien swimming to shore like professional swimmers. He looked to see Yoon moving in the kids' directions, and then it struck him that he could not feel the riverbed below him. He had two fears he could not stand, one was being in the middle of the ocean where he could not feel the floor and the second was heights even though he was a pilot.

Sai pulled up his feet and knees up to his chest mainly because he hated deep water not knowing if *Jaws* was lurking below, now his fear had multiplied a hundred fold. His imagination began to run away with him, he could feel the cold dead hands grabbing him, the teeth penetrating his skin for it was no longer *Jaws* he had to fear below, instead it was the jaws of the dead.

With the little girl in one arm Sai began to power swim his way towards the shore all the while holding his legs up to his chest.

Ta and Wien made it to the shore first and were now waiting for the rest as they sucked in air their hearts pounding a hundred miles per hour. Yoon clawed her way up the muddy bank of the river and turned to look at Sai and the little girl.

"Get her!" Sai pushed the little girl towards Yoon as he began to go under from not using all of his limbs to swim.

Yoon grabbed the girl's hand and pulled her to the bank when a cold dead hand locked on to Sai's ankle.

His fear of the deep had come true as the creature pulled him under. With his mouth opened and looking at Yoon he was dragged under the water. His throat filled with water as his eyes shot wide open, every sense in his body was now in overdrive as the attack happened in slow motion to him. He looked down and saw a pale arm protruding from the darkness of the deep causing him to jerk violently as his body told him to fight.

He tried to scream under water as he was pulled lower that only added to the panic. He jerked, he kicked he punched in every direction fearing that any second teeth would be in him. With a wild kick from his boot he hit his assailant in the face breaking the creatures jaw and causing it to loosen its grip. Almost simultaneously, he felt another hand grab his shoulder, its fingers digging into his collarbone, pulling him in the other direction.

He was pulled out of the water and onto the muddy bank.

Sai was saved again – this time by a man in his early twenties who was wearing glasses and had the look of someone who was a hardcore Trekkie.

Catching his breath and staring at the water that had almost claimed his life Sai's eyes had showed real fear. His eyes and face were red with fear. If there were tears, no one could tell because his face was mixed with water and mud. Only he knew that he had cried for his life in that moment facing certain death.

Yoon held onto Sai with one arm as she helped him to his feet still holding the rifle in her free hand. He sniffled as he regained his composure.

"Thank you, Khap khun khrap," Sai told the Trekkie as three other people stood behind him scanning every direction.

The man was followed by what appeared to Sai as his friends, two women and a fat man.

"What about those people from that boat?" Sai asked.

"They ran off on the opposite side of the canal," Yoon said, as she looked at Sai's wound that he had failed to notice.

"You guys know where to go?" Sai asked not expecting an answer.

"We go province," the Trekkie man replied.

"Fuck, what the fuck!?" Pain shot through Sai's right thigh as he tried to take a step away from the bank. He looked down to see that a small piece of the canoe was stuck in his leg.

Immediately he pulled it out of his leg.

"Fuck!" Sai looked at the wood.

The adrenaline had worn off and the pain was now setting in. It was not the best time to become a gimp when you had running, screaming dead folk hungry for your flesh.

The wound was not deep, but it was enough to cause some serious pain.

Sai held the wooden piece of canoe while Wien dug into her backpack to tear one of her shirts sleeve's off.

"P'Yoon," Wien said as she gave the sleeve, which had come from a sweater to Yoon.

Yoon quickly got the point and tied it tight around his thigh.

Leaving the water early had given him precious moments to seal the wound, but now it was a matter of time before infection would fatally cripple Sai and in a world where the dead were coming to life, the hospitals were not a place to go.

"Thanks Wien," Sai said as he tried to hold the pain in.

Yoon then helped Sai up the bank and into a wet field as drizzle began to fall from the sky.

More water, Sai thought.

"Khun chu alai?" the Trekkie asked to Yoon.

They began to talk to each other in Thai as the crowd took a knee around Sai still looking out in all directions, especially the river.

"Pom chu Sai" Sai interrupted.

Yoon smiled and told the four strangers the rest of their names.

As the names were exchanged they took a moment to rest after they had moved out of the rice paddy to the edge of the jungle.

They talked about where to go like military bases, hospitals, police precincts, schools, anywhere they thought the government still had authority.

Wanchai explained to the group about the smoke he had saw rising from the Minburi Rescue Station. It seemed to be safe to say that the dead flocked in the direction survivors were heading.

For the group, they needed somewhere that people did not know about, some kind of hidden fortress.

Sai's mind sent him thinking of his home city and the San Antonio missions. These forts were built to keep his ancestors out so they would not kill the local population. They were Catholic forts/churches and in the early days they were meant for war, as armies of the six flags of Texas launched raids on the Apache and Comanche lands from within.

Sai began to remember his trip to the Grand Palace a day before. The palace/Wat was built like a fort except opened to tourist and in the middle of down town Bangkok.

"We need to find a Wat, in the middle of nowhere." Sai looked around to the group.

He had admired the similarities they had shared with the missions of his city. Most were fortress shaped, with large Chedis (large pointy Buddhist towers) in the middle. The walls were like the barracks of the Alamo, living quarters that provided a long wall and as long as the gates could be secured a Wat would be their best bet if they wanted to ride it out the dead storm.

The more he thought; the more ideas came to him. They needed one near a river, close enough at least and perhaps a little uphill in case of flooding. It needed to be so secluded that the eight of them could secure it at ease, even with clubs and sticks if need be.

As the group continued their discussion, Sai cleaned the rifle since he knew that water would mean mud, sand, and rocks were now in the bolt and chamber. This would cause the rifle to jam in a critical moment if it wasn't dealt with. Not to mention the rust that would eat at the rifle almost instantly if he gave it time to do so. He had opened the butt stock to find the rifle cleaning kit a little wet and he quickly made use of it as the group discussion went on in Thai.

Soon the Thai discussion had Sai's name in it, he began to put the cleaning equipment back into the compartment of the M-16 as he tried to eve's drop. The sleeve around his thigh was now soaked red and the bleeding was not stopping. Sai sucked down two bottles of water from one of the packs in the group knowing that soon he'd be feeling dehydrated and sleepy from the loss of blood.

Wanchai, being the genius of the group gave Sai an option to stop the bleeding. No needles were necessary since Wanchai had seen Rambo one to many times. He'd always wanted to try it. And now was Wanchai's time to shine.

Holding a lighter, and with a branch in Sai's mouth, the group watched as Ta and the Fat Man held Sai's leg down. Wanchai held the wound closed with his fingers and lit it on fire scorching Sai's wound shut.

Tears rolled down Sai's cheeks, as his flesh was burned shut slowly as Wanchai welded the wound together.

Sai began to struggle to keep his mouth from screaming and soon the group was on top of him as Wanchai continued to seal his wound shut. The burning of his wound lasted two minutes, burning all of the infectious bacteria to a crisp.

Yoon cradle Sai's head as his body began to react and twitch. His will power was slowly giving in to pain. His moans turned into small yelps as Yoon covered his mouth with her hand after he had bit through the wood in his mouth.

The smell of burnt flesh was in the air as Wanchai finished the job. The pain was still present but now subsiding.

Sai's leg was stiff, but the wound was sealed burnt to a crisp with the danger of infectious bacteria being reduced drastically. Another bandage came out of Wien's pack, her wardrobe slowly being destroyed, the second sleeve found its' place on his leg.

Sai stood back up slowly as he looked at the others. "Guess its time to go," he said.

The group continued to head towards the unpopulated areas outside of Bangkok. Trying to stay away from the large groups of refugees when possible for large groups were nothing more than moving dinner bells to the dead.

The newly formed group made its way a mile deeper into the jungles north of Bangkok. The goal was simple: find Sai's Wat and hole up until this thing blew over.

****

It was now 7:50 a.m. The group had been walking as Sai used his rifle as a semi cane every now and again. Everything his Drill Instructor had taught him was now out the door when it came to muzzle control, before the Army, he had taken much pride of being a Marine and trained under the intense discipline the Marine Corps had bestowed upon him, but that went out the door.

Moving through the rice fields they had come across other survivors who were heading out to the jungle. At one point the group felt like they should seek the company of others but large crowds attracted the dead. Many large groups of the living numbering in the thousands were under constant attack from the dead, their numbers dwindling by the second as the slaughter in the rear of their rag tag formations came under attack as they continued to move out of the city.

Looking back at the skyscrapers that could be seen between the trees on the horizon, over a hundred black dots swarmed over the Bangkok skyline like flies on a carcass. Helicopters were still operating over Bangkok, a mixed of private security contracted to save the rich, Army pilots mostly single pilots with no families, Police and Med Birds. They had been ferrying people none stop since the fall of Victory Monument. Rescue Stations surrounding the city had taken in thousands and in the dawn of the outbreak many of those stations had become nothing more than a smoking carcass full of the dead.

Bombs dropped from aircraft continued to explode around the city recovering the retreat of the army now. The intensity of the bombardments had been reduced drastically since it had begun.

Through the fields and the jungles the group moved on paved roads and sometimes dirt roads as they continued to head north. The occasional car drove only to get stuck later in traffic down in the dirt roads as the rain continued to drop from the sky. It did not matter much though to the people in the cars if they got stuck in the mud for the Army had already set up road blocks on all roads leaving Bangkok. Lines of abandoned cars led up to the roadblocks as the occupants were forced to continue on, on foot.

At one of the roadblocks the soldiers along with monks gave out MREs to the crowds of people in which Ta had managed to snag two. A

98

triage was set up on the side of the road as a few doctors tended to the wounded and monks prayed over the dead, most of the permanent dead were those with bullet holes in their heads.

Yoon stopped at the triage and told them what happened to Sai. She explained to a woman in a white nurse outfit about how they sealed his wound and before long she came back holding two syringes of antibiotics and an ointment.

The group came to a stop as Sai took off the bandage. Yoon quickly injected him and rubbed the ointment on the crispy wound. A fresh bandage was put on and like a football coach always says, he "walked it off." The detour was only for a few minutes before they continued pass the triage and headed north back into the jungle as the road curved to the east.

The MREs, of course, were not enough since calories had been burning none stop all night. Everyone who had packs was now full with non-perishables, including Wanchai, Lek, Akira and Kluay but they needed to raid one of the local gas stations to maintain a constant food supply. For it was better to eat the perishables in order to ration out the can goods at a later date.

****

As time continued, some survivors pulled over to the side of the road, taking a few minutes break, eating their MREs and resting as the group found themselves passing them by. In a few hours the thousands of refugees would disperse across the country side each heading their own way to what they thought was safety.

Now Sai and his group were alone once again; only the occasional scream followed by gunfire told them they were not completely alone.

Leaving the jungle once more onto a hardball road, a few wrecked cars faced them as they watched the front of the Esso gas station with the American Tiger picture. Probably a decade or so it had been well kept place, but overtime it looked just like any other backwoods gas station. Now it was a graveyard to a few wrecked cars stained with the smell of a fire fresh in the air.

"Looks quiet," Sai mumbled.

"Whatever happened here, we missed it," Klauy whispered to the group in Thai as he looked to them for their reaction.

In a creek on the opposite side of the road, the group entered and watched for signs of movement. The dead had definitely left Bangkok, it was now 11:00 a.m. and they could be potentially surrounded, they were now behind enemy lines.

The car windows of the wrecks were shattered and bloody handprints were displayed on the bodies of many of the vehicles. It looked like most people had made it out before the dead came but pieces of gore were still stuck to some of the vehicles with flies buzzing around, pools of blood were still present.

"What do you think Sai?" Yoon asked as she put a hand on his shoulder.

Sai whispered back, "We need the supplies. Wanchai, what do you say?" He looked to Wanchai by his side.

"I don't know."

Lek interrupted in Thai as she whispered to her boyfriend.

"I guess we need it." Wanchai looked to Sai.

"I'll go but you're coming too." Sai then turned his attention to Yoon. "Yoon, you and the others stay here, stay out of sight. I'll try to make this fast."

"I want to go," Ta demanded in English while tugging on Sai's shirt.

"No!" Sai said softly with a stern tone. "I need you here, take care of everyone and listen to Klauy."

"But P'Sai…" Ta began to whine showing his youth.

"I said no. Do as I say and you can come along next time," Sai said as he rose to his feet and began to quickly limp his way across the street. Wanchai bit his lip and crawled out of the ditch quickly closing the gap between Sai and himself.

Sai had been trained to clear rooms when he was a young Warrant in the Army, but he never did it during the war. He guessed the semi training would pay off today as he kept a low profile walking across the road. The others watched from the creek with anticipation as the rain began to die down to a drizzle.

Sai was still in pain from the hasty treatment on his leg, but his body pushed the pain aside as the adrenaline rushed kicked in once more. With his senses heightened he led Wanchai through the twisted maze of dead cars that resembled animal carcasses. His rifle greeted every window, every opening as he passed the vehicles in case some dead person waited in silence. He left nothing to chance. Clear on the right, clear on the left he whispered to himself as he glided by the wrecked cars with Wanchai bringing up the rear.

Wanchai carried a handgun, Chinese from what Sai could tell. Wanchai had liberated it the night before from the owner of a truck, which had a sticker in Chinese that said, "You can have my gun when you pry it from my cold dead hands." The hand was all that remained of the man and it was considerately left on the driver's seat for Wanchai to find.

Continuing to trail Sai's back, Wanchai's breath grew heavier as they walked by a red car that was still smoking from a fire hours earlier. Only shreds of red paint remained under the blacken husk of the vehicle. Once he was within three feet of the car he smelt burnt flesh through the black smoke, reminded him kind of like Sai's leg wound, which he had sealed up close and personal. He scanned the vehicle and saw where the smell was coming from. In the vehicle he saw two remains of charred children; they were huddled in the back seat holding each other in a tight embrace their faces gone forever as if whipped by an eraser. He could only imagine the horror and pain that the children had gone through during those last few minutes as the flames consumed their lives. There was no sign of the parents in the front seat, only the abandon black husk of the children. Tears began to roll down Wanchai's cheeks as he stared at the remains. *Did they really just leave their kids to die?*

"Wanchai, cover me, I'm gonna clear the van ahead," Sai whispered over his shoulder noticing Wanchai's dilemma.

Sai quickly made his way around a station wagon and towards a white van with black windows.

Seeing Sai moved caused Wanchai to snap away from his grimaced trance over the two dead children and began to cover Sai who was making his way through the open ground ahead of him to the white van. Sweat rolled down Wanchai's cheeks as Sai neared the white van. Anything could lurk inside.

Wanchai's mind wandered to the past as he thought of the game *Left4Dead* he had played last month. He was now holding his gun out waiting for signs of trouble as he covered Sai like he was in some online game. He swore he'd never play that game or anything like it again.

Sai approached the van, which had one of the sliding doors already open. With his rifle at shoulder level he cleared the van and then disappeared out of Wanchai's sight. He entered the vehicle and was instantly consumed by shadows and the tinted windows.

Wanchai watched as he saw movement from the tinted windows. It felt like an eternity as he stood their watching the van. He felt expose in the graveyard of cars, scared, his hair shot straight up on the back of his neck. It was as if someone was watching him from the shadows of the wrecked cars. Panic slowly began to sink in causing him to scan every direction at once, expecting to see a dead creature jumping on him from anywhere, but there was nothing but silence and wind.

He sighed a breath of relief when nothing appeared, but then he heard something moving from the direction of the white van. Something was sliding on the asphalt. It sounded part metal, but mostly a soft rub as if someone was rubbing a couch with pebbles. Wanchai's eyes squinted as he focused in on the source of the noise. First he saw a hand that was missing a few fingers come into view from below the rear of the white van. Next was the other hand that was missing all its fingernails, its grayish blue skin exposed from a long shirt that had been shredded. The thing pulled itself out of the shadows below the white van exposing a face that had been disfigured from bites. Its eyes looked out at Wanchia piercing his soul. It raised one arm reaching towards Wanchai as if pleading to him to come closer and with the other arm the creature pulled himself completely away from the white van. Two bloody stumps were all that remained of his legs; both stumps wiggled like a puppy that had found a treat to eat. Its mouth dropped opened exposing a dark abyss as if it was preparing to send out its battle cry, the warning to all like him that food had arrived.

Wanchai aimed his Chinese revolver in the direction of the creature, his arms were shaking, his aim unsteady. His world closed in on the dead thing crawling before him. All sound disappeared except for the creature dragging its body towards him. He shut one eye trying to focus on the dead thing when a silver flash interrupted his concentration. The world rushed back in on him as his tunnel vision exploded into panoramic view and the sound of wind and drizzle could be heard once more.

Sai stood behind the creature with a machete in his right hand and the blade in the creature's head. He put a boot on the back of the dead things back and pulled the machete out, chunks of skull, hair and brains falling on the creature's back. Sai looked calm, almost as if he was becoming at home in this hell.

Gulping and about to vomit from the sight, Wanchai was glad to see Sai again. Sai gave the all-clear sign, signaling Wanchai to approach the van. Wanchai moved in a low profile and met Sai at the door of the van just to the side of the dead creature's body.

"Found some goodies you might like," Sai said as he held an olive-drab A.L.I.C.E. pack he had found in the back of the van.

Inside the pack was a claymore, ten 30-round magazines for the rifle Sai carried, two white phosphorous grenades and two M-67 fragmentation grenades. Inside the van were four more M-16 rifles and a box of MREs all conveniently left out for the Sai and his people.

The owner must have abandoned his military post with his family, only to be killed out in the boonies; some canned goods were thrown around the cabin along with some blood. Reaching for the box of MREs Wanchai noticed a child's doll lying next to it.

That was when Wanchai lost the contents of his stomach; it was not the blood, but the children that had caused him to throw up. Reminded him of his younger brother, who had been a freshman at his university and was staying late on a school project just like every other freshman; the last he saw of his brother was his teeth biting down on one of Wanchai's classmates.

"Go back to the others and tell them to open each MRE and take the contents out so we can stuff them in our packs," Sai instructed Wanchai. "Give a rifle to Yoon and Ta, keep one for yourself and give one to one of your friend's, whoever you think can shoot the best. Then wait for me by the van and cover my ass. You got that?" Sai noticed the emotional fatigue that was setting in on Wanchai as he nodded in return. "Wanchai, you're doing fine." He slapped the man on the shoulder smiling. "Hang in there man." Sai nodded to reassure him.

Quickly Wanchai scuttled across the road as Sai turned his attention to the Esso station. Nothing moved from what he could see through the windows, it was a desolate looking place. Sai just prayed nothing was waiting for them inside.

Sai began to walk towards the gas station as he flipped the safety to semi-auto again.

Clearing several cars on the way, which took only a minute, he heard footsteps behind him, turned to fire and stopped just before pulling the trigger. Wanchai stood there looking at him holding a rifle.

"I told you to wait by the van." Sai paused seeing Wanchai's terrified expression written on his face.

Wanchai didn't answer; he was still scared from everything that was going on.

Sai sighed. "It's okay. Stay close, then and watch our six."

Wanchai nodded and began to follow Sai. He did not need any instruction on how to use the M-16; as a bookworm, he knew exactly how to work the rifle. He pulled the bolt and loaded a round into the chamber Rambo style causing a loud click of metal.

Sai gave Wanchai an irritated look and pressed on for Wanchai was not helping much with the whole stealth bit.

The two slowly made their way to the entrance of the station when Wanchai stepped on a piece of glass. Three screaming dead people came running out seconds later knocking over a shelf full of chocolate Pocky by the door.

Hesitating only for a second to identify his targets, Sai opened fire followed by Wanchai.

Bullets ripped through the trio's shoulders and then their faces as the two took a steady aim. The last dead creature, a fat man landed face first just inches away from Wanchai's sandal.

Still inside there was screeching, but no movement and Sai knew it was either trapped or handicapped.

"Let's make this quick!" Sai shouted as he ran into the building.

Deep down inside, Sai knew the gunfire had alerted everything within earshot of their presence at the Esso Station. Nearly a mile away the dead heard the shots and began a fast paced sprint towards the gas station's direction all at once.

Once inside, Sai moved out of sight and a wet crunching sound could be heard.

Turning the corner, Wanchai saw Sai pulling the machete out of a boy who had no arms or legs.

"Hurry the fuck up!" Sai shouted fearing the dead were closer now.

Wanchai opened an empty backpack and loaded up on food, candy, water, and soda pretty much anything he could get his hands on as he hastily threw things into the pack.

Sai packed water and food and what medicine he could find along with some toothpaste, brushes and soap when he heard gunshots from the group outside.

"Time to go!" Sai ordered as he threw the backpack over his head like a shirt and began to run to the exit.

Wanchai did likewise not wanting to be left behind and when he exited the station Sai had already taken down another dead woman and was now running to the group who were returning to the jungle.

Wanchai scanned for targets but none were found and as he crossed the street he heard screams coming out of the Esso.

It was clear that the dead could easily triangulate noise and from then on noise discipline would become top priority. This lesson on how the dead reacted to sound would definitely be considered when planning raids in the future.

As the group fled north, a few minutes had passed and nearly forty of the undead zeroed in on Esso. They arrived only to find a few corpses and no live prey. The survivors had managed to escape and were now heading north as quietly as possible.

Heading deeper into the province the group moved on, exhausted from their near twenty-four hour day they've been through already. They would need to find shelter soon for the coming night would be quickly approaching and the last thing they wanted was to run through the jungle in near zero illumination.

****

In a prison east of Sai's position half of the guards had already fled and a riot was now in progress. From the halls of one in the cellblocks a lone cop fired his shotgun as men in rags charged. He fired buckshot after buckshot, blasting holes in the inmates, when a man who had been crawling in the roof jumped down on top of him with a elbow striking to the guard's head.

The guard's head slammed against his right shoulder, the blow breaking the man's neck instantly and with the momentum of the strike the guard slammed to the cold tile floor, his shotgun sliding to the sidewall.

Immediately another inmate went for the gun, bending over at the waist he was about to grab the gun when the Burmese inmate who had taken out the guard kicked him in the face breaking his nose. The inmate flew backwards and fell on the wall besides the Burmese man, landing on his ass. With tears in his eyes and blood running down his face he looked up to see a shotgun's barrel in his face. The Burmese man fired the weapon and the man's face disintegrated across the wall.

"Cousin, get down here!" the Burmese man said in Thai with a heavy accent. The man was from Myanmar or Burma to others, had been a drug trafficker, murderer, mercenary and soldier from the dictator run nation.

Now with the dead running around he had been the mastermind of the riot, his gang and him used the other inmates as cannon fodder, and with the guards distracted the gang easily took control of the prison.

"Than, you sure? I don't want to get my ass shot off?"

"Goddamn it, cousin, get your ass down here."

Another man jumped down from the ceiling. This man was much larger than Than. He looked as if he were part Chinese.

Upon reaching the floor, the gang assembled, those inmates who wanted to join were allowed in, the others either ran off or figured they would stay within the protective walls of the prison.

An hour later, Than and his gang left the prison.

****

Sergeant Wan was in the Tactical Operation Command (TOC) tent receiving a brief when he managed to hear the dispatcher who was talking on the radio to a frantic man from the prison. The dispatcher told the panicked guard that no reinforcements could be spared, they were on their own and he strongly advised the prison guards to abandon their post and headed north towards the second quarantine line.

The guard asked if Minburi Rescue Station was still operational only to receive a negative. The Army had lost contact with Minburi Rescue station in the early hours of the morning.

The name had been added to a list of deactivated Rescue Stations, which Wan could see on a dry-erase board. Bang Khae, Dreamworld, Mueang Boran, Don Muang, Hua Lamphong, Siam Park and so forth were just a handful of names on the board.

Hua Lamphong, a list of over a hundred names Wan zeroed in on that one. Lost a lot of good men there.

Lost a lot of good men everywhere he thought. He could see by the list that the army was dying now.

"Group Tench Hut!" someone shouted from within the TOC.

The men came to attention and the words "at ease" were soon to follow.

Another General in charge of the second quarantine ring walked in.

"Men I have some news," he said with a stern face.

"Infection has broken out in Chang Mai, Nakhon Ratchasima, Phuket, Pattaya. We have similar defense quarantines around each city. But all attempts to contain this disease have proven futile, from now on it will be search and destroy. Bangkok and those others cities will be gassed at 1500 hrs today. I want several of your companies from the second ring to march in tonight for mop up duties. Kill everything you see, living or dead, it makes no difference anymore."

The Generals of Thailand had grown desperate. It was easy to read the man standing before Wan; there was no hope anymore just one last hoorah of heroics for the Army's Bucket List.

Wan heard this, but still as a soldier he did not question it. Fortunately his company was not ordered to meet certain death in Bangkok and was held in the reserves, much to the relief of him and his men.

In a short time, the counter attack would begin on the infected cities and as Num rested by a tree he watched India Company load up in back of several trucks. The

Trucks fired up and began to roll as a whistle came from somewhere within the convoy.

****

Now promoted since there were so few officers' left. Wan was a Second Lieutenant but still wore the rank of Sergeant on his sleeves. He did not really care to be a Lieutenant, he was just a man doing his job and for now it was to lead the company, which should have been a job for a Captain.

He looked down to Num and a few men from the checkpoint and Hua Lamphong that were now part of his rag tag company studying their faces when India Company's convoy came under attacked. Turning his head he saw as the dead charged from all directions at the trucks that were heading to Bangkok.

A few grenades exploded followed by rifle fire and .50 Cals but the number of dead pouring from the jungle was overwhelming.

The convoy was swamped with bodies and came to a screeching halt when the men inside of the FOB came under attack.

Num jumped to his feet as Wan opened fire at what looked like nearly five hundred dead people and counting pouring from the jungle. Wan stopped firing as he realized what he had to do. All around gunfire erupted, disorganized the military did not stand a chance and that is when Wan ordered the men near him to retreat, he needed to save as many as he could for all was lost.

He threw his men in the direction he wanted them to run, some not budging still firing to the last second, those men were now being tackled every few seconds by three or more dead people at a time. That is when Wan began to run as he shouted retreat at the top of his lungs.

They sprinted into the jungle brush as the dead pressed their attack and within minutes the gunfire had ceased and only screeching could be hear.

Chapter 6: *Dark Night*

It was a few hours past noon and the sun was still in full bloom. The humidity was high, but the breeze was steady as the group walked along a forgotten trail. Earlier in the day, the group found an abandoned van several miles from the Esso Station, but now the fuel tank was empty and they needed to make their way on foot once again.

They had moved beyond the horizon of Bangkok and were now somewhere thirty miles northeast. The van was parked lifeless next to a trail, fresh footprints beside it heading into the jungle. It had ran for fifteen minutes with the fuel warning light on before it had died and when the vehicle coughed its last breath it rolled to a stop. Like clockwork the occupants abandoned the vehicle with not a moment to lose for fear the dead would triangulate their position and come screeching in.

It was day three of Sai's R&R and he wondered what the guys in his company were doing. *Did this nightmare spread that far? Were they even in the godforsaken sandbox anymore?* He was clueless and part of him wished he had stayed but then as he looked at Yoon talking to Wien he thought it was for the best.

It was amazing how the end of the world played out. One day on a hot date with a beautiful Thai girl and the next day humping it through the jungle with psychotic triathlon dead iron man team coming for you. He did join the Army to see the world and here he was in beautiful Southeast Asia doing just that; all he needed was a box of Tecate and he'd be set for life.

He was glad he met Yoon. Looking over to her she was covered in dirt and sweat yet she still remained beautiful. Couldn't help but think of it, even under the circumstances.

Yoon noticed Sai, as he was first in the makeshift trail formation. He'd look back at her every few minutes or so which caused her to smile sending him a reassuring look in return.

Yoon did not take it that hard, for her mother and father had died in her childhood. She had been raised by her aunt and grandmother and became an actress at the tender age of eight.

Now she had taken up the motherly figure for Wien and Ta since they had been picked up from their home early in the morning. She kept a steady eye on the siblings trying to cheer them up as best she could even as the burning heat of the jungle took a toll on everyone.

Wien being the younger of the two took it hard, but she was done crying. Deep down inside she knew her mom was still alive and could not bear to think otherwise. Things could have been much worse if it were not for Yoon coming to get her. She felt safe with Yoon, Ta, the little girl and Sai. Being in her mid teens she was full of emotions on most days but today she battled it out to take charge of her feelings, using Yoon as an example to follow.

Walking behind her cousin Yoon, Wien was taking her turn carrying the little girl that had not spoken once since this had all begun. She was wearing her sleeveless sweater now; more than anyone in the group, the cold December rain bothered her. Her sweater was now sleeveless since she had used the arm sleeves for bandages on Sai's leg. So she wore it like a vest on top of a Minnie Mouse T-shirt shirt while the little girl played with the strings that dangled from it which kept Wien pleased. The heat had gone unnoticed to her, her light built kept her cool and even as Sai and the others in the group were drenched in sweat she somehow managed to stay cool.

Ta was the most enthusiastic of all, armed with an M-16, he was on top of the world. Throughout the hike through the jungle he'd shoulder the rifle like Sai aiming at every chirp from birds or falling branch, but when they stopped to rest he felt the pain for his mom for he knew full well that she was gone. When no one was watching he found a corner to shed a few tears.

Several times Ta had tried to lead the pack only to be turned around by Sai who told him to bring up the rear. A gung-ho guy like Ta was best in the rear, no sound would get by him and Sai knew it. Now Sai could have his full attention to the front as point man.

Wanchai and Lek were a couple from what Yoon and Sai picked up on. Both were nerds in Sai's eye, which proved useful in the future for the meek shall inherit the earth. Besides, back in the states he'd always considered himself a nerd, and that is probably why he became a pilot, *Star Wars* and all, dogfights in space of course.

Akira, a girl in her early twenties, was thin and very plain. She wore a pink shirt and khaki shorts with hair down to her shoulders. She remained quiet most of the time and everyone could not help notice the blood stains on her shirt near her waist. Where the blood on her shirt came from no one knew for she would not say.

Klauy was always sweating profusely; this had been a great workout for him being the hold end of the world and all. Klauy would talk every so often between catching his breath to Wanchai, but his talking was mostly bitching about the heat.

****

Throughout the day the number of people they had seen in the jungle had diminished drastically, perhaps killed or hiding in the villages that the group had passed. It was nearing four o'clock when the group saw what appeared to be an American B-52 fly overhead towards Bangkok.

Through the streets millions of the dead now walked searching for flesh. The creatures stumbled as if blind, bumping into each other and other inanimate objects until food was found. The signal from one of their screams sent the rest charging with a purpose and after reaching the goal and devouring their prey they would go back to the same trance state as they searched for food.

Above the dead streets, people were giving all they had to thwart the tide of the dead that tried to reach them on the upper floors of the skyscrapers.

Barricades were eroding as thousands of screaming dead surged through the buildings pushing up the stairs in order to quench their thirst.

In the skyscraper of the Amari Hotel, the dead pushed up a stairwell when they saw a helicopter landing on adjacent buildings. The dead began to leap out the windows as they tried to jump from one building to the next. Falling to their deaths below they never lost eye contact on the helicopters until their bodies were smashed on the roads below. The helicopter they had seen was the last helicopter to leave Bangkok that day.

The roadblocks were now overrun as the mob of dead walked quietly by while in Khao San Road the Patton tank that had saved Sai, Yoon and little girl went silent.

The last Army helicopter was on its way out of the city when the pilot spotted the B-52 coming in on a bomb run. He saw a pair of bombs fall, followed by another pair in a different location.

The B-52 was strategically dropping something in and around Bangkok as it weaved in the sky with its deadly payload.

The people of the Amari Hotel and many other skyscrapers looked to see what was going on. It was strange that the bombs that were falling were not exploding and soon they found out why.

A whistling howl came out of the sky as the B-52 flew over their position, a pair of bombs dropped out of the sky and with a loud thud they smashed into the Water Gate Toll booth not to far from the Amari Hotel's position.

From their perch the survivors saw a white smoke growing from where the bombs fell. The smoke grew and grew as the wind began to take it through the streets over the walking dead.

People started jumping from the building next to the Amari Hotel where the helicopter had left. They were closer to the gas than the Amari occupants.

They watched as the people started screaming and more of those people jumped to their deaths below and then the Amari occupants found out why.

First, their skin began to burn, as if a painful sunburn had befallen them. Then their skin began to blister as every orifice on their bodies began to bleed at the same time. Those who had been fighting the dead in the stairwell found themselves easy prey as the dead took them down at ease. Their bodies burned and boiled as the dead began to bite into them, their minds going mad with pain.

The dead flew up the stairwell where they found the survivors trembling in pain on the roof, all cradle up in the fetal position as the gas continued to run its course.

For the dead, their skin burned, they bled from their ears, mouths and eyes but other than that it did not do a damn thing to them but help increase their numbers as the overwhelmed the resistance.

****

Ho Chi Minh City was the latest scene of an outbreak, the slums were burning and the army was now bombarding the city from a series of trenches from outside the city. Phnom Penh and Bali also burned as their respective Air Forces dropped Napalm on the cities.

Like a scene from Godzilla, Kyoto had been leveled upon request by the Japanese Government to the U.S. A nuclear explosion engulfed the city as millions watched from the countryside. All that remained was the fire and bodies moving not to far away from the nuclear cloud.

****

The group continued to move until it was nearing 7:30 p.m. 30 plus hours of no sleep, they needed to rest for the night. It was then as the moon began to rise that they stumbled on a four-man team of soldiers that had been hiding in the jungle.

Sai had seen the movement and knew what it was; it was a soldier lying in the prone and had his rifle held up by a Y-shaped stick sticking into the ground. Sai had done that as a young Marine prior to joining the army. It was the best way to fake out the drill instructors when sleeping and still act like you're on guard duty.

"Tahan?" Sai asked as he walked up on the sleeping soldier careful to keep out of the way of the muzzle.

The soldier woke up and his body jerked as he looked at the man who had scared the living hell out of him. He nearly pissed himself and for some reason thought the man was going to scream at him for being asleep.

Instead, Sai smiled and extended a hand to the soldier who now felt guilty for sleeping. If Sai were one of the dead he and his friends would be dead.

"Pom tahan American," Sai told the soldier softly hoping he said he was an American Soldier.

Ta was next in line as a group of soldiers gathered by Sai. Ta began to tell them their story as Yoon and the rest followed up.

Yoon walked up to the soldier who looked like the leader to exchange Thai greetings, which was followed by a dialogue that Sai did not understand.

The leader was Sai's height, dark skin and roughly the same age. His eyes were like everyone else's; he was running on fumes just trying to keep his men alive.

"The soldier said the dead have been reported farther north," Yoon translated as three of the other soldiers began to recognize her from a movie and began talking to each other in the background.

"They barely escaped and have been hiding here since this late this afternoon." Yoon continued as the soldier continued to talk.

"Ask him if we can join them, the more guns the merrier tonight."

Yoon spoke in Thai and the four soldiers listened. They looked over at Sai and looked a little more intensely as she said Tahan, immediately catching the leader's attention.

The leader began to speak to Sai. "I'm Sgt Wan" Realizing his battlefield promotion didn't mean shit anymore for the Army was on the run. "I'd be happy if you and your friends join us, where are you headed?"

The man's English was as good as Yoon's, which was a sure sign of how educated he was. He extended a hand and shook Sai's hand as he greeted him.

"I'm Sai, its good to meet you Sergeant." Sai smiled as he held his rifle over his shoulder shaking Wan's hand with his free hand. "Been a tough day, what do you say we bed down with your troop after we set up a defensive formation."

"Sounds like a plan, we'll talk more once we get our perimeter secured Sai."

"Very well, let's get some fighting positions set up and put the women and children in the center." Sai replied as he and Wan began to move together setting up those with guns on the perimeter. Since both were military men they knew it was best to set up security and get to know each other later.

They took a quick inventory of what they had which was not much. The soldiers were lightly armed and only had one SAW and the M-16s they had escaped with. There was now total of eight rifles, one revolver, a machete and one Squad Automatic Weapon among the newly formed group. The weapons count was three hundred plus rounds, five M-16s, two M-67 grenades, two M-15 white phosphorus grenades, one QSZ-95

Chinese pistol, one machete, and one claymore amongst the civilians and Sai. For the soldiers, they had three hundred and sixty rounds for the three M-16s and four hundred rounds for the SAW, eight M-67s, two M-9 Berettas and four bayonet blades.

The SAW was placed on the path where Sai and the others had come from, the thought being that the dead were likely to come from the direction of Bangkok following other refugees. It was very Basic Training stuff; cover your avenues of approach with your heaviest, meanest weapon.

Sai and Wan agreed that the strength of their group relied solely on the Thai soldiers who were placed strategically around the perimeter with Klauy, Wanchai and Ta in every other fighting position since they were the weak links.

Unfortunately for the newly formed group, not all was fine and dandy for one of the younger soldiers was in complete disagreement with Wan about babysitting the civilians. It was nothing a few kind words by the group NCO could not fix however.

Wan made it clear to everyone that fatigue had already set in on most of the group, including the three young soldiers and himself. It was safest to dig in for the night, for the group was in the chronic stages of fatigue, mental as well as physical problems were beginning to arise and at night they could easily run into a dead mob without any warning.

The order of the night was to keep their weapons tight, which meant no firing unless it was sure they were being attacked. Things would go bump in the night but to avoid an all out battle they would not fire and just let those things that went bump in the night move on.

Yoon, now holding an M-16 was placed in the center with Wien, the little girl, Akira and Lek who now had the QSZ-95. It may have been a new world they all lived in now but still some chivalry existed amongst the men except for the young soldier who bitched away.

Once everyone was in place, the group opened up the MREs that had been stripped down to fit in their packs and began to re-hydrate themselves with the bottle water that was passed out.

As night rolled on Wan talked with Sai about the last attack of the dead, he was not sure if the Thai Army was still in existence anymore from what he had seen. He hated that most of his men while retreating had ran into several ambushes, dwindling their numbers and scattering what was left to the four corners of Thailand. It had been a miracle that Wan was still alive and he regretted it for he felt it was his responsibility for his soldiers' deaths. When the shit hit the fan he had ordered the retreat that led to the men running in panic as the dead closed in on their six. He had played the scenario over and over in his head since they had retreated. He wondered what if? The deadly question that everyone wonders when your friends' lives are cut short. *What if I was just that much faster? What if I had just formed up the ranks and fought back?* Truth was, that Wan, caught in the open, flanked from all sides had only one choice to chose from and that was to retreat. In doing so he had saved three of his soldiers out of 42 that had been thrown together and tossed under his command. The rest were mostly dead, a few here and there, some even formed up with men from other companies and platoons that had fled all along the second quarantine line. But by the end of the night they would all be dead.

Wan was like a Gunnery Sergeant or Sergeant First Class, an E-7 equivalent from what Sai could tell. He was not an infantryman whom Sai mistook him for when they first met; instead his MOS was that of the Military Police. He had been in the Army ever since he was drafted out of high school and decided to make a profession of it. It was better than being a farmer in his eyes and the friendships he had made during those years always pulled him through the worse of things including the loss of his wife to cancer a year earlier. The Army had been his mother, father, brother and sister.

****

The perimeter guards were each given an hour to sleep in the center with the women and children. Nearing 11 p.m. it was Sai's turn to enter the center of the perimeter.

Inside the so-called perimeter Sai sat next to Yoon who had Wien and the little girl sleeping on her lap. It wasn't much of a sleep but more of total exhaustion and blacking out for the little girl and teenager. They moaned a little in their sleep, something that brought Sai's memories back to when he was at the Recruit Depot on Fire Watch. Walking the squad bay of the barracks down the countless racks, exhaustion causing the recruits to moan in their sleep, some losing their bowels while many others simply drooled on their pillows.

"Wish things turned out different?" Yoon asked as she stroked Wien's hair, her cousin responding with a sleeping smile.

"If it did, Yoon, I'd be back in the war some time next week." He paused. "It was just fate, Yoon. Something drew me here and you know what? If it were not for the whole end of the world thing, I'd be leaving you next week to go back to the war." He laughed a puff of air. "Yoon, I'm glad I'm here with you, and I promise things will get better. My friends are probably on the way. It's nothing my boys can't handle."

Sitting behind her, to avoid sitting on Wien or the little girl, Sai told her to lean her back on his back. A trick Marines and soldiers used to do in the field, their weight would hold each other up and make it more bearable to sit and sleep.

Facing opposite directions, Yoon continued as Sai looked up between the foliage above, a few stars watching down on him. It never failed to impress him how when you get away from a large city a vast ocean of lights always awaited for you above.

"I'm glad you're here, Sai. Your karma brought you here and that same karma got Wien, Ta and me out of Bangkok. I don't know what would have happened if we would have never met, Sai, but I'm glad you came to us." She began to tear up as she thought of the last day's events, all the pain and suffering she had seen, the people who could have used her help that she had left to their fates. If karma were real, her deeds would not go unpunished. Too many had died and during that time, when all she could think about was saving herself and her family.

"You did fine, Yoon, without you I'd probably be dead too. At least we have had one hell of a first date. I'm mean here I am sleeping with your already." He bit his tongue and waited to here her response.

She began to laugh, quietly placing a hand over her mouth and then continued to talk. "Sai, promise you'll stay with us," she replied.

"I...promise," he answered.

Yoon continued to stroke Wien's hair as a cool breeze blew through the jungle, a welcome relief for the group as the heat began to evaporate.

"Sai, are they really dead?"

118

"I don't know." He paused, thinking back to Victory Monument. "I shot one several times, I know I didn't miss. I hit him like I was trained to but he just kept on going like the damn *Energizer Rabbit*. Back at Victory Monument, the Private who gave me the rifle told me to shoot them in the head. I thought he was just one sadistic pup at first, until his shot brought that guy down for good; but then again you shoot any man in the face he will go down for good, I guarantee it." He gulped some water from the bottle. "Honestly I don't know. I've shot a lot a lot of them, and I mean a lot. I never shot a man as a pilot; I've never killed an enemy soldier so I have nothing to compare them with. I don't know if they have a heartbeat, I don't know if they are even aware of what is going on. Yoon, so far every one of them that I have shot never went down until I got them in the head." He paused. "Honestly, I have no idea what is happening. All I know is that we need to survive this, Yoon; we must survive this mess. I'm not going to let any of those fuckers get us."

"Sergeant Wan said it spreads through the bites, blood and other fluids of the infected. That is what he was told from his superiors."

"I figured if they were dead that the bites would be just like in the movies and stories I've read, but I completely forgot about the blood." He thought of the legless dead man at the Esso Station with a machete in his head. "Guess we better watch out for the backwash." If blood had hit his mouth or eyes he would have been done for instantly; it would have spread throughout his body and killed him by now though.

"Do you think this is happening outside of Thailand Sai?"

"A British man told me it was all over Asia. China was first I guess. What is strange is how it spread from China to Thailand so fast. I haven't seen any of those people drive cars so I'm thinking they are all on foot. It's hard for them to get here unless someone with a bite got on an airplane, but I think that is unlikely due to the security at airports but its possible." Sai continued now looking into the shadows of the jungle, thinking he saw something. "I have my money on this being some kind of attack, maybe terrorist or something along those lines, that would explain why it had moved so fast throughout the region."

"Why you think that?" she asked as she lifted her hand from the little girl to touch Sai on the side of the head as she reached back over her shoulder feeling for his cheek.

It felt good, comforting for someone to touch him. He sank into her smooth hands as she rubbed the side of his head moving up to his hairline. He took a deep breath and continued.

"Perhaps America will save us."

"My friends are in southern Asia, half in the Middle East, maybe their coming here." Sai said hopeful with a low voice unaware his military was in full retreat from those regions.

Sai turned around and rubbed Yoon's shoulders, then told her to rest as he leaned the side of his body against her back before he lied her down.

Yoon lay on Sai's lap with the children on hers; before she knew it, Yoon was asleep.

****

Not long after Sai sat asleep watching over Yoon and the two girls. It felt like moments for Sai when he felt someone tugging on his shirt. It was midnight now and time for him to return to the perimeter.

"That was fast," Sai said to himself, wiping the sleep from his eyes.

He slowly laid Yoon's head down on one of the backpacks and noticed Wien was not asleep.

"Nong Wien pye lop, okay?" Sai told her to go back to sleep as he put his hand on her hair trying to reassure her with what comfort he could offer her. She closed her eyes and Sai lifted his hand.

Sai looked at the little girl who had been asleep since they met the soldiers and laid a hand on her as if she were his daughter. Glad to see she was sleeping he limped with his rifle and went out to his battle position and took to the prone in the wet jungle floor.

Next to him was a sleeping soldier, looked like Wan had placed his rifle on the stick too, like Sai they were both mortal. Sai had been there, done that and understood what the soldier was going through, he was the leader of the group of Thai soldiers and had probably done much to keep the four of them alive. Sai had been trained to be sleep deprived for weeks in the Marines long ago, and thankfully that training was more use to him now than being a pilot was.

It brought back memories all right and now here he was doing it for real again.

****

It was now two a.m. and Ta had been tracking movement somewhere in the jungle. Sai had begun to nod off after fighting sleep all night when a screech was heard followed by another, then another from over a football away in the darkness.

Machine gun fire quickly followed the screech along with flashes from several rifles. A few SAWS went off there after and lit up the jungle floor like a techno club.

A flare shot up into the air and the jungle roared to life with living humans screaming and the dead screeching from every direction.

Ta watched in awe as he saw the flare coming down by parachute. Dangling from the strings, the light from the flare shifted back and forth as its rays penetrated the jungle canopy. The shadows danced like demons as the flare reentered the jungle. Then another flare went up and Ta's eyes tracked it go up from those firing their guns.

The soldiers and Sai quickly closed one eye an instinct that was learned from their training, a small tactic so they could maintain some of their night vision for when the light was gone.

Gunfire was erupting from every direction as panic began to set in amongst the group. Thai soldiers looked to Wan and the civilians to Sai for guidance. Sai pointed his hand over his head and made several circle motions with his pointer finger facing the sky, which was a signal to come together.

The soldiers immediately gathered on Sai which the civilians quickly copying them.

"Men on the outside, women on the inside, we take a nice slow jog to the north." Sai said as the gunfire lit up the area in flashes.

Wan translated and furthered the instructions by telling two of his men to take point. One man and Ta were to protect the left flank of the formation. Wanchai and Klauy took the right flanks so Sai and Wan could bring up the rear.

Pop! Pop! Pop!

The soldier on the left flank opened fire as one of the dead spotted him as the last flare faded to darkness.

Another flare went up and Sai saw two dead men running at them from the north and as the group began to run their shadows twisted in the jungle.

Num in front of the now-running formation stopped, exhaled, and fired. Three shots, two kills – and one of the kills fewer than five feet from his position. He started running north once more as the women and children followed close by.

"Conserve ammo!" Wan ordered the rest of the group in Thai.

Moving north, they ran right by an undead attack heading off to their right flank where Wanchai and Klauy were. The dead charged to the east as tracer rounds missed them nearly taking Wanchai's head off.

Unknowingly, the group had camped in the center of what was a refugee camp made of soldiers and civilians hiding and now on the right flank of the groups' formation a slaughter had begun.

Some of the dead from Bangkok had made it this far north already and were now attacking the remnants of the army that had been scattered in the jungle, some being Wan's men. They charged into the wall of bullets attracted by the weapon fire causing more to come from miles away.

Flesh blasted off their backs as the dead pushed their assault on the army. .50 Cals and SAWs did their jobs and pulverized the bodies. Yet still they came, tumbling over themselves missing limbs and large portions of their torsos. The flares the soldiers were firing were only adding to the problem for the dead were like the living, humans were not nocturnal animals and with the lights advertising the livings presence, they came in full force.

Wan thought briefly of helping out his fellow soldiers but knew better than to follow through with it. He just hoped his soldiers currently within his group were not thinking the same as him for they did turn to fight they would only die with the rest.

The screeching of their hellish charge continued, as miles away the thumps of the blast had alerted hundreds if not thousands of dead who had been stalking the refugees of Bangkok. Within seconds of the first gunfire, they had triangulated the position and were now in race towards the living.

With the attack continuing several of the party raised their rifles in false alarm as civilian refugees appeared running in every direction with no clear goal of where to go.

The group continued north when another flare showed about fifteen people hot on their trail, screeching for blood, some had been soldiers from the ambushed squad that had already joined the ranks of the dead and were now following. The dead soldiers showed no signs of fatigue and were beginning to gain on the group as they negotiated trees and rocks. Their cries becoming ever louder with each passing second

"Yoon keep running!" Sai shouted over the screaming dead and sounds of battle.

"Let's hold them off!" Wan shouted to Sai as if on the same wavelength, his face now in a snarl.

Wan looked over to Sai who was already taking a knee as the group continued to move north. Yoon turned her head to see what Sai was doing only to be greeted by Wanchai who motioned her to continue on as he gestured his arm in a waving motion.

Ta held Wien's hand as he guided his sister behind the two other soldiers who were clearing the way in front of them, taking down the occasional monster that had out maneuvered the group.

****

Sai hit the quick release on the A.L.I.C.E pack sending it dropping to the jungle floor before turning to pull out a claymore from the bottom of the bag. The cries of the dead grew louder.

He placed the claymore in the ground and made double sure to face the blast plate that read towards the enemy to his pursuers. Next, he ran the wire to the detonator as Wan opened fire on one of the leaders. Wan was accurate, extremely good compared to Sai. He had more experience in this field than the pilot who had scrambled to put the claymore in place.

Soon twenty of them would be on them as five more triangulated Wan's fire in the dark and time was beginning to run out.

Sai grabbed the pack and Wan, pulling both behind a fallen tree. He looked over the log as Wan continued to fire and then waited for the last moment as the dead neared five yards from the claymore. Satisfied, he grabbed Wan's head and pulled him down as he detonated the claymore.

The blast sprayed pellets towards the enemy as advertised and shredded the pursuers like Swiss cheese while the leaders were completely vaporized. It was as if a shotgun was aimed at a sparrow from five inches away, nothing remained, not even a finger.

"RUN!" Sai shouted at Wan, not waiting to see if the blast had stopped the dead.

Sai got up and began to run when pain from his wound electrified his body.

"Shit! Run!" he shouted again, mostly to himself as he picked up the pack and hand-carried it to the north.

Yoon and the group were now fifty yards ahead as they slowly moved north. Several muzzle flashes from Ta and then nothing. Wan and Sai began to close the gap, giving the rest of the dead the slip.

****

After ten minutes or more of running, the gunfire had died off and the screeching came to a halt. The battle was nearly a mile behind them. Whoever it was in the jungle had probably defeated the first wave of creatures coming out of Bangkok. Now they were in the process of regrouping as the civilians fled. A second wave was already moving in their direction.

If the group continued to run they might increase the risk of running into something they didn't want to. Wan slowed the group down and they began to walk north once more. Through out the rest of the night, howitzer cannons fired into the area that the group had camped out at. A second attack was on the way and by the sound of it; the artillery was landing on what was left of that group of soldiers. They had been overrun in the dark, and with the lack of NVGs it was only a matter of time until the dead stumbled on the survivors.

Everyone in Sai's group knew what was happening to those soldiers and civilians that stayed behind as they screamed out in bloody anguish. Torn to pieces and eaten in the dark they saw nothing as they moon hid behind the jungle canopy.

Even as burnt-out as the group was, their sheer willpower allowed them to move on; but at this pace they would eventually become victims.

They needed to find a safe haven and fast – for they could no longer stay out in the open.

Chapter 7: *A Tunnel Too Far*

The battle last night marked the impending doom of the Thai military, for now there were no more vehicles moving or aircraft flying in the sky anymore. The bases where most of the aircraft had come from had been overrun with refugees from Bangkok. The refugees' numbers were in the thousands and within that number many had concealed bites, which proved fatal for the bases. The medical tents were first to fall, battered nurses ran from their patients into the clutching hands of the doctors. The dead easily moved from one wounded patient to the next as if they were in a buffet line. All the patients could do was wait until it was there turn.

Confused the soldiers began to abandon the perimeter gates as the dead launched attacks from within the green zone. Mass panic spread like a plague from within the fences of the base as the soldiers ran to their vehicles trying to make a break for it as they busted out of the base gates into the hordes of the dead outside. With the gates open and all order gone, the dead swiftly moved in to fill the void of power.

The dead river of humans flowed in covering every square inch of the bases as they sought out their prey. Completely encircled and with nowhere to run, the soldiers and refugees only had two options, the sky or underground.

Those pilots who still maintained their sense of duty died in the dying bases with the rest. They tried to take to the skies, but the sheer amount of passengers boarding their aircraft was beyond their gross weight limitations. They pulled on their collectives breaking every limit they could, trying to get their birds off the ground. A Huey was never meant to carry twenty to thirty people in flight.

They had become sitting ducks in the center of the base as the dead ran straight into the cabin pulling out one person at a time sinking their teeth further into the helicopter's juicy occupants.

Where most held out for at least awhile was in the underground bomb shelters. Those that had managed to close the doors in time only saved themselves to face a new nightmare. Never ending banging came from the doors above sending the survivors into a state of madness in the darkness. Only those who committed suicide hours later were spared the weeklong torture of hell on earth as the survivors tore each other to pieces in the dark abyss.

****

As dawn approached, the group was now hopelessly lost in the jungle. They prayed and hoped that they were continuing north for the jungle canopy had become so thick that only a few rays of the suns light penetrated it. No sign of life remained as darkness turned to shades of gray then blue as the sun rose over the jungle. Steam was rising from the floor creating a white mist that only added to the disorientation. During the panic of last night's attack the only compass the soldiers had was lost forever to the foliage of the jungle.

They had taken brakes every two hours since the night. Upon stopping the soldiers and the men would create a perimeter. Lying prone, the soldiers and men rested but tried their best not to doze off.

Lying prone, Num's skin was flushed red; his skin was burning as his eyelids began to fall. His clothes were soaked with sweat and morning dew; the scent of mud was fresh in his nose as he rested his head on the stock of his SAW. It hurt to move, not that he was sore, but due to the constant grinding of debris in his uniform. The only soothing sensation was the metal that rubbed the side of his face as he moved his head from the stock to the side of the SAW. The cool feel of steel against his cheek felt great; it was the only way to feel fresh. Falling to sleep he could not help; his body had stopped moving and now he found his comfort zone. His legs were resting, his arms no longer needed to carry the SAW and there was nothing he could do as his eyes started closing. He knew they were closing; they were falling, feeling so heavy that not even his will could keep them open any more.

"Son, give me your weapon." Wan put a hand on the boy's shoulder causing Num's eyes to blast open with a sudden sense of fear. "It's okay, Num. Get some rest now; I need you frosty the rest of the day."

Num looked up at Sergeant Wan, a few rays of light stabbing Num in the eye causing him to squint.

"Get a going now."

127

Num did as ordered and moved to the center of the formation while Wan manned the SAW.

****

It was late afternoon when Ta heard a noise coming from up ahead. He was taking his turn as point man finally. It had been something he had been looking forward to since they entered the jungle.

Sai had sensed the boy's energy and figured it would serve the group best now. Since the attack during the night Ta was the only one in the group who showed little signs of exhaustion. Possibly because it was every teenage boy's fantasy to be hero and that was what he was doing, even if it was under the watchful eyes of Sai and Wan. Ta had found his niche in the group; he was now the eyes and ears for everyone.

Ta gave his hand signals just as Sai had taught him and now a closed fist was held up into the air. Everyone froze standing like perfect statues just as instructed. A deathly silence alerted their senses and the smell of iron became heavy in the air.

Next was the sound of the second hand of someone's wristwatch, tick, tick, tick the seconds went by as Ta zeroed in on the location of what spooked him. The noise came off of Ta's one o'clock position. His eyes focused as he tried to look through the foliage, his ear moved just a little as if trying to tune in a lost radio transmission.

Frozen the group stood until Ta lowered his hand in a waving motion down towards the earth. The group slowly took a knee in response as Ta looked to Sai for guidance.

Sai slowly made his way to Ta with Wan following close while signaling his men to form a 360-degree field of fire. The soldiers quietly took up their positions causing Wanchai, and Klauy to do the same. All weapons were now facing outboard as if they prepared for an ambush.

Yoon took a gulp as she watched Sai go to her cousin followed, she then turned to her left and smiled at Wien who was holding the little girl. Yoon then moved to an open spot in the perimeter and helped with the 360-degree formation.

"What is it?" Sai whispered barely audible.

Ta, in a heavy accent, replied, "I think several of those things are up ahead." He pointed beyond the sight that the jungle would allow.

Wan walked over as Sai put a hand on the boy's shoulder.

"Good job, now get back in the formation and take care of your sister and Yoon while we go check it out."

Ta looked at Sai proud of his accomplishment and then moved back to the formation.

"Dead in the rear, dead in the front," Wan continued. "Sai we have no choice, we need to push through whatever is out there."

Sai looked back at the formation, the dreary faces watching him.

"They're tired Wan." He paused, turning his face away from them. "We need to be careful, we've outrun those nasty fucks already but our luck won't hold up forever." Sai looked ahead towards the problem area. "We better go scout up ahead and see what the problem is."

The two men walked back to the group and briefed them on what was about to happen. Num was now in charge of the soldiers and Wanchai of the civilians. If anything went wrong, or gunshots were fired by the scouts or the main group, they were to make a run to the east in hope of avoiding the swarm of infected to the southwest.

A brief goodbye to Yoon, the little girl and her cousins and Sai was off with Wan heading through the thicket and disappearing from their sight. The pain of waiting had begun.

****

A few minutes after the two men entered the thicket, a howling wail could be heard followed by a moaning chorus of messed up vocal cords. A clearing began to open up as the two men left the thickets that hid their friends and the moans became clearer. Not risking any movement straight through the clearing, the two men stuck to the shadows as they made their way to the direction of the noise using the trees for cover. Upon entering a thin brush line they could see what stood before them. A highway, filled with thousands of cars that were bumper to bumper. Still worse was the dead pedestrians walking in the one direction. Only moans and the occasional wails came from the dead parade, filling the air with sound as the never-ending line of the dead marched to the east.

All around the area was carnage; fierce bloodied panic had gone through this road, maybe just hours ago, maybe during the last night. Some cars were still burning as the dead walked by. Other vehicles had their windows bashed in with pools of blood on the dashboards and seats from where life had been extinguished.

Now though there were no signs of violence anywhere along the dead road just the uncoordinated walking of the dead shuffling to the east. Sai thought it strange how these Olympic athletes could run, but when prey was not in the area they turned into stumbling idiots, bumping into each other as they continued on east, he thought it had something to due with being goal oriented. When prey presented itself what was left of the body just kicked into overdrive, kind of like a soldier feeling his surroundings during a battle. The brain just had a way of heightening ones senses in situations that called for it.

Looking towards the direction the migrating heard was moving, Sai could see dark clouds that were rising from the horizon. They were not clouds but smoking plumes that were being released into the atmosphere. It was a clear sign a battle was still raging over the horizon, too far for him and the others to hear the music of battle. Little did the two men know that the Thai military was still holding on by a thread. The remnants of the army were covering the retreat of thousands of civilians as they retreated towards the Cambodian border. If only they had a bird's eyes view they would see that coming from the other direction was nothing but dead creatures marching to them as the Cambodian army retreated to Thailand.

Of course it was not Sai's immediate concern, somehow they needed to pass the highway for in the south was Bangkok where the dead were coming from. The east was a battlefield and to the west another city that had been overrun, what city not even Wan could tell for they were now lost.

Nervously the two scanned the area, looking for a weak point in which they could pass, but even if they managed to sneak pass the running dead, the ones stuck in the vehicles would give away their position in a heartbeat, causing thousands would descend on them instantly, it was not looking good.

Scanning to the right and to the left they found two buildings on opposite sides of the highway. Just then, it hit Sai, one of his favorite movies from the eighties, *Maximum Overdrive*. Perhaps a sewage pipe was under the road near the two buildings and that could prove to be the lifeline Sai had been looking for. Sneaking through the tunnel, all they'd have to worry about were snakes and maintaining their stealth.

Sai explained that he would scout out the area near the building on their side of the road looking for a drainage tunnel, leaving out the part that he ripped off the idea from a movie when Wan looked at Sai's leg. "I'll go. It'll be easier for me," Wan said as he looked over Sai's leg again to make sure Sai saw his concern.

Knowing that Wan was a capable, if not better soldier than Sai, Sai nodded his approval. Hesitating and not wanting to leave Wan to do the work of scouting alone, Sai thanked him and told him to return alive. As Wan began to scout out area alone Sai began to move back into the thicket at towards the group in order to prepare them for the challenge they would face tonight.

A few minutes after Sai began to make his way to the group, Wan was paralleling the road. Staying out of sight from the dead Wan swiftly covered ground. He moved quietly, but quickly, only stopping momentarily when the occasional dead creature crossed his path, and then he was off again moving towards his target. Any noise meant certain death to Wan.

The dead had congregated on the road for a reason, and that was because of sound. They were attracted to the moans other made causing them to herd together in a swarm of death.

The moans formed a symphony of wailing. It sounded almost as if a strong wind was blowing through a home during a violent storm. It brought their sick twisted family together which kept Wan for the most part in the clear as the creatures.

Circumnavigating the dead, Wan walked a mile until he came to the edge of a bus motor pool. The buses were empty and no signs of battle had taken place in the area, the employees had long abandoned the structure, which was much to Wan's relief. The buses just sat there watching the dead parade as Wan scanned the area.

On the opposite side of the highway was another gas station with a small S&P bakery shop next to it. Cars were piled up there; the sign a battle had definitely taken place. In the center of the vehicles a lone jeep from the WWII era stood, with a machine gun that was slumped on the standing. Bullet holes filled most of the cars in the area and a few left over people still struggled trapped in the cars. Body parts and blood littered the ground and bloody handprints covered the jeep where a soldier had made a last stand. Other than the trap dead in the cars, the rest had converged with the dead parade on the road, leaving the gas station relatively clear now.

Wan continued his scan when he found what he was looking for. A large cargo truck had driven off the road and into a ditch resting on a pipe that extended out of the ground into a pool of filthy water. No one appeared in the truck and no signs of a struggle in the cabin, which meant it crashed early on during the outbreak possibly due to a panicking driver.

As Wan continued to scan a lady began to run towards him from within the jungle. Her throat had been crushed under the jaws of her dead boyfriend and her chest had glistering white ribs exposed to the elements. Where her lungs were supposed to be was a caked cavity covered in blood and flies. It tried to screech but the air escaped through the ribs and throat as it ran closer.

Alerted by her presence Wan pulled a large combat knife from his right bootstrap wanting to dispatch the woman as quietly. The creature pounced on Wan and the two began tumbling into the cover of the jungle.

Wan, making more noise than he wanted continued to struggle in the brush while the dead parade continued to moan, covering the noise the two were making, unaware of the prey lurking nearby.

The woman had achieved the mount position on Wan. She chomped on open air as her head shot up and down trying to deliver the kiss of death. Struggling Wan managed to put his hands underneath her chin, his right thumb lodged inside her throat. His thumb felt the squishy flesh as he struggled with the woman's face. With one hand he reached for the knife that had fallen during the struggle and all he could see was the jagged blood stained teeth chomping down over him. He cursed in Thai, as panic began to sink its white teeth into him.

Fear was rising as the teeth kept chomping down on air, just inches from his nose; that is when he remembered his combative training. She was on the perfect mount on top of him and he figured he would pass her into the guard. With his right leg he flanked her left leg and while pulling down on her shoulder and using the other arm to keep her throat and head at bay he flipped her onto her back.

The woman started going through spasms after Wan grabbed the knife that was next to her face and shoved it into her nose breaking bones and sending fragments shooting into her brain.

The woman twitched in her final death thralls, slowing down until she went limp as a noodle under Wan's weight.

Quickly he grabbed his rifle and began his retreat to Sai and the others scanning for any incoming danger that may have seen him.

****

After Wan had moved stealthy back to the group, Wanchai and Lek dispersed the food to everyone. It was already running low again and the water bottles were falling short as well but not in danger yet. Some believed they needed to make another raid to replenish their supplies soon.

Being a safe distance from the road they argued their point to Sai, but being in occupied territory of the dead Sai refused to launch any type of raid on the gas station and S&P and was backed by Wan. You could go days without eating, water was the big killer and at the moment they had water.

After the losing battle with Sai, Wanchai and Lek found allies with two of the three soldiers remaining. Young and of course over confident the two agreed to find food near the gas station when they made their way past the highway later that night. The two would take a little detour when Wan and Sai were not looking, sneaking off so they could become heroes.

Yoon had continued to hold the fort down with the little girl, keeping her as quiet as possible. Ta of course was alert as always and scanned the area with his ears while his sister Wien took an ammo count of all those with weapons.

Klauy had fallen to sleep almost as soon as the Sai and Wan went out to scout the noise earlier. Since Klauy did not snore the group decided to let him be, a big boy like him took up a lot of precious calories anyways and perhaps hibernation was best for him so that the food would last longer amongst the group and his pain would be less.

The meeting between Sai and Wan was a discussion on detail on the best course of action for the group to take for the operation that needed to be conducted. A plan was forming and under the cover of darkness they would make their move as they attempted to past the highway of the dead, it was do or die operation.

While Sai and Wan discussed strategy, the two soldiers influenced by Wanchai and Lek formed a plan of their own, Num the youngster and who been put in charge of the three was left out of the discussion for he was Wan's favorite, and would most likely report back to the Sergeant. So when the group was clear of the tunnel the duo would raid the gas station and the S&P simultaneously.

Though Wanchai had brought up the topic again to Sai and Wan, the risk of being spotted was too great for a few bites to eat; that is exactly what would happen if they attempted it, a few bites to eat for the dead. The dead would descend on them in seconds if they were caught and with reasoning slowly sinking in Wanchai agreed that it was too risky and turned to Lek, who joined in on the discussion halfway through.

Yet the two soldiers stayed strong to their commitment and kept out of the discussion since Wan still outranked him and Sai was a foreign officer, if rank still meant something.

Late that afternoon brought a peaceful sunset as the jungle glowed orange. The group was well rested as the last rays of light touched the jungle floor. Sai had made his way to Yoon, the little girl and her cousins and explained what would happen. If their position was compromise they were to run like they never ran before while Sai covered the rear. He swore he would protect them to the very end and with that said he gave them a reassuring look before returning to Wan for last-minute changes.

****

As night fell, the group waited for their eyes to adjust before setting out on the great escape.

Meanwhile across the world in San Antonio, the orphanage named Madison Square became the latest scene of carnage. The sun was rising over the United States and the cities burned since the military had concentrated all firepower on them. The battle for America was raging, the naval blockades had failed and somehow on the eastern port of New York the infected came. Sweeping across the nation the states were burning as Mexico closed off the border to America.

Mexican tanks, military vehicles and the local drug cartels lined the border preventing Americans from seeking refugee in Mexico, and even with the Mexican army present, Americans found ways to illegally go south of the border.

It was unknown to the government how something could have spread so fast within the nation. Only a small clip had made it to Internet from a CIA agent trapped in New York. He talked as if he was a preacher about the door to hell being opened because the sons of the fallen had been discovered, which led to genocide on the streets. What the crazed man meant died with him. The blast doors of his compound were blown off the hinges by explosives and the dead poured in. The last people saw of him was his body parts being thrown across the room live on camera.

****

The sun was long gone now, the time had come and the group was on the move once more. Quietly they made their way through the jungle following Wan's lead stopping every few minutes when ever few of the dead marched to close to them.

The moon had risen and the illumination was roughly 30%, which was a drastic increase from the previous night. The stars were twinkling again along with the moon that was watching over the group, waiting for the moment one of them would slip up and get everyone killed. Like spectators at a game, the stars stared at the world they had come to enjoy. The savage murders continuing for their entertainment pleasure.

Through the darkness Wan navigated his way through a mile of dead infested territory. It took longer than he would like as the clock turned to 3:10 a.m. on Sai's watch but that was to be expected when moving in a group. Almost six hours of walking cautiously for just little over a mile and now they were staring upon their lifeline to the unknown.

Stopping in the formation they had set out on was Wan, Sai, Yoon, little girl, Ta, Wien, Num, Wanchai, Lek, Akira, Klauy, and the two young soldiers who brought up the rear. Wan and Sai set up the order, strategically placing soldiers throughout the formation to provide a more experienced field of fire in the event all hell broke loose.

Weapons facing staggered outboard they moved until they came to the clearing near the buildings. As before, Wan scanned the area and signal Sai to come up. Upon reaching Wan's position Wan pointed out the sewage tunnel near the abandon truck. Not much in the way the dead who kept to the road moving east hoping that a car or two would have people hiding inside.

The scan was promising and soon they would make their move, Wan decided it was best to move in groups of two or three that way if they were spotted some of the group would survive as the group that was spotted was torn to pieces. It was brutal but logical way of thinking. Sai just hoped Yoon would not be the one to be found for if that was the case he would not let her die alone.

The plan was relayed to the rest of the group and Sai and Wan would be first to hit the tunnel. Wan would go through the tunnel to the other side and pull security while Sai held the other end and would signal the pairs to come. Lying in the tunnel, Sai would wait until the soldiers brought up the rear. Wan upon receiving Ta at his end of the tunnel would secure a safe location near the building and call up Ta, Yoon and the little girl, from that position.

Next Wan would take Yoon and the little girl to safety in the jungle as Ta stayed put. They would take turns pulling security where Ta would be and Sai would be third to last out of the tunnel followed by the two soldiers. A blue light was the signaling device. It was dull enough for those who were not actively looking for it would not find it and clear enough for those who waited for its signal. That was the plan and as the group sank the information into their heads Sai and Wan began a low crawl through the high grass to the drainage tunnel.

The weeds and grass was high, providing much needed cover for the two soldiers who low crawled their way down into a ditch where the tunnel was. Bugs and ants crawled over them as they slowly made their way, trying their best not to disturb the long grass too much.

Under the cover of darkness they continued pausing only when the slightest moan from the marching dead seemed too close. The humidity was intense, but soon a cool breeze began to flow as they closed the distance to the tunnel.

Wan was first to make it to the tunnel, which was next to a pool of cool jungle water. He slid into the water on his back holding the rifle out and Sai followed likewise so they could prevent their weapons from jamming the first time they needed to use them during this maneuver.

Sai's face went under the water as he entered the pool. The water was cool and immediately Sai felt the sand and mud all over his body as it flooded into his clothes. It reminded him of the Quigley course he had did as a young Marine.

Sai's lips tasted like salt and the burnt scab on his leg burned some more. His face slowly popped out of the water as he regained his balance before he opened his mouth for air. Sand and water poured out of his mouth as he moved. Then he opened his eyes to what he expected would be a thousand needles entering his eyes.

Wiping his eyes with his free hand, Sai cleared the water to see Wan already pulling security at the edge of the tunnel taking a knee and holding his rifle out at shoulder level.

With a nod of confirmation to Sai, Wan turned around and entered the tunnel as Sai moved to where he was and took a knee. Sai scanned the darkness and saw the jungle where he could make out Ta's silhouette staring at him.

Behind Sai, Wan crawled on all fours through the mush and litter making his way through the steel tunnel. The tunnel was stagnant, the air foul and the heat from baking in the sun all day around one hundred and ten degrees Fahrenheit. The tunnel forced him to crawl with only inches to spare from the top of his back. Jagged pieces of rusted metal hung from above forcing him to lower his body into the sludge until he passed the sharp jagged objects. He moved silently trying to avoid any unnecessary noise since the tunnel seemed to amplify every move he made. He controlled his breathing as best he could when he reached twenty yards into the tunnel; the moans of the dead were amplified ten fold in this portion, the sound bouncing from every direction. Chills were sent through Wan's body as the parade of the dead marched on above him but as he continued through the sludge the last twenty yards the amplification had calmed down. He took a knee at the entrance and began to pull security before signaling Sai.

At the edge of the tunnel, Wan scanned the area of the ditch while his body sank an inch into the soft mud. Looking towards the gas station he saw an escape route that would keep him and the members of his group away from the dead in the cars and out of sight of those on the street.

Turning around he moved back to the tunnel and pulled out his L-shape light, he began to flash the blue signal to Sai.

Sai saw the signal and with his dull blue light that he borrowed from Num he sent the signal for Yoon, the little girl and Ta. The three in turn left the safety of the jungle, each crawling on their bellies towards Sai. Yoon and Ta had their weapons slung on their backs, which made it easier for them to proceed with the little girl between them. They stayed close to each other in a line abreast formation. Slowly they crawled through the high grass as quietly as they could, stopping anytime a moan seemed to loud.

It took nearly ten minutes for them to reach Sai, but speed was not as important as stealth was. When they reached Sai, he pointed to Ta to go first. As Ta entered the tunnel raindrops began to fall from the sky, a welcomed relief for the group because the noise may aid in their escape.

As Ta, Yoon, and the little girl entered the tunnel, Wien and Num began to low crawl after being signaled by Sai. The rain was becoming heavier as the droplets impacted the ground and formed a steady stream near the tunnel. Still in no danger of flooding the tunnel and with the dead continuing to march to the east the group began to pick up the pace.

The dead shambled and crawled between cars, driven by the flashes of explosions far to the east. The lights bounced off the forming overcast clouds and into the eyes of those with eyes.

****

Pulling security on the opposite end of the tunnel, Wan was now joined by Ta who was looking sharply into the darkness of the dead buildings in front of him. The buildings looked like skeletons; the windows shattered, displaying themselves as black voids of death inside.

The moans and grunts of the dead kept everyone on edge, which was perhaps for the best, for nothing escaped their attention.

In the tunnel the last two soldiers entered followed by Sai who brought up the rear instead of the two younger soldiers instead as planned.

As word was given to Wan that all was clear in the rear he slowly began to low crawl to the shadows of the nearest building. The rain continued and a few minutes after he left he made it to the building where he signaled for Ta, Yoon and the little girl to move towards his position.

The three quickly made their way to Wan and once in position Ta was ordered to pull security. Ta watched as Wan, Yoon and the little girl walked around to the left and rear of the building, to the safety of the jungle.

Ta stayed put until his sister and Num came, then he proceeded to Wan with his sister.

As Ta and Wien made it to the safety of the jungle, thunder began to rumble overhead. Wan faced the road pulling security while Ta and Wien entered the jungle. Now the waiting game had begun as the group slowly began to proceed to the jungle in leap frog fashion

Unfortunately within five minutes lightning had begun to light up the area. The flashes from the lightning slowed the pace of the group down tremendously. The operation was going smoothly until the weather brought in this new obstacle. The lightning flashed and lit up the road of thousands upon thousands of stumbling dead followed by the pounding of thunder that caused all the dead to look up at once.

Watching the scene Num continued to pull security as Wanchai and Lek began to make their way to the jungle followed by Akira and Klauy. He felt as if he was in the open as the flashes of lightning destroyed his shadowy hideout. He quickly moved to the prone in order to avoid a high silhouette that the dead might see.

Finally the plan fell to shit as the two soldiers made their way to the right of the tunnel towards the S&P and gas station. Sai's heart dropped from his chest as he saw the two grunts move quickly through the flashing lightning. Num looked on in disbelief trying to figure out what the duo was up to.

Quickly Sai moved out from the drainage tunnel towards Num, fearing that any moment several thousand screaming dead men and women would descend upon the group.

Confused Num looked at Sai as Sai waved his hand for him to run. Num waited until Sai was upon him and asked in Thai if they should cover the two soldiers. But Sai had no clue what he said.

Sai only replied, "Pye! Pye!" in a low, demanding voice that told the soldier to run.

Sai grabbed the soldier by his right arm and pulled him hard to get him to start moving as the other two soldiers neared the station careful not to alert the dead trapped in the cars.

****

Nearing the station, the taller soldier began to move faster than the other while the other pulled security checking the six. The Tall Soldier's goal was to get into the gas station and load up on food and water, hopefully become the savior of the group and earn more respect from the others, maybe even steal a girl away from one of the other guys. Like most young inexperienced pups that entered the military straight out of high school, his dreams were big and didn't make much sense.

Nearing the entrance of the gas station, the Tall Soldier signaled his pal to hit the S&P store with a wave of his finger. Then he entered into the darkness of the gas station overlooking the bloody handprints on the floor of the entrance. He walked passed the broken glass doing his best to bypass the fallen shards on the floor. Each step a well placed strategically placed move across a minefield of potential noise.

Moving past a mountain of Pocky boxes that had been put on display, the Tall Soldier instantly smelled the aroma of rot in the stale air. Something was definitely dead in here. He turned on his L-shape light, using the blue light for low intensity to view what was before him. Quickly he found the source of the putrid smell, body parts of a teenage female were everywhere in the aisle that stood before him. Her bloody schoolgirl shirt was caked with bits of flesh and gore, and was hanging on a shelf with the other junk food. She'd been torn apart by a pack of the dead, and from the looks of it not all the blood was coagulated yet. The shelves dripped with blood and he zeroed in on chunks of hair on a Pepsi bottle that was knocked over on the shelf. Next to bottle was gore from god knows what part of her. The kill had just been hours ago at the most, perhaps when they were waiting for sundown to make their move, maybe even when Sai and Wan had begun their crawl to the tunnel.

The Tall Soldier heard the sound of bottles being knocked around from towards the front of the store. The hair raised on the back of his neck as a noise caught his attention, every nerve in his body fired alerting him that danger was close.

Turning around, a boy in a school uniform covered in blood, missing a nose and pale skin looked up at the blue light that was in his distorted face. The boy raised his lips back as if he was snarling while the soldier raised his weapon, that is when the horrible high pitch screech roar came screaming out of the boy.

A sharp report of the rifle went off alerting everything within ears shot nearby.

The Tall Soldier fired one round into the boy's head and began to run to the exit when the symphony of screeching roared from the highway causing a stampede to break out. In less than five seconds the first of the dead, a woman, had cut off the Tall Soldier from the exit and as the soldier fired a round into her but two more of her dead comrades hit the door at the same time, less than another second later ten attacking dead corpses smashed through the door and windows of the gas station chasing the Tall Soldier down the aisle towards the beer in the fridge in the back of the store.

After the first shot was fired, the Short Soldier who was about to enter S&P turned with a raised weapon to see a lightning flash light up the faces of a hundred walking corpses that all turned in his direction at once.

Before he could react he too had been spotted, he dropped his weapon and began to sprint towards the right of the building, the opposite side of the group who was now aware that the stampede had started, cowering in the darkness.

The Short Soldier managed to get ten feet before a man who was covered in a mosaic of bites tackled him. The man's jaws bit down into the soldier's arm as he struggled to block the mutilated man in a futile gesture. Less than one second later, the soldier's screams were drowned out by a mound of bodies that ripped the Short Soldier to shreds in seconds. The swiftness of the attack may have been a godsend in disguise for it was not long after he had been tackled that he was dead.

Sai, Wan, and the others did not take long to run deeper into the jungle when the second shot took place. Wan knew his soldiers could not be saved, and the thought of running was against his character, but as Sai and Num entered the jungle moments before the first shot and he knew it was already too late for the two young soldiers. Their foolishness would cost them their lives. Survival of the group out way the needs of those who did not follow orders, so he continued to run with the two soldiers in the back of his mind.

A third shot was fired as the group made twenty feet deeper into the jungle. The thunder and screams of the dead covered their retreat as they ran like gazelle running from a pride of lions.

The Tall Soldier fired the third shot before he broke through the restroom door to find another teenage schoolgirl hiding in the one toilet room. Pushing his back on the door to close it, he tried to hold the dead out as the girl looked up in disbelief that her hiding place had become compromised. Her jaw dropped down in slow motion as she screamed and as soon as the soldier put his back on the door to bar the dead out the door exploded into the bathroom, which was no bigger than a janitor's closest. The soldier was squashed on the floor and the girl was smashed against the toilet, her skull crushed under the pressure as several hundred bodies that tried to make their way into the small room. The stampeded had pressed nearly twenty corpses into the five-foot by seven-foot room and they continued to push their way into the room causing the walls to crumble. Inside the small station ten seconds after the first shot was fired nearly two hundred dead people had packed themselves inside with thousands swarming the area of the station walking on cars causing them to fold underneath their weight.

****

Running through the jungle at the lead of the pack, Ta and Wanchai had dispatched a man they had run across with a knife before it could sound the alarm. The group had made a mile of running in a few minutes and they could hear the undead Led Zeppelin concert still playing at the gas station as they began to slow down.

Yoon held the little girl and was catching her breath when Sai slowed down to a walk and grabbed his leg. Blood had seeped through his wound during the run, but not nearly as bad as the original thanks to the treatment earlier. Limping his way to Yoon he looked at Wien who was catching her breath and was white as a ghost.

"It's okay," Sai told Wien, not knowing if she understood.

They seemed dead free for the moment, even though the screaming was louder than a monster truck rally.

Yoon under the evasion from the gas stationed had dropped her weapon as she carried the child. The sling had undone itself while she was on the run holding the child and fell off her back lost forever in the darkness of the jungle.

"You good?" Sai asked Yoon as he and the others caught their breath.

Wan looked in the direction of the gas station knowing what had happened to his men. Thankfully his men did not bring the dead to them, it was sick that he was at least happy for that.

Gasping for air Klauy had been the slowest of the group. He was holding his side, forcing air to come into his lungs; the group watched fearing he was about to die in front of them. Num quickly poured water on the man's head trying to cool him off as he breathed erratically. He began to speak to him in Thai and made him laugh helping him to control his breathing, which caused the pain to subside.

A minute had gone by when Sai looked over to Wan to get the group moving again. Safety was definitely something that would not last and the group began to move once more as the dead finished feasting on the corpses.

The bones were crushed and devoured, all the marrow sucked out and not a single piece wasted. Like piranha on a chicken, nothing was left of the two soldiers and the schoolgirl when the dead stood up and walked east once more.

Chapter 8: *The Refugees*

The sun was rising and the group had made it nearly ten miles north of the highway to hell when they heard the sound of water flowing from a very tiny waterfall a sign that they were approaching a small creek or stream.

Slowing to almost a halt, Num who had been on point pushed some bushes aside to see a flash of red from a shirt of an elderly woman cleaning something in the water. He looked left ,then right before he led the group out into the creek that was flanked from the north by a small hill. The hill paralleled the stream that led into the jungle where the group was approaching.

A mother and father both in their early thirties stood in a defensive posture, two kids one around four the other an infant and a grandmother who was in her seventies looked at the group, openly weary of the newcomers. Everyone was unarmed except the husband who held his weapon in his right hand while gesturing to his family to get behind him. The fact that they had managed to survive for this long with just a sword and a rifle was a miracle.

The two groups exchanged a moment of silence, no one daring to break the silence; perhaps they just did not know how to talk to each other since all this hell had begun. Humanity had gone down hill in a heartbeat; people were preying on each other in the jungles now, murdering and stealing from each other just to stay alive a few minutes longer.

The Husband carried a sword that looked to be from an expert blacksmith and a packed duffel bag on his shoulders that was probably the family's supplies. With sweat rolling down his cheek he rubbed his eyes and was first to speak up.

Yoon responded before Wan could reply and they began conversing amongst each other in Thai.

The only word Sai understood was "Wat" that was thrown in the sentences that the two were sharing.

The family appeared to be fleeing towards a hidden Wat in the jungle from what Yoon translated to Sai as the others continued to talk to him. They had chosen this particular Wat because it had been one of very few that was hidden deep within the jungle away from all the main roads that led out of Bangkok.

Wan walked to the side of Sai as the other men except the Husband pulled security weary of their position caught in the open in the creek.

"It's your Wat, your Alamo Sai." Wan translated for Sai.

"The Alamo is not really a good thing, they all died." Sai smirked as his eyebrows rose up trying not to laugh.

"They say it is a two day walk from here."

Sai felt a little hope, two more days and they could rest behind the walls of the Wat this was some good news indeed.

"There are roughly thirty monks." Wan continued while he listened to the man talk to Yoon.

"He's not sure how many civilians may have seek refuge there, perhaps their all dead now, but for sure if they were dead there, they are a lot less of them then what is running around in this jungle Sai."

The conversation continued until Yoon turned to Wan and Sai.

"He wants to guide us to the Wat, says his group was bigger but they were attack earlier this morning and got separated from the rest. What to you two think?"

"I think it's a good idea, no telling how far behind enemy lines we are already. We need the rest." Wan said as he looked over his shoulder at the two groups.

"I'm with him, we need the shelter. Best we move out now, two to three days, means one or two nights depending on our speed and night is not a good thing." Sai added to the conversation.

Wan walked up to the man and his family and introduced himself and the members of his group. The man looked at Wan and the young soldier, hesitant at first but soon enough he gave in and introduced himself.

The man's name was Tran, a second-generation immigrant; grandparents had migrated from Cambodia to escape the Khmer Rouge in the early 80s. He was a blacksmith and farmer, something that would be of great need to the group in the coming months.

The woman was named Liu, a Chinese immigrant who ran away from her family at a young age to find herself on a plantation in the provinces; she never let the children out of her sight as she introduced herself to the group.

The little girl opened up a little as she smiled at the other little girl named Ni. That was a start for her, at least she smiled and hopefully the group would find out her name soon.

The grandmother was Tran's mother, Pakatip, she had lived as a villager in Cambodia before moving to Thailand; her knowledge of life in general would be a valuable asset in the future.

****

The next half of the day was for the most part uneventful, no action, no drama, no running. The dead were out there, somewhere, but they had not seen any for a few hours, no more gunshots, nothing but the birds in the trees and the bugs swarming the air. It was if they had dropped off the face of the earth and they were the only living humans left moving through the jungle.

Being December in Southeast Asia, it was still humid but not to the point of massive dehydration. The stream sang its soothing song as the group paralleled it. Tran leading the way through the massive vegetation on the sides of the stream used his sword as if it were a machete, cutting a path leading up a draw deeper into the jungle and away from the stream finally. Once above the stream he sheathed his sword and unslung his old hunting rifle.

Adrenaline was still moving the group, and each of them remained quiet. One foot after the other was all that kept them moving. The only motivation they had stood at the end of their journey and they all prayed they would live to see it.

The suns rays were now showing late noon as Sai looked down at his watch that had just stopped working. The night before, crawling through the water had finally killed it. Yet he kept it on, not one to just throw away old gifts away.

It was around five p.m. he thought as he looked back at Yoon who was struggling with the little girl.

Sai moved over to her and picked the little girl up. Rocking in Sai's arms as he moved through the trail Tran had hacked out, the little girl rested her head on Sai's shoulder and slowly fell to sleep. The rifle slipped once from his other shoulder but Yoon placed it back in its place and as soon as it was comfortable he continued on the gaggle of people moving slower than ever before.

Klauy was now being pushed up another draw by Wanchai and Lek, dehydration and exhaustion had taken a heavy toll on the heavy man. He's breathing had become harsh and erratic over the last few hours and the group feared he would soon be coming down with a fever. Yet even with this knowledge of what may come, the forced march was continued since stopping only meant being eaten by the jaws of death.

It wasn't until the screams of someone being butcher half a mile or more away did the group finally come to a stop. Crouching, the group stopped, listening to where the gunfire was coming from. Upon zeroing in, they quickly began circumnavigate the area where the conflict was taking place.

A small battle was taking place less than a mile away, and the group was hastily moving to avoid detection from the incoming dead that were moving towards the noise. Under the cover of gunfire, the group moved on and within ten minutes the gunfire had ceased and the group moved stealthily once more, whoever been firing was now part of the ranks of the dead.

Tran showed a trouble brow on his face when he looked back at the group from point, Sai figured it must have been the other group Tran and his family had been with the night before. The remnants of his group slaughtered, their misfortune had given Tran and his group a chance, for if they would have kept walking in that direction they would have been ambushed in their place. From death came life.

The evening had already rolled in and the group now lay prone, in their fighting positions once more, women and children in the middle with the men outside. Tran was now on the perimeter after some awkward discussions at first to convince him it was not just best for the group but for his family as well for him to be on the perimeter. It was only natural he wanted to be close to his wife and kids, but the group needed him as the extra pair of eyes, that extra brick in the wall since the two young soldiers had died and weakened their defenses. After Wan had finished explaining why his family would be safer in the center with him in the perimeter he finally found a spot next to Sai and was now pulling security. Safe in the center his wife and children fell asleep as his mother watched over them.

****

That night like the others was filled with fighting in the distance, several F-16s were dropping bombs somewhere along the road they had crossed the previous night which meant somewhere out there the military was still holding on. The Thai Royal Air Force could not exist if it were not for the Army and Marines protecting them, which gave them a little light in the pitch-black night; they were not alone yet.

Somewhere out there were battle lines, how they could actually draw it up was unclear but there were still safe zones that continued to shrink by the hour. What was clear was that at night people were fighting and they were also dying. The Thai military was unaware that the system was failing, the governments of the world were losing ground and the armies of the world were slowly but surely dissolving into the dead ranks as the world's military increasingly began to lose contact with their civilian governments and with their military leadership.

The night was like spending a night in the trenches of World War I. The constant bombardment of shrieking, screaming and dying rang out from all directions every hour. All the group could do was hunker down and hope that some lone zombie would not stumble upon them.

In the morning the suns rays were welcomed as they slowly poured through the canopy to the jungle floor. Everyone felt like crap, several days already without a shower, covered in mud and filth, the only thing that got the group up that morning was the idea of reaching the Wat, and there would be sanctuary.

They set out once more, everyone moving slower than ever before, their bodies already pushed way beyond the limits.

****

Roughly around noon was when they found the human scum of the earth hunting in the forest. Ta had warned the group like he had done in the past and they froze. The sounds of a girl screaming and a group of men could be heard somewhere up ahead. The men laughed somewhere in the jungle and her screams only meant one thing and it was not good.

Ta and Num were quick to make a ruckus; the two wanting nothing more than to find that girl and help her, at least some humanity was still alive.

Sai looked over to Wan, and Wan looked back, Sai nodded his head in approval. Ta and Num were to scout the scene and see if they girl could be saved, and if so report back to Wan. All the while the group would need to fear that the commotion might draw unwanted attention from a rouge group of the dead.

Wan and Sai both agreed the group out weighed the needs of the girl, but with her screaming and the laughter of the men, they both wanted to beat the living hell out of them. The only problem was that if they left to find her, they would degrade the protection of the group.

The group on the whole wanted to move on and circumnavigate the scene, but none of them said a word as Ta and Num disappeared into the brush, both young men eager to find the girl.

The group waited and waited as the sweat rolled down their cheeks, Sai crouched next to Yoon, and Wien as the little girl held Wien's hand opposite of Sai. Ever vigilante they waited, Yoon worrying for her cousin until the brush moved and Ta's head popped out.

Ta had returned with news that it was ten men, each armed and each of them occupied with the girl.

Wan asked Sai what he thought as the girl continued to scream while the men roared with laughter hurdling insults at the girl.

"Options suck, what we should do is go around it, but I know you are like me, we can't stand here and let those fuckers do this." Sai groaned, his eyes narrowing. "But this is not what we think, the group needs to decide." He looked around. "Let's get a vote."

Wan agreed to the vote and brought the announcement to the group. The vote began; the men were for the attack except for Tran, which was understandable due to his family being present. Half of the women were not in favor of the attack, Yoon agreed with Sai on this because if it were any one of them, she would want strangers to do the same. The golden rule was still no dead in this merging new world.

The vote was in, and the attack would begin. The assault consisted of Ta, Num, Wan, and Sai. Wanchai, Klauy and Tran, who were left to defend the women and children and bring up the rear when the all-clear was given.

The attackers would engage the bandits, killing as many as they could and perhaps causing the rest to retreat. When the sight was secure, Yoon and Lek would enter the vicinity to aid the girl as the group collectively came upon the victim. Once the girl was recovered they needed to leave the area within two minutes in order to avoid contact with the dead.

Wien, Akira, Liu and Tran's mother were responsible for moving the children as quickly as possible when the clear sign came and Wanchai, Klauy and Tran would bring up the rear as the attackers cleared a path towards the Wat.

The order was given and Sai turned to kiss Yoon who smiled back at him as he left with the attackers.

Yoon and Lek gathered up the first aid equipment from the packs, placing the items in locations that they could easily access if something went wrong.

On the opposite side of where the attackers moved out from, Tran, Wanchai and Klauy pulled security, watching for any incoming.

Wien and the women prepared to move the kids and told them to remain quiet even though some fireworks were about to go off near by. The kids of course knew better and realized something dreadful was about to happen. Tran's son, Tran Jr., began to tear up first followed by Ni and soon the little girl who was beginning to interact a little more with those two as well.

Moving through the jungle like he had learned in the Marines long ago, Sai followed Ta and Num as Wan brought up their rear.

Num signaled where the enemy was even when the girl's cries and bandit's laughter gave it away.

Line abreast formation was quickly set up as they closed the distance to the laughing men. Each man spaced out to five yards between each other. Soon the group came to the edge of the clearing holding their formation. Moving into the prone, four rifles began to pick the targets through the brush. Those who stood around as spectators and were immediately armed would be the first to go, and then they would aim towards the girl where the men were less aware of their surroundings, for their attention was drawn to the girl. Those men would be easy targets of opportunity, next would be the ones actively messing with the girl, they were sure to be fumbling in the chaos as they tried to orient themselves on the situation.

As the attackers zeroed in on their targets, they waited patiently for Wan to fire the first. Wan was the best shot of the group and everyone knew that his round would not miss.

All was silent in the minds of the attackers as they waited for that first shot. Ta was eager as he watched what they were doing to that girl. He felt a burning desire to send those men straight to hell.

Wan's rifle fired suddenly causing Ta to jump.

Wan's shot sent a distinct report through the jungle air. The round struck home on a man with a black shirt, tearing straight through the chest. Blood sprayed out the back as the round pierced through his lungs tearing up his inside and then out his back. Before the gang could react three more shots rang out each hitting home and sending a man falling back into the foliage of the jungle floor.

Now the shock of the initial barrage was almost wearing off on the gang as two more men who had reached for their weapons were gunned down. The man who was currently raping the girl rose to his feet, his pants still around his ankles, he turned his head to looked to where the gunfire had come from when a round from Sai's rifle hit him center mass.

One of the three remaining men fired back with an AK-47 as he retreated into the jungle shouting in Thai. The other two were quickly behind him and a few more shots were fired in their direction. Wan began to pursue followed by Num.

Sai and Ta made a beeline to the girl and took security in the flanks, Ta only pulling security for a second and then moved towards the girl.

"Get back you stupid fuck!" Sai shouted in the heat of the battle. "Pull your god damn security!"

Ta quickly moved back after being reprimanded by Sai leaving the girl on the ground still in shock when Wan gave out the all clear.

Sai relayed the message as he scanned the thicket and within a matter of seconds Yoon and Lek came racing into the area with weapons drawn and a medical pouch available.

Sai looked back to see Yoon talking to the girl in Thai while pulling a shirt out of her pack at the same time.

The girl was a teenager, her school uniformed laid beside her in shreds as she moaned covered with bruises and cuts all over her body. The medical pack would be saved for another day since none of the wounds were life threatening.

Almost a minute into it, Wien followed by the little girl and the other women and children arrived on scene. Wien stared at one of the gang members who was coughing up blood, the result of a direct hit to the lung. The man wheezed as he tried to suck in air, his chest bubbled as the air escape from the hole in his lungs, an awful smell exhaling with each breath he took.

Out of the seven, two were still alive, but incapable of doing anything. Quickly Akira and Liu picked up their weapons, seven more rifles for the group, five M-16s and two AK-47s. The two searched for ammo, ignoring the dying bandits plead for help and once done returned to watch the kids.

The rear guard was next to move on scene and the rape victim was still confused and struggling with her saviors.

The clock was ticking; somewhere out there the dead were running and she continued to struggle with everyone, emotionally detached from reality she allowed no one close.

With the dead somewhere in the jungle running to them, Sai turned around and ran up to the girl. He came from behind her and wrapped his right arm around her neck and grabbed his left shoulder with his right hand. His left hand found the back of her head and with a swift motion he flexed his arms cutting off the blood supply to her brain from the sides of her neck. Within three seconds the girl was asleep. Sai picked up her naked body and threw her over one shoulder and looked at the group.

"Gathered everyone up, we are leaving!" Sai ordered the group as he looked at a few shocked faces from what he had done.

Wasting no time, however, Wan and the Num now took off at a slow jog and the group followed behind as the rear guard brought up the rear.

"Wait a sec." For a moment, Num swore he saw a Chinese-looking man in the brush, aiming his rifle in that direction he blinked and he was gone. "Never mind." He followed the group as they sprinted off into the jungle.

Still at the rape site, two minutes later, five torn-up soldiers greeted the two wounded gang members and were happy to put the gangsters out of their misery.

Their screams confirmed Sai's foresight and brought the rest of the dead roaming in the forest to the bandits' location.

As the dead feasted the group traveled nearly a mile from the rape site and began to walk once more.

Twenty minutes later they would stop once more and deal with the unconscious girl. Yoon and Lek quickly put a shirt and a pair of shorts on her.

The girl slowly came through and was now fully alert, the gang was gone and women surrounded her. She now rested, crying in Tran's mother's arms.

Ta walked up to Sai and scolded him for what he did to the girl. He was apparently uneasy by Sai's little maneuver.

"Listen, numb nuts, did you not hear those fuckers back there?" Sai grabbed Ta by the shirt, adrenaline still rushing through his body since the attack. "Less than two minutes after we left they were being torn to pieces!" Still angry Sai continued. "Ta, you must learn that survival comes before kindness. You survived all this time because we did not turn to help those around us. We survived because we had to be cold. Don't you pull this righteous bullshit with me boy," Sai continued as Ta wavered before Sai. "Look, every soldier has had that done to them; I merely put her to sleep. Think next time before you start talking shit." His voice calmed down. "Now Ta, you're doing well but you have much to learn still. Think about your family and what you will do to protect them. What would you have done to that girl? Reason with her? Leave her? Now calm down and get some rest, I need you to stay frosty, we need you frosty, that girl needs you frosty, so tomorrow I want you to get that girl to the Wat in one piece, and I'll protect your cousin and sister. Do we have a deal?"

Wan said something in Thai to Ta and Ta apologized to Sai for scolding him in Thai.

Wan knew the girl was going to be a struggle in the confusion and approved with Sai's action to keep her quiet, making her easy to move for time was something they did not have during that moment.

****

The evening had rolled in and the group had found shelter in the center of a ravine. It provided shelter from any roaming walking corpses stumbling upon them, and with two steep walls on the side the women and children felt a false sense of security, which helped everyone fall to sleep. The perimeter was smaller than before since the avenues into it were limited. Yet four people remained on top of the ravine at all times, taking turns on shifts coming down into the mini canyon. One person on each side guarded the two entrances, allowing people time to relax as the night rolled on. Hopefully, it was the last night any of them would be sleeping on the jungle floor.

In the center Yoon sat with her back against the wall of the ravine. Sai approached her, careful not to wake the little girl. Wien leaned on Yoon with her head on Yoon's shoulders as her eyes looked up to Sai.

"Sorry Yoon," Sai whispered taking a seat.

"About what Sai?"

"For what I did to that girl earlier."

"It's okay, Wan has been talking about that to everyone, Sai he would have done the same if you waited a moment longer."

"Don't want you to think I'm some kind of psycho." He paused. "How is she?" He nodded his head to her.

"She hasn't talked much, but she is thankful. She asked for her sister. Said she had been with her when the gang found them. They took her out into the jungle as they raped her, five guys took her sister away Sai."

"We didn't see her or anyone else, when we fought we had no idea there was another group in the vicinity. I wish we would have known."

"Tomorrow we find your Wat P'Sai." Yoon changed the subject not wanting to trouble Sai anymore on the subject.

"Let's hope they haven't been overrun." He let out a restless sigh. "How's your cousin doing?"

"Ta talked to me earlier about you. He admires you, thinks you are like a Samurai Warrior. He was just scared about what had happened. He's not a soldier, Sai. He's still a kid. Wien, she's doing well. Noi is around her age, and she was keeping her company earlier this evening. But Noi fell asleep shortly after with Tran's mother. I don't know what to tell her about her mother. Wien believes she is alive. I hope she is, but I'm looking at reality. I don't know about things anymore."

"Yoon, I know it's hard, but don't look back now, especially now. What matters right now is that you keep your cousins safe, keep yourself safe and the little girl. Perhaps she is alive. I pray she is, but we must survive now, we need to live," Sai assured Yoon. "As soon as we are safe, we need to find out what the hell is going on, how far this has already spread." He thought it best to now change the subject, to keep her mind off of her aunt. "You know, I'm going to be officially AWOL soon."

"What's AWOL?" Yoon asked curiously.

"Missing soldier, basically," Sai replied. "If there is still an America, I'll be officially AWOL soon. Let's just hope there is. Maybe we can find a plane or helicopter and make our way there, or to a carrier, or something."

The two continued their conversation, occasionally stopping when a branch fell somewhere in the jungle. They talked and talked trying to brainstorm ways to stay alive and soon all was quiet and they were all asleep.

****

It was the first night not a single shot had been fired, a helicopter passed over around three a.m. but nothing else, no shrieks, no screaming. It was unsettling, either the dead were gone or every creature within ears shot was already dead.

During the night Ta had made his way over to Noi and tried to comfort her, he had wrapped up her bare feet with bandages after he had thrown the old ones away and then shared an MRE with her. He was unaware that some people in the group were still awake and watching. It was almost like a show for the group as Ta tried to make a move on her; Ta of course did not realize that Noi was still in shock from the gang. Ta would need to find another time to get to know the girl.

The guards on the perimeter had heard noises from time to time, but they were unclear if it was the jungle or something else walking in the foliage. The ravine had provided that extra protection the group needed and the psychological barrier to allow for better sleep.

When the morning finally arrived, Tran's mother had created an ointment for Noi's wounds and bruises, using the surrounding plants, she undressed the teen as the group was forced to look away and applied the home remedy. Wan held Ta by the neck forcing him not to look. When all was said and done it was time to gather up the supplies and make the final track to the Wat.

Moving out, the group had made their way towards an open field of sunflowers. The sunflowers towered above the group and were perfect for hiding from the dead or the perfect ambush site for the dead.

They moved through the growth, scraping their arms and legs on the jagged stems until the stench of death slowly became overwhelming.

Unnerved, the group continued on, following Tran through the sunflowers until they came to a clearing. In the clearing a slaughter had occurred, two elephants lied open up with their contents spewed out all over the ground. Large cavities resided in their stomachs and over a hundred human foot tracks covered in blood littered the area, along with a few crushed corpses that fell victim to the elephant's heavy feet.

"There must have been hundreds of them." Wan said in disbelief staring at the carnage while walking by.

Several human corpses had their heads bashed in by the feet of the giant beast. They were like crushed pancakes, barely recognizable if it wasn't for the bodies that were next to them.

As they moved by the little girl began to speak in Thai. The only word Sai understood was "Chang," which meant elephant.

She's probably sad for the dead elephants. Sai thought to himself. Still at least she was talking now, strangest place to begin talking again though.

The group continued their march pass the slaughter and moved back into the sunflowers unaware they were being stalked.

Moving through the growth, a silent killer was moving in, it's back and legs broken from the battle with the elephant and now it crawled between the sunflowers towards the group at a steady pace.

Tran and Wan had just walked by it unaware it was just a foot or two away. Num, Noi and Ta followed them. Behind them was Yoon, Wien, the little girl and Sai who were in turned followed by Akira, the two children, Liu and the grandmother with Klauy and Wanchai bringing up the rear.

What happened next was fast and brutal when Num cried out in pain followed by shouts of terror from Ta and Noi.

The dead man had successfully ambushed Num, sinking his broken teeth into his calf muscle. It was still in the prone tugging on Num's leg trying to bring him down to his knees. Dropping his weapon the soldier pounded on the creature's head to no effect with his fist. That is when Ta stepped on the back of the dead man's neck unknowingly severing the spinal chord and rendering the beast immobile but still alive.

The creature's grip broke and the Num's calf fell out of his mouth, but not before biting a large chunk from it.

Wan was first on scene followed by Tran and as he looked over the bite, the shrieks began from within the field in a matter of seconds.

Before Sai could say *fuck*, gunfire opened up amongst the rear guard, and the young girls began to scream.

Wanchai and Klauy opened fire; they had waited for the dead to get close before dropping them.

The shots pierced the shoulders, chest and finally the heads of two would be attackers when Sai shouted to run.

The group began to move as Wan threw Num over his shoulders and Ta grabbed his rifle and the SAW.

Gunfire opened up in front as Tran missed his first few shots until a dead elderly woman was within range; he then swung his sword cutting the head in half with one swift blow.

While running the group passed the half headless body that struggled to maintain balance before finally collapsing to the ground.

Still running Yoon and Sai opened fire simultaneously. Two battered people ran from opposite sides on the flanks only to be greeted with fire by both as Wien ran between Sai and Yoon following Ta and Noi.

Like before it was lucky shots that had brought the attackers down, and Sai knew their luck was not going to hold up forever in the sunflower field.

Amongst the commotion a grenade went off; it was one that Wan had given Ta a day earlier.

The blast shredded five attacking individuals in the front of the group sending up a cloud of dust and sunflowers flying into the air. The heavy debris did not stop the group as Wan carried Num through the dust. That was when Num forced himself off of Wan.

Falling to the floor the soldier shouted in Thai to Ta.

Ta quickly moved to his position and gave him the rifle and a grenade. Wan argued for a few seconds as the group ran past them, unaware of what was taking place as the shots opened up continuously from the flanks.

From the glimpse of Akira's eye she saw as Wan stood up and saluted the soldier. Not comprehending what was occurring she moved on followed by the rear guard. Wan rejoined them leaving the soldier to cover their escape.

A crow watched from above to see two dozen dead people approaching Num like Raptors towards their prey in the fields. It focused in and stared at Num who roared at the top of the lungs so the surrounding dead could focus in on him. Sai heard the Soldier roaring in Thai from behind when he realized what he was doing; he stopped only to be pushed by Yoon. His heart sank as he left the brave soldier behind but there was nothing he could do, he could go back and could die or run and live.

Tears rolled down Num's cheeks, as he continued to shout out alerting everything of his presence. The young soldier switched the selector switch of his rifle to full auto and began to give the dead hell, diverting them from the group's escape. His rounds hit their targets one at a time but they continued to come; his thirty-round magazines would not hold out forever, and his rifle finally clicked empty.

A strange sense of peace fell upon him in what felt like an eternity. Calm and collected, he breathed a sigh of relief; the nightmare was almost over. He watched as a man wearing a bloodied blue shirt, torn jean shorts and a Thai style farmer hat hanging from his back came into view followed by an old lady who was missing an arm.

He lowered his rifle by his side and placed the grenade by his chest, and then he lay down on his back amid the trampled sunflowers. His tears were now gone he looked at the eternal blue sky as several shadows covered his body. He felt a wet sensation, as if he was lying in a warm stream, his soul was leaving his body as his bowels let lose and before the pain from the dead registered in his mind he roared one last time.

Less than thirty seconds after the group left Num the fire from the soldier ceased and triumphant roar began, it was quickly followed by the loud thud of the grenade going off. A small plume of smoke went into the air and the group continued to run.

The soldier had waited for as many of the dead to gather around him and as they bit into his flesh he closed his eyes and pulled the pin, three seconds later he felt no pain anymore.

The group continued to run until they exited out of the sunflowers and ran across a small dirt road and back into the jungle.

The jungle was a welcomed sight; it was a lot more forgiving than the sunflower field. The group wanted to stop, but Wan and Sai thought it best to keep moving, there was no telling how many dead people had been lurking in the sunflower field and in a few hours they would be upon the Wat.

Not far away, the remnants of the gang that had attacked the girl heard the explosion and laughed, figuring their attackers had been slaughtered by the dead. Three girls were now in their custody, and the gangs numbers had improved as they linked up with several other groups including the main force lead by Than. Together they took the girls along with other prisoners and began their journey to find sanctuary. Even though they were the low of the low, the meanest of the mean, they too needed shelter from the onslaught of the dead. For the dead were the great equalizer of the world, you could be a Navy Seal, a Marine, a nun or a prisoner, they did not care who you were, how tough you were and for that reason alone they were becoming the main species of this world.

Chapter 9: *Wat Tatsunupi*

The smell had come again; that bittersweet stench of death was heavy in the air. The stench coated their noses as they stumbled upon the site of another massacre. Dogs, cats, chickens, ducks, cows all lied out in the fields as swarms of flies and black carrion birds circled above.

Instinctively the group became hyper aware as they neared another village that was located not to far from the river that would lead them straight to the Wat.

Surprisingly there was not much in the way of battle; the place had long been abandoned, probably a night ago judging on how fresh the dead animals looked. Still that meant that the dead must be close by, perhaps they were the ones that had attacked them in the sunflower field, or perhaps they had just followed the survivors towards the Wat, which meant they would see them soon.

As they neared the village, Sai and Wan took point, they believed it might be the last time they could liberate supplies from their eternal prisons. This time the risk of detection was acceptable. Thought being that when they enter the Wat they might not be able to leave for a while and could possibly die of starvation if they did not take this opportunity.

The insects buzzed as they left the fields and into the first cover of trees surrounding the village. Forty yards behind them, the rest of the group moved, rifles facing all directions. They were worn out, driving on a dwindling supply of adrenaline and as Sai looked back it reminded him of the pictures of Triceratops herds defending their babies from Tyrannosaurus Rex with the children being in the center of the formation.

Rifles had been passed out to everyone since their encounter with the bandits. Armed to the teeth didn't mean more protection however for Num had been a tremendous lost, for his training, discipline and aiming were something that would be sorely missed.

Wan was first to enter the center of the village followed by Sai at his seven o'clock, ten yards away. Nervously the two men walked, their eyes scanning the scene for danger, their ears honing in on any noise that tried to elude them. Silently the two moved on.

The buzzing of the flies continued, never ending, as a wave of humidity swept past the two men. From under the drone of the flies a sound came from the hooch to their left. The sound of a glass bottle hitting a wooden floor alerted both men of something's presence.

The two turned instinctively, weapons drawn in the direction of the noise causing the group behind them stopped immediately and then they slowly came to a knee as Wanchai waved them down.

Sai's heart began to beat hard; he felt his chest pounding as he moved towards the direction of the hooch. Suddenly his breathing became noticeable in the eerie silence that followed the noise the flies that seemed to have vanished. His world had closed in around him as fear gripped his ears. He tried to control all his noise as they closed the distance to the hooch.

Wan immediately moved to Sai's right flank and the two men moved slowly to the noise when another sound came from the hooch. The sound of wood hitting wood confirmed something was moving inside.

"Could be a gimp," Wan warned as he continued moving forward.

Sai moved towards the door and paused, his imagination told him a dead man with no legs and arms would snake it's way towards him like some kind of crazy sci-fi original movie Worm Man or some crap like that. Maybe a dead baby would crawl up and gum his leg to death.

Sai was first at the entrance of the hooch, when another sound of wood rubbing against something could be heard. He held his rifle at shoulder level and with one hand grabbed a machete that he took several days ago from the Esso station.

"If it is a gimp, let's dispatch it quietly," Sai whispered, Wan nodding his approval.

Sai moved through the doorway into the single room of the hooch. The windows were open at the far side allowing the sun to flood the room with its orange light that highlighted the dust particles that were floating in the air. Several mattresses were thrown near the corner where the family must have slept, and several steel pots and dishes littered the ground. Signs of an immediate evacuation were evident here, clothes littered the floor and the smell of death was present but not as strong, a steady breeze came in through the windows clearing it out.

Wan moved through the door next and covered Sai's flank, while Sai moved towards an over thrown table in the corner hiding in the shadow of the hooch. The table was on its side hiding what ever was behind it.

Their boots echoed as they walked on the wooden floor, amplifying each step much to their disgust as thunderous creaks announced their presence.

Something was moving behind the table, and Sai slung his rifle behind his back as Wan held on to his, ready to fire if things got out of control. Sai prepared for close combat with his machete now free to be yield by both hands if necessary. He pulled up the blade to his right cheek and cocked his arm ready to swing as hard as he could. Another sound came, almost like a cry from behind the table and they paused once more, relishing the time they had before hell would break loose once more.

Sai then moved closer and with one fluid motion he leaped to the open side of the table with the machete raised over his head and brought it down to perform the killer blow, but he suddenly stopped.

Wan looked over the sight of the rifle and began to relax as Sai lowered the weapon and crouched behind the table.

"What is it?" Wan asked as he lowered his rifle.

Sai popped up and held a little fat brown puppy no more than two or three weeks old.

"Thai pup," Sai said as the trouble brow on his face melted away with calmness for the source of the noise had been the puppy.

Wan was relieved and moved over to pet the pup and then looked around the room.

"Better get started, time to salvage what we can Sai."

"Yeah, I'll grab everyone then," Sai replied as the two men walked out the door towards the center of the village. "This place looks dead, lets be sure to clear the other homes before anyone else goes in them."

The group watched as Sai began to walk over towards them, waving one arm signaling them to come in.

****

After clearing the village the group had found several containers of rice the size of large propane tanks. The villagers had been farmers before the world ended and stored their reserves before they fled in case they were to come back.

Ta and Klauy kept a watch out as the group went from hooch to hooch bringing the contents into the center of the village for a final review of what came with them and what stayed, perhaps to be liberated at a later time.

Tran's mother and Wien took care of the children in the center of the village. The kids took turns petting the puppy they name Kaew. The puppy's gentle cute face gave them a moment to think of something else other than death.

The women worked by moving the light stuff as the men dug deep under the rubble to find a wheel barrel that would be used to haul extra supplies to the Wat.

Like an Easter egg hunt the group scattered each looking for something that would be beneficial to the group. Through drawers, closets and boxes they scavenged, under normal circumstances it would have seen as repulsive. For over an hour they looked and then the calling card of the dead came.

The first shrieks came from the sunflower field, which hurried the group along. Someone had gone through the sunflower field behind them and was now screaming in agony as the creatures ripped her apart over a mile or two away.

Stopping what they were doing, the group assembled in the center of the village and the last leg of their journey was about to take place.

Moving along they walked down a narrow dirt path that turned into a sidewalk and later a mini Sky Walk that stood six feet off the ground, which negotiated a marsh and paralleled a man made canal/river. Klauy being the strongest of the group pushed the wheel barrel with ease and was surprise that it made little noise unlike most wheel barrels he had used back in Bangkok.

On the sides of the sidewalk a few homes and hooch's stood. Some had vehicles still in the dirt driveways, debris everywhere but no signs of human life. The river however still sparked with life, fish and frogs swam below to their left, the occasional snake slithered into the marsh and large white birds that Sai could not identified swooped down to catch their prey.

The Wat was now in their sights after they had walked for twenty minutes down the path. The Chedi spiral of the Wat pierced the sky with red tile and gold trimmings. On the edges of the Wat were figures of demons, later it was explained to Sai that they were Giants, part of a story called the *Ramayana*. It was almost museum liked to Sai as he walked closer and saw how beautifully decorated it was. Many colors flooded the temple structure and several smaller towers rose above the all-important wall that surrounded the Wat. Gold lined the walls and buildings, not fake, but real gold for the Thais in the area had pitched their money together to help build this beautiful structure from the ground up. Later Sai learned that it was Thai culture that called for the elaborate Wats that represented the community.

The tallest part looked like seven stories and held a relic from the Buddha according to Lek who pointed it out to Sai as the group continued to move closer with anticipation rising and hope building to it's peak. Surrounded by jungle the Wat was the only man made structure around.

The group approached cautiously as they looked at their surroundings while moving south. The path they were approaching from was taking them straight to a heavy wooden gate, which had been left opened. The stench of death was present.

The ground immediately in front the wooden gate was smeared with blood, and the group stopped as a few protests to leave the place flared up but were immediately silenced by Wan and Sai.

So they stayed at the entrance, for there was nowhere else to go, it was time that they needed to forge a safe place or die out in the open.

****

Inside of the gate, the group left the supplies near the entrance closing the gate behind them and then proceeded to the first small house to their right that resided inside the Wat for the Monks. Wan had cleared the house and the group set up base camp within the Wat's walls. It was easy to defend; the stairway was the only way up for the house sat on stilts and was about five feet off the ground.

Inside hung several monks' robes, which were still fresh from a recent wash – a sign that whatever had happened here had happened recently. Besides the robes, there was not much else – a small shrine to Buddha, a few books of prayer, and in the corner some offerings that were given to the monks.

The women kept away from the monks' linen due to their beliefs and began to pray in Thai as the children huddled around the puppy.

Ta, Klauy, Yoon, Lek, Liu, and Akira were to defend the house while Sai, Wan, Tran and Wanchai were to clear the Wat, which was half the size of a small city block. Many houses, many places of prayers, the supply rooms, washrooms, restrooms all needed to be secure before they could wander around freely, but first they needed to secure the entrances of the Wat for what is the use of killing the residents only for more dead to pour in.

Sai kissed Yoon and patted the little girl on the head and then smiled at Wien and Ta. He was last to leave the safety of the house with Ta closing the door behind them.

"Good luck P'Sai." Ta said before securing the door.

Outside the house, Wan was on point, using his experience as a ground pounder to lead the group, as Sai brought up the rear in a Wedge formation that looked like a diamond to the layman. Three hundred and sixty degrees of cover fire made Sai think back to his Marine days. Perfect for when you did not know where the enemy would come from. It was designed so if fire was required in any direction three rifles could aim and fire at once.

The four-man team made their way towards the gate that they had entered from. There they needed to find someway to secure it other than closing it with a dead bolt. They wanted those doors to hold against dozens of the dead if it came to that.   Approaching the heavy door they noticed that it only opened in one direction, which was inboard. It would make it easier to secure from the inside.

Looking around the vicinity of the door they found no lock from within. It was designed so anyone could walk into the Wat at any time of the day seeking help from the monks. For a moment things looked bleak until Wan spotted something. Hidden behind what looked like a storage shed they found a small Nissan truck, the kind Sai had seen on his worldwide adventures with the Army. It was a skinny blue truck that could fit in the back of a Ford F-150.

Wan quickly got to what Sai was thinking after he had pointed it out to the group and entered the truck shifting the gears into neutral. Wanchai was ordered to get in the vehicle and steer it after Wan exited the seat and ran to the back.

Wan, Tran, and Sai pushed the heavy vehicle which looked light but wasn't, ever vigilant to watch their backs as they maneuvered the truck into position. The truck slowly made its way towards the gate with the sound of rubber rubbing on asphalt.

The truck was wedge against the gate; it was positioned with no inches to spare so it would make it that much harder for the dead to enter. The side mirror on the right of the vehicle was smashed off by Wan in order to get it as close as possible and they were met with success. One down, God knows how many more gates to secure.

****

Quietly they closed two more gates, using a trailer and a heavy statue of Buddha placed respectably behind the gate facing the compound. In Sai's eyes the Buddha sat Indian style, more like monk style. The Buddha had his right hand facing out, or palms out as Sai was later corrected. The purpose was to hold back evil that was trying to come in. Which was strange for Sai since it was facing the compound instead of the wall where the dead outside probably wanted in. Either way it was good to see a friendly face holding the gate shut, just in case anything tried to bang their way in.

As the group moved towards the final door, Wien heard footsteps from the small alley next to the house. Quietly she moved to the wooden window, which was held opened by a small wooden stilt that propped it up.

As Wien approached the window she caught the attention of Lek, who also began to move towards that direction when a scratchy wet moan came from the alley. Every person in the room stopped; holding their breaths, they looked back and forth to each other, each dreading what the sound meant.

Wien saw the top of a bald head move pass the alley, heading deeper into the compound. After approaching the window she quickly closed it and latched it. She took a deep breath and looked to the group, each person frozen in fear except Lek, who had already begun to quietly close the windows around the house as another set of meaty feet walked by. The sound of flesh slapping off the concrete floor of the Wat began to die off as it passed the home, heading towards the same direction as the other one had gone. The feet were moving towards Sai and the others, somehow they knew they were somewhere inside the Wat.

****

Tran had just latched the final gate as Wanchai rolled a large pot to help secure it. That is when a naked monk covered in bite marks walked into view. It was an awkward moment as the stared at them. The two men acted as if they were caught red handed looking through the girl's underwear drawers, waiting to be scolded by the monk. It stared at them for what seemed like a minute, its mind determining if they were food or not.

Wanchai, being closest to the creature was dumbfounded in that moment, still holding onto the heavy pot, he screamed in Thai, probably saying, "Oh shit."

As expected, the monk released its battle cry.

Wanchai release the heavy pot that weighed nearly three hundred pounds and ran towards Tran who was surprised to see that the monk he had given offerings to several days ago was now covered in bites, with lips pulled up over its teeth and coming towards him.

As Wanchai ran passed Tran, Tran quickly caught on to the danger that was imminent and started running towards Wan who already held his rifle up to his shoulder, his eye staring over the sight of the rifle at the monk.

The blood covered monk charged after Tran and Wanchai leaving a trail of blood droppings on the floor when a loud sharp report came from Wan's rifle. The monk's head slammed back, the back of his head almost touching the monk's back since the neck had been broken instantly.

Suddenly, the Wat became alive with gut wrenching activity. Doors shook while the sound of pottery breaking echoed through out the Wat. It was followed by the sound of barefooted people slapping their feet on the pavement as they ran towards the rifle shot screaming at the top of their dead lungs.

At the base camp Wien had withdrew away from the window and moved towards Yoon who was holding the little girl when the gunshot alerted the Wat to Sai's team's presence. Fear sank into the house and was written on their faces as the occupants of the home prayed they weren't discovered during the commotion.

Back outside Sai was next to open fire, this time it took him only one shot to get a kill when a teenage boy leaped out of one of the monk's homes and hit the ground running. Missing an arm and eye, the teenager charged forth towards Sai who calmly raised his rifle and put his sights on the boy's head and fired.

The teenager's brain matter burst out of the back of his skull, sending chunks of it splattering onto a sidewalk behind him. The teenager stood there as its body's life force left him when a monk in an orange robe pushed him out of the way sending the corpse into a shelf of plants and pottery.

Wan opened fire again and was joined by Tran and Wanchai who stood side by side next to their comrades.

****

Inside the house, the children cried out and the big bad wolf came to visit after finding the source of the cries. The pounding of hands on the door had begun causing Ta and Klauy to raise their rifles in that direction waiting for the creatures to break through. As they stood in shock, Yoon and Akira unslung their weapons and pushed a large wooden chest to the door to help support it before they broke through. Tears rolling down her cheek, Wien took the little girl to hide in the far corner.

Lek opened one of the windows near the front door, to see two dead monks and an overweight woman banging on the stairwell, which was immediately to the left of her position and out of reach from the dead.

"Ta, come here!" Lek yelled in Thai, as the three dead things continued to pound on the door.

Ta ran over immediately to see what she had seen and understood what he had to do next.

Taking aim in a speedy manner, Ta opened fire, over compensating for the recoil he had aimed to low and the first shot tore through the creature's shoulders as it continued to attack the door. The man looked at him and then jumped from the stairwell followed by the other two leaving the stairwell clear of the dead and the door free from the assault.

In panic Ta backed away from the window when Lek grabbed him.

"They can't reach Ta!" She yelled to Ta as Klauy made his way over to them peeking out at the dead below the window.

The creatures shrieked and banged on the side of the home while looking up at Lek who gave them the evil eye in return.

Klauy looked over and aimed and fire. The skull was pulverized as the monk's head snapped back sending the body slamming into the pavement while the other two took his place using him as a step.

Ta then took aim and fired realizing the dead could not reach him.

"Like shooting fish in a barrel." Ta laughed, attempting to calm his nerves, trying to hide his fear.

Relaxing a little they watched as the last of the trio, the old fat woman tried to leap up at them. Her nails tearing off as she tried attempted to climb up the side of the house.

"They're so dumb," Lek said, staring at the fat lady.

The last shot sent the woman to her grave.

****

"Did you hear that?" Sai shouted from the top of a stairwell as Wan opened a door allowing Tran and Wanchai to clear the house. He'd referred to the gunfire coming from the other group's hiding place. Yet before he could explain what he'd heard, trouble was on its way.

A dozen of the dead were now closing in on their location, monks, villagers and children. Sai slammed the door shut and pushed his back to the door as the first of the dead smashed his body against the door.

Once that body slammed against the door outside, Sai realized that three bodies were decapitated on the floor in front of him with Tran's sword stuck in the chest of one. Tran was stuck in the middle of a deadly fight next to the bodies. Rolling on the ground, a woman had received the mount after on Tran as they slammed into a small alter filled with Buddha images, statues and golden amulets.

Tran screamed as the woman clawed his army with her nails while he tried to keep her from ripping his neck apart. The woman snapped her jaws in the air as she tried to inch her mouth closer to his neck, Tran was beginning to give ground to her.

Wanchai moved in and grabbed the woman by the hair. He yanked with all his strength and the woman went flying off Tran kicking and screaming.

Sai pressed his body against the door, holding three people at bay on the small stairwell just outside. He began to shout in panic, fearing that any second he would go flying across the floor with the dead in hot pursuit.

Across the room Wan charged the dead woman that was being dragged by the hair and used a stone the size of a child's head to smash the woman repeatedly as it tried to tear it's self free from Wanchai's grip.

The sickening crunch and splatter of the woman's face was quickly drowned out by Sai who was now sliding inch by inch from the door as the dead began to get their fingers through the crack trying to grab anything they could.

Turning their heads, the group saw Sai fly from the door with the dead spilling in behind him.

Rolling as fast as he could and still holding onto his rifle, Sai managed to dodge the first of the dead attackers as the creature jumped out for him. Fast as his roll was he could not escape the second one who had already taken a shot to the chest by Tran.

Fear, pure fear was in Sai's eyes as the battle unfolded slowly around him. He heard no gunfire; he saw no one but himself and the dead monk on top of him. With his rifle he smashed the creature right in the mouth with the handhold of the rifle, breaking its teeth with the impacts. Behind the monk a shadowy image jerked back, a few shots peppering its chest and then someone ran by in the opposite direction towards the door.

Sai punched the beast in slow motion, his senses focused on the battle in front of him as people moved in a blur around him. The dead monk clawed at Sai's face with a branch that was imbedded in the hand of the monk. The fresh part of the stick that did not penetrate the dead monk's hand carved out a deep gouge on Sai's left eyebrow and cheek.

A warm sensation filled the side of Sai's face as the branch dug into his flesh. In response, Sai grabbed the creature's head and pulled it toward him, using the momentum to flip him over his head and send him crashing into the floor. Sai and the dead monk now lay head to head; it was only a question of who would get up first.

Sai's rifle was now lost in the shuffle but that didn't stop him. Before the monk could get up Sai turned while getting up and sunk his fingers into the creature's eye sockets, he felt the warmth of the eyes as he pushed them aside shattering everything inside the monk's skull jabbing at anything that seemed vital until he felt the pop of the brain. The monk went limp immediately under his hands.

Sai then reached for the machete on his back and as he turned around he saw a young boy running at him with no face. It had been completely devoured by his family before he turned.

Next, Sai swung the machete sideways slicing through the boy's face almost three inches into the brain. The body went flying to the side like a rag doll through a hail of led. Several guns opened up into the creature's chest as Sai's friends fired over his head and into the fray of dead pouring through the door.

Sai then got up and ran towards a monk who ran passed him. The monk charged at Tran who was still lying on the floor. Like a linebacker Sai tackled the elderly monk. He wrapped an arm around the monks' lower half and sent him into the wall, breaking the creature's legs, arms and ribs in the process. Sai then turned to face another person who was sneaking up on him and before it lunged onto Sai, he sent his boot into the creatures face. The impact sent it flying back into two more people that were now in a full charge towards him.

Stumbling over the flying monk, the creatures fell to Sai's feet and before they could react Sai's boot smashed down on one, breaking its neck and smashing the brain in one hit. The last of the dead rose to his feet before Sai and before Sai could pull the machete free from it's last victim Sai attacked it sending it back to the ground. He began to beat the monk's face until the bones cracked under the pressure of his knuckles, sending a rogue fragment into the brain, stopping the killing machine forever.

All was over, the group had survived and near the door were now a dozen bodies. The group's faces showed darkness they had never experienced since this had all started. Their eyes had watered, not just because of all the gun smoke, but in the sheer moment of terror fear had clogged their eyes. Each man looked the same as the smoke from the gunfire cleared and the fresh iron smell penetrated their nostrils. Stunned and in disbelief that they were still alive they stood their expecting more to come rushing through the doorway, none came.

The dead who had managed to break through the barrage of gunfire laid dead by Sai's feet. He looked battered but it could have been worse. A rage had taken over that left him alive, and with blood pouring down his face and dropping on the wooden floor he began to laugh, he was glad to be alive.

Tran laughed as blood poured down the side of his arm to his fingers into droplets that rained on the floor as he reclaimed his sword with his good arm. Tran like Sai had been lucky that the creature's fingers that had ripped his arm apart were not covered in its blood and very lucky that the he had avoided the creature's mouth.

The other men looked at him and then they joined in the laughter, each trying to play off their fears for their moment of death had never seemed so close. It was only a fight that lasted no more than two minutes.

The men laughed in relief but all around the Wat the sounds of fist beating from the doors of several homes within the compound could still be heard. Many had died after they had locked themselves away.

****

The group returned to the house where they had left the women and children to find three bodies below a window. They quickly regrouped inside and planned on killing off the trapped dead inhabitants that still pounded on the homes within the Wat.

Tran was bandage and Sai's face was cleaned up as it began to swell, he used the belt along with some robe from the monk's wardrobe to cover his now closing eye. He'd lose some depth perception, but without medical attention any cut could become disastrous if infected. Lucky for him Yoon still carried the medication that she had taken to the medics and applied it to the two injured men.

Cleaned up and ready to go, Sai and Tran followed Wan and Wanchai out the door and began to walk to the pounding of fist from the inside of one of the larger temples.

Upon entering the building Sai was greeted to paintings of what he believed to be heaven. Men with golden pointy hats and swords protected a kingdom of beings that flew through the air. While on Earth, a war raged on which looked like demons fighting these men or angels. His amazement in the painting was quickly pushed aside when the pounding continued behind a large statue of Buddha decorated with flowers and incense sticks.

Wan was first to reach the room behind the Buddha. It was a plain white room, no furniture, nothing but a few bloody footprints, perhaps from one of the dead they had killed in the skirmish earlier.

The door where the pounding came from was just to the rear of the room, near a window that allowed the suns rays to fill the void.

Sai noticed how the door opened into the room, which meant they needed to kick it in, into confirmed hostile hands.

Wan was about kick it in when a board on the ceiling moved catching the group off guard. They looked up and raised their rifles to see an Old Monk holding his finger over his mouth in a sign to keep the four men quiet. The monk moved the board completely to the side revealing an attic where he had been hiding. Quietly he lowered a rope ladder and waved the group up.

Without saying a word, the group climbed up the ladder before they spoke to the monk. They were trying not to give their position away to the dead who lurked in the next room while they made their way up the rope ladder.

The man quickly spoke in Thai to the group when Sai noticed the Old Monk had quite a few survivors with him. Some were old men and women, some teenagers; there were eight children and an infant. Three were obviously monks, not including the Old Monk who was now talking to Wan. Sai counted four men above the age of fifty, one in his late thirties, one in his twenties, three teenage boys near Ta's age, and four boys under ten. The room also contained seven women over fifty, eleven in their late twenties to early thirties, eight teenaged girls, four girls under ten, and the infant.

It was the most people Sai had seen for a long time, and he was thankful that these strangers were still alive; somehow they had managed to avoid the onslaught from the dead breaching the wall.

"Sai, he says that there is another way into the room," Wan began to translate. "Another fifteen people are in that room." He paused, then said: "He says all of them have lost their minds. Sai, they don't think they are dead." Wan looked to Sai, realizing the monk did not want anymore killing, but now that could not be helped.

"Wan you need to explain to him that these people are dead, and if we don't dispatch them we are all going to die."

Wan and Wanchai began to explain to the monk of what was dwelling in the Wat below. These things were killing machines, whose sole purpose was to extinguish all life they encountered. It had taken nearly half an hour to explain to the monk what needed to be done and when all was said and done the monk told Wan to do it as humanely as possible. Wanchai agreed to do it as quickly as possible and then the monk pointed out another latch on the ceiling floor that they could open to peek down into the room where the dead lurked.

Wan explained to Sai what was going on and the Old Man looked at Sai, examining the pilot and wondering why Wan was telling him something in English. Is he Wan's leader? The truth was no, but the two men did share a mutual respect for each other and still had a military bearing.

Wan finished his translation to Sai with, "We can take them out from the safety of the attic."

"Just like Lek said," Sai continued. "Just like shooting fish in a barrel. Lets do this quickly, you're ready?" Sai grabbed his weapon and pushed up from where he was sitting.

The Old Man looked at Sai as he rose to his feet and began to move towards the latch in the ceiling where the dead still pounded on the door in the room below. The Old Monk saw the machete on Sai's back and began to pray as Tran and Wanchai followed moved as well.

In Thai, Wan talked to the Old Monk. "We'll take care of them; just tell everyone that there will be some firing." He paused. "We are only giving them the peace they deserve. Try to keep everyone calm, I don't want to start anymore panic. When we're done, we'll talk some more."

Sai, Tran, and Wanchai waited by the wooden entrance to the attic. It was nothing more than a board covering a hole. Taking a knee Sai began to speak up as Wan took a knee beside him and looked to Sai.

Sai looked around at all the men. "We lift the board." Pausing, he emphasized the next phrase mostly to Tran and Wanchai. "Take our time. One shot, one kill. Don't rush this. We good to go?"

They both nodded that they understood as they readied themselves.

Calmly, Wanchai moved the board and a rush of rotting flesh penetrated his nose, the stench rising from the room and filling the attic with the sweet aroma of death. All around people covered their noses and mouths as the stench settled.

Below the dead quickly turned their attention up above the room as the movement of the wooden latch caught their eyes. They immediately began to congregate below the attic entrance reaching up for their prey above, calling out to them in their horrible language to come to play.

Chills were sent down Sai's spine immediately as the four men kept perched above looking at the mosaic of bodies reaching out for them. Whatever had happened had been brutal in this room.

Bones and bite marks were almost tattoo-like in appearance to the men above. They were covered in a grotesque artwork, some were missing limbs, eyes, noses, some were nothing more than piles of mush that reached up as the others trampled them and tried to use them as a human ladder. All ages and both sexes were represented in the horror museum below. Pools of blood that had not coagulated were being splashed on the walls of the once white room. Guts and shit mixed together as the dead pulverized the intestines and jumped up and down for the men, creating a nasty soup in the process.

Just below the men and above the dead the ceiling was dripping with blood that somehow managed to find the ceiling as a resting place when the slaughter had occurred. That had been due to jugular veins being severed sending spray in graffiti like manner across the room and onto the ceiling

The horror below sank in on the team's psyche, but slowly Sai took aim as he grimaced at the scene. He aimed at the first man he saw, face half devoured, a single brown eye staring up at him until Sai fired.

One round at a time the slaughter had begun; each man took aim and pulled the trigger, resulting in a body dropping to the pool of blood and gore. It was pitiful as the creatures fell one by one; stupidly they continued reaching out for the men oblivious of the doom that was falling upon them from the attic.

In less than a minute, they were completely dead and all was silent, except for flies buzzing around gorging themselves on the feast the room had delivered.

Sai lowered the rope ladder down and brought out his machete again as he slung his rifle over his back, Tran did the same. Close quarters with a rifle had proven almost impossible in the last skirmish and the two men were not taking any chances as they climbed down the ladder.

Sai's boots hit the pool of blood that was an inch thick around the room. He scanned the room looking for any signs of danger as Tran made it down into the slaughterhouse.

Wanchai slung his rifle and brought out his QSZ- 95 and descended as well as Wan gave everyone in the attic the signal to remain quiet before descending.

Wan reach the ground to see that Sai's machete was already covered in blood as well as Tran's sword. Each had found an immobile creature and had finished it off with one swift swoop of their blades.

Fifteen bodies were accounted for just as the Old Monk had said, many more people had been in the room, but with body parts in every corner there was no way of telling how many were actually in the room before the dead devoured them.

Wan returned to the attic and told the Old Monk to stay put and then asked for any volunteers to help clear the Wat of what remained.

Three men volunteered immediately, one with a shovel, one a pipe and the other a machete. They joined Sai and the group and after a few house greetings, there were no more fist beating on doors. They had repeated the process of finding a vantage point where they could pick off their targets at ease. It was simple and effective and no one complained about the strategy.

****

Once the Wat was cleared of all the dead, nearly fifty corpses littered the grounds; the once holy place of sanctuary was now a dead desolate place, void of life except in the main temple, where a golden statue of Buddha watched over the two groups as they finally met to become one.

It was a social event and cause for rejoicing, for the Wat was now secured from the dead. It was here where life would begin anew under the watchful eyes of Buddha. Yet death was all around the Wat, the shots fired had caused well over two hundred infected to the walls of the Wat. But their stupidity told them nothing of where the entrances were. Instead, they just beat on the stone walls; one or two found the gates, but, with the gates further secured, nothing would break in, at least they hoped.

As the darkness crept over the land, the group socialized until the late hours of the night, until all were asleep lying before the Buddha. The only movement throughout the Wat was that of Kaew chewing on Sai's fingers and Wan smoking in the darkness as they kept watched over the residents of Wat Tatsunupi. Yoon, Wien, and the little girl slept together knowing that tonight they would be safe inside the compound. The two men sat of the entrance, both soldiers taking it easy and thinking of what their next move should be.

Chapter 10: *Rebirth*

Dawn had come and everyone was asleep except for Wan and Sai who were standing outside of the main hall in the open air. There they looked before them at the work that needed to be done before they could turn this Wat into a fortress. Corpses littered the grounds; they were in the homes and some of the smaller temples from the battle the day before. Now they were stinking up the place and attracting bugs. Surrounding the bodies were thousands of flies celebrating over the feast in which they fed on since they bodies had stopped moving. They swarmed over the bodies, maggots already in the process of munching their way to becoming adults.

"The air is going to be rotten today," Wan told Sai as he took a drag from a cigarette he had saved, exhaling slowly while savoring the flavor.

"Got any ideas?"

"Sai, Thai Temples are not just a place for prayer, it is where we have our funerals, you see that white building with the silver door and golden fence over there?" Wan pointed with his cigarette in his fingers his eyes rolling back to Sai. "All we need to do is have one of the monks start it up while we put the bodies in." He took a drag one more time as if he were thinking.

"Well that sounds good, but what about the power, electricity. Doesn't it require electricity?"

Wan exhaled. "Yesterday while we were running around this Wat I saw several generators around, and more importantly, the crematorium has its own supply of gas from propane tanks, no public gas around here. Trust me Sai, this is going to work."

"Sounds like a plan, then."

"We should keep things quiet during the cleanup, hopefully those creatures outside will just wander off if they don't think anything is alive inside."

"Well, as soon as they wake up, we need to call a meeting. We need to get organized, our group is good, they got the basics down on how to survive in the wild, but now we're not running anymore. Nation building is a bitch. We are we are going to need to form teams, establish work details and fire watches. We need to identify what talents we have here and utilize them for the Wat's benefits." Sai paused as he looked at the trees beyond the walls. A bird chirping away had caught his attention. "We need to find out who lives in the area, see who knows the land the best. Many things need to be taken care of. Logistical supplies, weapons, food, et cetera. We need to prioritize things. We may even need to launch raids into the homes we saw yesterday. There is no telling how long this hell will last, and the last I saw of the Thai army was the soldiers in full retreat."

Wan took a drag again as Sai waited for his response.

"Nation-building, like W said."

"Pretty much."

"What a drag."

****

Two hours had passed and now Sai, Wan and the Old Monk stood before the new residents of Wat Tatsunupi. Hands raised in the air and back down as Wan asked questions revolving around skills. He asked who were the farmers, who were the construction workers, who were prior soldiers, who had medical training and so forth. Everything was asked to the audience from work experiences to medical histories, such as asthma. No stone was left unturned during the session.

Yoon who had quickly became a favorite in the Wat due to her celebrity status; she sat to the side of the three men with the little girl by her side. She took notes on the meeting and tracked the various skills within the community. It was the first census of this rising community in which she wrote down into a note pad for further review in the future. Once all the information had been written down the first work detail began. They needed to cleanse the Wat and burn the bodies.

This did not involve any particular skill set other than operating the crematorium in which the surviving monks had cover. Some of the older women however were put in charge of watching the children. They stayed in the Wat's main hall most of the day keeping the kids entertained and more importantly keeping their voices down as the rest of the residents gathered the bodies loading them up on several wooden carts and the wheel barrel that Klauy had brought from the village.

Yoon, Lek, Akira, Liu, and six of the women in their late twenties along with the teenage girls began to forage through each house and every attic for essential supplies. Medical supplies had been found by Wien in the attic of the house they had originally hid while the men secured the Wat the day before.

Canned foods, bottle water, blankets and fresh clothes were taken from the homes and brought to the main temple so they could begin to take a tally on what they had and see how long rationing would take them into the future.

With rifles slung, and handkerchiefs over their mouths and noses, all the men and some of the women took the tedious task of carting the bodies to the crematorium, each careful not to infect any wounds they had sustained since the outbreak had begun.

The smell became foul as the afternoon rays began to pour down on the Wat, which only helped to ripen the bodies. Bellies were swollen to the point of bursting as people carted them off to be burned.

The bodies were brought before the Old Monk who was now the operator of the crematorium and also the man who would send the dead with prayers to their final resting place.

It was late afternoon when the final body had entered the crematorium, her ashes floated harmlessly into the sky as the Wat was cleansed. The teenage boys were now cleaning up all the bloodstains with Clorox, using rubber gloves that one of the women had found to help prevent accidental infection.

Tran's mother, Pakatip, treated Sai and Tran's wounds again as Yoon helped the older women who were busy in the kitchen cooking for the evening meals, this was temporary until they could be medically treated by one of the other residents who was busy with a more in need patient.

It was not a grand feast that most would have liked to create, but a rationed feast, containing mostly fish and rice. Troubled times were ahead, but no one complained as the first bowl of steamed rice and fish was served.

The children were first to eat, followed by the rest of the group, and finally Sai and Wan.

There had been much talk of the Thai army rolling in to save the day, but Wan was quick to explain that the last he saw of the army was rolling east under hot pursuit of the dead. He did not give any details of what had happened during the battle in which he along with probably hundreds more were left behind, but Sai made it a point to find out eventually someday.

As the first evening in the cleansed Wat rolled in, Sai and Wan created the fire watch, this list had a four man shift who would patrol the night and day in twelve-hour shifts. It was only fair that those who ran the fire watch were given privileges for their duties and allowed to refrain from work details for twelve hours as they recovered.

The work details became more organized as the evening rolled in, Sai and Wan thought it important to identify the soldiers of group soon, for earlier that day Yoon had reported the results of the foraging and the news was not good. It would be two weeks until the residents of Wat Tatsunupi would be force to send out a foraging party. Identifying the soldiers soon would allow for ample time to train them into a tight nit group which in theory could go beyond the safety of the walls and quietly gather the supplies they desperately needed.

The group that Sai had arrived with was good, due to the fact that there had been plenty of experience to go around with the other now dead soldiers.

If this group of soldiers were identified, they would need to definitely be given lighter details due to the training that Sai and Wan had in mind. There may be protest to this but those who put their lives on the line on these future raids needed some kind of compensation for their services. Still like any other military unit they would need to be flexible enough to help out around the Wat when needed. This discussion would go on for some time.

Priority for now was in the defense of the Wat, plenty on the "to do" list before they could forage in the surrounding area. Sai's leg needed to be cleaned again, stitched properly with the supplies they had found; with the help of the local "doctor," he would be as good as new.

****

A woman, named Katsura Kurasawa, a Japanese widow of a local Thai man, was proclaimed the doctor of the group even as she explained that she was just a nurse. Yet her nurse status was quickly elevated due to lack of medical personnel in the vicinity and she found herself with a battlefield promotion.

Tran's mother Pakatip quickly made herself Katsura's assistant, she had taken care of a family for several decades and her knowledge of life in general would become extremely useful.

Two other women and Wien also volunteered to be part of the new medical team and when the meeting was over Katsura began to further organize the group and their first lessons on first aid would be Sai and Tran which proved quite painful.

Next they moved into Noi's case; the rape victim still showed the marks of a heavy beating. After her arrival of the Wat, Noi experienced Post Traumatic Stress during her recovery, which kept the medical team busy as they constantly kept vigilance on her.

After Sai and Tran ran the gauntlet of being used as a training tool, Pue, a girl near the age of Wien, joined in, allowing the knowledge of her biology class to help further the groups potential. A few days later Noi decided to be the third teenage apprentice under the watchful eye of her adopted motherly figure Katsura.

****

Tran, was made the head engineer of the Wat, he had extensive work experience building structures, welding, plumbing, roofing and being a blacksmith; he was the equivalent of the Mexican Day workers of the U.S since he was basically illegal in Thailand.

Being the hard worker like many from all over the world, he built a life for Liu and his kids, acquiring many craftsman skills over the years as he did what was needed to support his family. Never did he expect to be the lead man of anything in his old life, but today was different; he would never again be just another handyman again.

Tran's first priority was to take charge of the fortification of the gates, then build a sanitation system, and create a pumping system to pump out water from the ground in the center of the Wat. Since a river was next door it was only logical that below the surface of the ground water flowed or at least collected in the wet Earth. The Earth would provide a natural filter; upon being further sterilized, the water would be safe to drink and bathe in. He was doing his best to protect everyone from diseases and infection.

Second in command would be Wanchai, not as experienced as Tran but some of his college education in Engineering would help if not improve Tran's designs. Wanchai being the younger gladly took the position as second in command out of respect to Tran.

Later, Tran would turn his attention on the weather beaten roof's that had fell into disrepair after a storm that had passed a few days before Sai and the group had arrived. It had occurred when they Sai had been reenacting a scene from the movie *Maximum Overdrive*. That same night the dead had infiltrated the Wat causing the survivors to go into hiding.

Three other older men and a teenage boy joined the group. Of course for the early part of the projects that Tran cooked up involved fortifying the weak points on the perimeter like the gates. Sai, Wan, Ta and the rest of the men provided the muscle Tran needed for this.

****

Yoon took the role of head of logistics; she monitored what the Wat had and took a count of what the foraging party needed immediately. She also began to create a list of what they would like in the future if the foraging party was able to retrieve it. Along with several women they spent the next few days cataloging, and mapping what was within the walls of the Wat in preparation for the raids to come. She even became a mini armory as well, took the weapons count, ammo count, and cleaning equipment and turned one of the central houses into a warehouse full of logistical equipment, which was also the home for the SAW that Ta had salvaged from Num.

Her second in command was Lek, who found the job pleasing; she helped organized the work details for the day, and planned the areas of the Wat to be search by priority of what could be found first.

The Old Monk became an invaluable asset to the Logistics group for he knew where most supplies were kept and helped create a map of the surrounding area outside of the Wat for future raids. He drew on several sheets of paper for several days the outlying villages that surrounded the

Wat as best he could. His map was extremely precise and he marked the distances down to a few feet.

The Old Monk, working with Sai, Wan and Yoon, began to draw up routes to the surrounding buildings where supplies might exist. He went into great detail when it came to the jungle, the swampy areas, the dense vegetation, power lines, highways, dirt roads and sidewalks that would expedite or delay travel to and from the Wat. He even drew the route of the river and a trail to an Air Base that existed near the city of Lop Buri for Sai.

"A bird should fly," he told Sai knowing that the pilot could secure this Wat's future faster and safer than any ground raid ever could.

Six of the remaining teenage girls found themselves working for Yoon from time to time along with the important task of taking care of the children as the adults worked. They began a sort of preschool for the smaller children and an elementary school for the older kids to keep their minds off the hell that existed beyond the walls.

****

The remaining women volunteered for kitchen duty, which they happily took for themselves; with Yoon's help, they had gathered all of the Wat's dishes, plates, bowls, pots, pans, and cooking utensils along with supplies of firewood for cooking.

Their job was to feed this the fifty plus personal who now called the Wat home. With so many mouths to feed, they actually had the job that lasted all day, for they continuously worked to prepare the next meal.

****

Naturally the military function of the Wat fell on Wan and Sai. Being well experienced, the two men walked around the perimeter and marked points along the walls that could be used as lookout points where the dead could not see the lookouts but where the lookouts could see all while remaining invisible.

A fire watch list was created and the residents of Wat Tatsunupi took turns on the watch. In the beginning, the Army of Wat Tatsunupi was severely short on manpower and was forced to use men from other jobs to help fill the fire watch schedule. Only four men at a time were taken from the Wat to perform the fire watch so the majority of the men could

185

work around the Wat. In twelve-hour shifts, four individuals walked the perimeter night and day, making sure everything was secured. The list consisted of all the male individuals of the Wat's residents and their sole purpose was to alert the residents if the dead managed to infiltrate the wall. Upon being alerted the residents had two options, secure their homes and fight the dead off from the stilts of the home or enter the attics where the dead could not reach.

The fire watch was not an easy job from what most people thought at first, at day it was fine but at night when patrolling alone all the sounds of the jungle came to life followed by the sounds of the dead, their shrieks and moans sent shivers down the spines of all those who took the watch during the early nights of the Wat's transformation.

Soon after securing the fortress, Sai and Wan began recruiting and the ones most eager to join the small army were naturally the young. Ta was the first volunteer when he heard an "Army" that was forming for the coming raid.

Stephen Argento, a quarter Italian, a quarter Australian, and half Thai was another teenager quick to volunteer, followed by his brother David Argento, a man in his mid twenties. The two had been on vacation with their family from Australia when hell had fallen and if it had not been for David, Stephen would have been dead along with their parents.

Stephen joined for vengeance while David joined to protect his brother from what was sure to come to the fledgling army.

The third teenage boy had already been to the Thai boot camp that each male kid was required to do. His name was Tor, he was young and alone and he had escaped from Lop Buri a few nights ago when the airbase nearby had been destroyed by the dead army. Somewhere while on the run he lost his sister to a group of men. From what everyone could tell, his sister probably died.

Chit was the fourth teenager who had signed up. He was a nineteen year old, a college student in Bangkok that had managed to escape much like Sai and his group had. He had been the jock of the "soldiers," was on scholarship for soccer which he had played his whole life, resulting in him being the fastest of the soldiers which had its benefits in a world overrun by the dead. All he had to do was outrun the slowest and he'd be safe.

The last man of the fledgling army was in his mid thirties and Katsura's brother. He had come from Japan to visit his sister for two weeks when he was caught behind the lines of the dead. Luckily for him he had left Japan single with no kids and did not have the worries that some of the others of the Wat had to face alone.

Toshiro Kurasawa, had served in the Japanese Defense Forces as a flight engineer on the P-3 Orions. Not a ground pounder like Wan, but still had the training that put him ahead of the game amongst his peers in this fledgling. He was taller than Sai and Wan, had a beard, and was very tough looking; due to his experience, he was third in command of the makeshift army.

The eight were now the standing army of the Wat, in the early days of it's formation, they found themselves doing other tasks daily and when completed they would train with Wan and Sai the rest of the day in preparation of the coming raid. A perk however for being the first of the soldier cast was that they were given the extra side arm's and rifles to train with and use in everyday life. The men were always armed.

Part of their duty was to clean the weapons daily since the humidity would surely destroy them within days if rust were allowed to set in. A pencil was used to clean the weapons as well as oil. When rust formed on the barrels they took the pencil and drew over it, which dissolved the rust. This was to supplement the cleaning materials that were already in the butt stock of the M-16s, which was limited. Of course more weapons would be needed later and maybe even improvised weapons as well if things became worse.

Combative training from the United States consisted of a little bit Gracie Jujitsu that Sai had learned over the years from the Army. Neither a master nor one to even think he could stand the chance in the octagon, he found this gift of ground fighting to be something to use against the dead. He adapted it so he would perform no arm-bars near the reach of the lethal jaws of the dead; he was still unaware that a single bite meant death during that time, but he did know that was their main weapon.

Muay Thai was taught by Wan, the stand-up fight meant quick strikes and standoff fighting. Of course he did teach them the use of the almighty elbow and knee, a well place strike could disable an opponent if done properly.

Both styles were to be used in a last resort, the rifle being first when it came to dealing with the dead. Unfortunately the weapons had limited amount of ammunition so it was required for the seven to also arm themselves with axes, picks and machetes from the tool shed of the Wat.

Tran who was not part of the mini army did lend his services to the men by showing them the Cambodian style of sword fighting which was very similar to Thai swordplay due to the history of Cambodia once being part of the kingdom of Siam in the past.

Toshiro, literally a descendant of Samurais showed them the way of Bushido, he may have been just a mechanic in the security forces but the man was surely what you thought a Samurai should be, but he did have a few faults. He was the comedian of the group, a favorite with the children around the Wat. Womanizer was another word that came to mind when Toshiro walked by strutting his stuff to the ladies. Alcoholic, etc., etc., but still his swordplay was unmatched.

Naturally, Toshiro and Tran formed a rivalry when it came down to whom had the best sword techniques, causing both to go on fighting late into the hours of the night.

Amongst other training Wan trained the group to clear rooms while Sai taught them formations to use in the jungles that he had picked up in the Marines. Every morning the soldiers would run for thirty minutes straight followed by a push-ups, pull-ups and sit ups.

"You run on the attack, you run in the retreat and when you can't run no more it is time to die," Sai would say as the men huffed and puffed running around the Wat in a tight formation with packs on their backs to simulate the weight they would be carrying on their foraging missions. He thought of the *Seven Samurai*, a movie Sai had come to love as a kid, and that is exactly what these men needed to become in order to fight for the residents of the Wat, *Seven Samurai*. Luckily, they had an eighth man, which was a bonus.

The soldiers also discussed tactics to use against the dead and decided that their stupidity was their greatest weakness and best option to exploit. If needed they could climb a tree theoretically and kill the creatures one at a time as they charged from below with a shot from the gun, or blows to the head. The dead should fight them on their terms. The Art of Sun Tzu would be altered over the years to come when fighting the dead.

188

For the next two weeks the "soldiers" would train for the moment they'd leave the safety of the Wat, becoming the hunted once more as they raided the villages in the area. Only time would tell if their training, their preparation would pay off or if it was just a huge waste of time.

****

Some of the monks who had lived in the homes of the Wat had passed on for good and the houses quickly found new life as people moved in.

A men's house and women's house were two such houses, those without families or friends found themselves in these communal homes. A kinship was formed and as time passed each home had develop their own set of rules.

Tran and his family stayed in the house they had first hid in when they came to the Wat. Liu and Pakatip grabbed some blankets from the logistics house and made bedding for their kids. Pakatip being one of the most senior women found it her responsibility to take in four orphan girls to stay with her family in the evening, as time would past they would become her family as well.

Yoon made her household in between the main temple and the logistical house. The home consisted of a simple wooden floor, a wooden column in the middle, an altar for Buddha decorated with gold trinkets. Blankets were thrown on the floor for bedding. Here is where, Ta, Wien, the little girl, Yoon and Sai considered home. A sense of security existed in this house for it held three rifles that found their way to hooks on the wall next to the door.

Wanchai, Lek, and Akira made a separate home behind Yoon's and adopted four boys into their home which helped Akira cope with the situation tremendously, gave her some hope and a sense of responsibility being alone in the world she now had children to watch out for.

Klauy resided in the men's house while Wan kept to himself at night, preferring privacy rather than comfort. Noi would eventually move from the women's house to Wien's home in the coming weeks due to a friendship that would come.

The next two weeks were busy, no rest and all work; but, as the last meal of the evening was prepared, each person found the time to relax and melt away from a long day of work while the four-man fire watch continued to patrol throughout the evening and early morning, keeping ever vigilant on the wall that separated them from extinction. The occasional moan a constant reminder that beyond the wall thousands of people were dying every hour swelling the ranks of the undead.

Chapter 11: *On-the-Job Training*

Waiting anxiously, David looked around as he stood near the gate of the Wat. The sun's rays began to rise from the east sending beams of light into his face. He did not turn but instead watched the sunrise.

On David's back was an axe the size of a small baseball bat. He had found some belts over the last two weeks scavenging around the Wat and created a sheath to cushion it against his back when he needed to run. With the axe strapped to his back he waited thinking of the events to come in the hour ahead of him. It troubled him that he would be leaving the safety of the Wat so soon, but someone had to and he knew that his little brother was all too eager to prove himself as a man. He had remained against Stephen's decision since the moment he volunteered for this mission, but his brother's mind was set in stone and someone needed to look out for the boy, only family could do that job.

David knew that Wan and Sai would watch out for Stephen if he decided to back out now, but no one could protect his brother better than him and he was right. Only blood was strong enough to commit the sacrifices needed to protect Stephen. David pushed the thoughts of what was to come out of his head and turned his attention on all the nature around him.

The air was cool, blowing softly through the trees, and an attached spider web sparkled with morning dew. David watched as the glittering web waved at him from the roof of the main Wat. Then he heard chirping coming from a tree covered in ribbons and other Buddhist amulets. The birds had awaken at the crack of dawn and begun their morning song as they chirped to each other, something most people never realize until your out away from the big city. They started off slowly with one or two chirps before the sun rose but now the songs were pouring in from all directions. It was a welcome song to the haunted moans of the symphony of the dead. It was a peaceful scene and David took it in for it was the last moment of harmony that day. After a deep sigh he saw his brother approaching from their house.

With his Australian accent, he greeted his brother. "Hey little Brother, ready for the big day?" David asked as he forced a smile trying to lead his brother by example by hiding his true fear.

Stephen looked up, fear obviously in his eye but still willing to press on with the mission. He had a spiked club that Tran had made for him on his back and held his rifle at the low ready position.

It took awhile for Stephen to reply as he fought through the prewar jitters. "I'm good, I didn't get dressed up for nothing." Stephen smiled back as he tried a Scottish accent on for size.

David smiled and shifted his eyes to Sai and Wan who were approaching as a morning breeze flowed through the Wat again lifting the trees and the spider web once more. Sai no longer had the bandage or limped like when they had first met, his eyebrow and cheek were scarred but was healing just fine thanks to the Wat's resident medical team.

"Arunsuwap," Sai said trying to say good morning in Thai.

"Ah, Good morning," David responded in Thai as Wan went to work inspecting Stephen's equipment, then David's, while Toshiro walked up followed by Tor, Ta and Chit.

Sai's eyes caught the sword that Toshiro was carrying. Tran had loaned to him for the mission.

"Toshiro you didn't steal that, did you?" Wan laughed as he watched Toshiro strut his stuff.

With a deep Samurai movie voice, Toshiro responded: "This relic? Ah, Tran wants me to use this piece of junk; he says that Cambodian steel is the best. I just don't have time to finish my Katana yet, but you'll see her soon. Don't worry Wan, with Master Toshiro around I'll kill all the zombies before you get a chance."

"Let's hope we don't get the chance," David put in.

Toshiro grunted a laugh back for he knew he could take care of any dead head that tried to reach out and bite him.

Still though, Toshiro carried a rifle and like the group he would only use his sword as a last resort.

Sai looked around at the group as Wan had them fall in.

"How's everyone doing?" Sai continued not waiting for an answer. "Today we leave the gate; this is your last chance in backing down." He paused to see if anyone would bite on the chance to go. No one moved or showed signs of leaving so he continued on. "Outside these gates is a world of shit that we have all crawled through to get here. So now is your chance, so go ahead and fall out there is no shame here." Everyone waited in formation, each wondering who was going to do it, who was going to break ranks and leave the others to do all the fighting and dying. Sai and Wan were pleased as the men stood fast, each staying for their own reasons.

Sai continued on: "Today gents you are no longer just civilians on the battlefield, today you will become soldiers of Wat Tatsunupi." A few smiles grew on the faces of the younger soldiers, which was the goal of Sai. "Today is a good day to die gentlemen; it's our first of many missions to come. Today the training that you have received over the last couple of weeks will keep you alive. I want each of you to stay sharp out there, remember slow is fast, and fast is smooth. Fear leads to panic, panic leads to death, stay calm, stay collective and stay together once we leave these walls no one breaks formation or we all doomed to a world of hurt. Our mission is not too hard today, lets think of this as one hell of a training exercise or on the job training. We are only going three hundred yards at most beyond the wire. If for some reason we can't find the supplies we need we will go just a little farther up the river towards an area we know there is supplies. Our packs we will be carrying are waiting for us at the gates, so let's saddle up and start this day."

The men nodded and followed Wan out as Sai looked over to Yoon who was standing by the doorway of his home smiling at him. Sai smiled waving at her with his rifle. She smiled and waved back, the little girl and Wien walked out behind her doing the same.

The three watched as the soldiers put on their packs and two men who were on fire watch opened the gate for the soldiers to file out back into hell once more. The gate closed behind them and the QRF or quick reactionary force fell in by the door. These draftees stood there as a man on top of the wall watched the soldiers move out. If troubled happened they would be the ones responsible for sealing the door after the soldiers had returned.

Katsura appeared near the gate, obviously worried about her brother but more importantly waiting to see if casualties would return from the mission. It would not be long until Yoon, Wien and the rest of the medical team would assemble by the door.

With everyone set the waiting game had begun.

****

Beyond the wall was quiet, the last of the dead had left a few days ago in search for food but were probably still somewhere in the vicinity lurking, waiting for the soldiers to stumble onto them to start the beginning of the battle.

It was an eerie sensation that the group felt as Sai led the formation into the dead world. As briefed the day before two semi wedge formations were formed just outside of the gate. Three men formed a half diamond on the left and three formed a half diamond on the right, Ta placed directly in the center, with the eighth man who was Tor in the rear with the SAW directly behind Ta a few paces back.

Wan was in the right diamond as point man and Sai on the left diamond as point. They moved as brief towards the closest home, which was on stilts over by a tiny creek that emptied into the river. The formation held and silently the moved with their weapons lowered at the ready, each man scanning their sectors for trouble, relying on the other to do his job.

It was not long before the group paused as Sai held his fist up. The men froze and Sai looked to Chit, the fastest of the group. Chit moved as ordered from the brief yesterday. He moved to recon the high grass that led up to the stairs of the house, which lead to the front door.

Chit moved with stealth and made his way through the grass, careful to look through every blade of grass for anything that waited in ambushed. Through the glass he glided taking each step carefully and finally he made it to the wooden steps that led to the door of the home. He stopped listened for a few seconds, his mouth held open, his ears became in tune with his surroundings for the faintest sound as a precaution, checking to see if any noise came from the abandoned home. Satisfied it was clear he waved for the others to move.

Sai and Wan moved up as each of their formations followed each leader in trail formation respectively as Tor covered everyone while taking a knee. Tor's eyes scanned the area as far left and as far right as he could, relying on the guards in the Wat to cover his back.

Sai and Wan then reached the door while Stephen set up security to the left of Sai at the corner of the house facing outboard into the dense jungle. He looked underneath the home to make double sure that nothing was crawling towards him and the dead were not walking around the opposite side of the home.

David set up security to the right of the home him as Tor reached the center where Wan and Sai stood. He did a 180-degree turn facing the direction they had come from covering the entrance in case the group needed to retreat inside the home.

Sai opened the door and Wan burst forth with speed and agility carrying him in with his rifle at shoulder level followed by Sai, Toshiro and Chit. They quickly cleared the room and found neither traces of the dead nor any signs of a struggle.

Chit walked back out and signaled the two brothers to come in at set up security by the windows on opposite sides of the house.

The two brothers entered while Tor set up shop at the doorway covering everyone's retreat. As the brothers made their way to their points the others began to load up on the supplies that the Wat demanded as well as to make a mental note of the stuff in the home that could be useful on a later trip.

It was not a smash and grab, they did everything possible to maintain noise discipline and make this trip as efficient as possible. Within ten minutes they had gathered the resources they could find – food, water, medicine, weapons, tools, and so forth. The packs had become fully loaded and were now being strapped onto their backs as Toshiro and Chit took up David and Stephens position, this allowed the two brothers to stuff their backs while security was maintained for the team.

There were fewer vital supplies than they had wanted so non-essentials were now permitted, pens, paper, clothes, shoes, combs, brushes, silverware, toys for the kids, books for entertainment, beer, even electronics. Whatever could fit in the pack now could be loaded up. Whatever remained could be liberated in the future.

With their packs full they would need to make their first return trip of the day.

"It's ten till ten. Time to RTB," Sai told the group as he threw the pack over his head and onto his shoulders.

The group stopped what they were doing and gathered behind Tor whose pack was full due to Sai gathering supplies for him.

With their packs loaded, they exited and took on a different formation. One built for speed. Since the return was clear they wasted no time and took up a column formation with Tor brining up the rear. The two parallel lines marched out of the house covering their flanks and proceeded quietly until they reached the gate, which was already open for their arrival without incident.

Several men and the medical group were there to greet them. The packs were swiftly unloaded and supplies taken to the main temple to be accounted for while the soldiers prepared to make another run to the neighboring house.

One of the older men asked Wan why he did not leave anyone behind and just secure the house. The response was that they would leave no one behind in a group smaller than eight. If fewer, they could very easily be overrun and cut off from the Wat. They needed to be able to fight their way back and if they lost anymore of the numbers there would be no hope for the future.

****

Like the first trip they had moved out again without drawing any attention from the dead lurking in the area. It was now two o'clock when they were now closing in on their third objective, a house just beyond the tree line of the jungle. It was a house that resembled a junkyard; several worn-out husks of old abandoned cars littered the front yard. From the looks of it, the home it was the equivalent of a NASCAR hillbilly in the southern U.S. Racing paraphernalia littered the yard; old checkered tattered flags waved in the wind near the doorway of the home flanked by old leather seats that the residents had used as a couch on the wooden patio of the home. It was a good place to look if they needed parts for engines and so forth in the future.

Moving towards the home, Ta spotted movement just beyond the house to the right of the home and behind a car. A flash of orange rose from behind a rusted vehicle and began to move away from them.

Wan began to signal everyone to fall back for it was not worth drawing unwanted attention when the supplies they had gathered already could suffice the Wat for a little longer.

A twig snapped somewhere in the soldiers formation causing everyone to look at Toshiro who was grinning with a surprise look on his face.

The dead man walking away from the group stopped and sniffed the air. He turned his head back towards the soldiers and began to walk around the rusted car in their direction.

An orange NASCAR hat appeared from beyond the wreck followed by the pale dead face of Thai trailer trash.

The creature's eyes focused in on the group and its mouth dropped open with the sound dinner bell came screeching out. "Fucking rednecks!" Sai aimed and fired one shot into the creature's head. "Fallback!"

Still in the line abreast formation the second rank sprinted fifty yards back under Sai's order led by Wan as Sai, Toshiro, Ta, and Tor opened fire on the hillbilly family as ma, pa, the cousins, the twins, and so forth began to pour out of the home followed by their undead companions coming out of the jungle. The rounds hit their targets but the dead kept coming from the jungle and were reinforcing their fallen brethren in an all out charge.

"Fallback!" Sai shouted after he had counted to the number ten in his head.

The men near Sai turned and sprinted as fast as they could 100 yards back as Wan, David, Chit and Stephen opened fire from their position 50 yards away. Their rounds went around the oncoming soldiers as Sai's group members deliberately maintained five yards between each other just for that sole purpose. It was a tactical withdraw they had practice over the last few days.

Their rounds slowed the advancing dead, and as long as Sai and his men did not make any sudden movements the incoming rounds would not shoot them.

They ran past Wan and the others and Wan began to count to five in his head. The reasoning was that the zombie dead would be on them faster than Sai's group since they were already in a full sprint.

"FALLBACK!" Wan shouted, and they too began to run; they repeated this several times. Each rank stopped, taking aim and allowing their comrades to run by to set up a firing position once more. The dead were nearly upon them now and the path that they had retreated from held nearly three dozen of them, with dozens of more pouring in from the jungle.

The men on the wall of the Wat open sporadic fire over the soldiers' heads as the soldiers were now in a dead sprint towards the open gate. At the gate several men were firing from ground level towards the flanks of the soldiers as the area became alive with screeching.

The rounds poured down and the men entered the gate. In less than two seconds later two dead men had made their way in only to be greeted by Toshiro and Sai's blades as the other men helped closed the gate.

Wan and his group had been first to enter the gate followed by Sai and the others seconds later. The men who were at ground level firing quickly closed the gates with the two now really dead zombies squeezing through towards Toshiro and Sai. The gate crew slammed the door shut with seconds to spare.

Immediately a dozen, then several dozen, then a hundred creatures started banging on the walls and gate each with a desire to taste warm flesh.

The men on the top stopped firing and began to shout at the dead, drawing them away from the gate so they could beat on the stone walls and harmlessly batter their hands into stubs. The dead fell for the bait and followed the men towards the wall leaving a few stragglers on the gate.

Looking down a mosh pit of death, reaching and clawing their way to the men on the wall, there were nearly a thousand dead men, women, and children outside of the Wat now.

Under the commotion outside Sai looked around and was happy to see that everything had went to plan, supplies were gathered, enough to last another week at least. They had hit the second house twice due to the fact that several pots of rice had been found which proved to be a gold mine for the Wat.

Food was no longer an immediate concern, but it was now apparent that for the group to really survive they would need to secure farmland somehow. Raids were immediate fixes but not long term solutions and the risk was surely too great, they had been lucky now, but even with training, discipline and the use of formations an overwhelming force of the undead still could easily engulf whatever they sent beyond the walls.

****

That night, the citizens of the Wat came together to discuss their future, the eight man army was effective but they could not support the type of raids without more man power and yet they did not have the personnel in the Wat to support what needed to be done nor the food to support more people.

The Old Monk said they needed more people, to help construct walls to secure a patch of farmland just beyond the temples walls. He also mentioned they needed to secure an area of the river for fishing, which sounded easy but most knew the dead lurked below the waters as well. To survive they needed to expand and that was crystal clear amongst the group. A mixture of raids, farming and fishing was the key for an extended stay in the Wat and the priority of what to do next was tough. In the terms of food, expansion, more men, each was of equal value and all three were needed to survive.

Tran was now the lead of discussion followed by his apprentice Wanchai.

"To build these walls, especially now, we need to be able to secure large objects that we can place anywhere around the Wat. I can create a rice field easily that is no problem, I've done it before but the key will be the wall. I recommend trucks for now, big trucks. If we can line up trucks in a box formation big enough to surround a field and perhaps turn them on their sides near the Wat, we could then build the Wall without any direct harassment form the dead." He continued after he looked around the room seeing that he now had everyone's attention. "We need an outer layer for this Wat for what I have in plan. Sai and Wan, do you think you can secure us trucks?"

"If we can find them we can do it. But how do we overturn them when we get them into positioned?" Wan asked.

Everyone began to look around the room for the answer.

"We don't," Wanchai said. "You could park them out there, everyone get back to the Wat, and then we wait until the coast looks clear. Go out and secure the area between the tires and the bottom of the truck since there are large gaps there. The trucks our mostly a diversion so they do not see what we are doing behind the truck. You and your soldiers will be our ramparts while the rest of us work."

"In theory, it sounds good, but too many holes in that plan. First how do we get back to the Wat after we park the trucks? A thousand of those dead fucks are right outside our door and I don't think they are going to just let us waltz right in. Second we need to find trucks, how do we get there without being eaten? Third this sounds like a long project and we don't have months to spare, how long will this take Tran?" Sai asked.

"A few months, depending on zombie attacks and so forth." Tran saw what Sai was getting to. During that whole time of battling off the dead, supply raids would still be needed.

"Months!" Toshiro began to grow impatient.

Wan began to speak up. "Tran, Sai's right, this is going to take months to build, and time for the rice to grow. No matter what we need to hit a supermarket, something with enough food that is worth a raid. If we are going to build a wall, we need to secure a large amount of food before we can focus on the task at hand."

Sai turned to the Old Monk. "Where is the closest supermarket?"

The Old Monk speaking in Thai spoke to Wan while pointing at the map.

"Sai it is several miles out," Wan told Sai after the monk explained. Obviously the track to the supermarket was just as deadly as securing trucks. Someone was going to die, that was a given if they continue to pursue the annexed land project.

"Where is the Thai Air Base again?" Sai asked the Old Monk.

"Near Lop Buri." Wan answered getting to what Sai was leaning to.

"Well that is settled then. wW need food, materials and trucks, and each mission is us against the odds. I've spent my adult life dodging the golden B-B and I'll be damn that I'm going to get my ass bitten off by a bunch of goddamned zombies. If we are going to risk our asses, I'm going to risk my ass going for a helicopter."

Toshiro's attention was now turning to Sai, he would be the only other person who could help Sai get a helicopter running since you can't just go in and turned a key to get it started up like in most movies.

"I like where you're going with this," Toshiro responded with his rough voice, his teeth grinning and his eyes excited with the coming mission that would be forming shortly.

"This is how I see it. I'm a pilot, and I've done many sling -load missions in the past. Means I've carried all sorts of shit from the belly of my hawks. We do one mission to the base at Lop Buri, take a helicopter, gather supplies, find trucks or freight containers, and we can even find survivors along the way." Everyone began to nod with approval as Sai continued. "If we play our cards right, and we get logistical support for the bird like fuel and spare parts, we could use the bird for some time."

Tran's eyes lit up as he imagined the materials Sai could gather with a helicopter. His mind turned into a Home Depot as he thought of all the benefits such as tools, lumber, and other building materials that could be brought in for use of the wall.

"I could finish this much quicker and with just freight containers we could create a wall just using them, but I will still need to reinforce them with ramparts. Once the ramparts are done we could always use those same containers to keep expanding at a later time. Of course I'll build the rice paddies before I think of expanding and with the personnel we already have it shouldn't take too long. With the soldiers guarding the perimeter, I think this could work."

"Only problem Sai is how are we going to get to the airbase and if you do get there, how do you know a helicopter will still be there?" Wan stated.

Katsura stood before her brother and spoke up.

"The river Sai, there are boats still at the docks, some are motor, some are paddle. You could travel up river in relative safety of the boats."

"Sounds good to me. Boats it is then. As for the helicopter being there, we wont know until we get there. It is a gamble either way, stay here and do nothing or go out there and possibly have a chance of living or dying."

"Another problem," Wan interrupted. "The helicopter will draw unwanted attention; we've seen what a few gunshots did earlier today. A thousand zombies came almost instantly."

The crowd grew quiet as they tried to find a way to divert the dead from the Wat if Sai was able to retrieve a helicopter. Wien then stood up and spoke up in Thai filling the empty void as Yoon translated for Sai.

"We can take a motorboat back up river after they get here and shut down the helicopter." She looked around to see the responses on the crowds' faces, the teen growing red. "They will follow the noise; take them for a run up the river and at night paddle back under the cover of darkness. Wait until morning before you reach the rear gate and come on in."

It was a very simple idea and also very brilliant.

"I think Wien is right," Sai said as he walked over to her and put a hand on her shoulder acknowledging her idea. "Let's do it." He nodded looking around the room.

Yoon looked up at her younger cousin and smiled proud at her as Wien looked at the crowd nervously still blushing.

"We will come up with a plan to get to the base, and in a few days we will start this mission. I recommend that we hit the supermarket before we return to the Wat. By then, we will be running low on food." Wan stated

Sai agreed and the Old Monk adjourned the meeting.

The group was now excited, something to look forward to, unknowingly they had adverted cabin fever which would overcome other pockets of humanity. Psychologically people always needed something to do, something to look forward to before madness set in especially under extreme isolation and stress.

Overall the first raid was very successful, much needed supplies were requisition from the homes, enough food to last a little over a week if rationed properly and even new intelligence from the recon they did of the surrounding area was gathered. They had moved north a short, very short distance along the river and determined that behind the houses was a creek connecting to the river. Jungle was obvious piece of Intel and beyond the creek it continued north into a few more homes. The best way to reach that would be the sidewalk that paralleled the canal. There was good cover for the raiders if they needed, easy to hide and lose pursuers, but also a danger for ambushes if the dead waited to the last second before launching their attacks.

The homes were connected to the same gravel road that connected to the main parking lot of the Wat where a few abandon cars were. Surrounding the lot was jungle and the only way to the area was a gravel road that came from the west. A few more homes and a paved road which led north to south led to the graveled road, potentially carrying some dangerous pedestrians, luckily though the road was hardly used since it was a back road that led to more villages farther to the south and to the north. It was not connected to any of the main arteries coming from Bangkok, which was a good thing.

Boats were seen just like Wien had brought up earlier, securing those boats should be easy, only problem was that the engines could bring some unwanted attention and the submerged creatures had the potential to knock them over if they neared shallow water.

Wien's proposal had also given the soldiers a new tactic in which to exploit. Noise could be used to draw away unwanted attention and those slick long Thai style motorboats were extremely noisy. Very good for decoy operations and with paddles the new stealth fighter for this generation, perfect for raids if needed along the river in the future.

As the days passed, the Old Monk had drawn up a detailed map to the Lop Buri base. The plan was to take the canal to the north in what could be a day's worth of travel. Then they would pass a Chinese-style Wat that the crew could easily identify from the canal since a large statue of Buddha protruded from the Jungle Canopy along with a stone Chedi and other parts of the Wat.

The danger of course was that many had probably flocked to the Wat to escape death, but the odds were that the dead did get in. So extreme caution would be needed in that area. The raiders would proceed north about a mile from the Chinese Wat, and then disembark and a whole day's worth of a forced march would take place. They would parallel a dirt road where an elderly man would guide the soldiers to the base. He had lived in the area and used to walk the road with his brother as a kid.

Walking the dirt road would leave them open to attack but staying in the jungle would keep them hidden as they proceeded east towards the base.

Wan had been to the base a few times over his career and knew where the aircraft were parked. He'd be vital to the mission for he also knew the built up areas and where they would have most likely set up a refugee camp, if any. There could potentially be several thousand zombies wandering the base, but hopefully they followed their prey east towards the retreating Army.

It will be roughly around three weeks since the dead overran the area, which meant that battery power of what was left of the birds would be a matter of life and death. They would need to find a GPU "Ground Power Unit" to help start up the helicopter which meant they might need to enter a hangar to find it. Toshiro even brought up the need for spare parts which to keep up maintenance on the bird. Unlike the movies where helicopters were used in the end of the world without a care, helicopters in reality were probably the worst-case aircraft due to the high maintenance involved; so many moving parts meant Murphy's Law acting up was imminent.

With a helicopter there would be new requirements, Jet A fuel or JP-8 is what she liked to drink, and securing a truck full of JP-8 would mean another raid somewhere, hopefully into a friendly airport, which meant fewer zombies.

Sai knew that UH-60A`s existed in Thailand, something between seven to twelve of those birds existed here and since Lop Buri was an air base they could potentially find one. The UH-1 was also what Sai wanted to get his hands on; he had flown one after flight school at the NTC when the Army still had them. It was low maintenance and extremely durable and you could even use fuel from a gas station if needed, which would cut down on JP-8 raids. The drawback was that they were not Super Marine Hueys, which meant the sling loads would need to be extremely light since power would be an issue. To transport containers they would need at the least a UH-60 or even better a Chinook but Sai was no Chinook pilot and probably could not start one in fewer than three hours with a checklist. The Blackhawk was the only option; perhaps later Sai could get his hands on the Hueys.

Chapter 12: *The River North*

After two days of preparing for the coming mission it was time to set out once more. Sai said his goodbyes to his new family as he prepared to leave the gate. Unlike before Ta would not be joining in on the mission. Sai had a talk with Yoon and it was decided that Ta would stay behind. An older gentleman named Kwan or "P'Kwan" when using proper Thai courtesy when addressing elders would take Ta's place. Kwan would not be going as a soldier but as the guide once they landed ashore north of the Chinese Wat. There he would lead the men to the Lop Buri Air Station.

Kwan was a local man who had always been with Wat Tatsunupi before the civilized world ended. During the initial attack of the dead he had made his way to the Wat Tatsunupi and was the man who helped saved the lives of all those who went there for sanctuary. Along with Toshiro the two men managed to get what was left of the survivors up into the attic when the Wat was attacked.

Kwan had lived his whole life he in and around Wat Tatsunupi. In his early twenties was one of the monks at the Wat for a short time, he continued to serve the Wat in one form or another ever since. The man had been married for nearly thirty years before losing his wife to cancer, and with no kids and no one to hold him down he had come to save so many in Wat Tatsunupi during the initial outbreak.

When the dead had penetrated the gates of Wat Tatsunupi it was his idea to hide in the attic. He was the only other person other than the Old Monk who knew the Wat like the back of his hand. Now he would go on the dangerous mission using his knowledge to lead the way.

Kwan recommended they use his boat to move north which was nothing more than a slender, long yellow, blue and red canoe on steroids. His house sat along the river and in his backyard of high grass he had a dock where his water taxi was moored. On the dock were several fuel tanks of gasoline from the nearest Esso station. The house was off in the distance however, twice as far as their first raid and the team would need to take the sidewalk over the swamp land and high grass to the north of the Wat to reach it.

The Wat's residents had turned out to see the eight men off and before leaving the Old Monk presented each man with a Takrood. They were cylindrical objects made from bullet casings and etched with prayers and magical spells to protect the eight from evil spirits. It was a first for Sai, and he took great pride in wearing the Takrood around his neck and in Thai he said thanks, "Khap Khun Khrap."

LuLu, the name of the little girl that Sai had rescued held on to Sai's hand as Yoon, Wien and Ta walked to his side. LuLu had grown attached to her adopted family; she had finally opened up and gave everyone her nickname. It was probably the name her parents had used with her since she was still a toddler. Her full name still remained a mystery.

Yoon and LuLu kissed Sai as Wien held her hands together as if praying by his side and said Sawatdee ka P'Sai, which Sai responded with a Sawatdee Khrap. Then Ta shook Sai's hand and told him not to worry for he would protect the Wat in his absence and be sure that the LZ "Landing Zone" Tran was working on in the center of the Wat was done by the time they returned.

With the goodbyes said the gate opened, the soldiers and Kwan filed out into hell once more in a tight formation. With Kwan in the center of the large diamond formation they quickly made their way north through the clearing before coming to the sidewalk that paralleled the river. Single file they stealthily made their way north on the sidewalk.

****

The wind had picked up, and the humidity had lessened as the morning sun continued to rise. Kwan's home had already been secured while David and Chit took some essential supplies for the trip from the home. Tor sat at a table under the porch with his SAW set up to be a tripod facing the outbound jungle while everyone worked behind him.

It was better to use Kwan's supplies than the Wat's limited resources. They requisition supplies included can soups, can dog food, water bottles, a case of soda and one case of Leo Beer. If they were going on a suicidal boat trip might as well have some fun.

They loaded up the slick longboat with the faded striped paintwork on the sides. The engine of the longboat was from an old 1980s Toyota.

Since most engines were the same it had been converted to power a propeller with a long drive shaft protruding from one end of the engine into the water where a propeller was presumed to be.

The boat was docked in what looked like a patio made of weathered wood on stilts. Two benches faced each other with splinters sticking up from them, waiting for somebody's ass to pierce. The dock had a roof that resembled one of the countless spirit houses throughout Thailand but was made of tin and wood instead of decorated golden paint and other ornaments. Standing under it made you wonder whether the shabby roof could come falling down on you at any moment.

Walking into it the floorboards of the dock creaked under the weight of Sai's boot, very unstable from what he could tell, but it did not bother any of the others one bit. He stood at the small stairwell that led into the water. Before him were three wooden steps led the way into the canal, a few nails hanging out as decorations. Next to the steps was the canoe with Kwan already on board, waiting for the soldiers to hurry up and board it.

Kwan smiled at Sai realizing it was a strange sight for him; he wiggled the engine/propeller that was resting on an iron pole connected to the boat while laughing softly. The whole engine moved which in turn moved the propeller. Thai ingenuity at its finest. *Nothing a little duck tape couldn't build,* Sai thought.

Sai was first on the wobbly boat after Kwan gestured him on. Wobbly was perhaps an understatement as the boat felt like at any moment it was going to capsize over. Sea legs, river legs, Sai had none and quickly planted his butt down on one of the benches, his back facing Kwan at the rear of the boat.

This is going to be one hell of a long ride, Sai thought, as the rest of the soldiers began to walk towards the boat and boarded her as if everything was normal.

The soldiers had boarded the slick boat and as Tor took a seat Kwan spoke to Wan in Thai. Sai watched as Kwan spoke while Kwan gestured towards the land as Chit released the rope that moored the longboat.

"Sai, let's get ready to cover him when he starts the engine," Wan translated as he pulled his rifle from his lap where he was sitting and held it in a ready position.

Sai did the same as Kwan pulled a string that was connected to the starter. He tightened the string as everyone watched him. *This was going to be just like a lawn mower,* Sai thought, as he watched Kwan.

"Nung, Song, Saam." Kwan pulled the string hard causing the starter to ignite. The engine coughed several times at a high decibel and then died out just like a lawn mower, the motor sputtering to a stop.

Instantly shrieks came out of the jungle in response to the dying motor as Kwan primed the engine again and waited a few seconds before trying once more. The engine coughed louder, closer to igniting but failing once more as it sputtered.

The screams of hundreds moving through the jungle was growing closer as the soldiers in the boat began to say their prayers. They raised their rifles for the first sight of the dead.

Toshiro fired two shots first, followed by Stephen and David as three zombies rushed from behind Kwan's house headed straight up the lifted sidewalk towards the dock.

"Hurry up!" Toshiro began to shout over and over as Kwan readied the pull string once more. "In the name of Buddha, hurry up old man!"

"Nung, Song, Saam."

Kwan pulled again as several more zombies came into view, some of them moving through the thick mushy sludge area after leaving the jungle and entering the marshland.

The engine roared to life then sputtered out as Kwan talked to himself in Thai with not a care in the world.

Sai looked back at him and saw the calm composure on the man's face, which was nothing like his. Just another day with the boat according to Kwan's face. While Kwan was just going through the motions a teenage boy appeared on the dock.

The boy's roar signaled to its brethren that it found the prey that had made so much noise with the boat. It took a round a second later causing it's hands to clasp over its face on reflex.

Now the zombies moving through the sludge had increased to over thirty, all moving too slowly due to the route they had taken. Others still used the sidewalk but found Tor's SAW releasing a hailstorm of lead at them.

The soldiers all fired as they continuously scanned the bank of the canal for any who were smart enough to use the sidewalk. The sidewalk users were now down to zero, and now the dead in the swamp had increased to nearly a hundred, each trying to claw their way towards the boat through the mud.

Another useful bit of intelligence, the sidewalk may be one of the safest ways to travel along the river since they stood on concrete stilts nearly six feet high and out of the sludge which the dead were to stupid enough to use.

From below the water another teenage boy appeared, water pouring down from his bitten face, his eyes beyond milky dead. The teenage boy grabbed the side of the boat near David and began to pull himself up when David's axe greeted him. The thing's eyes rolled up back into its skull, its mouth when slack as David put a hand on the cleanest part of boy's head that lacked gore and pulled his axe out. The creature slid back into the water and disappeared.

The final attempt on the engine worked like a charm and this time all the passengers fell back on their seats as Kwan went full throttle away from the dock. The wake waves smashed into the remaining zombies who continued to follow through the sludge causing many of them to fall below the surface, trapping them in the thick waterborne vegetation forever.

****

Kwan had throttled back an hour ago as the group continued to head north. All was quiet now except for the engine, which produced a lower decibel. Kwan had stood like he had done so many times manning his motorboat without any desire to sit down and let someone else take over. Apart from working in the Wat, the boat was his breadwinner as a water taxi.

It was nice to feel a constant cool breeze over the water as the morning began to change to noon. The sun was out in full force but luckily Kwan had extra Thai style hats from his home that he had given the soldiers. The glare though was still a pain as the sun reflected from the water striking everyone in the eyes. Sai wished he still had his sunglasses, there had been hardly a day he remembered as a pilot that he never wore them.

Time was going by as the group headed north and a lot of time for daydreaming was taking place under the constant hum of the engine. Each man sank into their own worlds deep into their minds, the rocking motion of the slick boat forcing their bodies to shutdown. It was easy for them to doze off as Kwan continued north.

Traveling up the river they came across a crashed airliner. The plane had taken off from Bangkok International just prior to the fall of the airport. Soldiers, refugees, police officers fought tooth and nail to board the doomed flight not realizing that many of the passengers were already infected. Shortly after takeoff a gun battle had begun in the cabin causing the plane to go down just minutes after take off. Now there it was, the tail sticking out of the water, dwarfing the boat crew when they slowed down to idle trying their best to avoid the obstacles protruding from the water.

They watched as wiggling corpses still strapped to their seats in the cabin. The dead tried to get free from their safety belts, their heads and eyes tracking the boat crew as they idled by.

The crash was several weeks old but the smell of smoke and fire was everywhere. Jet fuel had burned the surrounding jungle down and corpses could be seen crawling towards the river but none were of any real threat. The crashed had destroyed most of their bodies and all they could do now was open their burned mouths and with their burnt vocal chords moan out to their prey.

Not far from where they left the plane a bus floated half buried in the water that had crashed through a railing of a bridge and was now resting below it. The longboat moved by slowly as the crew saw ripples on the surface of the water in the bus. Zombies thrashed below trapped by debris, responding to the engines hum as it went by. The hair of women was all that could be seen in the bus as it floated harmlessly to the surface. Their long black hair wiggled in the water as the women moved their heads back and forth resembling the dreaded Medusa.

As they proceeded under the bridge where the bus had went over a splash had caught their attention from behind them. Up above the dead had taken notice of the boat from the noise of the engine. Looking over the side they had saw the boat go under the bridge and immediately climbed over the broken railings and over the first one went.

Looking back, Kwan had seen another body fall, then another fall from the bridge, and it began to turn into a waterfall of bodies. He cranked the throttle again and off they went away from the dead human lemmings that tried to walk on air.

****

Every so often the group would hear gunshots off in the jungle, sometimes followed by a scream or several screams signaling a new member of the undead, other times after a gunshot the only sound was that of the wind. Silence could mean so many things after a gunshot. Suicide, hunting, killed a single zombie, mercy killings, murder and so forth.

In one instance they passed a house off the bank of the river that was on a clearing about a quarter a mile inland. Surrounding the house were forty to fifty people, each one banging on the walls. They had clawed so much against the wall that their fingers had peeled in layers exposing razor sharp talons that would last a few more days before becoming bloody stumps.

Something had drawn the dead to that home for they continued their siege as the longboat motored by.

There were no signs of life from within, however. Darkness was all the men could see under the afternoon sun from the farmer's home. For sure whatever had drawn the dead to the home was either a human or animal. Whatever it was it was either dead or dying for nothing stirred, even though it was clear a motorboat was moving by. The crew wondered what had happened to those inside and talk quickly went around about helping out but Wan and Sai made it clear that the needs of the Wat out way the needs of those they encountered.

Unknowing to the longboat crew a brother and sister lay dead underneath a bed. Both were still, dead from dehydration as flies buzzed around them laying eggs in their flesh. The sibling both under the age of ten had taken shelter underneath the bed when the dead came. Their parents had gone missing shortly after Wat Tatsunupi was cleared of the dead over two weeks ago. Crying, they had attracted the attention of the dead villagers in the area resulting in the never-ending siege. Slowly as time went by the humidity drained the life from the siblings and with dry throats and no more tears left, they fell asleep underneath the bed forever. The dead did not have the slightest clue that the siblings had escaped to the afterlife and had been trying to break it down ever since.

The boat pressed on to find few signs of life still present along the river of death. A cow stood near the river that had not been discovered by the dead, it stared at the boat as it drank unaware that death was all around. A gibbon called out to its troop somewhere in the jungle forest, it was on a lone tree surrounded by farmers who raised their hands towards the branches trying to grab the poor little ape. The luckiest of all creatures were the birds however, they who escaped the mayhem of the earth below. They had the worldview of the death walking below.

****

It was near three o'clock in the afternoon according to Kwan when a group of survivors on two separate motorboats appeared after they turned a bend in the river.

Kwan idled down his boat as the two boats came to a stop on the sides of the group. They passed out ropes and pulled themselves to Kwan's boat.

These were river people; a small portion of their village had survived the attack and had been going down river towards the coast in hopes of finding others. For several days they had traveled raiding homes along the river for supplies. Their looks showed signs of extreme fatigue; they were sleep deprived, malnourished and looked as if they had been through hell.

Wan began to speak in Thai to the people as Sai tried to listen in, picking up more words than he had when he first arrived in Thailand now. The passengers looked over to Sai as he heard the word helicopter. He also heard Wat Tatsunupi and the word Pye. It became obvious that Wan was going to be sending them to Wat Tatsunupi and was giving them detail instructions on when to cut the engine motors and paddle their way in.

"Sai, they have a radio just like the one I have," Wan explained as he filled Sai in. "Ta has ours at the Wat, I told them after they continue south for eight more hours to use 47.60 fox mike for the freq. They need a place to stay."

That was good news, an additional thirteen people for the Wat would strengthen it and their skills would come in handy when they were finally able to secure a portion of the river in the coming months.

"Sounds like you got it covered Wan." Sai responded as he noticed a teenage girl holding her arm, she held her hand over a wound with trails of dried blood spreading from it.

"She hurt?" Sai asked the man near the girl.

The man spoke up in Thai explaining of an incident they had earlier in shallow water up the river. The girl had been bitten, not to bad, just teeth marks that had punctured the skin and nothing more.

Wan talked back in Thai explaining to them that Katasura was the resident doctor at Wat Tatsunupi and that she would be able to tend to the wound.

The meeting was over and the two boats shoved off turning their motors back on simultaneously before heading south.

Continuing to push north Sai was troubled by the girls bite.

****

The Chinese Wat had finally come into view, a smoke plume rose into the sky from the center of the courtyard. The smell of burnt flesh filled the air as they approached the docks causing their eyes to water as they drew near. Flies buzzed around happily feasting on what was left of the residents there. Whatever happened here had been recent, most likely sometime during the previous night from the aftermath they witnessed.

A feast fit for the dead covered the grounds of the Wat to the Chedis, the parking lot and to the homes of the monks. Body parts littered the grounds of the temple, easily visible by the crew from the river; everyone had been torn to pieces, which was a sign that thousands of the dead had migrated through here. The pools of blood were almost fully coagulated and the sheer volume of blood in the pools meant only the top was crusty. Below the crust was a bloody ocean filled with bacteria and bugs.

Bugs were not the only things present in the hallowed grounds. A few dead stragglers were still in the vicinity of the Wat. They gorged themselves as they ate the flesh of their victims, their stomachs looked as if they were at the point of bursting yet still they ate like they were gold fish. Even stranger was their victims, most had been torn to shreds never

214

to reanimate as a killer corpse; some corpses were nothing more than heads thrown around the area. The bloodied heads had life in them however and they watched as the crew made their way past the temple. Their milky white eyes stared at them like hawks as their mouths opened and closed. They looked as if they were trying to suck the boat into their mouths like some sick twisted fish.

The crew made it by the Wat without incident while the dead continued to feast on their victims. Their teeth sunk into the flesh as they growled ripping the flesh from the bone. Jagged teeth broke as the bones were crushed in their jaws, their nails dug into the gore as the maggots wormed around the fingers and were ultimately consumed in handfuls.

There had been signs of battle all over the Wat, burnt houses of the former monks, and bullet holes along the columns supporting a patio near the river of the Wat. Moving a little farther upriver, they could see where the barricade had failed.

The ground before the former gate had once been a dirt road. Now it had been the seen of a stampede. Mud with thousands of footprints led to the gate where hundreds of dead bodies were almost completely buried.

It was from the muddy bodies that troubled looked up. A boy, who had been dormant in the mud, heard Toshiro sneeze, which caused him to stir. Its eyes opened under the black mush as its head turned right towards the river. There it saw over the other bodies, seven men heading north. It immediately pushed up from the mud, sludge falling to its side as it stood up and began to run towards the river with a high pitch scream.

Instantly other dormant bodies began to spring from the mud headed towards the little scout. A hundred maybe more began to pour from the shadowed areas of the Wat screaming to keep up with the child. They charged the water as Kwan motored the engine for the quick get away. The prop turned as the watered bubble behind it when the boy hit the water trying to reach them.

Sai waved his hand down trying to calm the others before they started wasting ammo while Kwan went full throttle.

The speedboat began to gain distance as a herd of dead entered the water behind them. Each one was trying desperately to keep up with the fleeing meat.

It was not long until the dead screams began to fade away as the long boat continued north.

The scene was a grim reminder that the men of Wat Tatsunupi must do anything to keep the dead from breaching their walls.

****

The evening had come and, due to the dead south of their position, they had traveled nearly ten miles up river before they came ashore. They were slowly falling behind schedule due to the extra distance they went up river. They had a day and a half before they were expected back home. If all went to plan they would have a UH-60 Blackhawk or a UH-1 Huey, plus supplies from a raid on one of the local grocery chains.

Quietly they had paddled to mile ten and steered off towards the bank. Wan followed by Sai and Toshiro were first to slide into the water. The three soldiers slid into the water as they held their rifles over their heads and proceeded quietly towards the shore.

In the back of their minds they considered the possibility of the waterborne zombies lurking below, but being so close to shore they were sure they would be standing waist high if there were any in the area.

Moving through the water quietly the three men closed the gap to the riverbank when Toshiro said, "I sure hope there are no kids or legless zombies by my feet."

The two men looked at Toshiro and shook their heads. He had a point but no use scaring the shit out of everyone about it.

At the shore the three men took up a kneeling position with their rifles raised into the jungle as the sun's rays began to fade. Only shadows greeted them from the darkness of the jungle. Their rifle sights were set for night fighting by order of Wan so they could pick their targets easier.

Kneeling and waiting for the others, it felt good as the cool water dripped from their bodies. It was a welcomed relief to the suns bright rays that had baked them all day. They waited for David, Chit, and Kwan who were already in the water behind them moving quietly towards the shore. Stephen the youngster of the group was to stay with the boat with Tor and his SAW as escort since speed was priority for the march and Tor lugging that machine gun around was only going to slow the group down.

If the plan fell to mush within the next hour or two the five men on the march would at least have a chance of making it back to the boat for an escape. Hopefully the engines would be running if the worst happened.

David hated leaving his brother behind but the boy was safer there than where David was heading. In two hours Stephen would be heading south along with Tor under the cover of darkness with only a flashlight and moon to light the way. He would eventually row the boat back to the Wat when he was closer and enter from the riverside wall with some rope that Ta would throw out over the wall just for them. Then the two young soldiers would only need to climb the wall and they would be safe once more.

Being parked behind the Wat would allow Ta later to have easy access to the boat without catching any more extra attention from the dead so he could begin his mission with Tor's help.

David looked back as he followed the others into the jungle fearing for his younger brother, trying to reassure himself that Stephen would be safe. David raised his rifle and Stephen did likewise and then disappeared into the jungle.

Stephen watched his brother disappear into the jungle and his senses heightened for now he felt vulnerable. He did as ordered by Sai and withdrew from the shallow depths into the center of the river where the water was deepest. There, Stephen and Tor waited as they watched for any signs of trouble, the clock ticking every second away towards the two-hour mark.

****

The first hour had been filled with intense fear; every noise coming from the water sent a dropping sensation down Stephen's chest. He tried to control his breathing, and his movements for every noise sounded like a dinner bell ringing next to him. Listening he watched as Tor sat quietly in front of the boat with the SAW in his lap. Stephen figured Ta was probably feeling the same way he did – scared shitless.

A fish splashed its tail in the water and Stephen's imagination pictured a hand trying to reach up from below him. A brush in the trees became a passing horde of the dead, but was only the wind. It had been the longest hour he had ever been through and as Stephen sat quietly his mind began to wonder of the horrors his brother might be facing. Questions filled his mind about David and the others, his mind raced with a bloody massacre of David and the others might be facing as he sat helplessly in the boat.

As the second hour came to a close he began fearing the moment he would need to start the engine. He prayed it would not be like P'Kwan back at Wat Tatsunupi. Several tries, really? Would the dead come? What if they were under him and tipped the boat over. Fearful as he was of that dreaded moment and with a few minutes left to go, he checked his rifle and looked to the shore where he saw a shadow move.

Stephen watched, as the time was less than a minute when he heard the wailing of a woman somewhere in the jungle.

A response came seconds later in the form of a moan on the opposite shore as if the two seemed to communicate. *Were they talking, did they know about him?*

"Fuck this." He mouthed as he checked his watch one more time.

He stood up at turned to the engine and when he grabbed the string to start the engine he took a deep breath as Tor nodded at him.

Just like he had feared the first pull only caused the engine to cough in place. The result was as predicted; the jungle became full of undead life. From all around they heard the screams, then the splashes as the dead entered the water around them.

Stephen's heart fluttered like a rabbit, as panic began to sink in; his eyes teared up as fear began to override his senses.

Tor began to fire tracer rounds at the black masses that moved closer in the water and with the muzzle flashes of the weapon they could see the bank of the river was full of people leaping into the water.

Snot came from Stephen's nose mixing with his tears as panic continued to sink in and on his third try the engine roared to life. Without any hesitation he throttled up and headed south never looking back at his pursuers who tried to swim for him.

Somewhere in that commotion Stephen swore he heard children giggling.

Chapter 13 *Hornets' Nest*

Two hours had passed when they heard the commotion of Stephen and Tor leaving the area at full throttle. The river roared with the sound of the dead, sending panic down David's spine. David turned as if he was about to run towards his brother when Sai grabbed him.

"Listen."

Just below the commotion of the dead the speedboat could be heard traveling away from the crowd. David listened and heard his brother moving closer to safety. Sai nodded giving him a reassuring look.

The men began to move once more as David sent a quick prayer and then pressed on following Wan's lead. David made his way to Wan's right flank about ten yards to Wan's four o'clock position. Toshiro was on Wan's seven o'clock, about the same distance that David had from Wan. Chit was at Wan's six; about twenty yards back with protecting the rear of the two VIPs.

Much to Sai's dislike he had to stay in the center of the wedge formation with Kwan. Kwan knew the way Lop Buri and Sai was the pilot, without either the mission would go to hell in a hand basket and the Wat's residents would most likely starve to death in the coming weeks.

With that in mind Sai took up position in the center with Kwan as Wan led them deeper into the jungle heading southeast so they could intercept a dirt road that was supposed to lead them towards the base.

Under the cover of total darkness the group moved slowly trying to evade the lone zombie and with the darkness nothing spotted them. It was two and a half hours when the bugs stopped singing; minute later animals could be heard fleeing towards their position from the north as they attempted to flee south from danger. The soldiers watched as everything from elephants to monkeys stampeded through the jungle heading south. The beast screamed, the elephants roared for the men to get out of the way. Toshiro narrowly escaped the moving tons of flesh as a trunk threw him aside and into some foliage.

Above in the canopy, gibbons howled as they jumped from branch to branch calling out to their troop in the darkness to keep up. The trees came to life as dozens of gibbon troops scrambled south.

A tiger ran by in a flash of orange causing Chit to piss his pants as several deer followed in the tigers tracks.

The animal stampede only lasted a few seconds and as the group heard the creatures moving south they looked around trying to figure out what the hell was that all about. That is when the sound of a Company worth of men running through the jungle could be heard coming from the north. The group raised their rifles and pointed towards the direction of the noise fearing the worst, not knowing what to do until Wan signaled the men to take cover.

A hundred yards away, nearly a hundred zombies were in hot pursuit of the live game. They crashed through foliage even as it tore their skin from their muscles. The only thing guiding them was the sound of the fleeing animals.

Sai grabbed Kwan and tossed him into a bush where he quickly followed. Kwan rubbed the dirt from his eyes as Sai put a hand over the man's mouth after wrapping his right arm around his face. Kwan watched as shadowy figures began to run by the bush, which was nothing more than the vanguard for the horde to come.

The main horde tore through the soldiers, trampling everything in sight. One of the creatures even tripped on David's boot; David had stuck his face in the mud in case he screamed. The creature just continued to run.

Lying on his back Toshiro saw several creatures jump right over him as he held his sword by his side and his rifle ready on the other side. One creature even used Toshiro's chest as a step as the dead things foot crashed down on his ribs and continued on.

The main force had now moved by and the stragglers were still moving through the men. Wan was in the prone when an old woman tripped on him. The shadowy figure looked back at him in the dark and it saw a silver flash of Wan's knife before it saw the darkness of the abyss.

Waiting several minutes now, the group lay motionless, quiet until the insects began to sing once more. The coast was clear, the dead were now several hundred yards south, at least when Wan rose to his feet first.

The other men followed suit and rebuilt their formation before continuing on in the direction Kwan told them to go.

The sounds of the insects singing in the night had proven to be a good warning sign for the dead and the close encounters and physical contact with the dead meant they could not hunt by sight at night, which was another plus for the army's intelligence. Darkness was their ally and in the future they would need to exploit this more often in order to maintain stealth.

Later they would use the tactic of listening to the bugs for when they stopped something was near. Cautiously they would wait as the lone zombie would walk by, heading off in a random direction and when the bugs sang again the group would move on.

A few animals crossed their path through out the night, most heading north, some of them were the lucky few that had escaped the jaws of the dead from the south. A lone elephant was the last animal they saw; it had been covered in bites and limping badly. It had moved south initially crossing the soldiers' path when it had literally come into contact with a wall of the dead. Thousands had forced the animals to push through the pursuers that had followed them from the north. It had turned and began to run in the other direction as several members of the heard continued south, taken down by the sheer weight of the dead. Alone this single elephant had charged straight through the dead, ranks to it's north, many climbing over its back, tearing at it s ears and just trying to get as many bites in as they could before it could escape.

While the elephant ran north, it saw a tiger, a mortal enemy now turned ally fighting off the dead. The tiger clawed at several, ripping the faces of its opponents but like so many others the numbers of the dead sent the beast to the floor and mauled it to death.

****

The constant stopping had begun to drastically increase the estimated time of arrival for the return trip home. The sun was already rising and they had barely gone a quarter of the way after they had reached the dirt road. Lining the sides of the road the men had been walking as the sky changed from dark black to gray then several shades of blue as the sun rose above the overcast skies. Cool drizzle began to fall from the heavens as the men moved in formation, weapons still facing outboard.

The ground had become muddy after several hard showers passed over the men. The constant presence of zombies always had the group kneeling in puddles of water as they waited for the enemy to move on.

If a quarter of the way during the night was the best they could do, the day would be worse. The lack of darkness meant the dead no longer needed to hunt by sound, if they saw you they were coming and the jungle was full of them as they continued to march east towards the base was at a snails pace.

The humidity was intense when the sun broke through the clouds; steam was rising from all the muddy earth. Heat exhaustion was now another danger they were facing.

Since the men had left the river, there had not been one moment when they were dry, the constant showers, lying in the mud and now the killer humidity caused them to sweat constantly. The result was that by midday almost all their water had been depleted; they were now reduced to drinking Pepsi, which couldn't hydrate them for shit. The beer was gone from the river ride, which no one seemed to complain about it; at their current rate, the soda would be gone by the evening, with nearly half of the march left to go.

They came to a complete stop after they found a ravine that paralleled the dirt road. It was decided that since the risk of zombie detection would prove to great that they would settle in for a few hours before setting off once more.

They lay down in a circle as they waited for the hottest part of the day to roll by, taking turns sleeping to conserve energy, calories, and water. The heat continued to pour through the jungle canopy and the humidity intensified as steam continued to rise from the wet puddles of the jungle floor. The men were covered in mud and dirt that penetrated their clothes and bugs crawled over them as they waited; they had become extremely exhausted as they waited in the steam room of a jungle. They no longer cared to even brush the bugs off their skin as the tiny insect legs ran across their faces.

As the noon sun moved by the group set off once more, their bodies covered with irritated skin, raw from the moisture that had soaked through the skin. It was painful to move as the skin broke underneath their clothes and with every step they could feel the skin on their feet peeling away, being replaced by blisters.

They pushed forth until they came upon a small hooch about four hundred yards north of the dirt road several miles later.

Water was in desperate need, and perhaps they could refill some of the empty bottles. To continue with the mission they would need to search the home.

****

Kwan and Sai waited with Chit in the tree line aiming their rifles to the flanks of Wan, Toshiro and David who were moving slowly towards the house. Toshiro led the group with Tran's sword in his hand and a rifle in the other. The Samurai was only too happy to use his skills for zombie killing.

The three men approached slowly and cautiously listening, searching for any signs of danger. Toshiro changed his combat stance as he walked up the two steps to the door; his stance gave him the edge to dispatch anything that might be lurking inside. The door was locked.

"Locked," Toshiro mouthed to David and Wan as he tried to turn the knob again.

As Toshiro tried again, he heard a whisper from the inside of the home.

"Mae?" a girl's voice asked.

A voice of another girl and an older boy began to talk to the girl who had spoken, scolding her for uttering a word.

Wan spoke up in Thai and signaled Kwan and Sai to approach the house.

The two made their way over as Wan spoke to the children. Not long after his first words the door opened up to the soldiers.

The door revealed two adolescent girls and a boy in his early teens. They were the children of poor farmers who like many children found themselves alone, hiding from the dead doomed and waiting for a slow death.

The group entered the home of the children and Wan asked for permission to drink their water before he passed out some of the soldiers' rations to the children, he was trying his best to show their intentions were good.

The children were malnourished and had potbellies to show for it. They watched with their sick little eyes as the soldiers filled their water bottles from a pot of rain water they had collected.

"What are we going to do with them?" Chit asked in Thai to Wan.

"What do you think Sai? What should we do with them?" Wan turned over the question.

It weighed heavily on Sai; bringing children on this nearly suicidal mission would put all of them at risk, but not bringing them would mean certain death from hunger and dehydration.

Leaving them and picking them up with the helicopter was out of the question, even if they left Chit to escort them to the bird. There was no way of telling how many of those creatures were in the jungles and surely they would rush the children and the helicopter when Sai tried to extract them.

"The best decision would be to leave them and let them die," Sai said coldly taking the others off guard. "But we're not assholes so we must take them, but let them know now that if they cry, if they scream, we will quiet them one way or another, a lot of people are counting on us and we can't afford to give our position away."

Toshiro nodded his head with approval as he sat Indian style resting his head on the handle of the sword; he obviously enjoyed his new life and all the drama that came with it.

David spoke up next. "I'll watch out for them Sai, you don't need to worry."

"Look, I'm sorry to be this way, but a fact is a fact, the people at Tatsunupi need this mission or they will die, your brother will die. We may not be able to protect them from what we are about to face at the base. If we get to the helicopter in one piece they only need to stay in the bird while I prep if for launch. Remember we run in the attack, we run in the retreat and when we can't run anymore it is time to die."

"I know, Sai," David responded knowing full well what Sai meant.

Kwan looked at Sai, knowing what it meant to bring the children. It was a tough call, and not an easy one, what if the dead caught sniff of them, they could not wait for their little legs to keep up with them nor could they carry them on their backs and expect to out run the dead. Like the dead world they now lived in these kids were truly on their own, if they could not keep up death was their fate.

The kids looked at each other nervously as Wan explained to them that they would need to be able to keep up and not make a noise.

****

Standing by the ramparts, the members of the Wat waited for signs of the helicopter, but it never came. Yoon and Wien stood by Ta on the wall standing on a crate they used to look over the wall.

All that they saw was darkness, complete desolate darkness and nothing else. Ta told Yoon that it probably just took longer to walk through the jungle than they had expected. He reinforced the idea that Sai and Wan were extremely careful when planning and executing the mission. Perhaps they just found it best to take their time in what ever they had come across in the jungle.

As the night rolled by Yoon talked with the Old Monk and they sent their prayers to the group so that they may return.

****

The sun had risen and the group had moved out with the children walking next to Sai in the middle of the formation. Not much to anyone's surprise the boy carried a rifle, which he was ordered not to use unless one of the adults fired first. The girls held hands and followed behind Sai as their brother walked behind them doing his best to protect his sisters.

The children remained quiet the whole time as the formation paralleled the dirt road to their left. Like the day before the group had to stop many times and for a brief moment the group feared the youngest girl was going to break down, but she stayed strong, probably due to the fact that it had been over two and a half weeks since the dead rose and their parents had probably been killed in the initial outbreak.

Perhaps Sai had no reason to fear for these kids were quickly adapting to the undead world. They had no choice.

As soon as the dead left the area, they pushed forward from their temporarily stops. The constant pattern of stopping and moving was quickly wearing everyone's nerves thin. It was only a matter of time until one of the dead sounded the alarm. The mission was taking much longer than anticipated and the nerves of the men were being pushed to their limits as they waited for the lone zombie to lurch by every twenty minutes or so.

This time, however, they had extra water and the group managed much better as they moved on with the humidity still high. As the afternoon rolled by, the dead had become scarce. The lack of the dead presence was a relief but still the discipline remained strong, not one word was said for hours at a time leaving only gestures for communication. They were doing their best to anticipate each other's moves.

It was the evening when the base came into sight, the dead were scattered throughout the area, several hundred of them, but not gathered in any one location.

Approaching the fence as the sun went down, Wan took the wire cutters he had taken from Kwan's house and began cutting through the fence line.

As soon as the wire was cut they entered the base one by one and waited by the fence line. Under the cover of darkness they continued and proceeded towards the flight line where several outlines of helicopters silhouetted themselves in the failing light.

It was a slow process for the group as they low crawled through the tall grass towards the transient ramp where some of the helicopters were moored. Beyond the transient ramp were more helicopters with two large hangers on the outer edge.

The children were like disciplined mini soldiers doing exactly what was needed of them and due to their small size they avoided many of the cuts and tears the heavier men had to deal with as rocks and other debris tore at their elbows and knees.

Sai thanked god that the children were doing better than he imagined and knew that deep down inside if worst came to worse it was against his nature to leave them behind. Yet he kept up his stern appearance not showing any signs that he would let the mission falter.

****

They reached the flight line and saw Huey after Huey on the ramp. All secured and tied down but no UH-60s in the area.

"It's not here," Sai whispered to Wan.

"Can we take that one?" Wan asked, pointing to the nearest Huey.

"Wan, we need to check the hangars. These birds can't sling a container," Sai replied as the group began to grow nervous.

Kwan spoke up knowing that something was wrong.

In Thai, he told the group that they needed to do what Sai said for if they could not fortify some farmland the group would eventually starve. It was best that they got what Sai needed.

Wan pushed on through the flight line parking in front of the hanger. He was heading towards the hanger Sai predicted might have the Blackhawk sleeping within.

The hangar was a large four-door structure. Each mammoth door was painted white and stood three stories tall and nearly fifty yards wide, weighing close to ten tons. The doors were closed and of opening these Goliaths would surely bring the dead rushing over to see what the commotion was all about.

Wan scanned the hangar and saw two normal doors at the side closest to him facing the south. Wan led the group straight for it, each man scanning their sectors for any dead.

Waiting for a few seconds with his ear against the door to see if anything moved inside Wan opened the door and moved in.

Upon entering the hanger they secured the side door as Wan, Chit and Toshiro moved forward with David at trail. They were to dispatch whatever they found with their blades as Sai and the others proceeded behind them in the hopes they would find a UH-60 waiting for them inside the dark hangar.

The hangar was a sharp contrast from the outside; it was cool and dry which gave the skin goose bumps. For a brief moment it felt good until from out of the darkness the sound of steel slashing through bone could be heard.

Sai moved his flashlight to the sound and found Toshiro with a bloody blade and a severed head rolling on the floor as a body fell in front of him. It was followed by a low moan from a woman deep in the hangar.

It was pitch black in the hangar and the only light came from the flashlights the soldiers carried that looked like alien ray beams in the darkness.

The group moved forward always listening to the loan zombie moan from within the hangar. They kept their vigilance for many more were surely inside with them. They walked by two UH-1s that had their engines being worked upon before being abandon. One UH-1 had no rotor blades and another had been gutted completely as they walked by.

The smell of oil and hydraulic fluids numbed the senses as they past two more aircraft and as the rounded the last Huey they found a body in an advance state of decay lying before them.

It was like an empty shell of a cocoon, the insides were completely gone, torn from the body for consumption by the dead. Besides the body several bloody hand and footprints covered the area, evidence that quite a few zombies were still here.

They passed the body and the strong odor of decay entered their nostrils, the oils and hydraulic fluids previously blocking the scent were now fully out of the way with the stench of death.

One of the little girls instantly began to gag and like a dinner bell going off the dead responded.

The dead began to screech and from out of the darkness bodies darted forth into the flashlight beams.

Stealth was gone now, and the group members, except for Toshiro, opened fire.

Sporadic gunfire filled the hangar as if a strobe light was going off. The flashes of light lit up the hangar with evil shadows as the dead charged from every angle.

Those that made it past the barrage of led met Toshiro's blade. His blade flashed under the light of the flashlights and gunfire as it struck head after head sending skull and gray matter into the air.

The youngest girl began to scream as her big sister held her tight while her older brother let loose with rounds of his own.

As the boy fired, Kwan pushed the girls behind him to cover them from the charging dead.

One of the demons made it past the barrage and Toshiro's blade. It made its way in the darkness until it got behind Kwan and the children who were distracted with the mass of shadows attacking from the front.

From the darkness its claws shot forth and grabbed the oldest girl by the face, her hair flew up as she was pulled backwards towards the ground, her eyes locked on to her attackers mouth and before the children and Kwan could react it sunk its teeth into the her face. Her eyes widened as her jaw broke under the tremendous pressure of the man's bite.

The children screamed in terror as they watched their sister thrown to the ground by this monster and attacked repeatedly. The dead man bit into her face over and over before latching on to her nose. With a swift jolt to his right he tore her nose off and began to work his way into her eye.

Kwan turned and attacked instantly but the old man proved too frail against it as the creature tossed him aside. Another zombie quickly jumped out from the darkness and attacked Kwan savagely.

The demon pinned down Kwan as Kwan screamed for Sai to turn around.

Sai turned to watch Kwan's hand stuck in the creature's mouth as the oldest sibling tried to take the other zombie off of his sister only to be attacked an old woman a second later.

The boy cried out as the lady pushed him back into a workbench, sending his head into the corner, piercing his skull with a sickening crunch. His eyes rolled up into the back of his head as he died instantly, spilling his brains all over the floor and bench.

The younger sister stood in shock to see her brother's brains spill out and her older sister being mutilated before her eyes.

Sai took his machete and began to hack at the zombie on top of the fallen sister.

His blade found the spinal column, and the creature fell limp on the bloody little girl.

He turned towards Kwan's attacker and smashed him in the face with his boot as the creature tried to bite off Kwan's arm.

Chit opened fire on the boy's attacker sending several rounds into both bodies while the remaining sister watched in horror screaming hysterically.

The battle was done as quickly as it begun and the banging from the outside of the hangar from the dead was almost a god send as the little girls terrified cries continued to send chills into everyone's spines.

"Chit, take the girl!" Sai shouted with tears beginning to roll down his eyes. "Take her!" he shouted again as he knelt down beside the older sister.

Wan approached to see what the situation was and it was far from good, the girl was drowning in her own blood as she cried in pain. Her remaining eye locked onto to Sai as if asking for help that Sai could not give her.

"Shhh," Sai cried.

"Shhh, baby," he said again, as he brushed the hair from her pulverized face.

Her body was twitching as shock set in. If she had a face it would have only showed fear and make it that much worse for what was to come next.

Toshiro approached, knowing what was coming.

Her eye was locked on to Sai who began to try to sooth her to fall asleep. He calmly told her to sleep the way a mother would a newborn that had been crying.

She nodded as she thought that comfort would come from it and as soon as she closed her eye Wan fired a single round into her head and crying was gone.

She never saw the handgun that Wan was holding in his hand.

Sai thanked the lord that he was not the one to put the girl down.

The other girl began to scream over and over as David held her, trying to give her what comfort he could as Chit dressed Kwan's arm in bandages.

****

If anything was worth what they had just gone through was that a single UH-60A was in the hangar. Hours had gone by as Sai determined the aircraft was flyable, after a long and thorough preflight.

The battery of the bird was low, too low for a proper start without assistance. If it was going to go anywhere it would need a Ground Power Unit, a.k.a. GPU to give it the juice to start up. Problem was that the GPU would be loud, an alarm to every stiff in the area.

The Thai maintenance book was similar to that of its American counterpart and Wan translated to Sai the history of the aircraft. It had gone through its preventive phase maintenance and the rotor blades had been recently tracked prior to securing it in the hangar. The pilots never made it to the base and their deaths had given Sai's people hope at the cost of two children.

Toshiro quickly scavenged the parts he thought would be useful, along with oils and hydraulic fluids. He stocked up the bird with over four hundred pounds of equipment with plenty of room still left for passengers, and the supply run they still needed to do before they returned home.

In the darkness, Chit had discovered an armory in the corner of the hangar and they brought out several M240H machine guns with tons of 7.62 mm ammo, plus over thirty M-16s, which they confiscated. They loaded the bird heavily with the equipment as the little girl sat in one of the pilot's seats still crying.

Sai explained how to load the bird for even though it could carry a lot it still had floor limits and g-force limits, and the last thing he wanted was to punch holes in the floor of the hawk or have a load come lose and flying into the cockpit while he was flying. They used several planks and removed some of the seats storing them in the hellhole, which existed in the tail boom at the rear of the cabin to accommodate the loads.

The planks were laid down and the equipment stored on them to disperse the weight on the floor equally and after a few hours of loading it up the bird was nearly ready to go.

While still loading up the bird with supplies, ammunition and more weapons, Sai looked to the front of the aircraft where one of the massive hangar bay doors stood. These doors were strong, secure and heavy. They would need power in order to get them open. A generator would be needed to open these doors.

So Sai now faced several more problems. First, the GPU was loud and noisy. Second, the generator was loud and noisy, third the hanger doors when opening were loud, noisy and slow, not to mention starting up the bird to begin with which was also loud and noisy. The dead could number in the thousands outside and they were not just going to let them roll out and take off.

Chit asked how he would fly the bird out of the hangar.

Sai responded with his next project, since the bird had wheels he would simply taxi it out. He'd start up the bird after they moved some equipment and any FOD that could damage the bird when the rotor began to rotate. It could be several more hours at least to make everything as fail safe as possible. The place needed to be spotless when they moved the bird for when the spooled up they could not afford any type of rotor strike or it would be game over. And perhaps just as important as taxing it out, was to get a decoy to divert the zombie hordes attention from the hanger so they could start up and open the doors. It was all or nothing, no half-assed crap tonight.

The men worked throughout the night in the dark using only flashlights to light the way, luckily for them they found plenty of batters and flashlights in one of the hanger's offices.

Toshiro who had wandered off in the middle of the night, avoiding the hard work at hand had stumbled on the maintenance pilots' lockers. There he pulled several helmets and a bunch of headsets that they could hook up to the ICS cords in the back of the aircraft. Unlike many movies where the actors are talking or even yelling in the cabin of the Blackhawk and completely understanding each other, in reality you'd go deaf if you were actually dumb enough to try talking without headsets.

Toshiro even found several boxes of earplugs, which he stored for later use in the future. As Toshiro wandered the office, David raided the vending machines retrieving all the junk food goods as the early morning approached. Every bit counted and nothing would be wasted.

Toshiro later found sling equipment, plus the netting they would need to conduct future sling load missions, which he quickly stored in the bird.

Through the night the men worked and scavenged until they found their diversion as the group stood on top of the hangar looking down at the airfield. One of them would need to be the bait to draw the dead away. A small white truck was parked just outside and within reach of the hangar with the keys still stuck in the door, the owner having leaving them conveniently there for them before he died.

Wan decided he should be the one to drive the decoy truck for he knew this part of the mission would be extremely dangerous and did not want to risk anyone else. All he needed to do was drive around the airfield; blow his horn causing several thousand dead folk to stampede after him. Very easy.

Then he would drive to the far side of the airfield so they could gather away from the hanger. There if all went to plan with Sai's portion, a helicopter ride waited for Wan. As long as he kept moving there should be no problem.

The night continued in the hanger as Yoon and the others of the Wat began to fear the worse for their time had become extremely overdue, but still she kept faith for Wien and Ta said they knew that Sai would find his way back to them.

****

The night went by very uneventful as the dead slowly dispersed from the hangar to the far edges of the airfield again. The sun was on the rise as Wan and Sai stood on the roof while the others slept inside.

"Sure you want to do this?" Sai looked over to Wan.

"We got no other option," Wan replied as he looked over the edge to see if any creatures were in the immediate area.

"We could wait another day," Sai stated as he looked over the edge too. "Let them disperse more.

"We don't have long until the food is out at the Wat, and besides I'm sure you have Yoon pretty worried by now, she's going to kill you, which you probably deserve since you are using me as bait. Come to my country and take our women," Wan joked, causing Sai to laugh a little.

"Well, man, you be sure to get to the bird," Sai said as he walked Wan back into the hangar. Sunlight was burning, and it was time to go.

Sai briefed the group on how to evacuate the bird if they crashed with the blades still running. He showed them how to buckle up and of course the quick release of the passenger belts along with pilot and copilot extraction points.

After the brief Kwan was helped into the bird, for his health had taken a turn for the worse. A fever had taken him since early in the morning and he was beginning to grow pale. They needed to get him home so Katsura could check him out.

The little girl was strapped in between the two crew chief seats just under the transmission of the bird. Toshiro took the port side seat manning the M240 while Chit took the other side with the other gun. David sat on the starboard side of the aircraft near the cabin door and was responsible for closing the cabin door after Chit had open it from his crew chief seat in order to extract Wan.

Toshiro adjusted his belt and then unbuckled it to exit the aircraft from the crew chief window. He then manned the GPU while Chit exited the aircraft to man the generator that would power the doors.

If all went according to plan, Chit would turn on the generator, then man the bay door controls, he'd wait there until the rotor blades started turning and then press the button to open the hangar door.

Before Chit could open the door however Toshiro would need to start the GPU, which was connected to the bird. Electrical power would flow through the bird giving Sai the chance to get the bird up and running. Then Toshiro would disconnect the GPU and move it out of the way so it would not hit the stabilator of the aircraft when it taxied out. With luck Toshiro would get in the bird before Sai flew away.

The signal to get the chain rolling would be the truck horn and five minutes later the door would open and the escape would begin.

The clock ticked as the soldiers manned their stations; at 0800 hrs, Wan would be on the move.

"One minute," Sai said, and signaled the group.

They held their breath as the minute slowly moved by and the sound of rifle fire could be heard from outside.

The clock was ticking slowly, every tick an eternity and then it the sound of the horn blowing could be heard with a vehicle peeling out of the area.

And now the five-minute countdown began.

****

Wan struck another zombie and closed the door of the truck before he started the engine. He pressed the gas, peeling out; he was off, blowing the horn as a dead man crawled onto the bed of the truck.

He did his best to avoid hitting any dead thing head-on, for any damage to the truck could prove fatal to him. He swerved in and out of zombie traffic as the dead took the bait and began to pursue. The screeching of the stampede immediately followed the swivel of heads from the dead on the flight line.

The screeching frenzy of the mob made every hair on Wan's body shoot straight up with fear, he felt thousands of eyes tracking his every movement as the truck burned rubber over the transient ramp and into the grass field. He was heading towards the runway.

Looking in his rearview mirror, he could be easily distracted as if watching a movie – for thousands were in hot pursuit. They dead were in an all out sprint behind him. They jumped over their brethren that were unfortunate enough to trip in front of the stampede. Men and women of all ages sprinted, grandmothers and grandfathers, sons and daughters including toddlers were on the run for food to extinguish their never-ending hunger.

As Wan drove on, the screeching calls of the dead pursuing could be heard from the hangar. In the darkness the crew waited as the clock ticked on Sai's watch. He would signal the start of the generators before he started the Blackhawk.

Four minutes until the group would know if they would live or die a horrible death and as they waited the screeching began to die off as the dead were drawn farther away like cats to a mouse.

"Tick, tick, tick." The clock's second hand moved, as the crew remained quiet, the fear now reaching near the boiling point as time barely moved.

Beyond the hangar walls Wan hit one of the undead demons, the creature smashed the right side of the truck, shattering the headlight and sending the bastard to the ground, his body bounced once and was instantly crushed by the truck sending the wheels out of alignment and the zombie in the back of the truck flying through the air. Wan swerved and hit another on the left side. This time the creature smashed into the windshield. Blood sprayed the passenger side as the creature found itself stuck in the safety glass.

The dead man gnashed and gnawed as his eyes tracked Wan, watching helplessly as he tried to free himself from the windshield. Wan pulled a sidearm and fired a round into the creature's head. The man's eyes rolled back and with the head stuck in the windshield its legs bounced from the right to the left as Wan continued to swerve to avoid other creatures as best he could.

The dead man stuck in the windshield bounced as Wan hit the edge of the runway, the body flew up and then smashed down on the hood once more. This time as he swerved to the left to run the length of the runway the glass ripped through the neck and the body bounced off to the side of the truck rolling several times until it came to a stop. In seconds it was trampled by hundreds of legs in hot pursuit with thousands more behind them.

Wan swerved again, this time to avoid a civilian 747 airliner that had crashed landed weeks earlier. It had lost a wheel upon landing and the aircraft came to a rest to the right side of the runway. The result was leaving tons of debris scattered across the runway.

Wan went to the left then to the right to avoid burn out seats and pieces of the wings of the aircraft. Gimped zombies littered the runway, crawling with broken backs, legs and so forth.

Avoiding the large debris, Wan trampled another creature that he failed to see, Wan bounced violently into the roof of the truck as the creature went under the truck. With no control he landed on a jagged piece of metal and his right rear tire blew out.

Like the show *COPs* of the 1980s, Wan was truly burning metal now, sparks flew yet his speed remained up. The burnt smell of rubber filled the cabin as he looked behind and cleared the 747 to see a trail of white smoke flying up into the air behind the truck.

His goal was complete, any second now Sai would be getting on his way, looking through the mirror he saw the ramp clear of the dead and he felt relieved that his friends would live through this.

The moment Wan was thinking of them he hit another creature which hit head on to the truck, it smashed the engine hard and like the others fell under the vehicle.

Black smoke began to rise from the engine as the oil began to burn. The smoke went through the cracked windshield and began to blackout the cabin when Wan quickly rolled down the window with his right hand.

The car was slowing; the speed was beginning to fade on him with only momentum carrying him forward now. The truck was dying.

****

The clock struck eight, and Sai shouted to Toshiro.

"Lets go!"

The GPU came to life with a roar and Sai automatically began to go through the checklist flipping switched so he could turn the bird's engines on. While Sai went through the motions Chit hit the generator to power up the doors. The hangar was deafening as the two generators ran like freight trains.

Sai signaled Chit to press the switch and the hangar door began to rise. Chit quickly sprinted to his seat as Toshiro disconnected the GPU and pushed it aside while Sai pressed the number one starter switch on the Power Control Lever.

As the door began to rise Sai saw a few dead people left near the ramp turn and begin to charge towards them.

The blades slowly began to move and Sai quickly pressed the number 2 starter on its Power Control Lever.

The green chiclet lights on the TGT, Torque, Rotor, and so forth began to rise as the blades turned faster and faster. The cockpit was coming to life with lights.

The TGT stabilized on engine one, and Sai pushed its PCL to fly as the number two starter continued to go.

Sai watched as the weaker engine, the number two, slowly rise on the chiclets of the CDU and PDU.

Sai looked out again and the dead had already halved the distance towards him.

The system instruments began to stabilize and Sai quickly slammed the second lever to fly noting that the tail wheel was still in the lock position so the aircraft would not twist out of control from torque.

Next, Sai lowered the parking brake by pressing on the pedals to release the breaks and raised a little collective as he pushed forward on the cyclic. He was supposed to be moving forward but nothing was happening. The aircraft had jerked forward and then stopped.

He pushed forward on the cyclic again and added more power and still it did not move.

"FUCK! CHALK BLOCKS!!!!" Sai shouted to Toshiro.

They had over looked the blocks under the main landing gear and Toshiro jumped out and took a peak at the incoming dead and saw they were now less than fifty yards away.

Toshiro then kicked the block away from the tire and threw it into the Blackhawk's crew chief window as Chit just kicked his side away and reentered the bird just as the first zombie entered the hangar.

"Close the Windows!" Sai shouted again, as he raised collective and pushed forward on the cyclic, which caused the rotor blades to lower in front of the bird, nearly cutting off the first head of the dead.

Carefully he avoided their heads for if one hit it they would just be seriously fucked.

The wheels were light and the hawk began to move forward as the first zombie hit the nose of the hawk and began to move around the bird towards the cargo doors.

The pilot doors and crew chief windows were locked but the cabin doors could still be opened easily. Toshiro and David held opposite sides of the doors and bloody hands began to bang on the windows.

The sudden light of the open hangar doors became dark again as the bodies surrounded the Blackhawk, blocking out the light from the cabin.

In the midst of the struggle, the girl began to scream in terror, fearing the rest of her life would last just a few more seconds.

Suddenly they felt a sinking sensation, as Sai pulled collective once clearing the hangar. The bird began to rise from the sea of dead and suddenly it was off, the dead hands disappearing sinking to the earth and the sun's rays penetrated the cabin's windows once more.

Toshiro looked around and smiled, then he moved to the little girl to check her while David strapped back into his seat.

Next they felt the sudden acceleration as Sai nosed over the bird and began to race towards Wan as he pulled the hell out of the collective.

The girl looked out as she saw the helicopters parked only 50 feet below turn to grass and then a runway as the Blackhawk accelerated.

"He's on foot!" Sai shouted again into the microphone. "Get on the guns!"

Toshiro still hooked up to the ICS box heard it and opened the window of the Hawk and told Chit to do the same.

Toshiro then locked and loaded the weapon and then took aim.

Leaning out of the helicopter Toshiro saw where Sai was headed.

Wan was in a dead sprint, with the dead closing in from all directions. He dodge an incoming zombie who rushed him head on and never stopped the pace as he heard the helicopter coming in behind.

Wan's lungs burned like never before, his legs felt as if every muscle was disconnecting from the bone.

Spit and tears began to roll down Wan's face, and he did not even realize that he had just pissed his pants. The brave soldier knew his time was up as two women charged from the front.

He threw his body into their legs tangling them up as he rolled back to his feet and continued his sprint. The two women got up slowly only to be trampled seconds later by their comrades.

Just then, Wan felt the blast of the Blackhawk's rotor wash pass right over him cutting a few zombies off that were charging at him from the front.

Sai kicked in some right pedal, nosed up the bird aggressively and lowered collective to cut the power and stop instantly in midair.

The bird sank and at the last second he raised collective to stop the descent just prior to hitting the ground.

As Wan ran, he saw Chit firing the 240, tracer rounds zipped by Wan's head as David opened the cargo door. On the other side, Toshiro laughed as he opened up on the zombies charging the bird from the other direction. He looked like a mad, drunken Samurai with a new toy, happily trying it out for Christmas.

David shouted for Wan to hurry as he pulled his rifle out and began to fire.

Wan never realized that only steps away the zombies were meeting a wall of lead, being pulverized by Chit's aim.

Their bodies twitched under the power of the 240 and parts flew off into their comrades pretty much stopping them in mid-charge.

Sai looked out from under the black visor of his helmet to see hundreds coming from the front while an unknown number came from the rear.

David helped Wan into the bird and saw Sai leaning over. Looking over his left shoulder, he saw Wan enter the cabin.

As soon as Wan jumped in, Sai yanked the collective and nosed it over.

The sudden pressure of the g-force sent David and Wan into the floor of the bird and as they regained their footing they looked out onto the airfield to see the hornets nest they had stirred swarming with undead creatures. There could easily be five thousand of them waving goodbye to the Blackhawk down below.

Sai gained altitude and David closed the door shut.

Chapter 14: *A Convenient Store*

Minutes after the flight, Sai was headed back towards the west to the river. On the two o'clock position of the aircraft, Sai spotted several large buildings, one with a sign that read "BIG C."

Sai remembered that from his time in Bangkok, at the hotel where he'd stayed, there was a Big C less than a block away. It was the Thai version of Wal-Mart, but on steroids; they were ten times bigger than a Super Wal-Mart with multiple floors. The typical Big C store contained food, camping equipment, clothes, shoes, toys, electronics and motorcycles. Dozens of other shops, from comic books, to 24-karat gold jewelry, banks, and gift shops were sprinkled throughout the building. On one floor, there was a food court that the building owned plus several fast food chain restaurants, arcades, rides for the kids, and Internet cafes. On the very top floor, there were was even a mega theater with eight screens, fancy first class seats, and several snack bars.

One thing about Thai people is that when they build, they create massive structures. The Big C that Sai had spotted was just as big as all those massive buildings in Bangkok.

He flew over the building, performing an aerial recon to see if the dead had breached the structure. The dead filled the streets but there were no imminent signs that the building had been compromised. Several of the floor windows had been shattered but a barricade was set up all along the ground level from what he could tell. *Could be survivors or a horde of the dead waiting inside.*

Wan was now on a headset and talked into the mic as he looked out the window.

"Sai, looks good, can you land it on the roof?"

"Lucky for us, they built a helipad." Sai paused, as he looked at the structure. "Hope it can support our weight," he responded, as he slowed the aircraft and came in for the final approach.

The rotor blades tore through the air as Sai pitched the nose up of the helicopter and lowered the collective. The bird quickly began to decelerate, as Sai found the glide path he wanted.

From below, the dead looked up as the Blackhawk appeared from a building to the east then over the street before disappearing over the roof of Big C. They reached out, hands up in the air as their food flew out of sight.

The tail wheel touchdown first since the Blackhawk always hovered nose high. Toshiro leaning out of the crew chief window strapped to the helicopter with a Monkey Harness began to call Sai in.

"3,2,1," Toshiro said referring to feet before touchdown.

The main landing gear touched down on the pad and the struts began to give way to the weight of the bird as Sai gently lowered the collective to flat pitch.

Sai paused for a few seconds, waiting anxiously in case the weight was too heavy; if so, he would yank the collective and be off in a second.

Satisfied he smiled, "Looks good." He turned over his shoulder to see Wan looking at him. "Secure the roof and I'll shut it down."

"Roger that, Sai."

Wan, David, and Toshiro got off the bird and scanned the area as they left from the three and nine o'clock positions of the Blackhawk to avoid the blades in the front of the aircraft which naturally rotated low and could chop of a head or two.

Sai set the brakes and Wan signaled him the all clear. Then Sai pulled the PCLs to idle and waited two minutes, watching the men outside move around double tapping the security check.

Satisfied that the roof was secured Toshiro quickly lit a cigarette and lowered his weapon and looked over the edge of the building, there he saw a mass of bodies staring up at him. The dead swarmed the streets below but from the look of things they could not get in.

The two minutes were up and Sai pulled both PCLs to the off position and the blades began to slowly come to a stop.

Sai stepped out of the Hawk and took off his helmet to a welcomed fresh breeze that blew through his sweaty hair. It was one of the small things he had learned to look forward to in the past after a long day of flying. The familiar sensation was welcomed and he turned around and put his helmet on the headrest of the seat before walking to Wan and the others.

****

The door on the roof busted opened and three armed men came running out. Two foreigners were in the trio, both men in their late sixties from what Sai could tell.

"How's it going?" Sai walked up to the men extending a hand.

With a Latin accent, the old man – who wore glasses and had a wrinkled face – spoke up.

"Good, see you boys are doing just fine. What brings you to our lovely casa today?" He didn't wait for a response; instead, he shook Sai's hand. "Name's George, George McKinney, journalist for the BBC. Just got caught here behind the lines with these gentlemen." George gestured to his left to the other old foreigner who had a camera hanging from his neck and then to the Thai man.

"Dario Bourne." Dario raised a hand and shook Sai's hand.

As Sai shook Dario's hand, Sai began to introduce the men he had come with.

David was already coming from the helicopter with the little girl holding his hand. He told the others that Kwan felt like staying in the bird for he was becoming too sick to move.

****

Sitting in the department store that had been turned into a well furnished home, two young women served beverages to the soldiers as George smoked a cigar in a leather recliner looking a little like Fidel Castro in Sai's eyes.

"Nice set up you got here," Sai said as he took a drink from one of the women.

"Well, at my age, you tend to like a nice place to call home. We figured we might as well live comfortably before we die," George replied. "Sai, why did you land that whirly bird here?" he said, getting straight to the point.

"We have our own set up just south of here along the river. We cleared out a Wat, fortified the walls and what you see here is our mini Army hard at work."

"Impressive." George raised his eyebrows and nodded his head.

"We landed here to scavenge for supplies."

Dario's eyebrows went up as he put a hand on the rifle that was on his lap.

Seeing this, Sai raised a hand in a gesture to put the two men at ease.

"We thought the place was abandoned, we had just got the Hawk and were on our way back to the Wat when I saw the Big C sign. We didn't know anyone was in here."

The two men looked at each other as Sai continued on.

"If you can spare some food and water, the people at our Wat would be forever grateful."

George took another puff of his cigar and then released an o-ring of smoke.

"Look, we got the helicopter so we can secure some farm land. When we get this built we could pay you back."

George stood up and took a glass of champagne from one of the women.

"Sai, there are only ten of us, ten of us that have survived this far, we once had twenty. We have enough food to last years here, all the can goods we could ever want. How many people do you have at the Wat?"

"Close to fifty."

"Fifty, damn boy. What the hell have you guys been doing?"

"Fifty," Dario muttered.

"Roughly, there was a bunch of people hiding there. When I got there, the dead had chased most up into the attic. A few of us cleared the area and so far nothing has gotten in. We can't last on raids alone; the demand for food is too great and the cost would be high, so we decided to secure some land for farming. If we stock up on food and essential supplies now, we can focus our attention on the land."

"Well looks like you've come to the right place, Sai, we have some of the finest dining you can imagine, frozen food, beer, canned food, wine, vegetables, liquor, and even Playstations. All we ask is that when you're done building that farm, you help us in our cause."

"Sounds fair." Sai smiled, as did the other men.

****

Toshiro, David, and Chit were busy fairing supplies to the roof as George and Dario gave Wan and Sai the grand tour of Big C.

They walked down several flights of escalators since the generators were only powering certain areas of the building that George considered necessary for survival such as the theater that smelt like weed.

It was a strange feeling to walk down the escalators where thousands had once used on a daily basis; now a fine coat of dust had settled all around the building, except for in the living quarters.

The group walked through a floor with many small shops that the dynamic duo had rummaged through and the smell of weed was strongest near the comic store for unknown reasons. The whole building smelled like it, though; no doubt the end of the world had these two living through some good times.

The dynamic duo was not just journalists but remnants of the hippies of the 1960s. Potheads, from what the soldiers could tell, but still none the less survivors, god only knew what kind of free love hippie crap went on here on a daily basis, for the place was full of interesting women.

At the end of the dark walk through the shops, they came to a stairwell with red letters painted on it. "HAVE A NICE DAY ☺"

Here, George stopped and looked at the soldiers. "On the other side of this door is the stairwell that leads to the first level. As you can see over there." He pointed towards the escalators that had been covered with all forms of debris from motorcycles, to computers and dirty laundry. "The escalators are out of service."

He used a key that he had found in an office and unlocked the door. "Remember, stay quiet."

Opening the door with as little sound as possible, Dario led the way, smoking some weed in front of the soldiers. He walked down the stairwell followed by Wan, Sai, and George.

On the first floor level, George unlocked the door and opened it up. A blast of humidity hit the men as heat poured into the stairwell.

They walked into the abandoned first floor; many shops were here, many which were clothing shops and purse shops. It was a place women had frequented before the end of the world

Looking around, they saw firsthand what the survivors of Big C had done.

In the beginning, twenty-five people had secured Big C; their small number helped them avoid attracting the dead in great number when securing the first floor. Chain fences had been set up on the lower levels around the escalator, with debris stacked on top of it, leading to the second floor. It looked almost impossible for anything to make its way up that shaft.

There were cars and Tuk Tuks from the parking lot that had been brought inside of the building from the service entrance. Now the vehicles served a new purpose, they stood on their side where the residents had flipped them and pushed them against the broken windows and doors around the building. To help support the cars and Tuk Tuks all manner of business furniture, refrigerators, stoves and anything heavy enough to prevent the dead from pushing the cars in was set in place.

Not much light entered the first floor for only a few cracks in the barricade allowed the sun's rays to make in through in beams highlighted by the dust particles floating in the air.

Sai looked to George who signaled the men towards one of the holes in the barricade. He stood there on top of a desk looking out into the street. Then he signaled the soldiers to look.

Upon looking outside Sai saw the dead stumbling around in an almost trance like state. A man sat in the middle of the street next to a scooter that was on its side. The creature studied the bike and began to play with the throttle. If it was coincidence or not, the thing looked like it may have remembered what the throttle was used for at one time. The creature just stayed there slacked jawed, something that Sai had not seen yet. When food was not present they were pretty much playing with things and hopefully they were not learning.

According to George, the barricade that they had crafted had begun just prior to the dead armies' arrival in the outskirts of Lop Buri. He and the others had heard the bombing from Bangkok the night hell came and saw from the Thai News channels of what was happening. Being old, the dynamic duo had no will to make a run so instead the two foreigners along with some Thai people secured Big C.

After watching the dead in the streets the men made their way back to the stairwell where George secured the first floor door and walked up to the second floor where the men waited and then he locked the second floor door.

"George, are those things learning?" Sai asked still amazed at what he saw that man doing with the bike.

"Sai, once I saw one walk a dead dog, well half the dog of course."

"You mean zombie animals?"

"Hell no, are you stupid?" George, Wan, and Dario laughed before he continued. "It was just some poor mutt who became the damn thing's lunch. I saw a kid walking his dog Spot, more like dragging him through the streets a few days ago. I saw another one holding a shovel. Sai, it looks like they remember things from their previous life. The shovel guy even had a hardhat on, which leads me to think it was just a memory. It looks like they just remember glimpses of their past lives."

"Memories could be dangerous," Wan interrupted disturbed of what he was hearing.

****

Sai offered the Big C residents refugee at Wat Tatsunupi, but the residents of Big C were not the only survivors. They had kept in contact with families, other groups who had somehow survived the dead assault on their city. They had lost members of their own fortress in attempts to rescue some of the others stuck out in the city. They were the last bastion of hope for all that lived in Lop Buri.

With his offered still on the table and most of the supplies loaded into the helicopter it was time to head off.

Sai, Toshiro, Kwan and the girl were to go with the first load. The helicopter now contained food, medical supplies, and a few toys for the kids. This would be the first supply run for the day.

Sai would return to the Wat and unload his cargo and with the help of Toshiro take out all the troop and crew chief seats that remained. This was so they could take a heavier load of supplies on the next trip so they could maximize the fuel the helicopter had left.

Wan, Chit and David decided they would stay behind to help with the movement of more supplies from the lower levels to make the operation run as smooth and fast as possible. Every trip was all about conserving fuel and this would be the deciding factor on how much they could bring to Wat Tatsunupi. Of course they would need to find fuel prior to the construction of the ramparts in the future.

With the decision made, Sai led his group back to the roof as Wan began to issue out orders to the remaining men.

Upon reaching the top step of the stairwell, Sai reached for the door, turned the knob and the door blasted open. Kwan charged into Sai who in turned slammed into the men behind him.

Kwan smashed his teeth together as he tried to bite Sai while on the mount position on top of him. It took Sai a few seconds to comprehend what had happened to the frail man. That is when Sai rolled over to his right on the concrete floor throwing Kwan off him. There he was looking straight into the eyes of the dead man he once knew. No soul was in that cold shell of the man they once knew; only darkness existed in the center of the milky gray eyes.

Sai grabbed Kwan by the hair on the side of his head and began to slam his head into the concrete. The head was pounded over and over until the back of his skull began to crack like an egg. Blood began to pour out onto the stairwell when gray matter beginning to spill out from the crack in his head.

Kwan's eyes grew wide as his brains left his skull. Now motionless below Sai's body he grinned with a permanent snarl on his face. Sai release the head of the man and stood up looking at the body.

Wan had heard the commotion and raced up to the roof where he saw Sai standing over Kwan's body.

"The bites, the bites had killed him and it was the bites that brought him back!" Sai said as he thought of the group they had met on the river. "They should be at the Wat now, with that girl." He looked up from Kwan's body to everyone who stood around him.

Sai immediately thought of Yoon and the kids. Panic set in as every hair on his body stood straight up. He hoped the girl had not changed yet, but deep down inside he knew it was too late. Kwan had only been bitten less than a day ago, just mere hours. What had happened at the Wat was already done. Sai could only hope that they had survived what he sent back to them.

"Wan, I'm leaving now. Send Chit up, we may need him. Don't tell David about this," he said, referring to his brother Stephen who was already back at Wat Tatsunupi.

Wan ran down the stairwell to fetch Chit and send him up as Sai began to start the helicopter with his passengers on board.

As soon as Chit was in the Blackhawk Sai pushed the Power Control Levers to fly and pulled pitch.

The bird raced through the sky leaving Wan and George standing on the roof of Big C. They watched as Sai raced off towards Wat Tatsunupi.

****

Half dead and running on fumes a man who was part Chinese, part Burmese, ran through the jungle. He had no idea how long it had been since the soldiers had killed his friends, it had happened so fast. He had left right before the fun had started with the girl. He could never hold his shit in.

Wandering for days, weeks, hell it could be months for all he knew and now here he was at a river.

He ran to the water and dunked his head straight in. He drank greedily failing to notice the pair of eyes approaching him.

Like a crocodile the dead woman's eyes had locked onto him. Unlike her comrades however she did not screech, she did not make any sudden movements, she just stalked her pray.

She had come to within a foot of his face; her hands were now reaching out through the murky water when the man lifted his head out of the water. His stomach was full of the vital fluid.

He wiped the water from his eyes when the woman struck. She moved like a crocodile taking down a gazelle. It was a ferocious attack but he was no gazelle. This battle harden inmate head bunted the woman in the face after he grabbed the side of her head.

The force broke the woman's neck and she went limp.

"Fucking bitch."

He smirked as he let her slide back into the water. That is when he heard the sound of a helicopter racing from the north.

In a matter of seconds, the helicopter had crescendo as it flew overhead.

The man felt the rotor wash that lasted only a second before leaving. The sound of the aircraft now dying off as the helicopter continued to race towards the south.

"Well, I guess that's my ride."

The man said and began to walk south.

Chapter 15: *Reunion*

The Blackhawk raced through the sky with the tips of the blades at supersonic speed, the aircraft shook threatening retreating blade stall at any moment as Sai pulled the guts out of her. The wind howled through the cracks of the closed crew chief windows and cabin door.

Below the bird Toshiro watched from his seat as the buildings turned into jungle then to a river where Sai banked hard left on a sixty-degree turn. The aircraft leaned heavily to the side as the G-Forces forced everyone down in their seats. Sai jerked the aircraft leveled never losing an ounce of speed or power.

Keying the helmet microphone from the cyclic he spoke into the blind on 47.60 FM.

"Whiskey X-ray, Dead Air." He paused waiting for a response, "Whiskey X-ray, Dead Air," he repeated several times as his main landing gear raced just feet over the water.

The dead watched from the jungles as the helicopter roared by. Many only catching a glimpse of the bird for when he past overhead the jungle helped blocked their view quickly.

"Whiskey X-ray, Dead Air. Fuck!" Sai said as Toshiro listened in. Sai turned his head to the center console to trouble shoot the problem, he looked at the FM radio to see if he had programmed it right as he called out into the blind again and could hear himself transmitting from his earpiece. No one was answering.

Something bad had happened and all Sai could do was hope and pray.

Sai was almost upon the Wat when he saw Ta and Stephen on the motorboat waiting patiently next to the Wat just as planned, it was a good sign, they did receive the transmission or at least hear the helicopter coming.

Sai banked over the Wat to see a single building that was in ruins from a fire. It had been the designated medical house, immediately he looked over his shoulder to Toshiro.

****

Upon landing the doors opened and the blades began to slow to a crawl as Sai shut the bird down. Yoon ran up to the bird and Sai opened the door leaning over to her giving her a quick kiss.

"Everyone okay?" Sai asked as he dismounted the bird putting his helmet back on the seat while the cabin shook as the men exiting the aircraft.

Yoon looked at Toshiro who was exiting the aircraft.

"Katsura, Akira and the parents," she said with a low voice as Wien walked to her side to listen in.

"The girl?" Sai asked referring to the teenager.

It had been early in the morning the day after the soldiers had left on the mission. The teenage girl had come down with a fever, the fever had hit her fast, her eyes were closed, and she was sleeping, moaning in pain as cold chills attacked her body. They had tried to hydrate the girl but she could not keep anything down. They had wrapped her up in blankets trying to keep her from shivering, but it was useless.

It was then when the girl's mother who was in the room with Katsura, Akira and Wien began to break down. The girl had begun to gasp for air; her breathing had become shallow when Katsura thought it best to bind the girl's hands and legs in case she turned into one of them. She had a feeling. The three medical team members began to hold the girl down when the mother punched Wien across the face sending her flying into a table. Wien was knocked unconscious as Katsura and Akira tried to subdue the mother. They failed to see during the commotion that the girl had taken her last breath.

After a minute of scuffling with the mother, they were finally holding her down after she fainted, that is when the daughter wrapped her hands around Akira waist and bit into her side.

Akira screamed in pain alerting the residents of the Wat.

First on seen was the father of the daughter who saw what had happened. He tried to pull the girl off Akira when she lunged at his throat. Her teeth pulled the flesh away and she tore into his throat while Katsura grabbed Wien who was still lying unconscious.

Katsura began to pull Wien out of the house and was almost at the door when the girl attacked Wien. Katsura shielded the teenager and was bit in the process, struggling on the floor with the girl while her father bled out near the mother. Akira ran towards Katsura to help her when the father grabbed Akira's ankle and began to pull her towards his mouth.

Akira's nails dug into the wooden floor leaving claw marks that left a deep gash of blood in the wood. The man bit into her ankle and then climbed his way up her waist towards her face. Akira's eyes grew big as the dead white eyes looked into her eyes before biting her face off.

That is when the mom woke up to see Katsura struggling with her daughter. Katsura was covered in blood as the girl continued to bite her repeatedly over and over. She saw what her daughter had become and then she saw Wien unconscious by the father who was tearing into Akira who continued to bleed out. The mother then pushed Wien's body outside of the house and shut it behind her. Wien tumbled down a few stairs and onto the concrete ground where Tran and Ta met her.

The mother now stood over the dying Katsura and in seconds was the only person left alive in the room. She reached out to a candle that had lit the room and tossed it against a pile of bloody linen. The fire began to grow as everyone in the home tackled the mother.

Standing outside with Wien in his arms Tran saw black smoke leaving the windows as the mother screamed one last time before flames erupted from the same window.

Immediately, the Wat's residents began to hull water with buckets as they started their firefighting efforts while the dead beyond the walls screamed in excitement hoping to be let in.

As bad as it was, things could have been worse, but for Toshiro the last of his family was now gone.

"I'll tell Toshiro." Sai hugged Yoon and Wien when LuLu ran up and hugged Sai's leg. Sai kissed her and hugged her before walking to Toshiro who knew something was wrong.

Toshiro began to call out in Japanese to his sister but had no response, he shouted out as Yoon put a hand on his shoulder his eyes tearing up.

"Toshiro, Katsura, Katsura didn't make it." Sai told the large man.

Toshiro began to curse in Japanese and roared into the sky as everyone tried to comfort him.

****

With the group and supplies unloaded Sai took off again over Ta and Stephen who were still in the center of the river waiting in the boat. There they waited for Sai to return again before they would finally lead the dead North on their night trip.

When Sai finally landed on what turned out to be three trips for the day he called the two youngsters and told them to head north.

Ta and Stephen quickly followed suit and turned the motorboat on and with a bell that Stephen had found he began to ring it. The bell and the sound of the boat engine called the dead to its location after Sai had shut down.

From the wall near the river, the residents watched as Ta flashed his white flashlight three times before taking off.

The residents then saw the dead follow along the banks, some entering the water behind the two as they led them to the north. It would be several hours before they would return.

George and Dario's group had remained at Big C just like they always knew they would, people trapped in the surrounding area of their location looked to them as leaders and with their radio they constantly kept the people up to date. They had become the new BBC of Thailand, transmitting news, rumors and drug propaganda along the airwaves. They would keep in constant contact with Sai over time, for Wat Tatsunupi as far as they knew was the only military presence in the area that could help in an emergency, even if their number was small.

****

The group rested for the next few days as they figured out the best places to look for containers and fuel were. The hangar they had stolen the Blackhawk from had the parts to sustain the Blackhawk. Unfortunately, in their retreat, they had left the door open, which was not a big issue, but was still a problem if they needed to return for maintenance. They could always land on the roof if needed and perhaps even man the station in the future. In everyone's minds, islands of human life now existed in a sea of the dead, and that was going to be the norm.

Fuel could be found at several airports, fuel trucks would be a good choice for they could be driven back to the Wat and used in safety, but the problem was getting them back to the Wat which they would need to figure out.

The Blackhawk was an Alpha model, one of the United States surplus older models, which was probably built the same time Sai was born. Still it had aged gracefully and if it would have been alive it would have been happy to be in service again. She would have been happy to know that with her around she would open the doors of new possibilities the citizens of Wat Tatsunupi. Of course those were still days if not weeks away for the immediate concerns of fuel would need to be met first.

Sai and Wan had discussed with the Old Monk what airports would have the fuel needed for the continuous operation for the coming sling load mission. Fuel would need to be found first before they could even start looking for a motor pool where they could come across cargo containers.

The airports in and around Bangkok were first in the discussion, but each one was out of the question. No operation would ever be conducted in that area according to Wan. Like a good Warrant Sai had been, he trusted the wisdom of the former NCO. If Wan said that place was no good, Sai said it was no good.

The airports of Bangkok had been ravaged during the initial outbreak; thousands, if not millions, ran to the airports praying that some plane take them away from the chaos. Now as they talked, the dead stumbled, shuffled, and moaned as they walked the flight line. The once-bright terminals of Suvarnbhumi Airport were now hallowed tombs. All the windows had been shattered, glass covered the once-polished floor, and at the Burger King at the international terminal, a Thai man in a Burger King outfit stared at his comrades as they walked back and forth in the dining area as if they were still open. Burger King Man watched a man pulling his rolling suitcase; instead of rolling on wheels, he dragged it as the wheels looked up at the ceiling helplessly. Burger King Man began to touch the register, searching for something, when his clumsy swollen dead fingers accidentally opened the cashier drawer. All sorts of money was in the drawer, green, pink, blue, all types of notes from all walks of life. The man grabbed the money and put it on the counter in front of him, where a boy looked at him with a burger king crown on his head, drool coming out of his mouth as his eyes stared at the money.

Nak Bin Bang became the airport of choice; it was just a short distance north of Lop Buri and big enough to have what the Blackhawk needed. It was big, but due to its vicinity near Lop Buri and Bangkok, the members of the coming mission hoped not too many refugees had fled to its location. Most fleeing refugees probably got stuck in Lop Buri or had fled to the safety of the Air Force base; their misfortunes were perhaps the Wat's best hope for salvation if they did not flee to Nak Bin Bang.

Nak Bin Bang being just a little bigger than a small private airfield had a small terminal for commercial airlines. The commercial airlines were small and had provided services to Bangkok, Bang Sean and Chang Noy. The flight line according to the Old Monk contained a few turboprop planes, private jets, and of course many small fix wing aircraft.

Fuel trucks were the target for this operation, get the trucks, two big ones full of fuel if they could, take them south, cross the bridge where the dead decided to reenact nature and become Niagara Falls during their river adventure and head home.

The plan would put Wan and David back in the hot seats since they would be the in each vehicle supporting drivers as Sai flew over with the Hawk with Toshiro and Chit manning the guns providing recon and cover fire when needed.

Sai assured the community that this was the best option. They needed the walls and in order to accomplish this they would need fuel. The demand by the Hawk for fuel would double due to the loads it would be expected to carry in order to build the walls. So fuel would be the key to sustain the operation and with that said the town meeting was over. Most were in favor of Sai's plan with a few still left arguing their point across to the Old Monk.

One of the men who had just entered the community of course was the opposition to the plan; he was one of the new comers that had trickled in after the last operation. His name was Ren Pi.

Ren Pi was a large man, bigger than Sai and Wan, about the same size as Toshiro. The man had arrived at the Wat covered in blood, which was not from the dead. The half Chinese man claimed came the blood had come from his wife when confronted by Sai.

From what Sai could tell the man was a coward and a criminal. He probably prefer safety in numbers, a typical gangster but a living man none the less. He was against the helicopter, against the fuel run and against the barricade. He just wanted to hunker down, avoid contact with the outside world and hide.

Sai saw the man as a possible threat to the peace, but being in the community they had rules and all were welcomed to join them even if they were assholes.

****

The next two days were thankfully slow, nothing much other than the occasional moan from outside. The motorboat Ta and Stephen had used days earlier had worked well, several hundred zombies that had come with the arrival of the helicopter were now moving north along the river still, searching for a phantom boat.

With the dead not banging on the doors of the Wat, life went on as the miniature army prepared to move out. Two more volunteers had entered the mini Army, now boosting the numbers to an all time high of nine.

The two men were brothers from the new refugees, both in their twenties. Eck and Arm Sornphan. Eck had been the leader of the group of refugees that arrived from the river; he'd lost his wife and daughter during the outbreak but managed to find Arm and his little boy fending off an attack from his neighbor. The two managed to take a small group of survivors and catch the river in which they would later meet Sai and his group.

Arm was eager to repay Sai, and with his brother's help the two volunteered to ride or drive with Wan and David.

Over the few days after the last mission Yoon and Sai had grown closer. When not training or carrying out other task the Wat required Sai would fine time for her. The old women gossiped as the two love birds spent their free time together while the old ladies listened in on their conversations. They discussed their future together and what may come in the future knowing full well that life in a dead world had made every choice a hard one. Should innocent life be brought into a world where it would fight every day of its life for survival?

As the lovebirds carried on, Wien and Noi managed the daily bumps and bruises in the new makeshift doctor's office following Pakatip's lead. Most of their patients were children who had ran around and scratched a knee. Of course they read about more of the medical field from some books that Sai had brought back from Big C. They learned how to stitch up wounds, dress up bullet wounds, sunken chest wounds, put a splint on a leg, mend broken bones and so forth. The books had given the two girls something to keep their mind occupied as time went by.

Ta had finally broken ground with Noi; he was a lovesick puppy in which he received a lot of flak from Toshiro and Sai who found his constant obsession with Noi quite entertaining. Watching, the two men saw how the girl just wagged her tail knowing full well of Ta's affection to her.

Tran was already busy forming sketches and making a list of materials they would need to begin to build the ramparts. The containers were a temporary construct and he laid out plans to engulf a large portion of the jungle surrounding the Wat. With the containers and the area secure his team of builders would then go out and begin construction. They would cut the jungle down and use the lumber for the walls. His vision for the end result would be to build several square ramparts surrounding the Wat. Each enclosed from the other in case the dead broke through in one the other sections so that they not be affected. He planned for farmlands, new settlements, and was already in the process of figuring out how to enclose a portion of the river with walls and underwater fences that would allow fish in and keep the dead out. In his mind, his fortress would engulf both sides of the river and escape tunnels leading out into the jungle near the river where he could set up a mini fortress with several boats in case of emergency. He smiled as he dreamed of the future city he would build.

Chapter 16: *Convoy*

As with the other missions, the community had come together to watch the soldiers leave once more. The morning sun was out, the sky was scattered with a small chance of afternoon showers from what Sai could tell with his crystal ball, but other then that it was clear blue 22. Humidity levels were high as always, drenching the crowd with sweat; the heat would be something he would need to worry about later on the sling missions that were sure to come due to power issues.

Sai moved counter-clockwise around the aircraft doing his final walk around, looking for any loose latches that needed to be secure, the last thing he wanted was for the engine cowling to open in flight and strike one of the rotors. He scanned every inch for anything he missed, for the smallest problem could build up later to something more. He walked around looking at his green checklist, triple tapping that he had indeed covered every area just to be sure. Unlike the wars he had been in, if he crashed now it would not be a few rogue terrorists out looking for his ass. It would be a full army of over a million dead people that he would need to evade.

Today however, unlike the last mission, it would not be a multi-day operation, which was much to everyone's relief. It was predicted to last roughly four hours depending on road conditions for the returning trucks. The drive was not that far but potential traffic hazards could come into play on the return trip and with the dead roaming the land the word hazards was an understatement.

The flight would only last thirty minutes to the airport. There under hostile attack it was believed it would take roughly thirty minutes at most to refuel the Hawk and steal two fuel trucks with three hours estimated for their return trip home. The tricky part would be to get back into the Wat with the vehicles at the end of the mission. The dead were not going to let them waltz right in without helping themselves come in as well.

Up in Lop Buri while Sai finished his walk around, George and Dario sat on the top of the Big C roof waiting in two beach chairs, next to them were two young Thai women they had rescued two days earlier. The duo knew what Sai was up to due to their radio and they were now waiting outside to watch the show from their vantage point. Sai would fly over in a quarter of an hour and the two old men would be waiting to offer any dead reckoning and undead reports to the convoy when they passed the outskirts of Lop Buri heading back south. Mostly the old men just wanted some hardcore entertainment as they sipped on their martinis waiting for the fireworks to begin.

Fun as it was the two men were still ready to help at a moments notice. Driving out of the garage with their ATVs they had liberated earlier from a sports store if the occasion did arise. The old bastards had been rampaging up and down Lop Buri on the ATVs getting the essentials, which was mostly booze and of course any survivors they had come across. They were old tough bastards and either insane or extremely brave for the ATVs offered no protection from the dead other than speed.

At Wat Tatsunupi Ta would be staying behind once again with Stephen. The two of them would act as a decoy as they sped their boat up river to draw the dead away from the convoy. Sai would do the same to the south using his helicopter, hovering just above the treetops. With the dead moving northeast and south, they hoped that the convoy could break through the dead lines and outrun the mob long enough for them to enter the Wat and close the gate.

It was time now as Sai entered the cockpit of the Hawk taking the right seat. He smiled at Yoon as she walked up to him where he leaned over to her.

Yoon gave Sai a kiss and rubbed the back of his head looking into his eyes.

"Don't worry Yoon." Sai kissed her back smiling.

"Be careful Sai." Yoon smiled as she drew away watching Sai put his helmet on as Chit entered the Hawk through the crew chief window behind Sai.

Wien walked up to Sai with LuLu in her arms and gave Sai a drawing that LuLu had made for him. It was of the Hawk with Sai in the front with stick figures of Yoon, Wien and LuLu holding hands and Ta in the back with a stick gun. All the faces of the stick family smiled at Sai causing Sai to smile.

"Thank you LuLu," Sai said as he leaned over and kissed her on the cheek.

"Good Luck Sai," Wien said.

"Hey girls, maybe someday I'll take you flying," he said in Thai to the girls in their surprise. It had only been a few weeks but Sai was quickly picking up the language.

The girls backed away from the aircraft as Sai closed the door and put the picture over the dashboard so it would slide itself down to wedge itself between the windscreen and the console with the drawing facing outboard.

The crowd began to back up as Ta and Stephen pushed them back to a safe distance when the APU was turned on. The high pitch mini engine howled causing the crowd to cover their ears yet still they continued to watch. Toshiro was standing at the nose of the aircraft and signaled Sai that engine one was clear to start with a thumbs up. He had taken the lost hard of his sister but still he insisted on being on the mission. He needed purpose.

In response to Toshiro's signal Sai ignited the number one engine and the blades slowly began to turn. Toshiro thumbed up the second engine and Sai responded by igniting it as well. The blades began to pick up speed causing the rotor wash to send debris through out the Wat.

Beyond the gates the dead grew wild as they charged the walls of Wat Tatsunupi. Hundreds of them responded immediately and charged towards the walls of the fortress desperate to find the source of the sound.

Sai continued with the checklist and finally had both PCLs to fly, all was set and the mission could begin. He turned to his crew and began to speak.

In the cockpit Yoon could see Sai talking into his mic to the crew and passengers and before he pulled pitch he looked over to her sending her a smile of reassurance as he nodded his head.

Sai pulled up on the collective and the main landing gear became light as the struts extended and then inch by inch the aircraft began to rise as Sai did his best to avoid tangling up the rotor system into one of the surrounding buildings. The tail wheel was next off the ground, as the entire aircraft began to take off straight up into the air.

Chit and Toshiro hung out the crew chief windows clearing the bird and when both men told Sai he was clear, Sai pushed forward on the cyclic and the speed of the bird began to rise. Once over sixty knots, Sai banked towards the river and began to head north.

The dead followed.

****

All the seats except for the two crew chief seats had been removed in case they had the opportunity load the aircraft with equipment that could be useful.

Sitting in the Hawk on their butts, Wan held his rifle muzzle down and explained to the others to do the same to avoid shooting the transmission or possibly the engine if there was an accidental discharge. The men were quiet, each one of them looking out the cargo door windows at the jungle below.

The dead were everywhere, as if a massive exodus from Bangkok had occurred. They were probably just searching for food but the sight of these herds or swarms were terrifying. With those numbers there was no way of waging a war of attrition against them.

Continuing on the Hawk was deafening and if it were not for Toshiro bringing earplugs those without headsets would have all had their hearing severely damaged.

After five minutes of flight the passengers had fallen to sleep, it was like a football game was about to begin. Something that all high school jocks once felt, a sense of peace, rest, but in twenty-five minutes the kick off would begin and they were the receiving team. One chance to make it to the touchdown, they were 4th and goal once they reached their stadium/airport it was game time.

Sai had looked back and then isolated the sleeping passengers on the communication system and began to talk to his crew.

"Toshiro, pax asleep?" Sai asked already knowing the answer.

"Yup, those bums," Toshiro responded before mumbling in Japanese.

"Gents, when we get there, we are going to land at the fuel pits. If the area is clear, I need you and Chit to hook us up for hot fuel. Chit, then start up the generator, which should be near the pumps so Toshiro can top us off.

"Try not to get bit kid," Toshiro stared at Chit smiling looking over his shoulder to see Chit's response. A little dark humor never hurts.

"Sai, think we should take the generator?" Chit asked looking to the back of Sai's helmet.

"Sounds good, if you get the chance just load it up, use a cargo strap on it though, don't need that moving around back there punching holes into the bird." Sai responded.

"Check this out," Chit said, as he looked out at the bridge the convoy would need to cross. Debris wise it was relatively clear, only a few cars, but several hundred zombies were on it walking east and then north after the helicopter.

"Probably use the Hawk as a decoy there, let them chase us a bit and then the convoy could move through, should not be a problem gents. Most of the roads don't have traffic in this area, so as long as the convoy doesn't stop we should be back in time for Monday night football."

"Manchester United," Toshiro and Chit said as they thought of the good old days.

"What the fuck? Not soccer, I'm talking real football, geez don't make me nose this bird over because you want to talk about twinkle toe sports." Sai laughed into the mic, the American inside him emerging.

The Hawk passed the burnt ruins of a Wat, smoke no longer rose, but the dead reached up and screamed at the helicopter as it passed by.

Sitting on the roof at Lop Buri the thumps of the blades pounding the air into submission could be heard on the horizon. Still smoking, a pair of binoculars was presented by the two Thai women to George and Dario.

George looked through his binoculars and used the hand mic to talk into the radio.

"Red 5, we got you coming over the horizon now."

"Hey, good to hear from you pervs. How are things with your new lady friends?" Sai joked.

"Fine and dandy I feel like Hugh Hefner," George replied as his main squeeze served him another martini.

"George, it's Toshiro! Find me a young Japanese woman," Toshiro said in a demanding voice.

"No problem, Tojo. I'll see what I can do. But, seriously, I've always been one for some Godzilla action myself."

"Don't make me go all Tora Tora Tora on you old Man."

"Don't you worry, Tojo. I'll keep an eye out. You guys just be careful today. Down below, I say we have roughly a thousand or more zipper heads running around so I'd steer away from here if I were you."

"Roger that George," Sai responded as he looked over towards Big C.

George watched as the bird traveled along the river a few miles away and headed north.

"Boys, remember if something happens don't be afraid to call us," George said.

"Thanks George; we'll be back in contact on the way back." Sai said.

"And Red 5, may the force be with you, always." George replied as his woman sat on his lap and began to kiss him.

****

It was five minutes out from the LZ, the crew grew quiet, no more jokes, nothing but business. The dead at the airport looked up at the sky looking for the source of the noise, but Sai was now Nap of the Earth or NOE. His landing gear was just feet above the canopy of the jungle, hoping the dead would not see the bird and come rushing to his location.

"Wake the pax," Toshiro ordered Chit.

Chit strapped into his monkey harness moved out of his seat to shake Wan's leg.

Wan woke to see Chit kneeling before him with his hand and all five digits out.

"Five minutes!" Chit shouted.

Wan nodded his head and began to wake up his team.

Wan grimaced as he said a prayer holding onto the Takrood around his neck. He thought back to when he brief his team before the mission. Sai would drop them off next to the fuel trucks if there were any. Next they would make sure each truck was topped off with JP-8. If not they would head to the fuel pits and refuel them. All the while they would need to cover their asses and the Hawk crew as they refueled. Then when the Hawk was airborne they would head out the gate and south using the Old Monk's map as a guide.

If one of the trucks were to be below what was expected, Sai would abort the refuel and draw the dead away giving the trucks in theory time to take the load.

Scenarios began to race through Wan's mind when the aircraft banked noticeably to the left, a signal that they were here.

****

"Thirty seconds!" Wan shouted as he took out his earplugs and slid next to the door.

They felt the sudden deceleration as Sai nosed up the helicopter and lowered the collective. Then they began to feel a sinking sensation as the Blackhawk lost altitude rapidly like an elevator and the ground could be seen rising up from the cabin windows with waves of tall glass moving like a green ocean.

First the tail wheel hit, then the main landing gear and Chit threw open the cabin doors as Toshiro opened up with his weapon from the opposite side of the aircraft, sending rounds into a few zombies.

"GO! GO! GO!" Wan shouted as the convoy crew disembarked from the aircraft.

Wan was first out and headed straight for the first truck he saw just beyond the grass, ten feet outside of the rotor disc. The vehicle was a full size sixteen-wheeler type truck with plenty of fuel waiting to be taken.

Wan scanned the area and then went to the fuel gauge of the tank behind the cabin of the truck It was topped off with the JP 8. He turned around and signaled Eck to get in and start her up as Sai pulled pitch to reposition over Wan as he moved towards the fuel pits. In the back of the aircraft Toshiro fired more rounds towards the wood line from the crew chief window.

Wan saw what was coming as he followed where Toshiro's tracers were flying, a few dead targets but nothing he and his team couldn't handle.

David made it to the other truck, which was half the size of Wan's but his fuel was below what he wanted.

"We need fuel!" David shouted to Arm under the noise of gunfire and the helicopter.

Arm jumped into the passenger side to see Wan taking aim and fired a single round at a time towards the incoming dead. The driver's door opened scaring the crap out of Arm as David entered and began to hot wire the truck as Eck did the same on his Truck.

Eck's truck came to life and Wan withdrew to the safety of the cabin as Sai landed in the hot fuel pit to let Toshiro and Chit run into action.

David started the truck and blew the horn as a sign he wanted to top his off.

Eck blew the horn back twice showing that he was topped off and held position as Arm pulled gears into reverse, backing up the truck then back into gear as he moved forward towards the Blackhawk.

Toshiro waved off Sai and Sai immediately pulled pitch and came to hover allowing Eck to reposition to the fuel pit.

Sai repositioned his bird closest to where the dead were coming from as Eck moved his sixteen wheeler near the fuel pits to help cover David and Arm.

Wan stepped out to see the status, Toshiro already had the JP 8 fuel flowing into the tank in the back of the truck and then looked over to Sai who had quite a few zombies reaching up for him as he pulled power to blow them off their feet. The Blackhawk was over a hundred yards away with a crowd of the dead gathering below it as Sai used the bird as a decoy to keep them from swarming the fuel pits.

Sai looked down through the helicopter's chin bubble as he hovered to see the demons reaching for him. He then looked over to the fuel trucks. He hovered stationary ten feet over the ground as he continued to draw the dead away from the trucks.

"You're doing good Sai," Wan said into the radio as he looked over at him. "You got their full attention, only had a few stragglers to deal with over here so far." Wan looked down to his boot where a child's body now lay with no head. "Few more minutes, out."

The clocked ticked and ticked as Sai moved his aircraft towards the runway and to the far side of the airfield. Now he had gathered fifty plus zombies with many more coming towards his position. He was the undead Pied Piper as the rats came out to follow his undead parade, which was being led further away from the fuel pits.

"Sai, Chit's been bit!" Wan yelled over the radio.

"What!?" Sai asked.

"Fucker with no legs came through the grass!" Wan's voice paused a few gunshots could be heard through Sai's headset. "Trucks are full now we are going to move out!" Wan continued. "Sai get Chit out of here!" he shouted again, a few more gunshots fired.

"Roger, you guys get on a move I'll pick up Chit and Toshiro."

Sai nosed the aircraft over as the trucks moved away from the fuel pit at the same time. Then Sai slowed drastically flashing his landing light to get the two crew chief's attention, signaling them to get into the aircraft.

Toshiro carried Chit and tossed him into the open cabin before jumping in. On his back Toshiro looked over his left shoulder to see Sai looking over his shoulder at him.

"GO!" Toshiro shouted as he fired a few rounds from his rifle.

Sai nodded and pulled pitch and the two crew chiefs dropped back to the cabin floor hard as the sudden acceleration forced them down. Below them the dead were knocked off their feet when the rotor wash blasted them away.

"Sorry Sai!" Chit cried into his mic after strapping into his seat. "So sorry!" He continued as if he let down the team's coach.

"Don't you worry Chit, you're going to be alright, I'm taking you to Big C, just strap in and keep your leg below your heart, put a tourniquet on it, Toshiro help him out!"

Toshiro looked over behind his shoulder to see Chit crying in his seat, the kid was scared to death.

"Toshiro, get a tourniquet on him ASAP!" Sai said again as he looked over to Toshiro who was not disconnected from the headset yet."

Toshiro unbuckled and moved about the cabin to Chit who was losing his composure. He was just a kid, no older than Ta and panic was quickly setting in.

Toshiro had a sincere look of worry on his face, he pulled out the tourniquet and tied it tight knowing what Sai wanted to do to the boy when they arrived to Big C. Toshiro rubbed his beard and looked up to Chit and disconnected his headset and then connected his headset into Chit's ICS cord.

"Sai, we might have time, it's a small bite. I fixed up the tourniquet nice and good."

"George might be able to do this. They have plenty of supplies there. I don't think Wien and Noi are up for the task yet."

"Humph," Toshiro groaned.

"Hang on a sec I'm contacting Wan."

Toshiro turned his attention to the boy; Chit looked more innocent with each passing second.

"Damn," Toshiro said to himself as he struggled to maintain composure as the boy began to pass out from fear.

"Toshiro, I've contacted Wan, looks like the roads are not too bad for them, so we are taking Chit to George."

****

Wan watched above as Sai flew over his position while the trucks were leaving the airport and turning right onto the main road. He said a prayer to himself as he continued to watch the UH-60 fly over trees to his left and disappear from view. His attention then turned onto the road as the massive 16-wheeler leaned heavily to one side before straightening out again after sending a few dead airport security guards flying to the sides of the road.

"Pye pye!" Wan shouted when he turned his attention to a man who was hanging on to his door. He pulled out his sidearm and fired once, the thing flew off the truck into a ditch of muddy water and Wan turned his attention back to the road ahead of him, continuing to ride shotgun for Eck.

The convoy pushed forward gaining speed, swerving in and out of abandoned vehicles.

"Watch it, remember we've got fuel!?" Wan shook his head as Eck scratched the side of another car sending sparks and debris into the air and the fresh smell of smoke into the cabins.

"Calm down, calm down, they can't catch us so take your time, figure this shit out, don't let panic take hold. Breath." Wan ordered Eck as he fired another round out his window.

"Hitch Hiker," Wan said before inspecting the magazine of the rifle on his lap. He then pulled out the radio and switched it to 47.60 in the green glowing box.

"David, how you doing back there?" Wan asked as he looked at the road ahead.

"Not bad, why you slow down?" David replied as he concentrated on the road.

"Better not to rush things David, we rush, we get into an accident, we all die. Just think about the movies, everyone who panics dies so just don't fucking panic."

"Wan, you sure about this, movies? You taking your god damn cue from a movie? There are fucking zombies attacking us."

"Trust me, I was dreaming on the bird and that is what I saw."

"Dreams now? You okay?" David asked as a zombie flew off the driver side of Wan's truck ahead of him.

"Don't worry we'll move fast enough where they can't catch us just not too fast where we are going to kill ourselves, we are rolling bombs of jet fuel, remember that."

"Where did Sai take Chit?" Eck asked on the radio.

"To Big C," Wan said with his tone changing. "Sai's going to have George cut the leg, maybe that will save Chit." Wan paused. "Let's concentrate on the mission now." The radio became quiet once more.

The convoy moved on and began to head south and as they rounded a bend Wan thought about Chit.

****

"Dario hurry up. They are coming!" George shouted from the roof into the stairwell that led down into the store.

Two women were helping Dario in the medical section of BIG C, grabbing bandages, towels, and antibiotics.

Dario cleared a table in the furniture section as the women brought the supplies needed and then they heard the helicopter landing on the roof.

Toshiro carried Chit off the bird and took him to George who was waiting with a wheelchair and a syringe in hand.

"Put him down, Tojo. We'll take care of him from here on. Go, go, don't worry, Tojo!" George shouted over the Blackhawk's engines and blades as he stuck Chit with a dose of morphine. George rolled Chit into the building disappearing into the darkness. "George, please save him," Toshiro said to himself, as a tear rolled down his cheek followed by a Samurai anger as he turned around and entered the Hawk.

The Hawk took off back towards Wan's direction as a chorus of dead hands reached up from the ruined streets below.

"Don't worry Toshiro, those two old farts will save him," Sai said into the mic as he looked at his fuel gauge. The Chiclets now read twelve hundred pounds.

"We're going to need gas Toshiro," Sai said as he lowered the nose and headed north. The dead watched from the shadows of the streets.

****

"Yes, yes I know," George said to one of the women before he placed two more tourniquets on Chit's leg, triple tapping to make sure that not much blood was lost when they cut the leg.

Dario was already wearing sterile gloves and had a hacksaw in hand when George put a little blue mask over his mouth like the others in the room.

"Well." George looked at Dario.

"Well what?" Dario stared at his patient.

"Going to do it?" George asked.

"Sorry, had one of those moments, lets get this over with."

George held down Chit's shoulders while the two girls held both legs and two more men held the torso.

Dario put the cold saw to Chit's naked flesh causing the hair on his bleeding leg to shoot straight up.

"Here we go," Dario said and he began to cut.

Chit woke from his drugged induced slumber and began to scream in pain as the assistants held him down while Dario continued to cut.

The flesh was cut down quickly and then the sound of wood being sawed could be heard as the teeth of the blade met the bone.

The saw's teeth moved in a rocking motion sometimes stopping when one of the teeth of the blade caught onto the bone. This would cause Dario to use more muscle to move it causing the blade to jerk in the flesh of his leg.

Each thrust pierced Chit's mind as Dario continued his gruesome task. The boy screamed as the mad scientist cut through the bone. His eyes went wild each spinning a different way as his mind began to shut down and finally like a switch, his brain turned off and his body went limp. Chit was lost in a deep unconsciousness and Dario continued to saw.

"It's going to be alright." George whispered as he held a hand on the boy's forehead with the sound of wood being cut filling the room.

****

"Wan, I think we got there in time, George and Dario were ready. I'm going to break off now and head back to the fuel pits. We should be in FM range, be back in thirty, good luck." Sai banked the aircraft to the right and headed north leaving the convoy in Wan's hands.

Toshiro's gruff voice spoke up as Sai looked out his window to the convoy. "I think the generator is still running, we left pretty fast, and I am sure most of those low life sons of bitches went south after the convoy. Once we touchdown I'll jump out and hook up the bird to the pump and if I can I'll load up the generator. Just be sure to cover me." His voice had become monotone.

A few minutes later, Sai said: "We're coming up on it now; I've got your back. Toshiro, just be ready to run."

The Blackhawk began to decelerate and Toshiro unbuckled then opened his crew window revealing a few left over zombies roaming the airport, most had gone after the convoy and were at least two to three miles to the south by now.

Toshiro unloaded a few rounds into the stragglers while Sai pulled the Blackhawk to a hover, turning the nose of the aircraft to the right and bringing the tail to the left before touching down onto the fuel pit.

Like Toshiro had said, the generator was still running and he quickly hooked up the hose to the Hawk.

Sai looked at the fuel gauge and saw the chiclet lights rising after Toshiro started the pump.

"We're taking fuel," Sai said into the mic to Toshiro who had a twenty-foot ICS cord connected to his mic.

"Sai we got incoming. At your three o'clock."

Sai opened he cockpit door, pulled out his rifle and took aim.

"I'll wait till they get a little closer before dropping them, watch your six Toshiro."

Toshiro pulled Tran's sword out of its sheath and put his rifle back fearing any stray shots near the fuel pumps could ignite and kill everyone.

Pop, Pop, Pop, Toshiro heard under the rotor blades as Sai fired from the other side of the aircraft. Toshiro was at his most vulnerable, there was only so much Sai could do from his seat.

Sai took aim with the helicopter vibrating the hell out of the cockpit. He narrowed his eyes as his firing sight bounced and then fired, instantly an old lady's head tipped back as a round exited the back of her skull. Behind her several more were moving towards the aircraft and at the fence line about a quarter a mile away a mob was forming. He bit his tongue and did not relay the shit that was about to fall upon them but instead took aim and fired again.

"Eighteen hundred, just a little more." Toshiro heard Sai's voice over the headset in his helmet followed by another burst of fire. "Toshiro, think we can grab that generator?" Sai asked. "Nineteen hundred pounds." There was another burst of fire.

Toshiro looked over at the generator, it probably was around three or four hundred pounds not realizing before how heavy the iron machine was.

"Sai, we're going to have to ditch it."

"No prob. Don't worry about it. Twenty-one hundred pounds. LOOK OUT BEHIND YOU!" Sai shouted, as he saw a woman rush Toshiro from the cabin door windows on his left.

Sai saw a flash of steel and then blood sprayed the window.

"Toshiro, you okay?" Sai shouted. "Toshiro!"

"Sai, my helmet came off."

"You okay?"

"Yeah, they need to be faster than that to get me."

"Twenty-four hundred, twenty-four ten. We're good now. Get in the fucking bird!" Sai said, as he looked at his fuel gauge and then back to a mob of dead creatures charging at full sprint less than two hundred yards away.

Toshiro unhooked the hose and turned the generator off before he got back into the aircraft.

"Good to go, Sai. Let's go."

With that, Sai pulled pitch and the aircraft was off again while Toshiro took his seat and looked out the window. A thousand dead men, women, and children waved at him as they left the airport. He had not realized how many of them were actually out there.

****

"Roger, Sai, we'll see you in a few." Wan looked up to see the Blackhawk fly over the convoy heading south to scout the bridge ahead.

Toshiro stuck his body out of the crew window and offered his version of improving morale. He extended his finger from the crew chief window at the convoy making a drunken face and sticking out his tongue. He of course got several fingers in return as the convoy crew laughed.

The Blackhawk flew down the road and within a few minutes arrived at the bridge.

"Toshiro, don't waste any rounds I've got an idea." Sai slowed the helicopter and came to a hover over the bridge.

Several hundred zombies stormed the bridge underneath the helicopter each reaching for the main landing gear of the hovering aircraft, which was only a few feet out of reach.

"Sai, what are you doing?" Toshiro asked before he coughed up some phlegm and spat it up on a dead man's face.

"Watch this, zombie kill of the week." Sai smirked trying to keep his mind off of Chit.

Sai hovered the bird over the side of the bridge until he was ten feet to the side of it.

Like a stampeding herd, the dead began to jump from the bridge at the helicopter, falling to their permanent deaths below.

Hundreds at a time were jumping as if they could fly through the air only to come crashing down into the water below. A small hill began to emerge from the river below. Broken bodies wiggled as their brethren continued to fall from above.

"Holy shit Sai!" Toshiro said astonished by the mass suicide that was taking place in front of him.

"Cool huh?" Sai laughed.

"Holy shit."

The bodies continued to fall, so many of them that they were forming a dam of corpses in the middle of the river.

Wan was closing in on their position and saw the last of the dead plummet to their deaths below.

Sai had given the all clear for the convoy to cross; only a few creatures remained. Standing perfectly straight, they stared at the helicopter as if their dead brains were trying to figure out how to reach the Blackhawk.

"Toshiro, check them out."

Close to twenty of them remained on the bridge. They stared at Sai with evil eyes studying him proving that there were some that possessed higher levels of intelligence.

"Sai, should I shoot them?"

"No, the bodies will make it hard on the convoy passing the bridge, let me lead them off the bridge first."

Sai landed the bird off to the side of the bridge on the eastern shore. Upon landing, the dead saw their opportunity to reach the Blackhawk and began a mad dash to the bird. Within fifty feet after they had left the bridge, Sai took the bird back up to a hover and began to move farther from the bridge leading these smart creatures away as the convoy snuck in behind them and over the bridge.

The crossing went smooth, a few leftovers that the convoy didn't even bothered with. A few of the walking corpses reached out but the speed of the convoy kept them from getting any real grip.

In one hour the convoy would be at the gates and the hard part of getting the trucks in without the dead coming in would come into play.

****

Wan checked the fuel of his truck, half a tank. "David how much gas you got?"

"Got a quarter left, we'll be on fumes by the time we get back."

"We're doing well. We've just driven through undead country, should not be a problem as long as we don't have to many obstacles." Wan fired at another hitchhiker.

David was not pleased the dead were still sprinting after them; their persistence was troubling.

The dead howled like rabid dogs and did not give up even as the convoy moved out of view. They had one single focus on their minds, food.

As the convoy continued south on the narrow road a car pulled up in front of them from a side street. Dust and rocks flew into the air as the vehicle fished tail in front of the convoy barely missing the lead vehicle as it headed in the opposite direction. The vehicles swerved drastically, threatening the tanker to overturn; as they narrowly passed, Wan got a glimpse of who was inside.

It was a man and woman armed to the teeth with two kids in the backseat. The man did a 180-degree J-turn behind the second truck and the convoy slowed as Wan decided what to do with them. The civilian vehicle began to follow the two trucks as David talked to Wan on the radio and continued to move south.

"They're just following us. Wat do you think we should do?" David asked.

"As soon as we are cleared of immediate danger, stop, run back there, and tell them where we are headed."

"Fuck that. You've seen how they run?" David fired back.

Wan bit his tongue. "You're right David" David was taken aback by Wan's unexpected response.

"Wan, don't worry about the car. I got them in view, as soon as there is a clearing I'll cut them off and get them on board." Sai said on the mic since he had been monitoring the whole conversation. The vehicle appeared under the jungle canopy behind the convoy but with the dense jungle below Sai would need to wait till they neared a rice paddy.

"Sorry, Wan, about the fuck that crap," David said.

"Don't worry about it. If something sounds stupid and it is stupid, then it's best to question it. You're a good soldier, David," Wan continued, as the group pulled into farmland again and out of the jungle canopy while Sai watched over from above.

Sai took the Hawk down off the deck at ten feet above ground level and paralleled the car. The occupants looked over to the bird. Toshiro began signaling them to come to the bird when they stopped.

Sai made a quick landing into a rice paddy, the tires sinking a little into the mud not too far from the road.

The convoy moved on as Toshiro jumped out of the helicopter and ran to the road with his rifle toward the car.

The car stopped and the passengers exited revealing an infant in a car seat who had been hidden from view.

The dead began to pour out of the jungle behind them as the couple sprinted to the rice paddy and began to slosh their way to the Blackhawk.

The dad turned around and opened fire as the wife carrying the car seat moved to the Hawk following the two kids who were ahead of her.

Toshiro ran out to the family to help them get to the bird while the dad covered their rear. Toshiro grabbed the smallest child with one arm and the other with the other arm after he had slung his rifle on his back.

Toshiro did a 180 and raced through the paddy, as Sai opened his cockpit door and began firing over their heads.

The cargo door opened and Toshiro threw the two kids in and helped the woman with the infant in; as he turned around, he saw the husband tackled in the mud by two of the dead creatures.

Toshiro closed the door after he entered the cabin and held the wife back as Sai pulled pitch. The wife fought and fought trying to reach for her husband but Toshiro's mighty hands held her down as the kids cried watching their dad being torn to pieces as more of the dead fell upon him.

"We got them. Minus the father," Sai said on the radio. "It could have been messy if they went through the gate with the convoy." He was trying to justify his actions.

"I know. It was the best call Sai we can't afford to have those gates open any longer than necessary," Wan replied.

"Sai, Sai, this is Ta, how far are you."

"Convoy is about thirty minutes, get that boat ready, and tell Yoon we have a woman, two children and an infant in need of medical attention. I'll be dropping them off in ten minutes."

"Roger, Sai."

Sai pushed passed the convoy scouting what he could see from the air; he found the sunflower field, the dead elephants, and the village he had first come across after losing Num, but no major road obstructions that would delay the convoy.

The Wat came into view and Sai began the final, descending slowly into the Wat, where Yoon and Wien waited with the other citizens.

The gate was already lined with men and as he turned 180 degrees over the river, where he saw Ta and Stephen starting the boat in the center of the river preparing for their part of the mission.

Sai brought in the bird while the rotor wash caused FOD to fly throughout the Wat and then in a matter of seconds the wheels touched down.

The cargo door opened and a mud-covered Toshiro stepped out and helped the woman and her children down, giving the baby carrier to Wien who stood behind her cousin.

With that done and everyone cleared of the aircraft Sai brought the bird back up and this time slowly began to fly west then south, leading the dead around the Wat out of the way from the convoy. The dead began to follow south as Wan brought the trucks closer from the north.

"Wan, this is going to be tricky, I'll take them as far as I can, the ones following you will probably be hot on your ass, I recommend you pick up speed while Ta uses the foghorn to draw any others north."

"Roger, Sai, picking up speed."

Eck pressed on the accelerator and the KMPH began to rise as the dead behind began to fall farther and farther away.

The road was clear and now Wan could see Sai in front of him about a mile away. He was leading several hundred zombies south while Ta and Stephen led another group north along the river towards Wan's east in the marshlands and out of his way.

The men on the Wat could now see the dust from the convoy rising through the jungle as they took aim at the dead closest to the gate.

"Hold your fire!" Tran shouted down the line.

Around fifty creatures still stood near the gate, the only obstacle left between the convoy and the Wat – still a deadly number.

As the men on the wall held their aim they saw the trucks rolling down the dirt road to the Wat.

"FIRE!" Tran ordered.

The men began to take down the nearest zombies as Wan fired out his window at the mob now charging his vehicle from all directions.

"Push it!" Wan shouted as he became excited with battle.

Eck slammed the pedal to the metal and the zombies began to smash into the front of the monster truck, disintegrating on impact like bugs.

"Sai, we need you here."

"Roger, inbound. Toshiro kill anything that moves."

"It's about time."

Sai nosed the aircraft over at full power and sprinted to the convoy. He zipped over the heads of the Wat's defenders towards the convoy.

Sai flew in on the convoy in less than a minute as Toshiro opened fire near the truck, killing a few and maiming many so badly they could no longer move. His rounds broke legs, necks, ribs, and crushed skulls. The convoy watched as his tracers rained down from above as they approached within less than a football field's length of the gate.

The dead had turned their attention to the convoy leaving the gate unguarded. That is when Eck punched his truck through the mob. The first truck acted like an offensive lineman for the second smaller truck who was the running back. The gates were now fully opened with the dead occupied with the convoy too distracted to enter the Wat.

The dead were peppered with rounds from the men on the walls and the two vehicles began to pull away from the mob who were now pursuing. Many broken bodies were left in the convoy's wake.

When the first truck entered the Wat Sai's Blackhawk flew over to engage the pursuing mob. Holding hover, Sai was now acting as decoy as Toshiro had a field day with the dead below.

The second truck entered and a few of the dead sprinted towards the gate after losing interest in the Blackhawk. But the defenders greeted the dead, forming a wall of lead, as the gate was sealed shut. A hundred dead pounding hands began to beat on the wall.

The trucks engines went off and the soldiers disembarked in awe that they had actually pulled the mission off.

"Wan, I'm going to take this mob to the bridge up north then head to George's place. Tell Yoon I'll see her tomorrow, there are over a thousand dead fucks down here and I need to lead them away before they get smart and start climbing over themselves to storm our home."

"Roger Sai, I'll tell her, let us knows how Chit's doing, see you tomorrow."

The hands on the door slowly stopped pounding as they turned their attention to the helicopter that was slowly moving north.

Yoon watched from the wall as Sai headed out of sight.

****

Hours had gone by and Sai had killed several hundred at the bridge before heading to Big C. Toshiro now stunk like a pig, covered in the muddy waters of the rice paddy, forcing Sai to fly with the cargo doors open the rest of the way.

On the roof of Big C, George greeted them and said Chit was under constant watch and had been secured to a bed in case he turned. The operation or butchery job had been a success. They had stopped the bleeding by burning the leg wound to a crisp and kept him drugged so he would not awaken to open the wound.

Dario had dressed the wound in white bandages and the women cleaned the blood in the furniture section of the store, as if nothing had happened.

Sai and Toshiro sat beside their sleeping comrade and hoped for the best.

Outside, millions upon millions of dead roamed the streets aimlessly in every city in Asia as the sun began to set. They moaned into the night with the occasional scream of death adding to the musical composition as the starving began to scrounge for food in all the cities under the cover of darkness, most turning into meals on wheels.

Chapter 17: *Time*

The next morning, Sai awoke to see the nurses tending to Chit's leg. Chit had been in and out of consciousness throughout the night, the pain must have been unbearable, for even in his drug-induced sleep he moaned and cried.

The bandages had bled through and had become soggy with blood. Sai watched the boy rocking in the bed with a fever and the lack of air conditioning was not helping any. Sai pondered if he should just ease that boy's pain and send him off to the next world. *What would Chit want,* if only he'd ask Sai for this Sai would do it without hesitation because he hated to see people suffer.

Finally Sai could not take what he saw and left the room as the women tended to Chit undressing his bandage and putting a new one on.

Stepping out of the office room to a walkway with a panoramic view of the city George sat on his butt with a bottle of tequila in one hand and a shotgun in the other.

"Sai, what happens, happens, don't beat yourself over it." George said as he moved to his feet, every aching bone sounding off as he stood up.

George was a tall man, much like Toshiro, and reminded Sai of a Cuban Obi Wan Kenobi, except this Jedi was drunk off his ass or high most of the time.

The two began to walk as Sai looked out at the morning sun rising on the ruined city outside the window. The scene was dreary, no lights, no life, just a bluish gray light between the buildings as the orange rays dance above on the rooftops not daring to touch the hell in the streets below.

"He was too young, but I needed him," Sai told George, as he continued to stare out into the city streets, where hordes of the dead roamed.

"No one is too young or too old now days Sai. This war is about survival. Those who can't hack out a life will see their end and then come back as one of them. I fear this is just the beginning. Those zipper heads out there are a prelude to the hell to come. I fear something worse than these stiffs is on the horizon."

George's last sentence flew by Sai.

"I've seen so many orphans, seen so many die over these last few weeks, more than I have ever seen before." Sai shook his head almost as if he was talking to himself.

Their footsteps began to echo as they walked down the stairwell from the offices to the main store.

"Yesterday, another family was destroyed, husband died protecting his family. Toshiro got the family on board but the man just stood there, knowing full well he would not see them again. I can't tell if this was my fault for picking them up. I hope, I really hope, we are doing the right thing. What if we would have just let them drive to the Wat? For god's sake, Chit lost his leg for fucking gas George. Gas for my stupid fucking helicopter."

"Sai, he lost his leg not for your helicopter, but for the people of Wat Tatsunupi. That fuel is essential to your survival. Without it, there would be no helicopter. Without the helicopter, you would not have a chance to build a barricade. No barricade, no farmland, and with no farmland, no food. From what I've seen," he said, putting a hand on Sai's shoulder, "you have done everything right, and I goddamn mean it, son. Before this is over, I guarantee you will lose more than a few more men, perhaps hundreds in the years to come. Now let me show you something."

The two moved into the department store and to the back where another office was set up.

In the office was the radio equipment where Dario was busy talking to the outside world and to his right a map with many tacks on it.

"The red tacks are the people who are running low on food and are basically trapped in high rises. No way to the roof, no way to the ground. Zombies in every level, yet with every raid of the vending machines, they manage to stay on the air even as their numbers dwindle. These poor bastards will slowly be turned into black tacks and, as you can see, most of our board is turning black. The yellow tacks are those caught in homes. With no access to a suitable landing area for your helicopter, they will be black soon as well. Now these blue ones, these blue ones are waiting for you. We have twenty-five of them around Lop Buri. Those favors you owe us, when you are done with the wall, please go get them. Sai, we've tried to reach those people by the sewer. That's how we found our lovely ladies, but we can't keep that up forever. We need your help."

"I see."

"Do this for Chit. Save these people when you are finished with that wall. When that wall is done, use that fuel to save more people."

****

The Old Monk discussed with Wan the best places to secure a container. As the morning sun rose, Toshiro showed David how to secure a container and rig it up for sling load operations.

Empty containers were preferred; they only needed to prevent the dead from entering, not taking incoming rounds from enemy troops. The less they weighed, the better; when the time came for the mission, they could only work a few hours during the day's heat. Heat would be a factor when it came to the amount of weight the Blackhawk could carry on the coming mission.

The group had also received word from Sai on Chit's status, he was in stable condition but in much pain, but pain was better than death.

Wat Tatsunupi waited and waited until the evening came and the familiar sound of Sai's Hawk grew in the horizon. Sai had left early that morning to scout the area and bring fresh bodies from Big C.

Yoon stood by the ramparts as Ta and Stephen manned the boat once again to drive the dead away.

This time Sai had a few more passengers, a work detail of men who volunteered to help Wat Tatsunupi build the ramparts. Some even left their families back at BIG C knowing full well the food situation at Wat Tatsunupi was being rationed, but if they could help Wat Tatsunupi to get up and running by producing food and become a solid fortress it would only benefit them in the end.

As the Blackhawk's rotor blades came to a stop, and the APU went off Yoon walked up to the cockpit and Sai opened the door to kiss her.

He flipped the battery switch off and unbuckled as the evening air swept across his sweaty face.

Toshiro was quickly filling up the Hawk for tomorrow Toshiro, David, Tran and Sai would head south to begin their fourth mission. Tran would ride shotgun with Sai in the cockpit and show Sai exactly where to put the containers. David would lie down by the hellhole in the cabin of the Hawk looking at Toshiro who actually volunteered to ride on top of the container loads after he hooked them up to the bird.

The plan would be to perform a limited slope on top of a container and drop Toshiro on top with the gear to hook up a container, and then he'd ride on top like a cowboy back to Wat Tatsunupi so he could show off to everyone. Doing his best to impress the ladies of course.

Once in position Sai would not drop the load like normal, instead he'd have Toshiro disconnect the load and hold on to the sling rope while he took him back to the Wat so he could ride climb in the cabin and repeat the process again.

****

The Wat had undergone some changes during the whole outings of the soldiers. Walls had been fortified and walkways along the rooftops had been constructed to allow guards of the Wat to have a clear view of the surrounding area.

The filtration system of the water pumps from the river had been altered; waterborne zombies were not the threat, but bacteria and other god-awful diseases they carried were. The rivers of the world were full of the dead and Wanchai knew he needed to find another way to get the water.

With Tran's experience building wells, the two set out two days earlier in digging right in the middle of the Wat. Several of the men dug around the clock for fresh water. It was Wanchai's idea that since the Wat was close to the river, the earth would be a natural filter. The mud would filter out all the unwanted germs and bacteria that those things could carry. Yet they still double tapped that filter and a pump was also set up in the well. Water was drawn to the surface into a filtration system once again and poured into a large boiling tank. Here, it was boiled until it was evaporated and went through a series of pipes to a collection tank that would collect the vapors and allow the steam cloud to rain down in the tank creating pure water for the Wat to drink.

The food stores were in the center of the Wat and handled logistically by Yoon and prepared by the older ladies three times a day. Yoon and Lek also managed the armory of new weapons that were being added from survivors and the raids done by the soldiers. Everyone was allowed arms, but to keep order and people like Ren Pi from going ape shit, many of the deadliest weapons were under lock and key. There had been talk of banning weapons in the compound by many after a fight had broken out between Ren Pi and a few others. But Sai and Wan argued that in this stage of the game they would need to hold onto them in case of an emergency came up. Still the soldiers maintained the heavy firepower which no one argued about for they were the ones who risked their lives on a daily basis for the good of the Wat, much to Ren's dislike.

Wien and Noi gave classes to the Wat on first aid and how to amputate limbs in the field. They had researched everything they could when they heard of what had happened to Chit. Even with Pakatip's help the trio would not have been able to do what George had done and took the initiative to learn how. It was a risky operation no matter what but the risk was necessary to save a life.

Klauy had lost twenty plus pounds and was constantly bugging Yoon for new clothes in exchange for his old ones. The Logistic Warehouse was always able to supplement what he needed; still, there was more that should be available to the Wat's residents; further missions would be required if the situation permitted.

Sai had been sporting Mexican gangster look over the last few days without a razor and was now turning into a bandito look-alike while others in the Wat grew beards. Razors, shaving cream were welcomed when Sai returned from his last trip from Big C.

There was also cause for celebration amongst the group for Wanchai and Lek were now expecting a baby. Wanchai had turned into a worry wart very fast over the news Lek had broken that evening, but the Wat assured him everything would be alright for the ramparts would go up, the land cleared and farmland would come. Life would be less harsh in the coming months.

As the night rolled in, everyone retired to their homes Wan stood troubled watching the dead beyond the walls. He was troubled about what had happened to Noi several weeks ago; it would not be long until someone like Ren's type of people came around causing trouble. Ren was the first of the bandit types, and Wan knew someday the Wat would need to deal with them.

****

That night Wien when awoke from a nightmare, she looked around the room to see Sai and Yoon sound asleep, her brother and LuLu knocked out beside her. It was a hot night and Wien decided a splash of water from the well might cool her off a bit.

She had walked to the well and splashed some water on her face. It was a refreshing feeling, which felt very good indeed. Water dripped from the side of her face and she could see the guard's performing their duties on the wall. Their silhouettes walking against the pitch black background.

The nighttime was different for Wien, the dead were out there but like everything else they seemed to quiet down at night. The insects however sang in the jungles. All types of little bugs called out for mates in the darkness.

That is when a voice startled her.

"Wien."

She turned around to see Ren Pi standing behind her.

The man gave a wicked smile.

Wien stepped back as he stepped forward.

"You know little girls shouldn't wander out here all alone, the big bad wolf could be out here."

Wien just looked at the giant man.

"Why don't you come to my place tonight, I'll take real good care of you."

"No, and if you come any closer I'll scream."

She turned around and ran back to her home leaving Ren Pi alone at the well.

Entering the room she found Sai awake waiting for her.

"What's wrong?" he asked, stepping closer to her, aware that she had been frightened.

She ran to Sai and hugged him. "It's nothing."

Sai knew instantly something was wrong. "What happened?"

She looked up at him. "Ren Pi, he scares me."

"What is it?" Yoon had awakened to see her cousin hugging Sai.

"It's Ren," he said before forcing Wien to release her hug.

Sai grabbed his rifle and stormed out the door waking Ta in the process.

"What's wrong?" Ta asked, his eyes shooting wide open afraid the dead may have infiltrated the walls.

"Ta, go get Toshiro and Wan, Sai's going after Ren Pi," Yoon ordered her cousin.

Ta just looked at her in a confused manner.

"Go!" she shouted, then turned her attention towards her cousin. "Now what happened?"

Sai walked through the darkness and saw who he was looking for still by the well. He was lying on his back smoking a cigarette he had stolen from some poor bastard.

Ren Pi turned his head to see Sai coming. His eyes grew wide knowing full well what Sai wanted from him. He sat up and reached for a shovel that was lying at the base of the well.

"Fucking bitch. I was just fucking with her."

"Fuck you!" Sai charged and butt stroked the man before he could swing the shovel.

"Sai!" Wan began to shout as he ran towards the commotion waking up half the Wat.

Sai proceeded to beat the giant man. He was like a wolverine attacking a bear. No fear at all.

Ren Pi managed to get a hit to Sai's gut before Sai pressed the handle bar into his throat. Sai was killing the man, crushing his throat when Wan and Toshiro pulled Sai off him.

Sai struggled with the two men as Ren Pi began to huddle at the base of the well's wall as if he was an innocent man.

"Wan we've got to get rid of this fucker." Sai struggled as Ren Pi ran back to his hooch.

"Calm down, calm down."

"I'm telling you this guy is bad news!"

The rest of the night Wan and Toshiro kept Sai from killing Ren Pi. Ren Pi had scared Wien but he had done nothing wrong. The man was a criminal and knew his limits; he was safe for now.

****

Far to the north, a blast exploded from the walls of a Wat much like Wat Tatsunupi. Men rushed the defenders of the Wat with two tanks that brought up the rear while a single APC leading the charge. The vehicle had stopped, rounds bouncing off the armor skin and then the doors opened from the rear. Pouring out of the APC the bandits began firing at the residents. The battle was quickly turning into a one way shooting range, the raiders shot everything that resisted and within minutes the battle was over. The only prisoners were women and children and under the gun of the raiders they were loaded up into cages that another APC pulled behind it like a medieval cart.

Beyond the burning wall two tanks stood waiting with a horde of zombies around them, behind them another APC with a cage full of male prisoners from another enclave were being used as live bait to keep the dead at bay.

The dead swamped the cage of the male prisoners as another cage full of women entered the Wat to help load up the fresh females and children that had been captured. In the cage was Noi's sister covered in bruises holding on to an older woman, her eyes wide with fear.

The number of the bandits had increased, former members of the Thai royal Army had been assimilated and now they had a compound to the west of the place they had just conquered.

In the compound to the west an enraged Than shouted at one of his messengers, asking if the raiding party had found his cousin. The man quivered before telling him the report and the news was not good. His cousin was still missing.

Enraged, Than proceeded to beat the man with a baseball bat until he left a bloody lump on the floor of his briefing room. Time was all that Wat Tatsunupi had left, for Than and his rogue group of bandits would find them eventually.

Chapter 18: *To Sling a Zoo*

Like several times before, the Wat's residents came out in force to wish the crew good luck. Tran's children smiled as Liu waved goodbye to her husband, watching him strap into his seat in the cockpit. On Sai's door was a yellow smiling face that LuLu had drawn for Sai to make his helicopter "More Pretty."

Sai smiled and waved to LuLu before he started the bird.

The rotor began to rotate and the wind started to blow as the residents watch the Hawk take to the air once again. Wan waved his goodbyes watching his friends leave over the wall and then began to walk towards the ramparts so he could keep up his vigilance on the dead beyond.

Airborne again, Sai took a peek at the company outside of the gate, less than a hundred and all following him south, which was a good thing. He'd stayed low for a while; then he gained some altitude to lose the pursuing dead, leaving them to walk blindly to the south. Upon reaching his target area, Sai would go flat pitch to create a simulated auto-rotation; this was so he could descend as quickly as possible since the noise would cause the dead to zero in on the containers. He hoped his rapid decent from altitude would confuse the dead.

The target area had changed a little. Instead of the motor pool where they would pickup truck containers, they would move a few miles farther south, where a train yard was located. The containers there were more of what Tran wanted. The problem with the trucks was that they were three feet off the ground due to the tires below the containers. The dead would still have a doorway through, which everyone except Tran had overlooked. Small detail but a big problem especially since the Hawk could not flip the containers without risking a crash.

The crew followed the river south until they came to several smokestacks protruding from the jungle canopy; the Old Monk's map had been precise with every curve of the river and dirt road that paralleled it.

From the stacks, Sai turned right and followed a dirt road that went west towards a clearing in the tree line.

If luck were on their side fewer zombies would be in this location since the train yard was small and away from civilization. Trains had come from Bangkok to here to unload cargo, passing it along to other trains in the pre-dead world. There were other trains headed towards Chang Mai and Nakhon Ratchasima with their loads.

Sai circled the yard and found where the containers were, no signs of zombies, but he could clearly see that a train had derailed just half a mile to the south of the yard. Trouble could be brewing.

The train had been one of the unfortunate trains to be leaving Bangkok with infected on board. Inside were hundreds of bodies, some twitching on broken glass – excited by the sound of the circling helicopter. The zombies that wiggled were broken beyond reason, mangled limbs twitched within the wreckage of seats and metal.

After derailment the real horror had occurred. Those stuck within the jagged confines of metal were slaughter like lambs. Corralled in the darkness the dead swept from coach to coach devouring the wounded.

Survivors who had fled into the jungles were under hot pursuit from the dead the train had carried; it probably took one night for most of the five hundred passengers to be consumed.

****

After flying over the area Sai brought the Hawk to a hover over an orange container with Chinese letters on the sides. Toshiro jumped off the Hawk onto the roof of the container and immediately unlatched the door on its' side from the safety of the roof. He slid it open and it was empty.

Toshiro gave thumbs-up to David, who was watching him from the hellhole of the helicopter. David was strapped to a Monkey Harness that allowed him to move about the cabin but still be safely connected to the hawk in case he fell out.

Toshiro then secured the door to the container once more and looked up.

David passed the word and Sai lowered the bird once again performing a limited slope with only his right wheel landing on the container. Below, the rotor wash blasted the high grass causing vortices of dirt to form, which floated harmlessly into the jungle.

David opened the cabin door and pushed out the sling gear to Toshiro who went straight to work as Sai hovered away from the container drawing any of the dead in the area away from Toshiro's position.

Sai maintained constant vigilance on Toshiro who was working feverishly with the dead charging from all directions.

The dead could still climb but being a solid wall on four sides of the container made it highly unlikely. Sai watched as two men approached the container. He figured that the men were not tall enough to reach the top for even if they stretched their arms up they still needed at least four or five feet to reach the edge. *This is going to work.*

It was not long until Toshiro was done. He stood up and looked at his work and then at the dead below him. Satisfied he waved his hands over his head signaling Sai to air taxi in.

Sai quickly air taxied to the container, and David began to call Sai in once the container disappeared from Sai's view in the chin bubble.

"5,4,3,2,1, come left 3,2,1, come down 4,3,2,1," David demanded of Sai, for Sai could not see from his position what was directly below the aircraft. After each command, Sai precisely manipulated the controls; finally, the Blackhawk cargo hook was in reach of Toshiro.

Toshiro hooked up the load to the hook and flicked David off with a smile to lighten the mood. Next, Toshiro quickly tied himself to the load as David followed Sai's teachings on what he wanted him to say next.

"Come up, Come up, sling is tight, load is tight, your up 1,2,3,4,5,6, come up, 20,21, come up. The load is yours." David sighed in relief as Sai now took command of the load and began to push forward on the cyclic while watching the systems on the Central Display Unit and Pilot Display Unit.

"Power's good," Sai said to himself and they were off, Airspeed came alive and altitude was rising.

As the bird gained speed, Toshiro had the ride of his life; suspended from a helicopter two thousand feet above ground level he heard nothing but the wind pounding his face as he screamed in excitement in Japanese.

The dead watched the strange sight.

****

The helicopter could be heard coming, and all of the residents made their way to the top of the houses to see the Blackhawk carrying something large below it as it approached in the distance. They watched as Sai closed the distance and came to a hover as the screaming dead ran to where he was dropping the first load.

Tran planned on extending one of the walls of the Wat first. The southern wall would continue west for at least four football fields wide.

In the cockpit, Tran was busy directing Sai, while in the cabin David looked down the hellhole at Toshiro, who was showing off to the kids and holding the rope with one hand waving.

It took some time to put the load down for it was rotating clockwise and when it was thirty degrees from where it needed to be David told Sai to bring it down.

"5,4,3,2,1, load is light, load is on the ground."

"Roger on the ground."

Sai began to lower the helicopter another two feet to give slack to the rope so Toshiro could untie the gear connected to the container. Normally Sai would press a switch and the cargo hook would open automatically but they needed a way to extract Toshiro out.

A minute later, the helicopter was coming up as Toshiro held on to the sling rope. Below the hanging man the dead were beginning to grow in number, well over a hundred of the stinking corpses surrounded the container.

The Hawk gently flew over the Wat's wall and put Toshiro down on the pad and when he was clear Sai pressed the release switch and the hook open dropping the cable. Two men helped Toshiro gather it up and clear the pad.

With everything clear, Sai brought the bird down on the pad as the crowd waved at the bird and cheered Toshiro on.

With Toshiro back on the bird, the process began all over again and they flew to the south once more.

****

It was now evening; Sai and the crew had stopped earlier around ten a.m., only to start up again at 5:30 p.m. until dusk began to settle in. They had carried twelve loads that day; two more and the southern wall would be done. They had refueled only twice; they tried to keep the bird light by flying with half a tank.

The containers extended into the jungle, which was beyond view from the residents, nearly four football fields wide on the first day. Tran figured the first set of ramparts would be only fourteen by fourteen containers wide and long, for it would go beyond the walls of the Wat when it headed north and he wanted to keep everything simple.

The following morning the sling loads continued without a hitch, Toshiro being on top of the containers was not only securing the loads but also proving to the crew that more importantly when the containers were all in place the dead could not climb them.

With that in mind Tran continued to pick out which containers he wanted, for some had ladders, others small nooks and crannies which the dead could utilize to scale the walls. So each time they arrived at the train yard, Sai would hover around the containers as Tran inspected each and everyone and when given the okay Toshiro would go to work, occasionally decapitating a zombie from the top of the container much to dislike of the crew, for they saw the act as an unneeded risk of falling and becoming zombie food.

The train yard now swarmed with the dead after the third day and Toshiro had a change of heart when using the sword for surrounding each container now was an *AC/DC* fan club throbbing and pulsating with activity. Thousands had flocked to the location since they actually spent more time hovering in the vicinity of the yard than dropping the loads at the Wat; when Sai returned to Wat Tatsunupi, he'd use altitude to shake them from moving north.

He'd head West sometimes, then East and South on other occasions. When he gained enough altitude slowly he would head north hoping the sound of the chopper was nullified somewhat. Of course he was no idiot, for even at five thousand feet the blades and engines of the Hawk were still audible from the ground, but maybe some of those dead bastards below had lost their hearing, not to mention the jungle canopy would probably confuse most of them, every bit of precautions he hoped would add up in the end.

It took a total of five days to box off the large piece of land that Tran had asked for. It had proven difficult to place the containers through the treetops but in the end they were successful; a fourteen by fourteen container wall had blocked off a large portion of jungle to include homes and other useful items.

****

The containers, however, were the easy part of the mission; a large part of the land had been blocked off from the dead, but a large number still inhabited the inside of this Zoo, which it came to be known as.

Several hundred dead folk inhabited the Zoo; they wandered the jungle, the open ground before the Wat and were now searching the homes that were located within the Zoo.

Wan at first thought he'd just shoot the dead from the walls but it was Sai and his fascination with ancient warfare that took the lead. Tran built pikes for the men, with a primitive spear like point covered in melted metals that could be sacrificed.

Sai figured it would probably be best to save the ammo for when they would actually need to enter the Zoo for mop up operations.

It took several days to construct the pikes and the day had finally come to use them.

****

A woman bitten on the cheek moaned, as she stumbled into thick vegetation when she heard a high-pitched whistle.

"Come out! Come out! The Samurai is here!"

Toshiro's voice had attracted the attention of all those within the Zoo.

A stampede of hundreds of bodies, including the woman, charged the west wall of the Wat. Dust rose when the dead's feet pounded on the dry dirt courtyard.

The woman was excited, her comrades on the charge once more, her eyes locked onto the meat on the wall holding long sticks which she did not recognize. She screamed with excitement; her heart's desire was being fulfilled. As she hit the wall, she clawed up, trying to reach her food, her mouth open drooling as her brethren did the same. She tasted what was before her; she felt like smiling, which came out twisted and wicked instead; her dead heart would have jumped for joy if it moved as she jumped up and came down with delight. She was like a child waiting for candy and as she looked up she saw something reaching out for her.

Her vision faded; she felt tired, her energy was draining; sleepy, so sleepy; *I think I'll lie down for a bit.*

Sai's pike rose from the woman's skull, as her body fell to the ground and was trampled by another person as a horde formed right below him.

The men on the wall were crushing the skulls with these metal-tipped spears. They felt the crunch and the suction as they pulled out of their intended targets' heads.

Each man with a pike had a rope tied around their waist held by two other men sitting on their butts directly behind them. It was a safety measure the group had come up with in order to prevent the dead from grabbing one of the pikes and pulling a man down.

Only twelve men were on the wall butchering the dead at a time, and behind them teams of men held the twelve with ropes and extra pikes for each in case their butcher's pike broke or was pulled over by the dead.

The butchering team started on the southern corner of the western wall. Logic was that the bodies would begin to pile up creating a ramp to the top if they killed enough in one spot. So they moved to another spot then another, moving up north along the wall until no more dead came out to greet them.

Toshiro whooped and yelled the entire day as he killed one after another, talking to them in Japanese, probably cursing them for all Sai knew.

Several times, the men switched out; by the end, many corpses had lined the wall. They would try again tomorrow and again the day after until no more dead came to the wall. When they were satisfied, they would enter the Zoo and begin the most dangerous part of the operation.

****

295

The search-and-destroy team consisted of the original members and Eck, Arm, plus three men who had come from Big C with Sai – two who had served as mules, carrying extra ammo and water in their packs. Unlike the days before, they would enter the Zoo fully armed with rifles, sidearms, and close-quarter weapons. They needed to be ready for anything that was still lurking in that jungle out there, not to mention the homes they would need to secure.

Wan, of course, had a major say as to who was placed where in the formation. Sai and Toshiro were lifelines to the outside world, and the only way for them to be placed in the more dangerous areas was if they began training replacements in case the worst came to be.

With that in mind, Sai and Toshiro were right smack in the middle of the line, abreast formation. Unlike before, the formation was tight; flanking the two were the three new men. To Sai's left was one new man was who wore a tight red shirt and two were to Toshiro's right. The new men would follow Sai and Toshiro's lead, for they lacked the training necessary in Wan's view to act in unison as the original eight had. To the left of Sai and one of the new men down, was Tor – armed with the SAW. Wan placed him there to give Sai the most protection in case things went to shit. To the left of the red shirt man and Tor were Ta and Stephen on opposite sides, since they were the youngsters of the group. Flanking them on opposing sides were Wan and David. David had proven himself quite capable over the last few missions. Wan saw the outer edge as the most dangerous and trusted David to hold his side. Behind them, forming a box formation, were Eck and Arm; the two would cover the flanks and bring up the rear.

The morning had come and the group filed out of the gate where no bodies lay since they had intentionally did their best to avoid killing them in that area. Around the wall however the corpses rotted filled with maggots.

The smell of rot outside the gate was worse than from within the Wat. The mangled bodies lay in the morning sun and the soldiers immediately tied cloths around their heads in an attempt to block out the stench. It didn't work.

With the formation set, the group began to move towards the tree line to the west next to the newly formed southern wall. The formation remained tight as the group followed Sai to the edge of the jungle stopping twenty feet from actually entering.

Here, Toshiro made his call and the group came to a knee with rifles at the ready. Two screeches came from the jungle and the foliage began to shake when a man missing an arm came running out towards Wan's side.

Wan immediately put a bullet in the brain when another came straight out towards Sai. Both Sai and Toshiro fired this time and the head exploded as both rounds hit home sending brain and skull fragments flying.

Another scream came from the Northern tree line, where the houses were followed by another.

The formation moved back ten feet and then wheeled in place with Sai now facing North and Wan and Eck covering the western jungle.

A football field away, three dead people came charging out.

"Hold your fire," Wan ordered. "Hold," he said again after the three dead creatures made another twenty yards. "Hold." Twenty more yards. "Hold." And twenty more. "Fire!"

The rifles cracked in the line and bullets tore into the shoulders and faces of the three individuals who then came crashing forward landing thirty feet from formations position. So far, so good.

Wan's rifle sent a shot through the air as another one came from the western tree line by surprise.

The creature's head jerked back, the impact breaking the neck and sending gore out back onto the lush vegetation.

All was silent after the skirmish, so the formation headed north along the tree line towards the homes on the northern edge of the courtyard/parking lot, as Toshiro provoked any others in the area with strange yelps and yells.

The people of the Wat watched as the group came to a stop, took a knee, and a rifle fired. The formation wheeled again facing the west and the rifles cracked once more. This time while holding this formation they continued on, keeping the majority of the rifles facing the Western jungle since they were in close proximity to it.

They moved smoothly to the north, staying out of the brush, and came to a stop in front of the homes. The formation changed once more facing north, and they continued a few more yards before coming to a stop.

It was the same house they had raided on their first raid. The door was open due to zombie exploration; signs of shuffling were everywhere inside.

Ta, Stephen, and one of the new men moved the door from the formation and came to a stop, then they climbed the stairs and peeked inside. Immediately, the formation heard the sound of three gunshots and then the wind once more. All they needed were tumbleweeds and they'd be in an old western.

With the wind blowing gently and all silent Sai and Toshiro ran up to the doorway as the last four men took up security on the sides of the house while Ta, Stephen, and the new guy went inside the home.

Sai and Toshiro followed in who were in turn followed by the other two new men. Next Tor went in and a few shots were heard once more.

With the first team inside the home, the remaining men followed in, with Wan the last to enter.

****

"Clear!" Ta shouted from the far window facing the north.

The house had been cleared; a few corpses littered the floor. The stench was strong and it was clear it was time to clear the next house.

"Let's get formed up and the last one out close the door," Wan told the men.

"It's a trap!" Ta shouted his voice full of fear.

Coming out of the jungle the dead charged. They had waited until they could encircle the soldiers and now they began their attack.

From Ta's window, he saw the charge firsthand. It was actually as if they had waited in the tree line, waiting to see if someone's face would appear from the window.

"Close the door!" Sai shouted as he moved towards the nearest window.

From within the house, Ta, Stephen, and the new guy opened fire from the northern windows.

"Alok, wait till they get closer!" Ta shouted, as the smell of gunpowder filled the room.

Alok took aim at one of the dead men who was reaching for the window and fired. Behind the falling corpse, there were thirty more coming in full force from the house directly behind the one they had entered.

Tor stood beside Alok and sent hell down range. His SAW shredded the faces of all that got within his sights.

"It's a goddamned ambush!" Sai shouted to himself, as he made his way to another window to see more reinforcements arriving from the west. Sweat was rolling down his cheek as he felt a sinking sensation in his chest, for he understood that this had been a planned attack. They had lured him and his team out; they had learned not to attack the walls, and they had learned to wait until they had them encircled with no way out. Either one of those dead fucks or something was beginning to think tactically for them.

All those thoughts raced in and out of Sai's mind as he fired round after round towards the undead silhouettes appearing by his window. His shell casings bounced off the wall of the house.

Outside the door, the dead used a log like a battering ram. Inside Wan held the door shut by leaning on it with his back as the pounding continued. David quickly rushed to Wan's aid by pushing a wardrobe to help secure the door shut.

"We're surrounded!" David shouted, loading another clip and pressing against the wardrobe as Sai raced to the window by the doorway.

With the wardrobe holding the door for now, Wan and David pushed with all their might to keep it closed as Sai took down a few who assaulted the door. But they kept coming; that is when Sai pulled a pin from a grenade Wan had salvaged for him and tossed it out the window.

"Fire in the hole!" Sai shouted taking cover from the window.

The room browned out as the explosion sent debris into the air; before it cleared, Sai was already at the window firing.

The undead battering-ram team was obliterated; in its place were the typical mindless dead folk they had been used to. They were dumb but superior in numbers.

Sai grinned as he took aimed and his bullet casings continued to slam against the wall. Sai felt no pain as the bullet casings bounced back off the wall slamming into his exposed neck burning the tissue.

Each round from Sai's rifle took an eternity as he watched in disbelief, still in shock from the springing of the trap. Finally, when the bolt of the rifle was pushed back, he released the magazine letting it drop to the wooden floor. He looked down as the magazine floated to the ground and turned his head to see Alok crying by the window near Tor who was still spraying hell out his window like a madman jerking his weapon in every direction as fast as he could.

Reaching for another magazine from the utility belt Sai wore, Sai saw Eck running across the room towards Alok who had been carrying extra ammo that Eck needed.

Sai slapped the magazine in with the stinging smoke tearing his eyes and moved once more leaning out the window to take aim at the dead who were rushing up the stairs over the mangle bodies of their predecessors.

****

From the walls, the residents of Wat Tatsunupi saw fifty or more zombies surrounding the wooden hooch. The dirt from the grenade had died down and the pops of gunfire continued at a steady pace as white smoke from the guns began to fill the area with a misty haze.

"HEY! OVER HERE!" Yoon began to shout to attract some of the dead to the walls of Wat Tatsunupi.

The crowd around her began to shout and a few of the dead began to turn their attention to the crowd on the walls. The creatures charged the walls as the door to the house began to give way.

Wan and David were being pushed inch by inch back as the dead forced their way in. Their muscles were failing as the two men over exerted every last ounce of energy they had to seal the door. The fuel in their bodies was burning faster than ever as adrenaline from the battle flowed double its normal pace.

"Not again," Wan said in Thai, as he saw his boots giving ground and dead fingers beginning to protrude from the opening in the doorway. The fingers wiggled through the cracks of the door like snakes hidden behind the wardrobe.

Sai saw what was happening and ran to the door, which was being held by the wardrobe and the two men. Slamming his shoulder into it he pushed the door two inches back towards the dead severing many fingers with brute force.

"Ta, Stephen, stop fucking around by that window. We've got company!" Sai shouted catching the two boys' attention.

Toshiro wasted no time taking his sword out with his left hand and held his rifle in the right, while Tor took position next to him on one knee behind a table.

"Let them come!" Toshiro shouted in Japanese his eyes filled with rage. He wanted to get close and personal to avenge his sister death and what had happened to Chit only made him more pissed off.

The new men stood by the boys and Toshiro to form a firing line aiming at the door while Alok still crying continued to break down, that is when Ta grabbed him by the shoulder and shouted something.

"Sai get to the line!" Wan shouted, spit flying from his mouth, every ounce of energy still pressed against the wardrobe. The door was giving way once more inch by inch under his boot.

"Sai go now, think of Yoon and the kids damn it!" His eyes rolled to Sai knowing it was not in Sai's nature to leave a man behind. "Go, please." Wan began to tear up knowing what he was going to do for Sai and the men.

Sai's face was grim as the three men pushed with all their might to keep the door sealed.

"Sai, please, the Wat needs you, now go!" Wan pleaded. "It's my time Sai, I've lost many men, and I'm not going to let you die."

David began to shout from the other side of Wan. "Sai, protect my brother!" David began to roar as all his muscles pulsated with the final surge of adrenaline.

"I'll save them!" Sai shouted as he pushed the wardrobe, tears rolling down his dirt filled cheeks. "I'll save them!"

With that said, Sai retreated from the door towards the firing line.

The pressure of Sai's weight was gone and the door began to slide faster than ever before.

"It's been an honor, Wan," David said, knowing what would happen very soon. The door opened more and arms – some missing fingers – began to break through the crack of the door.

"Same here, David. On the count of three, retreat to the line!" An arm reached around and grabbed Wan's wrist, the clammy cold dead fingers digging into the flesh.

Wan looked at the dead hand and began to count in Thai, knowing he could not escape the grip.

"Nung…Song…SOM!"

David ran as Wan stayed with the door knowing full well the dead thing had a firm grip on him. Wan reached for his sidearm as the door blasted open, sending a tide of bodies flying into the home.

The dead thing on his wrist was an old woman who was first through. Wan pressed the gun on her temple and her temple exploded on the opposite side of her head when a boy bit into Wan's leg.

In slow motion, Sai began to open fire watching Wan butt stroke the boy on the head with his sidearm.

The boy's head caved in as the old woman who was still holding Wan fell to the ground with her death grip. Just then, a foreigner tackled Wan followed by three, then four more people.

David pushed towards the firing line, as the line continued to fire. Bullets blazed by David and he could see Sai reaching for his machete with his left hand. Hot in pursuit, the dead were on David's ass, the bodies tumbled and became caught in David's legs. He fell face first into the floor and felt a warm sensation throughout his body as the bites tore into him. His eyes widen as he lost his bowels and the dead continued to swarm him.

"Hold them with what you got!" Sai roared his eyes burning with fury.

The bodies fell continuously when close quarter combat erupted as the first of the dead made it through the wall of lead.

Toshiro's blade flashed in and out of heads while Ta used his rifle as a bat to smash in the closest creature near him, each swing shattering the rifle into jagged edges as blood and gore swung wildly into the air across the room.

Sai struggled with a woman who had somehow got on his back while Alok pulled her hair to fire a round with his rifle into her head. Alok's crying was done, now he was in the fight for survival

Without hesitation, Sai struck an elderly man who was reaching for Stephen who was busy clubbing a kid in the face with his spiked club repeatedly. The elderly man fell limp to the floor and Sai kicked a boy in the face with his boot sending the kid backwards with a broken neck. Sai then turned to punch a teenage girl who was already biting into Alok's neck when a woman grabbed him. Sai was forced to fight her bumping into Tor who had dropped the SAW and now used an iron pipe sharpened into a short spear fighting off two men who were engaged in a gridlock battle with Tor.

Alok's blood gushed out spraying Ta's back while Ta stabbed a man through the jaw towards the brain with a combat knife. Ta cursed in Thai as the man's eyes rolled into the back of his head when another zombie pushed Ta's victim from behind sending Ta flying back into the girl who was biting Alok.

The girl who was biting Alok did not even flinch as Ta pushed into her and like a rabid dog she kept a firm grip on Alok while he continued to scream. "Mae!!! Mae!!! MAE!!!"

Alok's throat gargled as he cried for the help of his mother, the blood rushing in threatening to drown him in seconds.

David was screaming still, covered in bites and being torn to shreds as the dead moved their heads from side to side trying to rip away a piece of flesh.

From the fray, Wan got to his feet, firing his sidearm at all those around him. Even after being tackled by a mob he continued the fight making every second count, doing his best to protect the men. He was a bloody mess, half his face already eaten away and still he fought on as more creatures tackled him back down to the floor again which gave the rest of the soldiers precious time to fight on.

As Wan was taken back down, one of the new men, the one in the red shirt retreated towards a window on the northern part of the house. He stopped and turned back at the rumble and then without hesitating he jumped out of the window into the waiting arms of a mob outside.

Inside the home Eck and Arm stood side by side at one corner of the house firing nonstop at the doorway. They were creating a no man's land between them and the dead. All had been going well for the brothers until Tor and a woman went through the line of fire tumbling around. The woman's face exploded from a round from Eck's gun. Another round hit Tor in the shoulder sending him down to the ground with the melee still raging on around him.

Sai, now covered in gore, dropped his boot on a gimp, crushing the head under the pressure; satisfied it was dead, he pulled his machete from the creature's spine.

"Ta!" Sai shouted moving again through the battle taking a swing at the occasional zombie that crossed his path.

Ta had killed the girl that was killing Alok and was fighting to the side of the last new man Sin. They were now fighting together against the dwindling number of ghouls.

Passing Toshiro, Sai brought a dead woman with him that had been chasing him. Toshiro swung his sword in one quick swoosh and the ladies head went flying.

"You can thank me later!" Toshiro shouted in Japanese before he turned his attention to the four who had David pinned down.

Sai rammed a woman who was charging Ta and sent her through the wall back outside, where a few of her comrades took notice.

Ta was first to charge into the incoming dead, picking up a rifle that had been dropped in the combat. Sai who was closest to the opening pulled his sidearm and fired at the hole in the wall where the woman now lied with wooden shrapnel protruding from her body.

She growled and rushed back to her feet only to fall over again after Sai sent a round into her head. Her brothers and sisters were not far behind, they were now charging the hole in the wall. Ten of them came running and were creating a bottleneck effect at the opening giving Sai the time to shoot them down one by one.

Ta, Stephen, and Sin rejoined Toshiro, who was now fighting alongside Eck and Arm who had never stopped firing. They moved slowly moving towards the doorway and the opening in the wall as the enemy was slowly being killed off.

From the walls of Wat Tatsunupi, the men were using the pikes to crush what was left of the zombies at the wall as the gunfire began to trickle to a stop. The residents waited to see who was left from the hooch, to see if any of the soldiers would come outside at all.

From the wall, gunpowder was all they saw flowing out of the house and into the sky; nothing stirred, not even a mouse.

The soldiers were quiet, each catching their breath as they looked at nearly thirty bodies that had somehow squeezed themselves into the small home that could only hold fifteen comfortably. The only sound now was of Alok.

Alok began to convulse as he continued cry out again in Ta's arms. Blood continued to pour out of the wound in his neck but still he somehow remained conscious, probably due to the sheer amount of pain he was in.

Sai moved to Ta and Alok as Toshiro checked the other bodies for life with his sword.

"Shhh, shhh," Sai soothed Alok. "Ta, tell him to close his eyes, tell him it's going to be okay, calm him down."

Ta began to talk in Thai to Alok who looked up at him still sobbing for his mom. It did not take long for Ta to calm the young man down, the gargling in his throat began to slow and that is when he closed his eyes with Ta rubbing Alok's hair with his fingers.

Ta looked up at Sai who held his sidearm. Sai gestured to Ta to look away.

Ta turned his head and before Alok could sense anything he felt a ringing in his ears and then he fell asleep.

Sai laid Alok down on the ground with a gunshot wound on his head. Ta began to cry as he watched Sai walk off.

He moved on to David who had just died a few seconds earlier. Toshiro sent a round into his head when he opened his eyes and stared at him. Stephen knelt beside his brother crying as Sai walked behind him towards Wan near the entrance.

Wan was still fighting for life, still making every moment count. Covered in blood he looked at Sai and smiled. Wan stood by the doorway swaying, barely catching himself after losing his center of gravity. The smell of iron was heavy and Wan looked up at the men that were left and smiled.

"Live." Wan raised his sidearm and pressed it against his temple and fired.

"Wan!" Sai shouted too late to stop him.

The soldier fell to the floor onto the bodies of those he helped kill.

Sai walked up, knelt down beside Wan's bodies, tears finding their way out of his closed eyelids. He sniffled and then opened his eyes looking outside of the door to the blue sky.

"Is anyone else bit?" Sai asked, turning his head toward the men and then zeroing in on Stephen who continued to cry for his brother.

"No, but Tor's been shot." A voice said in the group.

"Tor, where are you?" Sai asked loudly looking around the gunpowder that still heavily obscured everyone's vision.

"I'm okay, just a bullet," Tor responded, leaning against the eastern wall of the house with his SAW back in his hand.

Just a bullet wound, it was better to be shot than to be bit; what a world, Sai thought before he talked to Stephen.

"Stephen, I'm sorry, but your brother saved our lives. He wanted us to live, he wanted you to live," Sai said, now walking up to him. "Stephen, I know it hurts, but turn it into something else, turn it…" Sai grabbed him, as he pulled him towards his chest. "Turn it into something else, man," he said as his eyes teared up. "Let's just turn it into something else."

Toshiro nodded, and Eck and Arm knew they were lucky not to end up like David and Stephen. Stephen cried into Sai's chest.

"We got to move now. Let's bring our brothers home," Sai said as he looked at the men, his eyes watering from tears and gunpowder.

"Sin, Toshiro, take David. Eck, Arm, take Alok. Ta, help me with Wan, and be careful not to get any blood in your cuts. We'll come back for what is left of that guy in the red shirt. What was his name?" Sai looked around the room, but no one answered.

"And them, Sai?" Toshiro asked gesturing his head with a snarl at the corpses.

"Torch them," Sai responded, as he grabbed Wan by the shoulders and pulled him up as Ta grabbed his legs. The two began to walk out of the building towards the Wat, where the gate was already open with a group of men standing outside. Tran led the group accompanied by Wanchai and Klauy who were armed with spears, a few rifles, and blades. They were already walking towards them as Ren Pi looked down from the walls.

The men met with the soldiers and grabbed the bodies; then they quickly made it back to the Wat as Toshiro lit a torch and began to set the home on fire.

The blaze roared while the bodies burned everywhere. Since the fire was in the open, there was no danger of a forest fire, especially since they were in the middle of the rainy season and within minutes the home came crashing down, cremating the bodies of their enemies within.

****

The residents watched as Wan, David, and Alok were taken to the center of the Wat – each with a hole in his head.

Wien, Pue, and Noi kept the children away, not wanting them to see what had happened. Kaew, the puppy, was all the entertainment the little ones like LuLu needed, but some of the older children knew something had gone wrong.

Wien knew soon that they would be treating the soldiers in her makeshift hospital; the books that Sai had brought over time would be in use today.

Yoon, Liu, and Pakatip stood together as they saw Ta enter the Wat first.

Yoon ran up to her cousin and cried, knowing she had almost lost him.

"You okay? Are you hurt?" She sounded like his mother, as she grabbed the back of his sweaty head and held her cousin tightly.

Sin walked in, as his friends rushed to him fearing he was gone.

Tor, Eck, and Arm entered followed by Toshiro who looked like he needed a drink.

Pakatip went to comfort the four men, feeling that they were her adopted grandchildren and Toshiro was another son. Quickly, she began to escort Tor to Wien and the others.

Sai and Tran entered last and Sai walked up to Yoon who was still holding her cousin.

Yoon quickly pulled Sai to her and held him and Ta as she sobbed. Sai breathed a sigh of relief as he took in her scent. The freshness only a woman could bring.

Tran was last in and told the men to shut the door. He looked out into the Zoo, knowing that soon they would need to once again go out there to clear what was left of the dead.

The Wat's door creaked as it was pushed shut and the Wat was left to their mourning as the day came to a close.

The clouds looked down on the Wat, and tears from the sky began to fall.

Chapter 19: *Taming the Zoo*

Tran and Sai were quick to realize the events that had taken place the day before could not slow down the pace of their operation in the least; the faster the farmland could be built, the faster that food could come in, reducing the number of raids necessary to sustain the Wat.

With many people still in a state of mourning, the gates of Wat Tatsunupi opened once more with Sai and half the men in the Wat leaving to form a giant L-formation in the open courtyard of gravel inside of the Zoo. The L was actually a backwards seven if you looked at it on the map. The long portion was to the west and connected itself to one of the cargo containers to the south. This large portion was also the most dangerous portion to be in for they were actually ten feet deep into the jungle that went to the west. Quietly each man in the jungle waited kneeling down, each holding their breath with sweat beginning to snowball down the sides of their faces. They listened, listened for any signs of disturbance and as they waited motionless the mosquitoes made meals of them.

The small portion of the L faced the north and connected itself to the original western wall of Wat Tatsunupi. Inside that area within the so-called safety of the L, people would be working under the constant protection of the formation.

The men were armed with everything they had; tools, guns, shovels, you name it, they used it. Prior to leaving the wall, Ta had been banging a gong on the wall for hours bringing a few dead stragglers to the wall to be greeted by a pike.

It was hoped that most of the dead had died in the battle in the hooch, but it was now certain that some of the dead had the capability to perform ambush style attacks. These smart dead or Brains as they came to be known became the most feared undead foes the residents would need to watch out for during the early years of the Wat.

With the knowledge of the alleged Brains the formation stood ready as others began to work inside the safety of the formation armed with tools, axes, shovels, and so forth. As soon as the formation was formed they had already begun clearing the trees and other obstacles. They were now clearing the land.

****

Tran and Wanchai's detail of workers, mostly young men and teenagers, began to feverishly get to work. Their axes and shovels began to clear the vegetation closest to the cargo containers, they hacked away not caring for the noise they were causing for outside of the cargo container perimeter hundreds were now banging on the walls and shouting for the food inside the perimeter.

Sai and Toshiro stood in the center of the L formation just behind the work detail, both armed to the teeth looking on, they were the Generals of the Wat now that Wan was gone and as the detail continued they began to patrol the perimeter of the L, making sure the men were holding steady and reassuring them of doing a good job, trying to take their mind off the fear they knew most were facing.

The pair came across one man who had already pissed his pants; the urine smell was fresh as the two men approached the jumpy sentry.

Sai spoke up in the Thai, which he had learned swiftly – like a character in the *13th Warrior*. He patted the man on the shoulder and gestured to the other Thai men just five feet away from him to show the man he was not alone on the perimeter. Everyone relied on each other and for that reason alone that man should maintain his cool for they all relied on him as well.

"Sai, it's going to be a hot one today," Toshiro commented as he looked up through the jungle canopy at the sun bearing down upon them.

"Toshiro, do you mind taking this guy's place for a moment?" Sai looked over to him. "Going to turn him into the water boy, the guy needs something to do or he's going to have a heart attack or go postal out here," Sai said in English looking at the fidgeting man.

Toshiro nodded, happily taking the man's place under the tree where he could rest and relax.

"Thanks, Toshiro. I'll get someone to replace you soon."

"No rush, Sai. Take your time."

After Sai and the Thai man left, Toshiro leaned up against a tree and crossed his arms, sitting Indian style, and began to nod off as the two men flanking him looked on wide-eyed in constant fear, jumping from any movement the jungle could offer, for death was near.

****

The water boy was hard at work ferrying jugs of water over the next few hours and within the confines of the L formation his tension had eased up. Toshiro had now rejoined Sai who was near the gate of the Wat talking to the Old Monk about what to do after the farmland was secure and so forth.

The Old Monk was a wise man and knew that Idle Hands were Evil Hands. The people needed to stay busy, there always needed to be something that needed to be done even though that was still farther down the road. The Old Monk was neither the leader of the Wat nor just another survivor; he had quickly taken the role as the wise mentor, or teacher. His wisdom would help propel the Wat in the future.

An hour later Wien had check up on the stitches that Toshiro and Sai had received with Yoon's permission. Wien, Noi, and Pue also left the Wat to do their part by helping to bring water to the guards in the formation that could not leave their post. The girls worked under the watchful eye of Sai.

The three girls were thankful to leave the Wat and the excitement was intense being out of the safety of the wall just behind the men. At first they were skittish about actually going to the perimeter; but, with time, they had taken to their job as if born to help. Soon, they had become brave enough to walk up behind the men on the L-formation; it was the farthest and most dangerous area they had been in since their arrival to the Wat. At the perimeter, they determined who was next to becoming a heat casualty and relayed the information to Sai.

Sai, knowing what it was like to be a heat casualty, took Wien's recommendations and even began to alternate some of the men around to Wien's pleasing. He gave some breaks in the shade and safety of the Wat all the while leaving the gate open in case of an emergency retreat was order.

With the gate open, more and more women began to leave the safety of the walls some even coming to help with the clearing of the brush with tools they had scrounged up. It helped the work pace tremendously.

Yoon had come with her cousin and the two other girls on occasion only returning to make sure LuLu and the others were doing fine.

In the center of the Wat Pakatip and her group of cooks busily made lunch for the Wat and took count of how much food was left and when the three girls returned with empty pots of water the three began to ferry the food out to the work site.

****

The group continued to work and had cleared an acre after a few hours allowing the formation to press another five feet deeper into the jungle. Trees that had been chopped down had been dragged to the edge of the entrance of the Wat, not to close where the dead could use it as a ramp to scale the walls in the event of an attack but close enough to use it in the future.

Men and women lifted the heavy tree trunks onto the carts that had been pulled out from the Wat and pulled back towards the Wat's entrance in what could only be described as ants busily dissecting a grasshopper – in this case, the jungle – and carrying its contents back to the hive.

Wanchai was now busy determining how much wood would be needed to build fortifications behind the cargo containers and what kind of wood would be best for what purpose.

****

However, the day did not go without incident; the first sign of trouble came when a gimp crawled up under the brush within a foot of a man armed with a hatchet and a slingshot.

His scream of terror sent Wien and her friends running for the Wat and sent Sai and Toshiro in the direction of the scream.

When Sai arrived on scene, a hatchet had found a home in the back of the gimp's head and the guard on his feet was kicking the body. Toshiro had been diverted from the screaming guard for some in the formation had actually begun to retreat towards the Wat without a fight. With his sword drawn, Toshiro's show of force sent the men back to their lines.

312

Wien and her friends walked back out after waiting for a moment after seeing Sai walk out of the jungle with the work detail working once more. The girls laughed like schoolgirls who had been frighten at a movie as they walked back out.

Yoon was quick to arrive on scene with Sai and asked if she too could help on the work detail.

After moments of talking she found herself along with Sai helping to push the carts loaded with lumber towards the entrance of the Wat to be dumped in piles near the wall.

****

Throughout the day, the members of the Wat worked together until it was late in the afternoon. It was then that the work detail and all those on security began to withdraw to the safety of the Wat and the doors sealed shut.

Overall, the day had brought good results; two and a half acres of the jungle had been cleared. There was enough lumber to begin fortifications; with the new area of land cleared, more women could join in the work details.

With the daily death toll at zero on the good guys and six with the stenches, it was cause for some celebration once more; with some alcohol George and Dario had donated a few days earlier, it was a good evening.

****

Sitting around the fire drinking, the Wat relaxed as each person carried on a conversation. Yoon, who sat in the arms of Sai, talked to Liu as LuLu and the other kids played in the area.

Pue flirted with Arm as Wien and Noi giggled on. Ta, in a trance state, looked across at Noi like some kind of crazed stalker.

Pakatip brought bowls of rice to her adopted son Toshiro, as Tran and Wanchai discuss tomorrow's work details.

The Old Monk even brought out a Thai instrument that resembled a guitar and played music for the group. He may have been a monk but he played a mean tune from the Northeast of Thailand.

As the group celebrated, Tor talked with Dario and George on the radio. The two perverts had a harem going on over at Big C, and Tor heard women laughing on the other end of the radio. The two old geezers celebrated, for the Wat and Tor turned to rejoin everyone, trying to make his way close to Wien. Everyone except for Ren Pi celebrated; the man stared out from the northern wall. He was looking for something or someone; it was obvious that the man did not want to stay here, but why, he would not say; trouble was brewing.

****

Days began to roll by; then weeks went by, as the whole Wat population was now outside, with only the children and a few old ladies remaining inside the Wat. The last of the brush was now being cut down; it was one acre, one small acre that would not even take an hour, since the whole place had been secured and every bladed weapon and hand was now busily pulling on the vegetation and cutting down the trees.

With the last tree came applause, as the men loaded it into the wagon and took it to the staging area. A few homes had been saved outside of the Wat. The homes would become areas where workers would eat as the land was being developed for farming, later on more homes and fortification would be built within the Zoo.

Wanchai took charge in the building of fortifications five feet inside of the cargo container perimeter, the point being that the helicopter could lift the containers easier without worry of hitting the walls in future expansions, which were already planned. To survive they would need to continuously expand.

The first of the wall was already being built, connecting from the southwestern Wat's wall and heading west along the cargo containers. Not being an immediate necessity with the cargo containers most people found themselves plowing the earth in the center of the Wat as Tran constructed an irrigation system to flood the field for planting rice.

****

Several trips to Big C had become necessary, along with several refueling stops to the same airfield Sai had gone to earlier. Tools, ropes, lighter fluid, and more medical supplies were brought in, boosting Wien's team's capabilities. No deaths had occurred from the Wat since the battle of the hooch and even a few survivors whom Dario and George had found made their way by flight to Wat Tatsunupi, boosting the numbers of workers and helping to finish the farmland that much faster.

314

With the farmland completed, the field flooded, the residents turned their attention to the fortifications that were now being reinforced. The ramparts were a mixture of earth that had been plowed from the fields to fill the two wooden walls with a deck built on top so people could walk around. The southern wall was roughly five feet thick and fifteen feet high, now towering above the cargo containers, they were being built to withstand thousands of rotting hands beating upon them and with the dirt filled inside the walls they could take a beating and never fall. Of course later on Wanchai and Tran thought it best to bring in stone to further strengthen the walls.

On top of the southern ramparts, devices to drop large stones on the dead below were being constructed; these mini cranes could load up a few rocks on what looked like a giant shovel. Pushed over the edge and with the tug of a rope the platform holding the rocks would open unleashing death from above when the time came to move the containers so they could farm more land.

Stairs were not constructed, instead ladders, the thought being that in the event of a battle they could pull up the ladders and kill the dead from both sides if needed using pikes.

With the rice already growing and a few months going by the ramparts were looking gorgeous and the last part to be built was a gate facing the west. This gate was heavily fortified; the door consisting of melted iron from the Wat and heavy ten inch thick boards, the gate were that of a medieval castle, designed for siege warfare. It would go up by a system of pulleys that moved up by a wench and when closed three metal bars were wedge in just the right angle that there was no way the stiffs could raise it.

Wanchai, not being one to rely on just one gate built a second gate, this one was made of pure iron and looked more Gothic for it looked like a big tic-tac-toe game with the sharp points sticking into a metal frame in the ground that Tran had built. The metal frame stretched from one rampart to the next under the gatehouse. With the Iron teeth in the center of this metal device, if the dead did break through the first gate the Iron Jawed gate as it came to be known would definitely hold them.

The gate was designed to dip into a hole from the entrance and back up a hill onto level ground. If the dead did break through the two gates they would need to go straight ahead and up a hill while taking fire from the flanks by men with guns, pikes and blades. Up the hill was a moveable fortification armed with spears six feet long, which could be wedged into position so that all that entered the dip would be held up.

The moveable fortification was on two wheels with all the spears facing one direction, presumably the direction the dead would come if they broke through the gate. On the back of the device were several metal poles that were designed to lodge themselves into the ground and no matter how hard the dead would push on it, the device would just lodge itself deeper into the earth while men behind it fired with guns and most likely bows and arrows if things got really bad in the future.

Chapter 20: *Neighbors*

Eight months had gone by, and the morning rays of the sun were striking the Wat's golden Chedi's. Two UH-1 Iroquois helicopters parked in the Zoo on two makeshift pads were now beginning to spin up, as two more birds and a fuel truck watched from the brand new airfield Tran had built a month earlier.

Sai and Yoon were the pilots of the gunship, armed to the teeth with guns and rockets, Tor and Stephen being the crew chiefs/gunners. To the right was Toshiro flying single pilot, having being the first person Sai had trained to fly. His crew chief was Eck with Arm riding as a pack with binoculars looped around his neck and a recent arrival to the Wat was accompanying him.

Talking on the Fox Mike, Sai readied the flight for takeoff.

"Waiting for the Beacon call, we're red con 1," Sai said in Thai to Toshiro, who had mastered the language as well.

"Roger, we're still spooling up give us a sec."

Sai turned off the anti-collision lights of his aircraft as Yoon talked on the radio to Ta.

"Beacon." Toshiro said now spooled up for flight.

"Roger beacon. Torch." Sai began to pull on the collective from the left seat and applied left pedal. Unlike the Blackhawk, this bird had no mechanical mixing unit to help adjust for various aerodynamic issues; he actually needed to fly the bird. The Huey was the same as flying a dinosaur and much older than him.

Sai's bird began to take off as it dust blew into the field where people worked; they did not even look up at the bird take off anymore for they had grown accustomed to the sight. They held their straw hats as Toshiro began to pull collective and make a pedal turn to the left to follow Sai as he headed south down the river on a scouting mission to Bangkok.

Toshiro watched carefully as he flew within three rotor discs of Sai and over the fortifications of the Wat, which in the process of blocking off another large piece of land with containers once more.

Thousands of the dead looked up, but unlike before where they were identical to a mosh pit at a concert, most had begun to slow down, some drastically due to decomposition.

Finally, decay had slowly set in on many. Over the last month, they had noticed most were no longer eligible for Olympic competition; now reduced to shambles, a few were still joggers, and even rarer were the sprinters. Different states of decay, the residents figured; some even had primitive functional minds, but that was the least of their problems.

There were stories of something else, something smart that was out there controlling the hordes in a war against man. It was just rumors from refugees rescued in the north, but rumor or not the Wat was going to be prepared. The residents had seen what the dead could do during the ambush that had killed Wan and David; from what the refugees claimed, that event may pale in comparison to what was going in the northern regions of Thailand and Laos.

Other than the dead, the bandits had become an issue as well. Somewhere north of Lop Buri, Than and his gang had set up shop where they launched raids on survivors when they could find them.

Over a hundred bandits raided the area, using military-grade weapons and vehicles; fortunately for Wat Tatsunupi, they had not engaged in direct combat with Than.

In the bandit camps, there were over a hundred slaves, many of them were women and children, some were those condemned to live out the rest of their lives in decoy cages, others who were fathers destined to fight for Than under the threat of executing their families.

Noi's sister was still alive; the worst was over for her, for she was now one of the girls of Than, who had his own private harem the rest of the boys could not touch. Safe as she was, she still prayed to find her sister someday.

****

The Huey's blades chopped through the air as they flew low level towards Bangkok. Sai insisted his pilots be trained to fly low level for they never knew if hostiles would be lurking in the ruins or jungles with AAA or SAMs, even though the odds were against anyone left knowing how to use them but with the threat of Than's bandits closing in it was justified.

The brown water danced under the sun's light as the river snaked its way south. Yoon was on the controls and Sai was guiding her down the river using a map they had taken from a local airport months earlier.

Yoon wore an OD Green helmet like Sai did; it was something else he insisted his crew wear. His reason being that if they did crash, the last thing they needed was to be unconscious only to awaken to something biting them. Like Sai, she also wore a green pickle suit with a Thai flag and the King's flag on her right sleeve. Sai, on the other hand, had an American and Thai flag woven together as one. The countries of the world may have been gone now, but the flags gave them a sense of pride.

Under Sai's ALSE gear he had his patch for Dead Air, which Yoon was working on trying to earn.

Soon there would be more pilots, for Sai planned on expanding his fleet in the near future, which meant more patches would be needed.

While the two Hueys raced south, more and more of the dead came into view. Thousands upon thousands littered the landscape as structures began to appear on the horizon.

The mission would take them to the outskirts of Bangkok, to a rumored safe haven for those still alive in the massive city.

The man riding along with Toshiro had come a week ago; he had been attracted to the sound of the helicopters that were moving containers to a new piece of land.

He'd come by boat with Ta being the first to spot him. His name was J; he was ex-special-forces Thai Royal Marine. He left his Eden in Bangkok as food began to grow scarce and through a network of sewer tunnels his people had been using he made it to a boat. He was a scout from his safe haven known as The Vault.

The vault was a large Bank that was in the center a city neighborhood that was under human control. It was cluster of buildings, not buildings like New York but mostly one-story buildings with over a thousand hungry mouths waiting around it. All the people of The Vault could do was wait for their scouts.

In the lead aircraft Sai pointed to his right gesturing for Yoon to turn right and she pushed the cyclic right and pulled back a tad causing the bird to enter a shallow turn. Toshiro was quick to move after her, knowing she was on the controls for Sai was much more aggressive on the controls then she was.

The jungle was gone now; only a sea of ruined buildings now lay before them with some pillars of smoke coming from parts of the city, signs of battles that had taken place from the fighting locals. People were still alive all over the world, fighting day in and day out for the war was far from over.

****

The thumps had caught the guards' attention, and soon the sound of helicopters coming had the residents running out of the buildings into the secured streets, some running to the top of the roofs with mirrors to signal the birds.

People began to scream and wave their arms while a large man with a flare gun shot up into the sky.

The red light raced through the sky and caught Sai's eye.

"Flare, two o'clock, three miles," Sai said into the mic.

"Tally," Toshiro responded as he began to talk to his crew.

Ja began to tell Toshiro a green flare should be next, a signal meaning all was well, it's was meant for Ja.

As predicted a green flare raced across the sky over The Vault seconds after Ja had said it would.

Toshiro slowed back as Sai had briefed earlier to almost twenty disk. Sai was going to take his gunship in first to be certain it was not a trap for Toshiro. Than's past acts had caused Sai to be uneasy when bringing Dead Air to a place they had not been before. One of Sai's pilots had been ambushed but managed to escape to tell the story and now Sai was not taking any chances.

"I have the controls." Sai grabbed the controls and Yoon let go of the cyclic and collective as her heart raced with excitement.

Sai pulled a steep turn towards The Vault and brought the aircraft to NOE again.

He wanted to be sure he would avoid visibility in case they were tracking him with anti-aircraft weaponry.

The residents lost sight of Sai but maintained visual with Toshiro who was now circling, orbiting waiting for permission to begin the landing into the vault from a distance. He was a small dot to the residents slowly moving just above the building tops.

Closer to the vault, racing between the buildings, Sai could not help but think of *Star Wars,* taking his X-Wing through the trenches as buildings flew by the cockpit doors.

Yoon's eyes were wide now, as the ground raced past her, the buildings quickly turning into a blur.

"Weapons Tight, but Lock and Load Boys," Sai told his gunners.

They pulled their bolts back chambering their first rounds as Sai flew another thirty seconds. Each gunner was now at the moment of truth, live targets could await, but each prayed they would be friendlies for they have never killed the living.

Sai now raced down the final stretch of road, The Vaults residents hearing the pounding of the Huey's blades growing extremely close as he flew. At the end of the road a single building stood between Sai and The Vault and at the last second he snapped the cyclic back and began a cyclic climb. The G-Forces caused the crew to sink in their seats as Sai nosed the bird up to thirty degrees.

People watched in awe, as the helicopter climbed and nosed over aiming all its rockets and guns at the center of their camp. Down it dived and over it went as the rotor wash blasted the citizens of The Vault.

On the quick pass, the crew observed, looking for signs of betrayal but there was none, only people waving, not knowing that if the crew felt threaten they could have easily made a mess of The Vault.

Sai began to orbit The Vault with long wide left turns so he and the gunner on his side could inspect The Vault just a little longer.

The citizens waved at Sai, some armed, some not. There were women, children, and elderly all residing within the fortress of The Vault and with two low orbits it was time to bring Toshiro in.

"1-2, Indiana." The signal was sent and Toshiro began to pull his bird into a steep turn headed towards The Vault.

"1-1, I'm at your seven, 10 disk, going to begin final into The Vault."

"1-2, Roger, at my seven, keep frosty when you land, I'll make a few more orbits, just be sure to let me know what you see."

"Roger, beginning final."

Sai passed again over Toshiro's three o'clock. Toshiro hovered at ten feet bringing it straight down to the ground causing a crowd to begin to grow just outside of his rotor disk.

Sai watched from above as Ja and Arm exited Toshiro's aircraft, people ran up to meet Ja with the look of excitement written across their faces. The man had accomplished his job and here was Dead Air.

"Looking good 1-2."

"1-1, I'm shutting down. I'll call you on fox in a few."

Toshiro's blades began to slow down as Eck took his helmet off, the cool breeze now hitting his face. He looked to his brother who was already talking to people in the crowd, Ja introducing him to everyone.

Eck looked up to see Sai over the 9'o clock position continuing to orbit above.

Sai was not one to lend his trust easily, especially since the reports of bandits recently, so he continued his orbit, he covered the bird as Toshiro and Eck exited the aircraft, the blades coming to a complete stop.

Toshiro headed towards Arm while Eck carried a red rope with a hook on the end. Eck walked to the front of the bird and threw the rope over the blade and caught the rope on the other side. He began to pull the blade counter clockwise towards the tail boom of the Huey in order to secure the blades from damage from Sai's rotor when he landed.

Two orbits had gone by and Toshiro began to wave up at Sai as he walked back to the aircraft and turned the battery back on.

"1-1, Chocolate, we've got chocolate."

"Roger chocolate, I'll begin my approach now. Yoon you got the controls."

"I've got the controls," she responded as trained.

"You've got the controls," he said again, the three way positive control he had bestowed upon his pilots.

With Yoon on the controls, Sai let go of the cyclic and collective while Yoon began to set herself up for an approach into The Vault. She was still in training and now that no danger was present she once more found herself controlling the bird.

She took a sigh of relief for a moment and soon her nerves were back up. She felt all the eyes of The Vault's residents staring at her, watching her as she began to start her final approach.

"Slow it back, a little more, powers good, rotors good," Sai instructed as she maintained her focus outside with a horde of zombies screaming for her from the streets below. A crash meant certain death; the crew's life was now literally in her hands.

The Huey began to shutter as their airspeed slowed. The vibrations rattled the crew in their seats, which was normal, especially for a Huey.

Her focus intensified as both crew chiefs cleared her of The Vaults walls, in response she began to descend from twenty feet, then to fifteen as she slowly kept moving forward at a snails pace.

Close to the ground now the rotor wash began to send debris up into the air through the compound. The residents shielded their faces with their hands as tiny dust and rocks blasted their faces.

"Doing well."

"Ten feet, forward 5,4,3,2,1," a voice in her headset said. "Bring her down here, 3,2,1, skids light and your good." The crew chief announced with Yoon pushing down on the collective.

"Good job Yoon." Sai smiled at her as he lifted his dark visor to reveal his face.

Yoon smiled, her lower face giving it away for her eyes were covered by the visor looking all around for approval. Outside the residents cheered and clapped for help had finally arrived. Next to her Sai had begun to shut down the aircraft while the crew chiefs exited the bird.

****

The Dead Air crews were introduced to the leadership of The Vault, a police officer and former homicide detective from the Chit Lom district of Bangkok. He'd been at the Central World Mall, the same exact mall that Sai and Yoon escaped from so long ago and he too narrowly made it out of their with his life.

His name was Konkrit; he was a man a little older then Sai but who had aged way beyond his time over the last few months. His hair was turning gray, his eyes looked worn and like the others from The Vault he was definitely showing signs of being malnourished. Life in the big city was far worse than where Wat Tatsunupi was. The residents' faces were worn, worn to the point they resembled the soldiers who manned the trenches of World War I. They had been under constant siege with millions of the dead beyond their walls and their bodies had bared the brunt of that kind of pressure.

Konkrit came straight to the point when he met the military leadership of Wat Tatsunupi, he needed for Sai to take some of The Vault residents with him for they could no longer support the number of mouths living within The Vault's walls. Over the past few months the raiding parties had come to a screeching halt. The dead had overwhelmed the majority of their parties and the amount of resources arriving had begun to dwindle.

Behind Sai, Toshiro was eager to take the refugees with him; he greedily rubbed his hands together as he inspected The Vault's women outside the bank while the others talked with Konkrit.

The problem now was that Wat Tatsunupi's farms were only big enough to support their own residents at the current time. Sai explained to Konkrit the endeavors that were taking place in order to secure more land for Wat Tatsunupi. He also emphasized the dangers that came with clearing the land of the dead that may have been enclosed inside the containers. Clearing the land would be hell again, and the lost of more of Wat Tatsunupi's men was almost guaranteed, however, The Vault still had manpower available if Wat Tatsunupi needed it.

Konkrit was quick to volunteer some of his men for the danger in clearing more land for Wat Tatsunupi and of course weapons from The Vault was almost unlimited. During the outbreak many weapons were never fired and only dropped once. The Vault had a full arsenal including several tanks inside it's perimeters, something that would make clearing the land easier, only problem being that the tanks would probably never leave Bangkok with one bag of gas and with the cars and debris on the roads they would burn to much gas trying and just end up like many tank crews early on. Surrounded by the dead with nowhere to go.

No matter what, though, Sai was going to help the people of The Vault and the extra man power and weapons would make clearing The Jungle that much easier, The Jungle being the new area which resembled The Zoo. It was then agreed upon and in two days time Sai would be back to pick up the men and weapons.

Sai discussed the evacuation of The Vault by those who wanted to leave; those who would leave would be first up when it came to clearing The Jungle, but more importantly a semi trade agreement was decided upon. Medicine, technology, generators, fuel and anything the modern world had to offer. The Vault could probably get their hands on these times with raids after they secured the Bangkok sewer system. A project that involved The Vault troops securing block by block of the underground world in hopes it would make it easier for raiding parties to secure more goods. Eventually Konkrit planned on securing the sewer passage ways to the river that led north to Wat Tatsunupi, but for that to be done it would involve a joint force of both "city-states" as they came to be known as.

The next few hours of talk eventually led to a conclusion for now at the end of the talks Sai had agreed upon an alliance with the people of The Vault and speaking for Dario and George of Big C the three states became one. Wat Tatsunupi, Big C and The Vault were now part of an alliance. All for one, and one for all; they were the largest and most powerful settlements that were known to exist in central Thailand. They would become symbols of civilization in the future.

****

Yoon, being the celebrity she was, had spent most of the day talking with the people of The Vault, many were impressed that she was now the pilot of the gunship. Her fan base may had been devoured months earlier but it may have grown stronger now that she was probably the only actress in all of Asia still alive, top it off she was flying the gunship Dead Air.

Dead Air 1, was a souped-up version of a UH-1 that Toshiro had overhauled. It was OD green like many others of her kind, but had been gutted of all nonessentials to make room for guns, rockets, and whatever creative thing Toshiro could put into her. It was a beast on skids, extremely dependable, very durable and effective in killing whatever got in her way. She was the lifeline to the known world.

Arm, Eck, and Tor had stayed with Sai as they toured The Vault with Konkrit while Toshiro and Stephen made a name for themselves with the local women.

The heart of The Vault was a bank where they had their meeting. The Vault of the bank was the last resort in case the perimeter was breached. Inside the perimeter, Sai observed four tanks and three APCs, along with a few cars. Still in working condition, they would use the vehicles only in emergencies since the perimeter had been compromised several times in the past. Only with a combination of claymores and flamethrowers did the soldiers of The Vault manage to fight off the dead.

The residents were from all backgrounds, it was just luck that had kept them alive so far, in the right place at the right time and that was all that matter. Many had just stumbled on the fortification early on during the outbreak. There under Konkrit's leadership many large trucks and buses had been overturned helping to block several streets leading to the bank.

The sun was near the horizon, and the day was beginning to come to a close. Konkrit finished giving his tour to Sai and the others when it was time to lead them back to their aircraft.

The residents came out as the crews began to strap themselves into the birds and with Yoon waving goodbye Sai began to start up the bird as her fan base waved back.

It felt good as they made their way home that late afternoon. They were not alone, and even in the destruction of Bangkok, life was finding a way; but the ever-dreading tide of the dead screaming from below kept lurking deep in the back of their minds as they flew towards the safety of Wat Tatsunupi.

****

The three enclaves of Wat Tatsunupi, Big C, and The Vault united as one in the name of survival. Commerce was opened up as a search-and-destroy party under Konkrit secured paths through the sewers of Bangkok to the river and other places closer to the malls. Barricades were set up throughout the sewer system so it became like an underground highways as carts traveled back and forth under the eyes of The Vault's soldiers.

Finding the exits to the river was the beginning; a joint water assault was launched and led by Toshiro, who led several members of each city-state down the river in motorboats from Wat Tatsunupi and the Big C region.

Three boats were sent with five men on each. It was a daring nighttime raid into a harbor south of Bangkok. There they acquired two fishing ships that they planned on converting into cargo vessels and Toshiro even got a new toy, an old PBR River Rat boat from the Vietnam era which suited his life well when it came to drinking and fishing. After killing the occupant who was stuck in his seat due to a seatbelt on the River Rat, they fueled up the boats with gas cans The Vault provided and headed north. The River Rat ship went to Wat Tatsunupi as Toshiro's trophy and the fishing boats went to the other two ports one that was not physically connected to Big C and could only be reached by air.

Over the following year, Sai had expanded Wat Tatsunupi's barriers tremendously using the same tactic that they had done while constructing the Zoo. Wat Tatsunupi now stood on both sides of the river with a bridge connecting the two, which was built by Tran and Wanchai. The river in the middle of the Wat Tatsunupi Fortress was now secured; trees that had been cut down were anchored into the river and below nets kept the dead out of the area between Wat Tatsunupi's two sides. The dead that did inhabit the area between the two sides were disposed of in one night.

Sai and his troops had lit torches on the banks of the river and waited. The dead who still had eyes saw the flames above and rushed to the sides of the bank, there they met an end as spears, axes and swords greeted them for the sides of the river were lined by two separate formation of soldiers standing side by side.

Wat Tatsunupi was still constantly in a state of siege like that of the people of The Vault, the dead knew where they were since machines ran there daily giving the dead hope that they could reach the tasty morsels inside someday. At any giving day there could be over a thousand moaning stiffs outside beating on the walls that Tran had created. There were no longer walls of cargo containers, but walls of reinforced ramparts

327

made of earth, stone and wood, almost like a medieval castle. His construction teams worked day after day and with the resources coming in from the other city-states construction time was reduced. Technology, not what it once was, slowly was coming back.

Sai's fleet of helicopters had also begin to grow, 1 UH-60A, 2 UH-1Ds, and 2 EC-145s also known as LUH-72As Lakotas to the US Army, one of the first birds he flew out of flight school. Great avionics package, but with no GPS signals that didn't mean shit. Still though, the bird was dependable and required less maintenance than the UH-60, which he saved mainly for sling loads.

A combination of raids by ground and air had recovered enough vital supplies to keep his fleet running for at least two more years, sadly, one day the parts might stop coming in, the fuel would go bad, but as long as they could maintain what they had they could keep them going. Perhaps even start producing fuel. Sai was no longer the only pilot of Wat Tatsunupi which was a god send for him, Yoon, Stephen and Tor had joined the ranks of aviators along with Toshiro who now rarely flew due to his eyesight beginning to fail another pilot that had flew early on had died of natural causes.

Wat Tatsunupi was the largest of the three city-states, housing nearly two hundred people and counting to grow. The Vault had a hundred exactly and Big C was approaching a hundred.

The three states were not the only ones to thrive, other smaller enclaves were sprinkled throughout the sea of the dead, some unreachable and some not.

Some that made contact wanted no part of the Alliance and wanted to start life over from scratch, however others fell under the protection of the Alliance, in return the Alliance soldiers would be allowed to use their enclave on long range missions into unknown territories. Most small enclaves however would simply evacuate to the larger states.

The Alliance was not the only ones to prosper, Than had carved out a large territory in the undead world. They pillaged and burned many enclaves over time and found that it was more useful to enslave the population and force the men to fight for him under threat of killing there families. To Sai, Than was considered the Axis of evil for wherever he went he brought misery. It would not be long until the two factions would meet in all out war. Skirmishes had already begun in the alliance most northern territories.

Bad as Than was, Sai feared the dead more for they had failed to decay twenty months after the war had begun. Some were smart and used the others to charge smaller enclaves causing the occupants to defend one side of their fortress while on the other side a pyramid of bodies would form to scale the walls. The Brains led the ones who committed those acts; however, rumors continued of something else far to the north that controlled the dead for the sole purpose of waging war against man. These stories had Sai nervous; and, with Than running around causing mayhem, his sense of security was dwindling. The two men needed to face each other soon.

Chapter 21: *Battle for the Big C*

A young Thai boy was climbing the ladder to a wooden lookout tower above Wat Tatsunupi. Upon reaching the top, he crawled into the bird's nest where an old-fashioned, wind-up siren stood watching over the compound. With sweat rolling down his cheeks, he grabbed the handle and began to crank it as fast as he could. The siren started off calmly in a whine before it began to crescendo its way up so everyone could hear.

The aging siren yelled far beyond the compound, whining in intervals and catching every creature within earshot's attention. Sai who had been talking with the Old Monk near the Northern wall looked towards the tower as he stopped in mid sentence with the Monk. There he saw the boy cranking the siren. Immediately he began to run towards the original part of Wat Tatsunupi while Stephen, Tor and Yoon began to scramble from their previous duties around the Fortress Temple.

Wat Tatsunupi had awakened with a flurry of activity. The soldiers ran to the perimeter like they had rehearsed so many times before while others formed ranks in the open fields. Wien and her friends began to set up the hospital in The Zoo for the mass casualties that the siren said were coming. At the school the children were herded into the original part of the Wat for added protection.

Sai ran through the Wat's original western gate to see Toshiro already untying the bird, a UH-1 gunship, fully loaded and ready to kill anything that was waiting for it. A crew chief teenager shortly followed Toshiro's lead and began untying the bird as Sai entered the cockpit and began to strap himself in. Strapping the belts on Sai saw a runner approaching the bird from the radio station with a message.

"P' Sai, it's Big C. They are under siege. Tanks have broken through the first barriers and moving west towards the secondary walls. It's Than." The boy huffed and puffed trying to catch his breath.

"Did Arm pass the word to The Vault?" Sai asked, while the boy handed Sai the coordinates of the attacking armor.

"The Vault is launching two boats to head to the extraction point for the survivors. Our convoy is about to roll out. Ta's getting the River Rat ready to go, and everything is going as rehearsed, sir."

"Good job, thanks." With that said, Sai put on his helmet, tightened his chinstrap, and wiggled his fingers through the nomex flight gloves.

Toshiro slapped Sai's helmet, a signal saying all was ready with the bird and they could spool up anytime.

With that said Sai went through the checklist by memory and began to spool up Dead Air. The blades turned as Sai began to talk on the Freq Hop secure channel.

"Yoon, you up?"

"Roger, Sai."

"Hey, babe, no heroics today. The boats are on the way to the rendezvous point. We've got tanks incoming. I don't know about triple A, but it's going to get rough. Wait for the Ice call. Love ya and happy hunting."

"Be careful, Sai."

Yoon sat in the Blackhawk with the APU running waiting for the two gun ships to launch first. Tor and Sai would provide cover while two slicks – aircraft with no rockets and only the crew chiefs gun for protection. The slicks would pick up the refugees and begin ferrying them to the rendezvous point. The rendezvous point was Big C's docks that always had an armed team on the walls. Logic was that instead of the birds traveling back and forth to Wat Tatsunupi and wasting time/fuel for every round trip, they could drop them off there and let the boats ferry them to Wat Tatsunupi or The Vault as needed.

At the Northern gate of Wat Tatsunupi, a barrage of gunfire erupted at the dead who were swarming the area. The *Mad Max* Thai versions of Road Warrior vehicles rolled out with a covered M117 with a makeshift plow leading the way driven by Eck.

Stephen watched from where his "Lakota" was parked as the convoy crushed wave upon wave of dead as they moved through the gate and once the vehicles were gone the gate was sealed up by the soldiers and the convoy was on their own.

The convoy raced out, rolling over bodies but not opening fire; the vehicles had been proven many times over in the past and the occasional thump on the heavily modified bumpers was no cause to worry.

Eck drove out through the slit in the M117, knowing what had to be done as he led several modified kick-ass two-tons and a sixteen wheeler that resembled a B-17 Flying Fortress. The M117 he drove also had a periscope-type device on top of it that could be extended if the dead covered his sight.

"1-1, Red Con 1," Sai said in the mic as his crew secured themselves in the crew chief seats.

"1-2 Red Con 1 Beacon," Tor said as he waited to pull pitch.

"Roger, TOWRICO, Torch."

Five seconds on the second Sai pulled pitch and he along with two of his crew chiefs, Dead Air 1-1 rose straight up before noising over and gaining speed.

Sai could see the Blackhawk with the blades not yet turning and then he saw Tor's bird as he flew right over it and behind Stephen's bird, then he flew over The Zoo and over the wall.

Tor pulled pitch as soon as Sai flew over and turned left to follow Sai who had already turned northeast towards the river.

"1-2 Closing.1-2 Convoy," Tor said after a few seconds of flight.

"Roger, convoy, accelerating."

Sai nosed the aircraft over again and the Huey began to pick up speed.

Yoon watched as Tor's bird dipped below the trees and followed the river after Sai.

"2-1, Red Con 2," Yoon said to her sister ship.

"2-2 Red Con 2," Stephen replied.

"Roger, we'll go Red Con 1 in five minutes." Yoon took a deep breath and prepared for battle.

From one of the walls, Ren Pi looked at the Blackhawk and smiled. It was time for him to go home.

"George, those guys are ruining my vibes, man," Dario said, as he loaded his rifle and headed out of Big C's building towards the main barricade that had been set up a year earlier.

George followed out the door as several women and children ran inside the building. Gunfire was heavy on the eastern wall. Massive explosions were taking place as the two old farts raced to the primary wall as fast as they could which was at a snails pace compared to the younger men around.

At the wall, snipers were trying to pick off the enemy snipers who had taken up residency in several of the ruined buildings. The tanks were coming, single file and were almost in range for the RPGs, behind the tanks were cages being pulled by APCs full of living human bait, mostly children and elderly. The dead swarmed the cages, reaching for the juicy flesh inside the iron bars.

Upon reaching the wall George and Dario looked out to the outer perimeter. The tanks had pulverized it; fortunately, this wall was thicker and should last longer.

Dario saw several of his men who had been retreating from building to building get mowed down by the tanks machine guns and then swarmed by the dead beyond the main wall.

"Fuckers!" Dario fired a few rounds downrange, a useless gesture.

"Dude, you're just pissing them off more, don't you think we have enough hostilities already man?" George said, still high as a kite from the pot they had grown that year.

Another explosion this time closer sent gravel raining down on the two old men.

"Sai where are you," George said to himself, as he took aim and fired pissing off the tank crew just a little more.

****

The tanks stopped about two hundred yards away; the second and third tanks moved up, flanking the first tank in the debris-filled road. Undead poured over them, but the crews were used to it; they could care less about a hundred corpses pounding on the hull of their iron beast; on the top of each tank turret was a makeshift periscope. The tank commanders used it to get around when the dead swarmed their armor.

"This doesn't look good man." Dario fired his RPG, which bounced off the front the tank shredding the dead around it and causing minor damage to the Patton tank.

The tanks opened fired. Their rounds tore into the barricade, but still it held.

A few more RPGs fired, but the armor proved too tough to penetrate.

All around, George's men began to fall as the tanks' machine guns opened up on the RPG crews. Tracers flew over George's head in what would have been an awesome trip of LSD but he had run out of that a month ago.

George stood up when the firing stopped and fired his RPG again but to no effect again. He went back to his butt just as the gunner crews fired their main cannon into the thick wall.

The blast of the main cannons was beginning to rock the barricades.

"Retreat!" George ordered as he pulled Dario and the other young men away from the wall.

As if on cue, the tanks fired on the wall again, causing chunks of it to give way. The cannons fired several barrages on the wall and the cracks were beginning to give way to tons of dead that were on the other side.

Another barrage and the explosions sent the retreating men flying through the air as the concussion waves felt like they were going to shatter their insides and with another barrage the wall finally gave way.

George turned around and picked up a young man who was on the ground near him and told him to run to the safety of Big C. He bent over and picked up his AK-47 and with his last RPG still slung to his back he knelt down as the first of the dead made his way through the wall.

A sprinter, a dead woman with a missing arm, rotten clothes, and a permanent grin came charging forth. Calmly, George took aim and fired.

The top of her head flew off and dark rotten matter was sent rocketing to the sky as a young sprinter followed by a shambler made it through the wall, followed by a jogger and a crawler.

George made his stand as Dario heard the gunshots from behind. He turned to see his old friend alone roughly a hundred yards behind him.

"George! You old fool, have you gone senile?" Dario was about to go back for him when two of the younger men quickly grabbed Dario by the arms and pulled him towards Big C as he fought every step of the way.

George had taken down over a dozen, and still they poured through the gap; he could hear the tanks moving closer as they approached the hole in the wall behind the dust.

From behind the dead, another explosion caused that the last section of the wall to fall. The number of dead began to decrease; most that entered now were shamblers, which George had no problem dispatching.

From the smoke and fire on the wall, he saw a long olive drab cannon pop out of the dark cloud as the dead approached his position once more.

"This is it."

George fired the last of his rounds of his rifle and unslung his RPG as the dead reached within striking distance. He charged forward as the tank's turret turned towards his position.

The gunner of the tank saw an old man running past his sights and out-maneuvering the dead around him. Now at the side of the number 1 tank that was first through to breach the wall, dead hands reached for George, jagged fingers tearing into his flesh, teeth sinking into his arms. He looked like a running back trying to make a touchdown in the end zone as he pulled the defensive team of the dead with him.

His vision was decreasing as the bites took effect, his blood was flowing, his muscles were dying yet he forced every last ounce of energy to move around the tank.

The second and third tanks saw George and his undead groupies move behind the first tank where he stop right behind the first tank.

In pain, he lifted his RPG up at pointblank range of the number 1 tank's rear.

"It's a Good Day to Die!" He squeezed the trigger; a swoosh of hot air was the last thing he felt as his RPG struck home.

Dario saw the tank erupt into a bright fireball as his friend reached nirvana. The turret flew up over a hundred feet into the sky before landing forty yards to the north onto one of the ruined buildings.

****

At Big C, Dario's remaining forces rallied as they fired at the tanks with everything they had; the dead were no longer an issue, since they were still attracted to the human tuna cans on wheels just outside of the wall.

The two remaining tanks began to move towards Big C; they were intent on capturing the building and not letting the dead in it; they fired at the roof, at the soldiers on the top floors and not at anything ground leveled.

The tanks moved closer as two APCs carrying Than's troops shadowed their movements. Than's elite were going to storm the building as the last two remaining APCs outside of the perimeter pulling the living bait that kept the dead outside of the burning wall.

The tanks closed the distance, this time just feet away from the building, where they began to open fire with their machine guns.

Bullets tore through the barricade and the defenders at the ground level as the APCs backed up with their rear doors facing the barricade.

Bleeding and shot in the arm, Dario held his rag tag group of defenders at ground level. Most were wounded, many were dead and all hell was about to break out as the APCs backed up.

A grenade came rolling towards the entrance of the building and seconds later the structure shook as a loud thud burst through the front door, several popping sounds could be heard nearby as smoke and CS gas began to fill the bottom floor of Big C.

The sound of the barricade being smashed was next followed by gunfire from the entrance and more grenades went off.

Coughing from the CS gas and blinded by smoke, a grenade rolled next to Dario as he rubbed his eyes just in time to see it come to a stop by his foot.

"Fuck this." He grabbed it and threw it back towards the entrance.

The explosion helped clear out some of the gas and smoke and sent several of Than's men straight to hell.

Dario began to fall back with snot and drool falling out of him as bullets whizzed by his head striking others around him when the sound of a Huey closing in caught his attention.

****

"1-2, just like practice."

Sai was diving down at the tanks and APCs outside of Big C.

"Guns, Guns, Guns, Rockets, Rockets, Rockets," he said to himself as he unleashed hell.

His tracer rounds found his targets followed by the rockets penetrating one of the tanks. He pulled up and banked hard right as his crew chief opened fire at the soldiers like a wild man killing and maiming many of Than's best on the first swoop. Sai could hear him music coming from one of the crew chief's seats, coming from the wild man who fired like a rabid dog. *Whoa Black Betty Bam Ba Lam.*

Tor dived in second opening fire just like Sai had done his tracer rounds bounced off of one of the APCs before his rockets shredded everyone in it.

The crew of the APC ran out covered in flames as their comrades tried to put them out while still taking aim at Tor, who was banking hard right following Sai's path. Seconds after they saw Tor bank right, Sai who had already done a 360-degree turn was diving down on them once more.

The second turn for Sai was a little different he could see large caliber rounds coming up to meet him from somewhere down below.

"Triple A, ten o'clock!" He spotted the Anti-aircraft artillery.

Sai broke contact with the burning APC as he banked hard left between two buildings for one of the APCs on the perimeter had been modified with an Anti-Aircraft gun.

It lost lock on Sai as its rounds smashed into Big C and another building Sai had taken cover behind. The gunner then turned to Tor, who was diving on his position.

Tor opened fired with guns and rockets and took out the AAA in a hail of glory pulverizing the crew and the dead alike.

"1-1, got him!" Tor shouted with excitement.

"Great kid, don't get cocky!" Sai always wanted to say that as he banked around Big C and brought his guns down on another APC near Big C.

The men fired and Sai could feel a few rounds hit the bird when he opened up with guns and rockets.

He flew over a smoldering APC and a tank that Ta had just killed as he headed towards the perimeter to see the two more APCs pulling cages behind them.

"You see that 2?" Sai asked as he flew over the two vehicles.

"Tally."

****

From Wat Tatsunupi, the residents felt the waves of explosions shake their homes. Smoke was rising in the distance from Big C; a large black plume of death was spiraling up into the sky as the battle continued on.

From the lead APC in the convoy, Eck could see through the jungle at the black plume that was waiting for him. Unlike before, the road had been cleared of vehicles and the ride was much quicker; they were now already turning right onto the bridge to cross the river.

"Dead Air, Rolling Thunder, twenty mikes out."

"Roger Rolling Thunder, watch your asses, Than was organized for this, keep your eyes peeled."

"Roger."

"Rolling Thunder, we have friendlies on the eastern perimeter at the Echo Wall of Big C, looks like thirty people stuck in two cages surrounded by Z. Two APCs accompany them, they are using the friendlies as bate, keeping the dead for the most part out of Big C."

"Can you take out the APCs?" Eck asked.

"Negative, they are danger close."

"Roger, we'll take care of them, Sai."

Eck and his convoy crossed the bridge sending a few zombies over the sides of it. The convoy was thirty men strong, armed to the teeth and ready for what awaited them.

****

Yoon and Stephen were already in a stag right formation with Yoon leading the way. The two helicopters crossed over the Rolling Thunder convoy towards the plumes of smoke.

Through the windscreen, Yoon could see two helicopters circling several black plumes of smoke around Big C.

"1-1, 2-1. We're Diamond," Yoon said, her voice entering Sai's helmet.

Sai looked to the south of his position to see the two helicopters inbound.

"2-1, we got enemy in the wire, threat should be minimum, use eight hundred feet as your hard deck, and we'll stay low to draw their fire. Call us when you're Ruby." Sai pulled a hard right as he took fire from a building to his left.

Toshiro lit up the side of the building, sending chunks of concrete and flesh to the swarming dead below; he always preferred to be the gunner rather than the pilot.

Yoon and Stephen were now in a cruise formation, giving the two birds enough room to maneuver in case they took fire. Stephen now trailed ten rotor disks behind, covering Yoon's rear with his crew chiefs, scanning for any tracer fire.

The Blackhawk shot straight up to eight hundred feet followed by the stripped-down Lakota as they maneuvered to the west of Big C.

"I'm setting up for a right base 2, follow me in." She continued: "1-1, Ruby." She began her steep approach onto Big C's roof. She rode the shutter in as the two Huey gunships flanked her side, following her in.

She was now four hundred feet from her target when she heard her crew chiefs open fire. The helicopter jerked for a second as the sound of the guns going off shook her nerves. From her seat she could see people on top of Big C waving for her and crowding her LZ.

She continued forward as tracer rounds zipped by the nose of the Hawk. The LZ was now cleared as men forced the crowd back as she came within a hundred feet over the LZ.

Below in the building the firefight continued and grew more interesting as the dead entered the fray. Both sides found themselves being tackled by their dead enemy and it was not long until the bandits were fighting side by side with the Big C soldiers as the dead attacked both sides with no prejudices.

"5,4,3,2,1, wheels light, you're on the ground," the crew chief said before he jumped out his window and began to load people into the back of the helicopter. He stuffed as many bodies as he could into the bird and forced a leg back inside the cabin before he shut the cabin door. He then jumped back in and the other crew chief told Yoon she was cleared to take off.

Yoon pulled pitch and headed straight between the two Huey's, then turned right 180 degrees back to the river towards the Big C docks.

She waved as Stephen landed his bird on the building and began to load up passengers while Sai escorted her from trail.

"Yoon Break Left!" Sai shouted as he dived down on her two o'clock position.

Yoon did as ordered, turning away as Sai opened fire with his machine guns sending tracers into the jungle canopy. Nothing shot back as the two birds continued to the rendezvous point.

Yoon landed the Blackhawk and this time the other crew chief stepped out as Sai circled above. The passengers exited the aircraft and a pool of blood was in the back along with one of Yoon's crew chiefs and a refugee.

"Pull them out and get a volunteer to man the gun Yoon." She listened to Sai's voice and then told her crew chief to get a volunteer.

The two bodies were pulled out of the aircraft and a bucket of water splashed into the cabin as a thirteen year old boy got a quick lesson on how to use the weapon.

"We still got several more loads, Yoon. You're doing fine. Now let's get back to work."

"We're taking fire!" a voice shouted on Eck's headset.

The convoy rolled through tracer rounds and RPGs. The flying fortress truck opened up with cannons and flamethrowers spewing its contents on the sides of the road as it brought up the rear.

Eck could hear the rounds bouncing off his vehicle as he kept his convoy together and rolled through the ambush.

"Keep moving!" he ordered.

Rolling Thunder left a trail of flames and wounded. Than's forces were incinerated not expecting the fortress to be so powerful. They became easy pickings for the dead as they tried to scramble back to their vehicles.

Eck turned left and began to head north when he drove straight through a crowd of thousands of zombies. The convoy slowed to a snails pace as the tracks of the lead APC crushed all that stood in its way.

"Hold your fire," Eck Ordered as his vehicle went up and down from over fifty bodies that were popped below his tracks like zits.

"Tank!" a voice shouted. "Three o'clock!"

The periscope style tank approached through the crowd, the turret aiming at the second two-ton in the formation.

Pa…POW!

The two-ton exploded into the crowd, sending bodies in every direction.

Eck floored it again and pushed harder through the crowd as a piece of the two-ton crashed on top of the APC.

The men on the next two-ton began to lob grenades and everything they had when they heard.

Pa…Pow!

This time, the tank erupted in flames as the fortress rolled right in front of it and fired two howitzers from the roof of the iron beast. The dead surrounding the tank disintegrated as the blast shattered their bodies into a million pieces.

****

"1-2, RTB for fuel. I still got half a bag."

"1-1, Roger, returning for fuel."

Tor broke off of the Lakota's wing and made a beeline straight to Wat Tatsunupi as Stephen landed with five passengers at the port base of the Big C

Ta had arrived with his River Rat at the drop off point. Men mounted the guns on the boat and they patrolled both sides of the river waiting for the two boats from The Vault to arrive to assist in the evacuation, which Konkrit was leading.

Already twenty-five had been evacuated and were awaiting their rides down river at the dock. Big C soldiers patrolled the walls of the port scanning the jungle for anything other than the dead that had flocked to their location.

A hundred dead arms reached out from below, the dead moaning and screaming for a bite to eat. They pounded their torn fists against the wall made of earth, wood, stone, and steel, not even denting the structure, which proved too strong.

Inside, the frightened survivors of Big C huddled together as the Lakota dropped off its load and began to turn around for another run.

****

Firing from behind furniture, Dario was dropping the dead that were now walking up the stairwell and onto the second floor. Big C soldiers and what was left of Than's forces were now fighting the dead from behind a barricade, the enemy shambling ever closer.

"See what you started, numb nuts!" Dario shouted to a fat enemy soldier, who was firing next to him.

"Than made us, he has our family!" he shouted back, as he fired into the fray.

The floor was covered in bullet casings rolling in every direction and the air was clouded in a white smoke. From the smoke, dead arms reached the barricade where they found the soldiers using baseball bats, swords, and spears to hold them at bay.

"Don't give them an inch!" Dario shouted, as he smashed one of the creatures in the head with a golf club.

Along the furniture-built line, the soldiers fought as they ran low on ammunition, yet held strong as they heard the Blackhawk land on the roof once more.

Above on the roof, Chit was in charge; he helped loaded the next batch even while on struts and one leg. He had a rifle and a sidearm strapped to his body and kept the area calm for the most part as he directed the refugees to the heliport.

Hovering above, Sai's Huey began to make an approach to pick up five passengers as the Blackhawk became airborne once again with another twenty, mostly women and children, crammed in the cabin like sardines.

Sai landed on the pad to see Chit loading the next batch. He nodded at Chit and Chit nodded back in return.

"Sai, they're secure."

"Roger on the go."

His helicopter began its return trip and Sai noticed he was close to BINGO fuel.

"Yoon, I've don't have long on station. I'll take you to the docks but then I'll have to RTB. Tor should be up shortly, stay high out of the small arms and keep your eyes peeled for AAA or smoke trails."

"Don't worry. I'll be fine."

****

At the docks, the first batch was now on Konkrit's boats. They began to pull out of the dock when they instantly came under fire.

Ta opened up with his River Rat, and the battle began on the river.

Motor rounds were now dropping into the river aiming for the boats. From below the water the explosions rocked the waterborne dead as they saw the boats disperse above.

"Yoon, take them to Tatsunupi!" Sai ordered as he saw the mortar rounds falling in the vicinity of the rendezvous point.

"Roger."

Sai flew towards the dock and Toshiro dropped large propane like object from the helicopter, which was filled with cocktail called napalm.

The jungle exploded into flames, sending the dead stumbling on fire – but, more importantly, causing whatever enemy forces that had been mortaring the river to begin to flee.

"Ta, continue to hold your position and fill those boats to max occupancy, do you understand me!"

"Roger, Holding, it's fucking hairy down here!" Ta said, as the water exploded next to his boat and tracer rounds continued to fly from all directions.

"Sai, its Konkrit. I've landed. We will hold this position. Don't worry about us. We'll get everyone out.

Konkrit and his men began to race to the walls, one of his men was armed with a Javelin missile since the threat of tanks was high.

"Jesus," Sai said, as he looked over the side of the wall. What had been hundreds was now turning into thousands outside of the wall of the dock and worse was that they were beginning to do that pyramid thing. Somewhere in the swarm were several Brains directing the others to form the ramp to scale the wall.

"Sai, the dead are building a ramp."

"Shit, hold them with everything you have. Rolling Thunder is closing in on Big C. Get everyone on the boats. I'll get the other gunship to start moving pax. Hold them."

Sai's fuel was running low, and it was time to return to base for refuel. He hated doing this, but he had a crew and five passengers who depended on him to keep them alive.

Sai's crew chiefs fired randomly through the jungle as he headed south to Wat Tatsunupi.

****

Plowing through the dead in the streets, Rolling Thunder had arrived at the perimeter; two APCs stood there silently as the dead swarmed the cages that were pulled into the area.

"Looks like the APCs were abandoned," Eck told the convoy, still taking fire from a building to his three o'clock. "Can someone take care of that asshole please?"

The fortress turned the improvised turret Howitzer on the roof towards the direction.

Pa…Pow!

The explosion caused half the building to fall on the crowd of dead below. Squirming body parts wiggled beneath the rubble.

The two-ton behind Eck's APC was under attack; covered in barbed wire and spikes that faced downward, the dead tried their best to scale the vehicle's sides. But with the trained soldiers on the back of it, they were kept at bay.

Sin, who was sitting in the turret of the Howitzer, heard Eck's next order. The fortress was going to try to pull both cages to safety. The hard part would be attaching two cables onto them with thousands of dead surrounding the convoy.

"Should be fun." Eck said to himself.

"Fire!" the wheeled fortress commander shouted to the flamethrowers. Flames shot out from the bowels of beast. The jelly formula latched itself onto the dead and froze them in place as wave upon wave of napalm slammed into them, creating a Texas barbeque.

"Sin! Get the track moving!" the fortress commander ordered.

Sin hurried down from the turret into the fortress where a tractor that now resembled a spaceship waited. They had used it in the past to clear roads when entering the city; this time, however, Sin would drive up to the cages and attach cables to them.

"Prepare to launch Sin!" the voice shouted to the crew.

Sin took his seat in the armored tractor that had an enclosed driver seat with four slits in it – one in the front, two on the sides, and one on the rear. The slits were not meant for driving through a horde of the dead. Behind the driver was an extra seat, for whoever was unfortunate enough to ride shotgun in the bulldozer from hell.

A woman took her place behind Sin and slapped him on the head. "Let's get this shit moving, Sin."

"Prepare to lower the cargo door! Evacuate the loading bay!" The men surrounding the Tractor left the room and closed an iron door behind Sin.

"Opening cargo door!" the voice shouted.

Light penetrated the rear of the fortress and the smell of death slammed into Sin's nostrils once again. The door lowered in front of him revealing a horde of dead waiting for him. Pushing the gears around, Sin made the tractor go forward and into the fray. The tractor was swamped immediately as the dead climbed all over it and into the cargo bay of the fortress where steels doors stood.

Upon leaving the Fortress, a periscope made of steel shot straight up from the roof of the tractor. The operator was Sin, who looked over the crowd that was covering the slits of his vehicle now. He turned the scope around to the left 170 degrees and found his targets.

He pushed the gas and the Tractor began to move through the crowd with a few surprises.

Chainsaws were at every end of the iron beast and were operated by his passenger through a series of controls.

The jagged teeth began to tear creatures off the tractor by sawing their bodies in half. On the lower level of the tractor, heads were sawed in half as it slowly moved towards its targets.

The vehicle bounced as bodies popped under its wheels for several minutes as the tractor crawled to the cages.

From behind the tractor several men appeared on the roof to draw as many of the dead within killing range of the flamethrowers. Many lost interest in the moving iron beast and went straight for the bait, but the sheer number remained too great.

"Almost there, Sin," the voice said in the headset.

Sin brought the vehicle to within inches of the iron cages. Through the mass of dead bodies surrounding the cage Sin could see the civilians cowering inside. His heart raced as he grabbed several Flash Grenades from a stump inside the cabin of the tractor.

"Cover me!" he shouted to his passenger. He pulled the pin on several grenades, as his passenger unlatched the hatch of the tractor and popped it open. She went out first shooting the dead on the tractor first, hands reaching out for her simultaneously.

"Fire in the hole!" Sin dropped the grenades on all sides of the tractor.

Loud bangs shook the vehicle as bright lights engulfed everything within the vicinity.

The explosions rocked the dead, the civilians, and the tractor crew; but, unlike the rest, the tractor crew had expected it.

The dead had fallen all around, confused and in a daze while Sin hooked the closest cage to the tractor with a hook and cable. He had jumped from the tractor onto the street floor that was littered with squirming dead, still too messed up to get their footing, while the girl from the tractor fired at those who reached out for him.

With the second cable in hand, he was about to latch the second cage when he saw that no one left inside was alive. They had been infected and torn each other to pieces. He dropped the cable as the dead around him began to rise to their feet at an increasing pace.

"Oh fuck! Oh fuck!" He began to panic, as arms started reaching for him.

The girl opened fire and heads exploded as Sin ran like hell to get to the tractor.

Upon reaching the machine, he climbed it as fast as he could when dead hands grabbed on to his ankle.

"Oh fuck!" A second later, he felt several bites around his foot.

His eyes widened as he looked up at the girl.

"Nana!"

He was pulled back into the street and disappeared below the ocean of the dead.

"Sin! Sin! Sin!" Nana shouted as the dead began to crawl up the tractor towards her.

"SIN!"

Hands reached out for her, and she hacked them with a machete before closing the tractor door.

"Sin," she cried.

****

Wave upon wave came through the second floor of Big C. All soldiers from both sides were now in the fight for survival as sprinters busted through from the stairwell. The shamblers had eaten up ammo and now the cavalry was on the attack once more.

"Hold the line!" Dario shouted as he continued to fire. "We need more ammo!"

"Fire in the hole!" someone shouted, tossing a grenade.

Boom!

Several of the sprinters were shredded; mixed in with their shambler brothers and several smart zombies, the dead were beginning to get the upper hand.

"Form your ranks!" Dario ordered as he fired the last round from his rifle. "Phalanx!"

A group of men rushed up from the rear of the battle lines. They lined up shoulder to shoulder in front of the escalator as several men armed with homemade shields, short swords, and tridents took a knee in front of them.

"FALL BACK!" Dario ordered the gunners along the barricade.

The men began to run through the phalanx formation as the dead penetrated the first barricade in hot pursuit.

Dario was now behind the phalanx as the first of the dead hit the line.

The wall of tridents impaled the dead, as the men with short swords and shields hacked at their heads. Bodies quickly began to pile in front of the Phalanx as the tridents continued to hook their prey and the short swords hacked away.

"Steady! Fall back slowly! Keep the formation tight!" the leader of the Phalanx ordered.

The formation slowly moved back as the dead continued to pound the formation, the shields and wall of tridents preventing them from penetrating them as the ancient formation was proving deadly once again.

On the roof, the crowd grew restless as the Lakota landed once more. On the radio with Chit, Stephen told him the bad news. The trips were going to take longer now that passenger drop-off was diverted to Wat Tatsunupi; they needed to hold as long as they could for Yoon and Tor's choppers to return for evac.

With that said, Stephen lifted off and headed south with five more passengers. Chit moved towards the stairwell and began to head down the stairs, leaving a young Thai man in charge on the roof. He went down several flights of escalator stairs towards the smoke and gunfire until he came to the third floor, where the soldiers were reloading along with Than's men. From there, over at the escalator, he saw the phalanx holding as they slowly backpedaled towards the secured escalator behind them. It was a strange sight to see, for in front of the men was a never-ending horde of dead, and immediately behind the phalanx was open ground. How long it would be open ground? It was probably just a matter of minutes.

There, Chit waited for his turn to hold the dead at bay.

****

"LET HER GO!" the Old Monk shouted to Ren Pi.

Ren was holding Wien hostage with a Beretta in hand. The Wat's residents surrounded him, as he demanded to board the Blackhawk.

"Fuck you old man!" He fired a round into the Monk's head.

The Old Monk lay dead at the heliport as Yoon told her crew to leave the helicopter. Her eyes fixed on her cousin, who was going into hysterics struggling against the stronger Ren Pi.

"Move, you fucking bitch!" Ren shouted into Wien's ear almost deafening the teen.

Arm was now in the area, his rifle at hand; but with Ren using Wien as a human shield, there was nothing he could do but watch Ren throw her into the back of the Blackhawk. He then pointed his gun to Yoon and forced her to climb into the cockpit. Immediately, he put a gun to her head while holding Wien down with his knee.

Ren put on the head set and began to speak as Yoon took off north away from the Wat. Arm rushed back towards the radio room where he would contact Sai of Ren's treachery.

****

The port was about to be overrun; the dead were now just feet from reaching the top of the wall. Konkrit and his men held as hands began to reach over out for them. Their gunfire was slowing down, and bayonets, swords, and spears were now doing the job.

Konkrit continued his fire as the first of the dead breached the top of the wall. He sent it flying back down the ramp of wiggling bodies only for another to take his place.

"Get a helicopter here Ja!" Konkrit shouted to his radioman. "Tell them the port is about to fall!"

Ja took the radio from his back and began to call in the mayday.

"Mayday! Mayday! We got Z in the Wire! We got Z in the Wire! Any elements, this in an emergency. We need immediate evac!"

Ta and his gunboat disengaged from the firefight in the river and began to pull into port as the sound of a Huey coming up the river in the distance could be heard.

The boat slammed into the docks and upon stopping and Ta got on the PA system. "Get in the boat!"

The civilians piled on as many as they could take as the dead continued to scale the wall. Konkrit was now in a vicious hand-to-hand battle with two dead people. All around the compound the dead were entering the ramparts to find the soldiers were not giving an inch of ground. Fierce bloody battle was still raging as Ta pulled from port and headed south towards Wat Tatsunupi leaving many to wait for the Huey.

The Huey landed in the center of the carnage, the crew chiefs opening fire at the walls that were now mostly dead now. The Huey was swamped with people instantly but not all could fit and with a heavy burden Tor pulled pitch leaving the soldiers to their doom.

As his helicopter gained altitude he saw the end as hundreds of the dead, mostly Sprinters began to charge up the undead ramp and over the walls. It was obvious to Tor that whatever was controlling the masses down below was not a Brain, but something much more sinister. It had waited until the last possible moment to send in the sprinters.

The soldiers were torn to pieces as the last of Konkrit's men began to make a run to the river. All around Konkrit his men were being tackled until only five were left. They jumped into the water and began to swim to the other side – always careful about letting any of their body parts go too far below the surface, for the dead were surely lurking down below.

****

"Sai, Ren took Yoon and Wien and are heading north," Arm told Sai.

Sai looked down at his fuel gauge; he barely had enough fuel to land, and there was no way in hell he could follow.

"Fuck, I should have killed that fucker!" Sai said to himself as he punched the cockpit door's window.

"Sai, Big C does not have long," Toshiro said, trying to keep Sai from making rash decisions, for the needs of the many outweigh the needs of the few or the one.

The gunship landed at the same pad that Yoon had left. There, the ground crew immediately began to hot fuel the bird as he thought of what to do next. A leader's decision was to stay in the fight, but his heart's decision was to go after Yoon and Wien.

****

"Dead Air 2 is on the way. Set up the fortress for helicopter operations five K south of Big C. The Port is gone. Big C is about to go, and we are now down the Blackhawk. Big C, hold as long as you can, help is on the way."

The voice on the radio said as the dead were now battling on the third floor of Big C. Chit opened fire again but was now running low on ammo. The smoke was thick here for it had risen from the lower levels and continued to rise and out of Big C.

Tor watched the many plumes coming out of the city; he had heard word of what had happened with Wien and Yoon. Wien and he had grown close over the last year and it hurt like hell for he was not going after her. He had heard of the decision Sai had made with Yoon and tried to be cold and calculating like him, but the pain was still strong. Sai was right, though; as long as Wien and Yoon remained airborne, they were in no immediate danger of being torn to shreds.

Tor began his approach to the roof that was now swamped more with people.

Landing, Tor took on as many passengers as he could before pulling pitch again. The helicopter dropped over the side of the building and flew south. In the distance, he could see Sai already returning.

A flare went up to the south where the convoy was set up. Tor slowed down as Sai passed out his right door headed towards Big C.

Tor flew another minute or so and saw the LZ, which was on top of the fortress, and around it were thousands of zombies, some already on fire from the flamethrowers.

"Come forward, 3,2,1," said the voice in the helmet set. "Clear to land."

Tor lowered the collective, and the Huey began to sink until the skids touched down on the top of the fortress.

Sai landed on Big C to see the fighting was now just on the floor below. Dario appeared from the stairwell just as Sai had landed. The man was covered in bites but was somehow managing to hold on. There was no sign of George and Sai, who would never know of the man's sacrifice in the streets of Lop Buri.

Dario smiled at Sai when Toshiro told him they were ready to roll. Sai pulled pitch again and that was the last time he would see Dario.

Dario walked back down to the floor below him as Tor began an approach onto Big C. Below, half his men were bitten and would never leave this place. Chit was gone, died a floor below, tackled by Sprinters. The Phalanx was breaking, the men worn and tired from an enemy who would never falter and never grow tired. Inch by inch, the phalanx was falling back, until Dario ordered all the wounded to throw everything they had at the dead.

"For your women, for your children, give them hell!" Dario shouted, as he tossed the joint he had been smoking.

In one last hurrah, the soldiers, bandits, and anyone else who was fighting on the floor, charged into the dead, with swords, bats, pipes, empty rifles, torches, everything that could be used as a weapon, employed in a charge into the ranks of the dead.

If the dead were human, they would have been in terror for the ferocity of the human attack was fierce. The soldiers plowed through the dead, as if they were weeds beneath the feet of horses.

Dario smashed everything as he swung his sword, left, right, up and down like a Viking warrior. They managed to push the dead back to the elevator before attrition took effect. Dario found himself surrounded by the dead; his men were all gone now. He looked around as the Shamblers closed in on him.

He reached for a joint in his pocket and lit it up. "See you dumb fucks in hell." He smiled.

He grabbed two grenades from his cargo pockets and laughed as he pulled the pins.

Sai was now on approach to Big C again with the dead beginning to scramble onto the LZ. Toshiro opened fire into the stairwell trying to slow them down.

A cloud of black smoke shot out of the stairwell as the grenades exploded. The last of the passengers were loading up into Sai's bird. Through the smoke the dead came out once more, shambling towards the helicopter.

"Time to go Sai," Toshiro said as he patted Sai's helmet to reinforce the thought.

Sai pulled pitch and headed straight ahead, gaining speed and altitude with a full load of passengers. He banked hard right after gaining sufficient speed and pointed all weapons on top of Big C. He unleashed everything he had at the roof of Big C.

Rockets pounded the roof creating a large explosion as one of them hit a propane tank. Fire erupted in the building causing hundreds of zombies to catch fire instantly. He watched the building burn and he swore that Than would pay for this day with his life.

Chapter 22: *Eye for an Eye*

"Sai it is not his fault." Ta held back Sai from beating the man's face in again. The man had already suffered a broken nose and jaw; many of his teeth were either in his stomach or scattered around the floor.

"You had a fucking choice! You could have fought back you stupid piece of shit!" Sai spat in his face.

"They have my family, please!" the man cried as he begged for mercy.

Sai threw Ta off his back and smashed the man's face again with his fist. Teeth went flying once more as the Thai man pleaded for his life.

Ta was about to hold Sai back again when Tor grabbed Ta nodding his head side to side.

Sai grabbed the man by the ears and pulled him towards the floor to find Sai's knee breaking his nose into more pieces.

"You stupid fuck! That is not my goddamned problem, you weak son of a bitch!"

"Please, I'll show you where they went. But please save my family. You can kill me if you want, just please save them." The man coughed up blood as Sai looked upon him with a look that no one had ever seen before. Hell was in Sai's heart, a passion for revenge, hatred. Darkness was consuming Sai's soul in front of the other men.

"Where are they?" Sai slapped him before he took a step back. "You better not be fucking around or I'll make sure you die a slow death." Sai grabbed a map from one of the men in the room and laid it out on the table. He then grabbed the man's face and slammed it on the table after turning the chair 180 degrees. "Where are they?" He pointed as he grabbed the man's broken hand and slammed it on the map.

The man pointed to an area just south of several steep hills and west of the river north of their scouted area.

"Ready my bird!" Sai shouted before turning his attention to the man. "If Yoon and Wien are dead, you are dead, your family is dead."

Everyone in the room stood quiet, fear gripping them. Sai looked around.

"The bird will be ready Sai," Toshiro said. "You need to calm down, be the Sai we know, not the Sai of death."

Surprisingly Toshiro had another side other than the drunken Samurai that he had displayed proudly.

Sai left the room thinking of Yoon, Wien, Ren, and Than.

"Calm down Sai, we will get them back, I promise," Toshiro continued as he walked out with Sai who was headed towards the armory. "Goddamn it, Sai," He said, grabbing Sai. "Sai, they are not dead. They are safe. We do this right or we are all dead. They are safe, maybe not with good people but the dead are not tearing them to pieces."

"Sorry, Toshiro," Sai apologized, his eyes full of anger.

"Listen man, I know you, if it weren't for you we all be dead three years ago. Everything is going to be alright, trust me we will get your family back."

"Toshiro, she's pregnant." Sai's mouth twitched, as his eyes teared up. He had been strong for so long and now more than ever he needed to stay strong for Yoon, the baby, and Wien.

****

"Cousin, it's good to see you again." Ren Pi hugged Than, both men laughing at their reunion.

"I see you brought me some gifts." Than smiled looking at Yoon and Wien, examining the two as he walked around them. "I know you." He walked up to Yoon getting extra close. "Ren, this is a good catch. I'm impressed. Fai, take them to my room for later and get them out of these filthy clothes." He paused. "Give them something less complicated." He grinned before turning his attention towards his cousin. "Now, Ren, tell me more about this Sai asshole."

A woman approached Yoon and Wien; it was Noi's sister, Fai.

"Please come with me," She told the two politely. The three walked out of the room through the catcalls of the bandits that were waiting to have a turn with the new comers. Vulgar expressions and verbal abuse was tossed at them as Yoon looked for a way to save her cousin. She scanned for weapons that were within reach for she did not want her cousin going through what she knew was coming.

Upon reaching the center of the camp, they approached Than's home. It was there that their bonds were cut by one of the guards. Immediately Yoon made a go for the knife but found a quick punch to her stomach stopping her in her tracks. Fai immediately began to yell at the guard. "You think Than wants marks on her?" The guard stepped back and looked at them.

"Get in there!" The guard raised his rifle.

The three entered the so-called home, as the guard locked the door behind them.

Inside the home, there was nothing but a bed. Being former prisoners the convicts knew that anything could be made into a shank and for that reason there was nothing for the sex slaves to use against their attackers.

"Wien, don't worry I'll get you out of here." Yoon turned to her cousin as she held her in her arms.

"Don't try to escape. They have this place set up like a prison. All the women here are slaves, their husbands off to fight for Than. Than has total control here," the woman warned. "I've been here since the dead rose. Trust me, I have tried."

"It will be okay, you don't know Sai. He will come for us and he will not hold back here. I promise." Yoon held her cousin tightly and ran her fingers through her hair. "Wien, Sai is coming for us. We just have to be strong. He will come."

"I know." She cried as she thought of what was coming raced through her mind.

****

"Before the dead, treachery amongst humans happened daily. But now we are an endangered species, outnumbered and killed on a daily basis by an enemy that does not want to die. Every day has become a struggle to eat, a struggle just to stay alive, but yet we have prevailed." Sai paused, looking around at all those that sat in the middle of the Wat.

"In the ashes of civilization, we have united against our common foe, and have fought him hard. But, as in all ages of man, there are people who want to have total control and these assholes who would take everything from us if we give them a chance." He took a breath.

"Today, on this peaceful Sunday morning, the forces of Than savagely and ruthlessly attacked the peaceful people of Big C. Caught off guard, the walls were breached by tanks and it became clear that it was only a matter of time until Big C was gone." His facial expression changed.

"We've lost many men, women, and children today. We lost loved ones and friends. We've lost soldiers and mentors." The crowd grew angry as emotions began to run deep.

"Their deaths will not go unpunished today. Their deaths will not be in vain, for today we have declared War on Than and his evil empire. It was only a matter of time until this war would come. We've all foreseen it and now is the time to strike. For if we do not act, Wat Tatsunupi and The Vault will suffer the same fate as our brothers and sisters of Big C." He looked around.

"Now, as many of you know, Ren has taken Yoon and Wien from me. I'd be lying to you if I said I was going to war and not rescue them. I was ready to go as soon as I found out where they are being held. But Toshiro has shown me the light; we are currently planning an assault at the heart of Than's empire. We have the intelligence that says he is where we think he's at, just south of Phi Mai. Now, who among you will take vengeance, who among you will be willing to put all of his soldiers to the sword?"

Sai finished addressing the crowd then sat on the floor in front of the main temple of Wat Tatsunupi. Toshiro and Tor were first to stand to their feet, followed by the men of Big C, then the soldiers of Wat Tatsunupi, and those from The Vault.

"Tonight, we prepare for battle! And tomorrow will be a Good Day for Than to Die!"

****

As the night rolled in, the alliance forces prepared for battle; tanks had been brought up from The Vault, helicopters were repaired and rearmed. The boats were refueled along with the two-tons. A garrison of men was selected to stay behind with the Wat in case of an undead attack.

Sai, Toshiro, Konkrit, the prisoner and the highest-ranking member of Big C's remaining forces came up with a battle plan in the TOC. The assault would take place; prisoners would be rescued, if possible. Sai and Tor would search for Yoon and Wien during the chaos of battle once the tide favored the allied forces. The objective was to kill Than and Ren Pi, and to destroy any chance of their forces rebuilding their armies for a counterattack. It was all or nothing for the Triple Alliance.

Not too far away, time rolled by as it approached midnight. Waiting in the rape room, the door opened. Ren Pi smiled heavily as he looked at Wien. "My cousin said I could have you." He grinned greedily.

Ren walked up to Yoon, who held her cousin; the two backed away until he was within striking distance. Yoon high kicked him in the chin, sending teeth up into the air. She then attacked his throat but was backhanded across the face, knocking her out on the floor.

Wien rushed to her cousin's aid, when she felt the man's arms pull her off of Yoon.

She cried as the night rolled on while the first force, a convoy from Wat Tatsunupi headed towards Than's camp, led by Konkrit and Eck. Three tanks, four two-tons, five APCs, two refuel trucks and the fortress with over fifty men moved out through the dark jungle, their headlights engulfed in darkness as soon as they left the compound.

"Five hours to go, Sai. Ta will be moving out with his Marines in two. Get some rest," Toshiro told Sai.

"Not tonight. I can't. I can't.. They are my responsibility. They are my family."

Toshiro knew there was no way Sai was going to let his guard down, for he was still enraged.

"Let's go over the plan one more time," Toshiro said, trying to distract Sai from thinking too much of his family.

****

Yoon opened her eyes to see her cousin covered in bruises from head to toe and naked on the bed. She squeezed her eyes and prayed for Sai to come.

At Wat Tatsunupi, looking at his watch as the rotor blades turned. Sai waited anxiously for ten more minutes. "Fuck!"

Remember your training, time on target, plus or minus thirty seconds. We can't get there early until our forces are set up. Sai thought to himself as the second hand barely ticked along at a slugs pace.

"I know," Sai said to himself before continuing on. "1-1 beginning commo check."

Tor and Stephen listened as Sai commenced the check.

"1-1 on fox mike, 1-1 on victor."

"1-2 on fox mike, 1-2 on victor," Sai heard Tor's voice say.

"1-3 on fox mike, 1-3 on victor," Stephen's voice entered his hearing.

"Flight, this is lead, switch to fox internal," Sai said.

All the men switched to 30.34 fm and kept Arm, the radio operator, on Victor where he'd be monitoring the operation as the acting battle captain.

"It's almost time," Sai said to himself as Toshiro listened. "I'm hoping this works."

"Sai, don't worry. You are Sai, last of the Apache and Comanche people. Make your ancestors proud today. Give your enemy hell!" Toshiro laughed, as he talked like a scruffy-looking Samurai once more. "Sai, it's time."

"Flight, going blacked out." Sai switched off the lights of his bird and switched on his goggles.

"1-3 Beacon," Stephen said.

"Torch."

The residents watched Dead Air fly off over the Chedi and over the farmland they had built before disappearing into darkness.

Minutes had gone by and the sounds of the rotor began to fade from the ears of Wat Tatsunupi and the three birds were now flying stag right as they headed up the river and to the east once they reached Lop Buri. Big C was still in flames sending smoke and burnt flesh smell into the night air, which was all that illuminated the earth. It appeared as a black blob in the night vision goggles with light shades of green showing the flames hiding within the building.

****

"Rolling Thunder in position." Konkrit said as Eck looked at the enemy encampment with a pair of binoculars. They were surrounded by the dead but not in any danger of being killed. The soldiers waited patiently inside the vehicles as the dead clawed at the iron skinned.

"The Duke is in position." Ta and his Marines waited by the river with a barge that had two up armored humvees and a two-ton.

"Dead Air, 2 minutes, on my signal unleash hell," Sai said as his men armed their weapons.

****

Monday morning, 0548. The encampment was asleep; today would be their Pearl Harbor in the worst possible way. A night of bloodlust and drunken orgy had been held the night before from the news of Big Cs defeat. The women and slaves were back in their cages, as the bandits snored secure in their compound protected by a few slave lookouts unaware that snipers were watching them from the jungles and river.

It started low, as it always does – the thud of the blades coming, thud, thud, thud. The sound barely audible as the Dead Air ships flew closer. *What was that noise,* the guard wondered as he felt his chest begin to vibrate as the thuds grew just a little over the audible level. It felt as if their heart was beating to the rhythm of the thuds.

Not far away, flying NOE again, Sai covered the noise using the trees and surrounding jungles as he flew closer. He nosed the bird over and began to charge ahead with the other birds following suit.

Feet above the river, which was cleared of wires from Ta's reports, the three helicopters raced, their Hueys shook violently as the birds vibrated from the wind pounding on the fuselage and blades.

Sai could now see Ta's forces up ahead waiting patiently in the river; the Marines were ready to kick some ass. That is when he pulled back on the cyclic thirty degrees nose up. He sank into his seat as the Gs increased and the bird shot up into the air before he nosed the aircraft over while simultaneously pulling on the collective to load the rotor, preventing it from snapping off as the negative Gs hit the aircraft.

Nosed over thirty degrees, the guards watched in shock as tracer rounds zipped through the sky towards one of the guard towers followed by rockets. The tower caught fire from the rounds just before it erupted into a ball of fire as the rockets hit something inside of it.

Panicking the Bandits had awakened to see Sai's gunship fly right over them with a yellow smiling face with an O expression for a mouth painted on the bottom of the fuselage. The two crew chiefs on his bird opened fire from both sides into the compound aiming for the piles of awakening bodies that surrounded the bonfires from the night before.

Seconds later bullets from Tor's gunship tore through the guards of another tower turning them into a red mist just before the rockets leveled the structure.

From the open land that led into the jungle Konkrit and Eck led the ground assault. The aging tanks fired into the walls, causing the walls to explode into wooden splinters as the tanks moved forward, followed by the APCs and two-tons with the fortress bringing up the rear.

On the river, Ta and his Marines landed. The vehicles crushed the dead as they sped off the barge and headed west towards the fortress.

"We are under attack. We are under attack," a voice said repeatedly on the speakers from within the bandit camp while the bandits ran to the walls.

The bandit tanks took fire from the circling Hueys and Lakota circling above. Toshiro and the other crew chiefs cut down many of the men as they continued to open fire at all that moved towards the tanks. Their rounds destroyed all the bodies that they hit as they released a steady stream of fire.

"Man the guns!" Than ordered as he walked onto the ramparts.

AAA started firing into the morning sky. Tracer rounds zipping by all the helicopters as the alliance tanks continued to approach the perimeter from the south.

"Eck, see what you can do we're taking fire!" Sai banked hard right, and then hard left, jinking the enemy fire.

"Long rifle, long rifle, fire mission, fire on that wall, level the fucker."

The fortress howitzers opened fire in the direction of the tracer fire. One of the AAA gun crews erupted into shrapnel as the howitzers hit home using Kentucky Windage to aim; still, several AAA positions kept firing safe out of the line of sight.

"I'm hit!" Stephen shouted in the radio.

Stephen jinked left then right as an AAA round entered the cabin below the right crew chief's seat. The crew chief exploded in every direction as the round went straight through him and out of the roof and through the rotor disc.

"Fuck! I'm hit!" Stephen shouted again as the controls began to vibrate violently. He looked back to see a hole where the crew chief once sat. "Oh fuck, Sai!" he shouted again.

Several more rounds left the AAA gun at the direction of the Lakota as the last crew chief continued to fire back shouting into his microphone. "Break left!"

Stephen banked hard left as the rounds narrowly missed the Lakota; he swore he could feel the rounds missing the skin of the fuselage by inches.

The Lakota banked over almost seventy degrees when something appeared from the ground.

"Oh shit!" the crew chief cried, as he saw a smoke trail rise from one of the tents in the camp towards them.

Point five seconds later, the Lakota erupted into a fireball. It appeared almost zero G for a moment, as parts flew in all directions before raining down on the camp below.

Flying over the other side of camp, "We got SAMs Sai!" Toshiro shouted, as Sai responded to the threat while the fireball dissipated in the sky, leaving a black cloud while the wreckage of the Lakota crashed down into the camp.

"Get lower, Tor!" Sai ordered Tor, while he himself took his Huey to the deck once more narrowly missing an antenna cluster.

Sai dived between the encampments minimizing the exposure to the stingers as trained and continued his attack strafing a few bandits who were running south towards the southern wall.

362

"Where was the SAM?"

"At our six o'clock!" the other crew chief shouted.

Sai banked hard left missing the ground by his rotor blades with just feet to spare.

The stinger crew tried to lock on to Tor but he too was flying in and out of buildings and could not get him in their sights as Sai turned towards the stinger crew without their knowledge.

"I see the fucker."

Sai opened up with machine guns; his tracer rounds found his target and managed a direct hit on a fresh stinger they were using to aim at Tor. The crew exploded when Sai flew over and out of the compound.

"Two, watch for more missiles."

****

RPGs started raining down on the first tank as it approached the gate. Inside the gate, Than's forces waited in their two remaining tanks, waiting to fire when their main gate was breached.

The howitzers from the Fortress continued to rain down death into the camp as the Marines crept in from the east unnoticed.

All eyes of the compound were focused on Konkrit's forces, which left the Marines to plant IEDs concentrated on one spot of the eastern wall. With only a few zombies in the way the Marines quickly placed the bombs and loaded up the vehicles so they could back away from the wall.

At a safe distance from the eastern wall, Ta exited the humvee holding the detonator as his Marines dismounted and searched for cover.

"Duke ready to detonate." Ta looked up as Sai flew by.

"Clear to blow." Sai said.

"Clear." Tor responded.

"Roger," he told the crews. "Fire in the hole!" he shouted to his Marines.

Ta twisted a fuse device that ran from his vehicle to the wall a football field away and the morning sky turned bright.

The earth shook as the massive explosion sent a wave that shook everything within a mile-blast radius. The air bent as the concussion wave sent a distortion throughout the area.

Sai and Tor struggled to control their helicopters as the wave threw the two birds high into the sky in what was equivalent to severe turbulence.

Banking to get back into the fight a mushroom cloud was now where the eastern wall had been.

"Holy shit." Toshiro looked on in awe, amazed to see the cloud rising into the sky before turning into a single large column of smoke.

"Keep firing!" Sai ordered as he dived the bird down into another run on the compound followed by Tor.

The pressure wave had squashed everything alive or dead in the vicinity of the eastern wall. The dead were almost nonexistent in that area as the Marines stormed into the compound attacking the tanks from the rear with RPGs.

"Duke has got them by the balls," Ta shouted as he fired RPGs into the rear of the tanks that were defending the main gate.

Konkrit and Eck breached the gate charging straight into the lion's mouth.

The bandits fought fiercely as they tried to defend their sacred shithole. The first tank to breach was hit by an IED and sent over to its side.

"Eck's down!" Konkrit shouted into the radio as he entered on the second tank followed by the third.

Eck popped the hatch of the tank and crawled out under fire. Rounds bounced off the iron skin of the tank as he took a knee aiming at a bandit when he noticed a green object rolling next to him. Eck's eyes focused in on the object, his eyes widening once he identified the grenade that stopped rolling next to his boot.

A cloud of shrapnel engulfed Eck and he was gone as another APC entered the gate, the gunner on top firing his 50. Cal wildly.

Pop! Pop! Pop!

"Sai, I'm hit." Tor stared at his caution advisory panel, which had the Eng Chip light illuminated. The engine was tearing itself apart after taking a few rounds in the accessory gearbox.

"Stay calm!" Sai's voice said as Tor's eyes widened.

"I'm going down." Tor's engine caught fire; the drive shaft was now breaking up, causing the rotor RPMs to drop, sending a steady tone into Tor's ears.

"AUTOROTATE!" Sai shouted, looking at the smoking Huey, seeing the rotor blades beginning to slow before his very eyes.

Tor lowered the collective and the helicopter dropped out of the sky as the Rotor RPM shot straight up over the limits. In what could be considered a controlled crash, Tor kept his bird in trim and raised the collective to keep the Rotor RPMs within limits as he had done many times when training under Sai. He was in a state of total awareness as he looked simultaneously at the warning and caution panels while keeping his eyes on the trim ball, the rotor rpm, the air speed indicator and still looking for a place to land.

His eyes searched the area as if he was in a state of rapid eye movement sleep until he found what he was looking for. Tor found a suitable landing spot inside the compound in the middle of a firefight but at least he would not play the numbers game against the living dead if he crashed outside all alone.

At sixty knots, he pulled back on the cyclic to slow himself down and felt the bird sink when he raised collective to cushion the landing, maintaining the heading with the pedals.

The skids hit the muddy ground and he began to slide through the gun battle that was taking place as his crew chiefs continued to fire.

The Huey skidded across the battlefield taking fire from all sides as the bandits took pot shots. The crew chief's valiantly returned fire for a football field's length until the aircraft came to a complete stop shot up full of holes.

Tor unbuckled his safety harness and kicked opened the door that was full of holes and fell out of the bird to see both his crew chiefs had been shot to pieces.

He looked around as tracer rounds began to zero in on him, causing him to take cover behind the skids of his aircraft. He took his M-4 and fired back as he went for cover away from his aircraft to the north of his position. Behind the cover, he pulled out his radio from his ALSE vest.

"One, this is 2, I'm at the Western wall, taking fire, need assistance!" A round shattered his radio and sliced his hand.

"Wien!" Tor cried as a grenade exploded near him. "I'm sorry, Wien!"

Just then, Sai hovered over his head, the machine guns firing in every direction and then Sai was flying forward once more.

Tor looked up to see the Angel of Death killing nonstop as Sai nosed the aircraft over once more. His helicopter flew over the battlefield like a demon as Tor watched from behind a few sandbags. That is when it hit him; he looked around and nothing was alive, his crew chiefs were lying on the cabin floor still hooked up to their monkey harnesses and surrounding him were now over a dozen dead bodies.

Tor picked up his rifle with his good hand and headed east towards the center of the camp as Sai and his crew continued to pick off the remaining soldiers in the area.

On the north wall, Wien, Yoon, Fai, Ren Pi, Than, and a small entourage of bandits climbed down a ladder as their men were being butchered by the Alliance forces.

Sai caught a glimpse of the three women and flew over the top of their heads as he saw Wien climbing down the ladder and heading into the jungle with two men behind her.

He banked hard right when he felt the familiar thuds of rounds hitting his aircraft. The fuel-low caution light illuminated. The so-called self-sealing tank was hit and leaking, a steady stream of fuel pouring from the tank.

"Toshiro, we're hit, going to land. Ubei, those flying lessons were not for nothing now. I'll touch down. You get on the controls and land this bird on the barge. Do you understand me?"

The crew chief looked at Sai. "Yes, sensei."

"Atta boy."

Sai broke left and landed behind one of Konkrit's tanks firing its main cannon. Dust and mud flew into the air as Dead Air 1 touched down behind the alliance lines, and after the brown-out conditions had dispersed the young Japanese man, Ubei, hot swapped into the cockpit and took the controls as Sai jumped out holding his M-4.

Standing behind Sai was Toshiro. "Let's get going."

Ubei pulled pitch and headed east towards the barge that was to be used as a precautionary landing site in the event one of the birds could not make it home on its own.

"You should have stayed with him," Sai said to Toshiro as he watched the Huey leave under the care of his pupil.

"We are taking the Blackhawk?" Toshiro asked as he ran after the last tank.

"It's probably on fumes by now. We'll take it later. Just a second."

The two men moved behind the tank after taking fire, there Sai opened a small compartment from the rear of the tank and pulled out a phone that was connected by a cord to the vehicle and began to shout into it.

The turret turned and fired once more into a log cabin sending splinters flying in all directions.

"What you tell them?" Toshiro asked.

"They are heading north towards the wall. I'm going after Yoon. Stay with the men."

"Sai, you can't do this alone. We're brothers, sprout."

"Well, if you get shot you'd better not complain to me."

The tank commander began to turn to the ten o'clock position and made a bee line to the north as Sai and Toshiro followed behind it's safety.

****

The battle was coming to a close as the tank Sai was behind fired at a bunker full of Than's men. The slate had been wiped clean and now IT was time for them to rescue the prisoners.

The dead were kept at bay from entering the compound with the fortress on the southern wall and two APCs on the eastern wall blocking the breaches.

The slaves were freed from their cages and loaded up into the secured vehicles as Tor met up with Sai and Toshiro on the northern wall.

"Weapons check," Sai ordered the men.

They each pulled out their magazines and took a quick count of what they felt was in it. Satisfied, the three began to descend down the wall where a dead man found a bullet in his head. The three were now on the pursuit deep into the jungle.

Konkrit and Ta policed up the compound and within thirty minutes their mission was completed.

Chapter 23: *For My Love*

Close to two miles north already, seven Bandits, plus Than, Ren Pi, and the three prisoners navigated the dense jungle, only encountering a few Shamblers that they dispatched at their leisure. They were pushing north towards the mountains, towards their version of a FOB or hideout. The hideout was manned day and night by Than's troops as an emergency shelter in case the dead had breached the main fort's wall.

Trailing behind running as fast as they could, Tor, Sai and Toshiro moved with a purpose and were now beyond earshot of the encampment. They had left Konkrit as acting commander of the mop up operation while Ta waited at the perimeter to help transfer the women and children that had been held captive.

The trio moved like deer in the jungle, easily dodging the low level branches and hopping over logs at ease.

Below the jungle they continued to hurdle, through the brush they passed and up the hills they went, with Tor, the expert tracker, keeping the tree men on track. Tor, as the youngest of the men, was also the fastest, he glided through the jungle slowly gaining a lead on Sai who in turned was leading Toshiro.

Sweat rolled down the sides of their face as they pressed on. They dispatched the occasional rogue zombie that came to close with a quick shop from their short swords. Sheathing their swords once more they headed north with their rifles slung around their backs, muzzles facing down while using both hands to traverse the harsh terrain that was quickly turning into rolling hills and streams.

Their boots sloshed through the mud as they climbed the wet hills as the pursuing dead tried to do the same only to slide back down. Upon reaching the top they did not hesitate with a break as the three men slid down the north side of the hill on their butts as fast as they could, keeping their eye on the goal as they grew closer and closer to the two women they had lost.

Sai felt as if he had wasted too much time; he felt panicked he needed to find his wife and soon. He needed her more than ever and he was not going to lose her to some madman.

Tor was like Sai, though he had never confessed his love for Wien he knew deep down inside that she was his and everything would be alright if he could only find her.

****

Wien was shivering, still in a state of shock from the beating and rape the night before. Holding onto her cousin she continued to move at gunpoint as Ren Pi and Than walked in front of the two with the other bandits bringing up the rear.

Yoon put her head against Wien's, and whispered: "Sai is coming. It won't be long."

Yoon was sure of Sai; he would come no matter what.

The group continued north in silence to the second enclave that Than's forces were waiting at. It was unreachable by road or vehicle and the only way was to hump it out there.

Time was rolling as both parties headed north and the afternoon sun was now gone, as a cool breeze began to enter the jungle the parties had traveled nearly five miles.

Walking by a cliff on the edge of one of the rolling hills, the bandits pressed forth unaware that less than a quarter of a mile away Tor was closing in fast followed by Sai two hundred yards behind and Toshiro another quarter of a mile away.

Tor raced by several zombies who reached out for him but proved to slow to catch the young man. They turned to pursue Tor and a minute later Sai ran by hitting both in the head with his sword. The bodies fell to the stony ground as Sai went up to the cliff his calf muscles now in pain from the rolling terrain.

Tor was now closer as he unslung his rifle and while running took aim at the trail of bandits.

He stopped and fired.

The bandit's chest exploded causing the bandit to fire his weapon continuously before he slammed face first into the stony ground.

The bandit next to him turned to take aim and was brought down by Sai as Tor continued his charge. The man's chest imploded as Sai's round tore through his ribs and lungs before exiting his back.

Yoon and Wien turned to see Tor coming up the path. The bandits opened fire, causing Tor to hit the ground rolling for cover.

At the prone by a boulder Tor took aim and fired hitting two more as Sai hit three more simultaneously.

Sai continued his run as Ren Pi grabbed Wien to use her as a shield. Wien struggled in the man's embrace.

A grenade exploded behind Tor as he continued to move up shooting at the bandits.

Toshiro who had now passed the two dead zombies moved up the hill cursing in Japanese and pulling out his katana, he needed to quit the booze.

On top of the hill, Tor hurdled over a boulder as he closed the distance on Wien when he felt a strong punch to the chest. Looking at Wien, Tor stood there motionless as Ren Pi took aim again smiling from behind Wien.

"Tor!" Wien shouted as another round impacted Tor's chest.

Ren Pi dropped his weapon and pulled out a large hunting knife laughing as he tossed Wien aside failing to realize Tor had friends. She slammed into the ground, her body struck with pain.

Ren Pi walked up to Tor who was stunned. Tor looked down at his chest as all sound left his hearing; his rifle was no longer in his hands. He then looked up to see Ren walking towards him. Tor pulled out his combat knife when he realized he could no longer breathe. Looking up at Ren he struck out at him with all he had left.

A flash of silver danced in front of Tor and he felt a burning sensation in his back as Ren turned him around and stabbed in through the kidney. Looking up at the sky, Tor saw the clouds and felt a sense of weightlessness as Ren held Tor up laughing at the young man. Tears rolled down Tor's cheek as he tried to look over to Wien who was crying in her cousin's arms now.

Ren stabbed him several more times, the energy draining from his body. Tor then felt the sensation of falling. His body was flying through the sky after Ren pushed him over the side of the cliff.

Rivers of blood flowed through the rocks around Tor's body. Ren Pi smiled, realizing that he had fucked this young man's love. He failed to realize that Sai was coming up the path with the face of a demon burnt upon him.

Sai fired a three-round burst and obliterated the man's head like a watermelon and he continued running up the hill.

"FUCKER!" Than shouted as he pulled up his gun to shoot Sai and fired.

Sai's gun exploded as the round hit the stock of his rifle sending shrapnel into his arms.

Yoon grabbed the weapon and struggled with Than as she tried to wrestle it away from him. Than head-butted her and fired. A round went right through Yoon and out of her back as Wien ran to her falling cousin.

"Yoon!" Sai shouted reaching for his sword, the sharp piece of steel unleashed from its sheath to drink the blood of a living man.

Than raised his rifle back up at Sai and smiled as he pulled the trigger. Nothing happened in his shock. The weapon was jammed; the cartridge of the round used to shoot Yoon had jammed the weapon.

Than's eyes grew big as he realized Sai was coming at him with a sword. He quickly changed his stance taking his rifle up like a baseball bat.

Now a few feet from Than, at a dead sprint Sai charged as Than swung. Sai evaded by rolling underneath the weapon and appeared upright behind Than.

Sai swung with all his power and chopped Than's left arm off with one swoop. Than's weapon flew into the air with the arm attached as Sai kneed Than in the back of the spine bringing down the sword on his right shoulder.

Than's eyes were full of fear as he realized his shoulder was hanging by muscle alone. Then Than fell to his knees and was now in a state of shock. Bleeding from his mouth as he looked at Sai who walked around to face him Than's bowels released. Shit and pissed filled his pants when he saw the sword in Sai's hand. Blood and flesh fell from the steel weapon, as the holder of the weapon's face grew enraged.

"Sai, Don't, please," he pleaded, with Sai realizing that this killer before him was his nemesis.

Sai put the sword to his chest and knelt before him. He held the back of Than's head and with a little force he slowly shoved the blade into him.

Than screamed out in pain as Sai took his time slowly pushing the blade into Than's chest while Wien cried over her cousin behind Than.

Than could feel the bone stop the blade and Sai pressed a little harder, the blade digging into the bone before it broke through. Sai felt the bone give way; the man's chest became deformed as the ribs broke through the skin. Than cried but could not move for he was paralyzed in Sai's deadly embrace.

Next Sai felt the man's lungs pop as the blade pierced it. Sai snarled in the man's face before he twisted the blade causing as much pain as he could and before Than's life gave out Sai pushed with all his might and the blade tore through Than's back as he continued to twist it.

Than's eyes full of tears and fear began to close but not before Sai pulled the sword out of his chest and brought it down right between Than's eyes.

Than was now dead, lying in a puddle of blood, his body was a mutilated mess.

****

Sai rushed to Yoon who was holding on to see Sai once more. Kneeling beside Yoon, Sai took Yoon from Wien.

"Stay with me," he cried as he held Yoon close to his chest.

Wien knelt by Yoon holding her hand as she watched Sai cry for her cousin.

"Please, don't leave me," Sai begged.

"Sai." She smiled, her eyes clear of the clouds.

"Yoon, please don't go."

"Sai, I'll always be with you. Take care of Wien for me." She smiled to Wien. "Take care of Sai for me, Wien. Sai, tell LuLu and Ta that I love them."

"Please," he said, and could not speak anymore as Yoon continued.

"Sai, this is only the beginning, promise me that you will fight till the end, never give up on life."

"I promise." Sai kissed her holding her head his tears falling more rapidly.

"I love you, Sai, let me give you my last breath." She began to struggle.

Wien watched as Sai gave her cousin one last kiss.

Her eyes smiled at Sai and Wien as she looked at both of them.

"Bye, my lo…"

Her eyes closed as if she were falling asleep in Sai's arms. Sai held Yoon tightly as Wien watched her cousin fall into the never-ending sleep.

Behind Wien, Toshiro waited as he kept his eye on a few Shamblers that had been drawn to the location.

"YOON!" Sai shouted to the sky with an inferno now raging where his soul once was.

Wien and Toshiro watched Sai, not saying a word as he cradled Yoon. He stayed that way for a few minutes holding Yoon.

"She's gone," Sai finally told his companions with a crack in his voice. "I'm not going to leave her here for them."

Sniffling, Sai picked up her body and one of the dead bandits rifles.

"It's time to go."

They began to move north as Toshiro called in for a pick up in a clearing he could see not too far up the hill.

Moving north, they fought their way through the dead, until the came to a plateau where the Blackhawk that was being piloted by Arm and Ubei waited. Under pursuit the crew chief's fired at the increasing horde of the dead as the passengers entered the cabin. Sai held Yoon's body on the cabin floor as Wien sat by his side looking at her cousin, wishing she could have done more.

Over the rotor system the sounds of children laughing could be heard from the tree line.

Ubei pulled pitch when from the shadows of the jungle a woman in white appeared, her face was soulless and an entourage of children's silhouettes appeared behind her in the darkness of the jungle. Everyone in the bird saw the ghostly figures that stared at them as they left the scene of the crime.

The flight back was long and quiet. Toshiro watched as Sai let loose along with Wien for Yoon. His best friend in the world was changing before him for Sai's loss was heavy on his soul.

****

The next evening, the residents assembled for Yoon's funeral. One of the most well respected and loved members of the community was gone forever. Under the largest Golden Buddha, her body rested; flowers surrounded her as people came to pay their respects.

His family, Ta, Wien and LuLu, surrounded Sai. The cousins cried, but Sai was done crying. His despair was changing him. He could feel the anger, the hatred growing inside him as he watched people walk by him saying goodbye to Yoon.

As with Thai custom, the funeral lasted three days and on the final day he watched as people put his wife and unborn child into the crematorium. They closed the silver doors behind her.

The war against the dead had just begun.

Epilogue

That was six years ago, a time I remember all too well. Yoon, the baby, all of them, I still carry deep inside me and even though she is gone I can still feel her here with us, especially now for it has become more dangerous than ever.

The dead still roam the land but the rules have changed, it is no longer the walking dead we have to fear, there is a hell of a lot more that has surfaced over the course of the time. We've been at war since Khao San Road against an enemy that brought us years of misery. Hell has come to earth and only the strong shall continue the struggle to preserve the human race.

Through death, life has come; my daughter is now four years old with curly hair like mine when I was her age and she has striking resemblance to her mother. Her brother is two years older and even at the age of six he has become a deadly weapon. Their older sister is my adopted daughter LuLu who is now fourteen and just because she is not blood does not mean I would not die to defend her, she is my daughter. Without her I would have given up after Yoon's death and without Wien I would have been long dead by now. My children are waiting for me now.

They are the reason why I have fought all these years and now is our chance to end this nightmare once and for all.

Through the years I have flown over the dead world, Dead Air lives on till now, my helicopter fleet is still efficient as ever and soon they will fly once more.

The clouds are growing on the open field ahead of me here in the plains of China. I can hear Dead Air flying off over the horizon as the hordes of hell gather for this final battle.

I've always wanted to check out China and here we are like the Three Kingdoms of old. Will I be known as the next Lu Bu? I could only hope.

A dust cloud can be seen from here, they are on the move. To my right the holy men have left my side and have begun to bless the formations of men standing tall. Holding their weapons, spears, tridents, swords, rifles, handguns, bows and arrows, the battle-hardened veterans prepare for war. On the flanks of my formations are my motorized vehicles, including a few tanks along with my War Elephants that would make Alexander the great feel proud.

It's a good day to die.

"Here they come Sai," Toshiro's voice warned.

"Men! Prepare for Battle!"

About the Author

Flying the friendly skies for the military, Samuel C. Garcia has had plenty of time to think of the "What If" questions. What if the dead rose? How could he use the aircraft he has flown against them? Garcia's discussions with fellow crewmembers quickly turned into the book *Dead Air*. Garcia called on his real-life experiences in the military to write many of the out-of-this-world scenes in this book. In *Dead Air: First Flight*, Garcia's goal was to create a realistic horror adventure where the main character is no superhero but a member of a team. For updates, visit Facebook.com/DeadAir1. Happy hunting!

www.ingramcontent.com/pod-product-compliance
Lightning Source LLC
Chambersburg PA
CBHW060153260626
47160CB00001B/240